PENGUIN BOOKS

The Mind Game

'How hot can a first novel be?' *Nova*

'Very exciting, very shocking and surprising . . . *The Mind Game* is a huge achievement, crammed with new ideas about science and morality' Charlie Lee Potter, *Open Book*, BBC Radio 4

'Part dystopian science-fiction, part exotic contemporary thriller, *The Mind Game* will replace *The Beach* as the read for travel-sure, techno-savvy 20-somethings' *Jocky Slut*

'There is sex, and there is violence, but the main thrills occur as Macdonald takes a size ten boot to the limits of social behaviour and proceeds to kick' *Maxim*

'An excellent first novel . . . brilliant narrative' *Mail on Sunday*

'In Alex Garland, things-aren't-what-they-seem mode . . . cue sinister games, double bluffs and paranoid emotions, as everything turns into the holiday from hell. Psychologically thrilling' *Elle*

'A cracking thriller' *Express*

D1151224

The Mind Game

HECTOR MACDONALD

PENGUIN BOOKS

PENGUIN BOOKS

Published by the Penguin Group
Penguin Books Ltd, 80 Strand, London WC2R 0RL, England
Penguin Putnam Inc., 375 Hudson Street, New York, New York 10014, USA
Penguin Books Australia Ltd, 250 Camberwell Road, Camberwell, Victoria 3124, Australia
Penguin Books Canada Ltd, 10 Alcorn Avenue, Toronto, Ontario, Canada M4V 3B2
Penguin Books India (P) Ltd, 11 Community Centre, Panchsheel Park, New Delhi – 110 017, India
Penguin Books (NZ) Ltd, Cnr Rosedale and Airborne Roads, Albany, Auckland, New Zealand
Penguin Books (South Africa) (Pty) Ltd, 24 Sturdee Avenue, Rosebank 2196, South Africa

Penguin Books Ltd, Registered Offices: 80 Strand, London WC2R 0RL, England

www.penguin.com

First published by Michael Joseph 2000
Published in Penguin Books 2002
1

Copyright © Hector Macdonald, 2000
All rights reserved

The moral right of the author has been asserted

Set in Monotype Dante
Typeset by Rowland Phototypesetting Ltd,
Bury St Edmunds, Suffolk
Printed in England by Clays Ltd, St Ives plc

To my parents, Rosemary and Alasdair,
who gave me the best African childhood a
mzungu boy could have

PART ONE

I can think of few things in this life that matter as much as emotions. From a collection of electrochemical impulses in the limbic system come the driving forces that have led man to achieve his most sublime triumphs and to commit his foulest acts. Emotions give reason to our actions yet cause the most pointless damage to the fabric of our society. In building relationships they are our greatest allies, but when they refuse to lie for us they are the most insidious of traitors. Emotions distort the truth yet preserve morality. Above all, they are central to what we define as humanity. If the scientific community continues to relegate emotions to the obscurity of academic appendices, we shall be immeasurably the poorer for it.

Professor Anthony Carrington
– Address to the Royal Society, 1973

I

Recording No: 4

Date: 15 December   **Time:** 7.30 am

Situation: Coral headland overlooking ocean

Sensory Context: Visual: magnificent seascape, early morning sun; Auditory: waves breaking on reef; Olfactory: fresh salt

Cognitive Context: Minimal cognitive activity

Emotional Context: Happiness, sense of peace, relaxation

Somatic Response: None

Facial Response: Musculature relaxed

Global Viewpoint: Optimistic, unconcerned, free

Action Impulse: None

A Chinese guy once told me that deception is like boiling a frog. Drop it in scalding water and it will leap out immediately. But start cold and it will never notice the rising temperature. You can fool all the people all the time if you do the groundwork slowly. It just takes patience: inching the temperature up, degree by degree, until the victim is cooked.

Cara knew how to boil a frog.

The first thing I ever heard her say was just one small piece of the groundwork: 'I have never stayed with the same guy for more than a week.'

3

How do you answer that?

'Hello,' she added, looking up as I walked through the door. A quick smile, almost colluding, crossed her face. It was a finely balanced smile, drawing warmth from chestnut eyes and raising delicate muscles around her cheekbones. None of the others seemed to notice me. Piers' face, marked in devilish black-white patterns by the flicker of the candle, was fixed on hers. He was desperate to come up with some clever remark. But his creativity failed him and he simply said, 'Challenge.'

'Aren't you going to welcome your guest first?'

Piers flicked his head round briefly and nodded at me. Irritated at the interruption. Captivated, for sure. 'Well?'

'True.'

The girl leaned across the table and helped herself to two red chips from the pile in front of the host. There was a brief silence. Duncan broke it.

'You shouldn't admit to that kind of thing. I was about to invite you to dinner, but it hardly seems worth it for a mere week.'

The girl smiled, her eyes laughing at the joke but acknowledging the serious message behind it. 'Maybe I'm just waiting for the right man,' she said.

I left my bottle on the drinks trolley and filled a glass from the jug. Piers had been mixing cocktails again. In five years he wouldn't remember a single one of his tutors, but he'd still be on first-name terms with every off-licence manager in Oxford.

'Sorry I'm late,' I said, aiming the apology mainly at Jenni. Leaving her alone in this company for an hour was hardly the kindest thing to do to a friend, and her face was already showing the strain. She sat two places away from Piers, holding a half-full glass and a half-empty hand of chips. I recognized the floral print dress from the last time I'd got her invited to a party. It still looked painfully cheap, even tacky in this circle of denims and pullovers. Piers was in black Versace jeans and black polo neck. When he stood up and held out a stack of chips I noticed an unusually strong smell of aftershave.

'Thirty quid. Reds are one pound each, blacks are two.'

'You've got to warn me earlier next time you want to fleece me. I thought we were just going to get drunk.' I tried to make it sound light-hearted.

'You've got to not care about thirty quid. You're a big boy now, with a nice big student loan.'

I grinned to show I didn't care and went to sit by Jenni. Her mouth was already set in a defensive grimace. I whispered some hollow assurance and slipped a few chips into the half-empty fist.

'Good of you to turn up, darling,' said Sal as she leaned over for a kiss. Always more friendly than the rest, I could never decide if her style was just a subtler form of mental torture. 'Have you met Cara? Piers discovered her and now she's taking us to the cleaners.'

I waved at the girl across the table, using the excuse to glance again at the curve of her upper lip, the steep slope of her nose, the long black eyelashes that never seemed to blink. She smiled back, clearly and coolly amused by my interest.

'Good. Now you have,' said Piers. 'Rules are: unchallenged truth pays one to the pot, unchallenged lie takes the pot.' He pointed to the large heap of chips in a silver ashtray. 'Challenger pays two for truth, gets four for lie. OK?'

'Sure.' I smiled again to prove my enthusiasm.

'Ripper. Your turn.'

Ripper drained his glass and got up. He made his statement on the way to the drinks trolley, his back turned. Interesting tactic.

'I have personally destroyed forty-eight point three thou of high-performance sports car.' Ripper often spoke like that.

I glanced at the new girl. She seemed a couple of years older than the others. I was glad to see she wasn't impressed by the boast, true or otherwise. Her eyes remained partly on her tapered hands and partly on me, as if she didn't need to see Ripper's eyes to know he was lying.

'Challenge,' called Charlotte. 'I saw that pile of scrap before you totalled it. Can't have been worth more than twenty.'

Ripper finished pouring his drink and walked back to the table. 'Twenty-six actually.' He flicked two black chips across. So he'd been going for the swollen pot. Failed tactic.

Beside me, Jenni gave a small choke. There wasn't much I could do to extract her from the mess I'd landed her in. A fresher among finalists. A country girl among urban sharks. Easy prey. I put an arm round her shoulder. A week ago it had seemed like a good idea to introduce her to this set. She needed social roots; they were the central pillar of college life. In my haste to try and get myself accepted, I was blind to their faults. But tonight, something was different. No amount of blindness could disguise the cruel anticipation, the impatience for blood.

True or False was not just a poker game to that crowd. Winning or losing meant nothing. The essence of the game was the elaborate, grandiose manner in which the contestants could phrase their claims. And it wasn't just about boasting. A lie could enhance status even more than a truth, so long as it was sufficiently imaginative. The very fact that the liar was staking money on his opponents' inability to detect the lie implied it could easily be the truth. When Charlotte claimed to have slept with a Russian prince in Mexico there was real hesitation before someone called her. All were left with the distinct impression that she *might* have done. Jenni couldn't begin to penetrate this looking-glass world.

'I met the Prince of Wales last summer,' she began bravely. 'He came to school in June and congratulated me on being the first Oxford entrant in ten years.'

'Challenge,' drawled Alex. 'He was sleeping with my mother in June. They were in Barbados.'

'It's true,' stammered Jenni.

'Nope, that was his double you met. Been filling in for him a lot recently.'

'Don't call me a liar!' Her nostrils were flared wide in fragile fury.

'He's just teasing,' I said gently, lifting a couple of red chips off Alex's pile and handing them to her.

'It's true,' she repeated, the sense of injustice flooding her face.

It was my turn. The atmosphere was getting aggressive. I needed something new: unthreatening to Jenni but entertaining to the rest. And of course I wanted to win.

'My tutor is working on a new sensor that detects neural impulses in the brain. It can measure emotions and he's asked me to be the guinea pig.'

Scalding water. But in this game sometimes you want the frog to leap out.

'Challenge!' yelled everyone immediately. Perfect.

'Challenge,' repeated Piers. 'I'm host, so I said it first. Even your tutor's not that crazy. Pay up.'

'True,' I said. 'You pay up.'

Piers looked incredulous. 'What kind of idiots do you think we are? It's obviously bullshit.'

I shook my head.

'OK. We'll vote. Who thinks Ben is lying?'

I laughed. 'What is this? Lie detection by democracy? A jury?'

But Piers ignored me and stared at the others. I could feel Jenni's loyalty struggling with her honesty. Around us every arm went up. Except Cara's. I looked at her in surprise.

'You lose. I declare you a liar and claim an extra fifty per cent as penalty,' said Piers. He reached across to seize his prize.

I was six pounds poorer. Justice had lost. But Jenni was safely forgotten for another round.

She had arrived in college two months earlier and something about her had struck a chord. Perhaps it was that sense of isolation. Or perhaps the cautious uncertainty with which she watched the swaggering, hearty student committee welcome the freshers. Whatever the link, when I drove past her in the street and saw the listless pace of her steps I stopped without thinking and offered her a lift. She had been walking back to college, she said. At that speed, you'll never get there, I said. At first she laughed with me, then suddenly she started crying. I never found out why.

Her room was no different from any other. A few photos of favourite pets by the bed. A small stereo. A line of empty folders, waiting to be filled with the wisdom of her professors. She dipped one teabag into two mugs and told me her life story. I didn't ask for it, but then there wasn't much to tell, so it felt like casual conversation. Life in the slow lane. A farm in Norfolk. And now? Well, of course, this is where it all took off. Now she had this incredible opportunity. And she was going to make sure she used it to the full. A first in engineering, an athletics blue, and then the world. It was that simple. Sounds ambitious, I said. Lots of hard work. Exactly, she said. And that, together with the sharp, quiet humour, is what I liked about her. Straightforward honesty. But it was an attribute that was doing her no favours in the present company.

I looked up as I heard my name. Everyone was laughing. 'What?'

'And you can't say anything,' said Piers.

'About what? I missed it.'

'He says you're impotent,' laughed Charlotte. 'And that he's seen it for himself.'

'That's funny?'

'Of course,' she grinned. 'Absolutely.'

Through the laughter, Cara's voice was calm. 'Challenge,' she said.

'Really?' said Piers. 'You know our friend so well already?'

Cara ignored the question. 'I'll double the stakes and bet, with the chemicals you've probably got in your bloodstream, you have a harder time getting it up than him.'

There was an amused silence. Piers raised his eyebrows and tried to look shocked. 'You expect me to admit that?'

'Unless you're willing to prove otherwise, I expect you to pay double.'

'I think we'll spare the guests.' Laughing, in a weak attempt at self-recovery, he passed her four black chips. 'You're a little too good at this.'

Cara nodded. She had been winning consistently. But she had also been laying the groundwork, heating the water. Each of her statements had been tailored to construct a certain impression of reality, a particular image of the girl no one knew. Now the pan was at boiling point. She leaned back in her chair and fixed her eyes on Piers.

'I have no underwear on.'

No expression. She simply waited for a challenge. None came. The frog didn't move an inch.

'You know you're going to have to prove this if you claim it's true?' said Piers.

'Is that a challenge?'

He shook his head. 'I've lost enough to you.'

She looked across at me. The tiniest smile appeared. 'Well?' she seemed to say.

I held the gaze but said nothing. The smile broadened to show the edges of her teeth.

'False.'

'Damn!' shouted Piers as she emptied the pot. A fortune in coloured plastic. But he didn't care about the money. 'How disappointing is that?' he growled. All round the table, the men were looking aggrieved. A succulent, invisible fruit had been held out to their imaginations, only to be torn away before they could enjoy it. The other girls were watching their new rival with admiration and apprehension. All except Jenni, who had retreated into a protective shell of silence. But for the first time that evening, I had forgotten about her completely. I too was captivated.

'Hell of a babe, isn't she? Haven't seen a figure that perfect in a long time.' Piers was unpacking thick-base pizzas. 'All the guys started drooling over her the moment she arrived. Charlotte's really pissed off not to be the centre of attention any more. How many of these do we need?'

'Four's plenty. She seems fun.' I started opening bottles of wine. Piers crammed six pizzas into the Aga. I wasn't surprised.

'More than fun. You were drooling, too; you're just better at hiding it.'

'OK. So she's more than fun. Happy?'

'Well, don't even think about making a move on her. I'm very nearly there with that girl. She was flirting outrageously with me back there. I've just got to find the right moment.'

The kitchen, like everything else in Piers' house, was unnecessarily large. He paid for the privilege in a sense, as it took him fifteen minutes to drive into town. His father hadn't been able to find him anything sufficiently grand within walking distance of the university. Once Piers had visited my flat near the Iffley Road and marched about the cramped space I shared with two others, a look of disgust on his face. Only after a couple of beers did he stop noticing the cigarette burns on the carpet or the tears in the wallpaper.

Not that I was the poorest student to have ever enjoyed Oxford's riches. Many of us who chose to escape the suffocating confines of the college walls ended up in run-down housing which no one felt moved to renovate. But Piers and his friends could never really come to terms with the relative squalor that the rest of us endured. His solution was to remain in his castle and make Oxford society – as limited in his eyes as it was – come to him. That night was just the last in a long series of parties that allowed Piers to act the part of patron to those of us who fitted the bill. What the criteria for selection were I had never been quite sure. But it was clear that Jenni had not met them.

'I mean, why her for Christ's sake?' He pulled a bottle of whisky from the cupboard and swallowed a mouthful. 'It was a bit awkward – no, frankly, it was embarrassing – having her moping around before you got here. Looked like I'd invited her. Hell's that going to do for my credibility? Why couldn't you have come together?'

'I'm sorry.' It was pointless trying to defend Jenni. Her qualities would mean nothing to Piers. I had learned early on that, despite their self-assured and seductive strides through life, this crowd considered it their birth-right to value personal achievement somewhere below a cheap cigar. 'She wanted to bring her own car so that she could leave before me. I meant to be here earlier. I got held up.'

'You got held up,' he mimicked.

'I had to hand in an essay.'

'What? You're not serious? The term's over.'

'It's just an extra topic I wanted to cover. The only time my tutor could make it was tomorrow.'

'Crazy.' He wasn't going to let the real crime drop. 'I still don't understand what you see in her. Bloody flat-chested, mousy-fringed thing. And so boring! Can't you liven her up?'

'I don't see anything in her. She's a friend, that's all. I'm sorry she's not on great form, but that was a heavy atmosphere in there and she's not used to this kind of party. She needs time to adjust to Oxford life.'

'Fine. Let her adjust. But why do you have to get involved? Are you running a charity for socially inept bumpkins?'

I swallowed back the rebuttal as I always did when Piers touched a nerve. Any progress I had made with this group was entirely through playing by their rules.

'Aren't I the original country boy?'

Piers opened the Aga to examine the pizzas. 'Why do I keep buying these disgusting pineapple ones?' He started picking off the fruit. 'Yeah. Yeah, you are. But at least you're vaguely amusing to have around. That one, though, what can anyone do with her?'

'She's really sweet.'

'She's really sweet on you, anyway.'

'No, she's not.'

'Oh, come on,' said Piers. 'You're her knight in shining armour. A big, beautiful finalist who actually talks to her. She looks at you like she's wetting her knickers. Which she is undoubtedly wearing. Probably thick, white M&S stuff.'

The door opened. Jenni looked in timidly and offered to help. I cringed at the timing. Piers just laughed. Grabbing a couple of bottles, I led Jenni back across the hall into the drawing room.

'I'm sorry. I didn't mean to break up your conversation,' said Jenni. The rest of the party was spread across the room, some standing in classical cocktail pose, some sprawled on the sofas. Cara sat on the floor talking to Rachel.

'Oh, we were just waffling. Creating noise while we got the food ready.' I smiled at her anxious face. 'Are you enjoying yourself?'

'Definitely.' She hesitated immediately. She was one of those people who found even a white lie difficult to sustain. 'I was pretty useless at that game though.'

'Listen, I'm sorry about that. I didn't realize there'd be gambling. I'll cover your losses.'

'No, don't worry. I'm doing fine for cash. I haven't spent nearly as much as I expected.'

'Really? Most people end up badly overdrawn during their first term.'

14

Even as I said them, I regretted the words. Most people! As if that was what the outsider wanted to hear.

'Well,' she shrugged. 'You know. I don't really go out that much.' Before I could backtrack, she asked: 'Where can I find a bathroom?'

I was doing so badly.

As I stood alone, waiting for the unwelcome fresher to return, Cara appeared by my side.

'Either you're extremely imaginative or you're involved in some fascinating research. As you're a friend of Piers, my guess is it's not the first. Care to tell me about the emotions device?'

I looked round in surprise. I'd forgotten that someone had believed me. 'You're interested?'

'As a biologist. Certainly.'

'You're a biologist? I'm surprised we haven't met before.'

'I'm a post-grad. Finished my first degree in Edinburgh this summer. I did some psychology on the side. Emotions are relatively unexplored territory.'

'True. But this sensor uses some new technology which should change that. Apparently it's the first time anyone's been able to sense emotion impulses without opening up the skull. I haven't seen it yet, but James Fieldhead's impressed so it must be good.'

'Dr Fieldhead's your tutor? I would kill to work with him.'

I smiled at her sudden enthusiasm. 'Have you met him?' She shook her head. 'If he saw you I expect he'd feel the same way.'

She seemed annoyed by that, but let it pass. 'So when are you doing it?'

'I'm not. I can't afford the time with Finals coming up.'

She glanced around her in amused contempt. 'Of course not. I can see you've got much more important things to do than groundbreaking research. Such sophisticated company that you keep.'

'And that you keep.'

'Keep implies coming back for more.'

'You're not planning to?'

'Not unless I run short of cash.'

'Piers will be disappointed that you think of him as nothing more than a bank.'

'I doubt it. He seems utterly uninterested in what anyone else thinks.' She stared into my eyes for a moment, as if searching for similar deficiencies in me. Then her gaze flicked sideways. 'Oh look, here comes your sweet little friend. That means I've got to go and put up with our dear host's self-satisfied sneer again. Tell me more about it later?'

So much for being very nearly there.

But Cara had put the optimistic Piers in a pleasant mood. It made him entertaining and generous, and reminded me why I had spent a year building a bridge from my own world of rural tranquillity and family to his elitist domain, populated by foreign holidays, port bottles and other people's sisters. Even the sweet little friend was now getting the occasional kind word from the king. At one point he went so far as to mix her a Bloody Mary, encouraging a grateful smile. Jenni was never going to relax completely, but at least she lost a little of the defensive look with this attention.

Then she gagged on the drink.

'What's wrong?' I asked quickly.

'It's . . . it's really hot. Strong. Ugh . . . could I have some water?'

'Yes, of course,' said Piers, picking up a jug and filling a tumbler. 'I'm terribly sorry. I must have overdone the Tabasco.'

Jenni took the glass quickly and drained it. 'Thanks.' She smiled apologetically. 'Perhaps I'll stick to wine.'

Pouring her a glass, I stared angrily over her head at Piers. He held up his hands in baffled apology. The bastard.

'What are you playing at?' I demanded ten minutes later in the kitchen.

He shrugged. 'Just wanted to liven her up, old chap. My party, my prerogative. Dull guests need to be livened up.'

'With Tabasco?'

'No, with vodka,' he said calmly. 'I just needed the Tabasco first so she would drink half a glass of spirits and think it was water. Speaking of which, I must change that jug before someone else ends up legless.'

Not waiting for a reply, he wandered across the hall. I followed him back into the drawing room, where Jenni was deep in conversation with Ripper. Slurred conversation.

'So why are you called Ripper then, eh?'

'That you don't want to know,' replied Ripper.

Jenni's whole body seemed off-centre, as if pulled

sideways by an invisible cord. One hand rested on the back of a chair, the other raised the wine glass at increasingly frequent intervals. It was almost empty, but Ripper's hand held a full bottle, ready to add explosives to the flames.

I interrupted as casually as I could. 'Ripper, my friend, you're monopolizing my date. Have a heart.' Pleasantly surprised to be released, he sauntered off towards Charlotte. 'Come and sit down?' I suggested.

Jenni smiled happily. When she was on the sofa, I prised the glass from her hand.

'I've had such an exhausting day,' I began.

But Jenni seemed uninterested in my words. She placed her liberated hand on mine and giggled.

'Did I make you jealous?' she asked. 'Is that why you tore me away?' With a contented grin on her face, she tried to focus her eyes on mine.

Oh, God.

I noticed Cara staring at us, an amused smile in her eyes as she ignored Piers' monologue. My cheeks were burning. The host looked round.

'Time for another truth game?'

'No! We're just taking a rest. Anyway, we're bankrupt.'

'That's OK; we'll play a different one. With a different currency. But this time lies are out. *Verboten*, understand?'

I nodded.

'Absolute rule. No lies. Ben, you know the flag on the roof? Be a darling and get it, will you? Please?'

Reluctantly, I got up and walked to the stairs. On the landing, a second staircase led to a roof terrace. I opened the door and felt the freezing December winds cut into my face. Already the terrace was icy. The pot plants, tenderly arranged by Piers' mother, lay dying of exposure and neglect. Expensive wooden furniture was rotting from having been left too long in the rain. Only one item received Piers' proper attention: the full-sized Union flag that flew from a makeshift standard on the balustrade. Fairly ridiculous, really, but that was Piers. I unfastened it and carried it back down.

The whole party was once again seated around the low table. Cara had taken my place next to Jenni. It seemed to me the move was deliberate, somewhat provocative, although what she was trying to provoke I wasn't quite sure. That ambiguity was quickly becoming a defining characteristic of this disconcerting girl. I handed the flag to Piers and took the stool they'd left me.

'Good. Thank you,' said Piers. Seizing a corner of the table, he jerked it upwards – sending ashtrays, glasses and pizza crusts sliding to the floor – then spread the flag over the top. 'This is your bond. From now on, everything you say, you swear on this flag. If you have a shred of patriotism in you – no lies.'

As I said: fairly ridiculous, really.

'Simple rules. Someone asks you a question, you answer straight or you take a dare. If not, you leave. Clear?'

'Crystallico, dearest,' said Charlotte.

I looked across at Jenni. She seemed reasonably upright. But I hated to think what she might start to say. I pushed the thought out of my mind and switched my gaze to Cara. She was watching Piers with a disinterested curiosity, as one might observe the movements of a locust in a cage. She felt my stare immediately, flicking a few blonde strands behind her ear as she turned to match it. I looked down again.

'Please don't say you're bitten as well,' whispered Sal beside me. 'I know at least two of us, not counting your little friend, who will be awfully disappointed.'

But Piers had started the game.

'My turn first, gentlemen and others. One for you, Ben. What's the worst thing that's ever happened to you? On the flag, remember.'

Such a casual question. What if I'd been through something really terrible? A kidnapping? An assault? It irritated me that Piers felt so confident in his assessment of my straightforward, Dorset life that he could ask it. Nothing but forgettable amusement from Ben on that one. So I supplied forgettable amusement.

'When I was six, I got locked in the cellar at home with no light. I was only there for about twenty minutes, but I was terrified of the dark for weeks after that.'

Laughter. Amusement. But it hadn't been so forgettable for me.

My turn. I let go of the flag and looked across at Cara. I couldn't help it. Any excuse to have her speak to me again.

'What do you despise in life?' I asked her.

She gave me a look that assured me she wouldn't provide the answer I wanted. Truth can, after all, be politic.

'Hypocrisy, time wasting, and people who take pride

in being dull,' she said. Her voice was as neutral as always. The audience had no reason to guess they were being insulted. I wondered if I was included in her grouping. It surprised me how much that bothered me.

'In your opinion,' asked Cara, turning to Piers, 'what is the single most important idea to come out of science?'

I had an extraordinary sense of being linked to her by some secret confluence of thoughts. The meaning behind every one of her words, her looks, was utterly clear to me. The question seemed such an obvious invitation to stupidity. Piers happily walked into the trap, with some small-minded response that confirmed her scorn. But no one noticed. Sitting back, they just waited for the hard-core questions to begin.

Eyes were heavier now. Grins a little less refined. Backs were slouched and make-up was smudged. Brains were running a few notches south of optimum. I knew the flag was a gimmick, an excuse our host provided so that his guests would have something to blame their indiscretions on. The real truth-inducer had been siphoned into our bloodstreams over the course of several hours. Or, in the case of Jenni, seconds. Piers, for all his failings, understood the dynamics of a party. The game of Truth or Dare had been timed to perfection.

It didn't really matter who you asked. The question was everything. Forget specific references to sports cars or underwear. The best questions could make anyone uncomfortable, could send a shiver of delighted anticipation through the gathering, whoever the subject was. The answer would be savoured, appreciated for one tour of the mental goldfish bowl, and then forgotten by the time the next sufferer was ready to reply. No single individual was supposed to get victimized. But just occasionally the rules changed.

The first worrying question came from Max.

'Jenni, you gorgeous girl, this one's for you. How many boys have you kissed this term?'

I felt a stab of sympathy for her, wanted to answer for her, wanted the question disqualified on the grounds of unfairness. Max knew perfectly well what the answer was. I waited for the piteous look to appear in her eyes, the apology and the humiliation. But Piers' medicine had transformed his patient. Unsteadily, she leaned forward and grasped the edge of the flag.

'None,' she announced proudly. 'But I've found a . . . a . . .'

Immediately I knew what was coming. I couldn't say anything.

'. . . a . . . very special boy,' she decided, settling her lopsided grin on me.

I closed my eyes, listening to the hilarity erupt around me.

'What?' she muttered. 'What's so damn funny?' I opened my eyes to see her gazing around in confusion. 'He *is* special. He's a million times better than you tossers.'

'Your turn, Jenni,' I said softly. 'Ask someone a question.'

Her face brightened and she turned to Ripper. 'So why . . .' she asked, 'why *are* you called Ripper?'

Why did she have to keep asking that?

Leaning forward until his face was just inches from

hers, Ripper waited until everyone had gone silent. 'You know those two ducks that wander about the quads in college?' he asked.

Jenni nodded happily.

'There used to be three until someone got drunk and tore the head off one of them.'

Once again the room filled with laughter. Ripper leaned back in his chair with a broad grin. I glanced at Cara. She showed absolutely no expression. Did that mean disapproval? Or was she just trying to spare the sweet little friend sitting beside her with a face twisted as if it had been stung?

Jenni had gone white. It might have taken five seconds for the response to register in her brain, and another five for her to decode it. But when the message finally found its mark, her alcoholically induced serenity was obliterated. Breathing heavily, her hunted look back, she sought me out in the sea of dangerous laughter. I winked to give her some sort of reassurance, but the last thing I could do after her earlier declaration was to comfort her.

The game was no longer just about safe amusement. Piers was leaning across to whisper in Ripper's ear, Rachel was signing to Charlotte, Max was watching Jenni's discomfort through serpent eyes. The Union flag looked redder than normal.

Ripper cleared his throat. 'My turn, I believe. Cara. Carina. Carinella. Carissima. Now you've seen us all in our true colours, which man here would you most like to sleep with?'

She didn't flinch at all. She too had seen the whisper,

had understood Piers' hopeless attempt to force her to closure. She looked at Ripper in silence for a moment.

'I'm afraid I can't answer that.'

'Then, Carinellisima, you must pay the forfeit and take my dare.'

The slender, sober stranger just smiled.

Ripper paused and his eyes flicked towards Piers. How obvious did it have to be? 'Carissimillina, I would like you to demonstrate the depths of your affection. A strong kiss, please, dear Cara dear, to anyone you like.'

I waited for the refusal, for the disappointed deflation of bated breaths. But Cara just nodded and turned to her right, bringing her hand round behind Jenni's head and pressing lips against lips.

Too shocked to react, Jenni went rigid. When Cara let her hand fall away, she stayed locked in position. A howl of amazement and objection rose from the group.

'Won't do, Deara,' said Ripper. 'You hear the crowds. Forgive our old-fashioned society, but you have to choose a man.'

'OK,' smiled Cara. 'You should have said.'

She stood up and stepped outside the circle. The room went quiet. Cara walked up to Piers and dropped an arm over his shoulder. The host smiled up at her, already tasting in his mind the sweet flavour of victory. He rested his hand on her black silk trousers and leaned forward.

'Thanks for inviting me,' she murmured.

His smile disappeared. 'You're leaving?'

'I don't know,' she said, detaching herself and walking round the circle towards the door. 'You'll probably want me to,' she added as she reached me, seized my head from behind and pulled it backwards.

Cara's mouth closed on mine in an instant. My eyes focused on her soft white neck as her tongue slipped easily between my teeth. She moved as naturally as if we had been lovers for months. And once she had started, she didn't stop. Applause was coming from the girls. I didn't dare to imagine Piers' reaction. But then I didn't need to. He quickly made his anger clear by lashing out at the easiest target. His voice was cruel and cold:

'Fine. Then here's my final question. Jenni, on the flag, what are you thinking now?'

We both looked up to see the unwanted fresher leap from her seat with tears running down her cheeks. She stumbled towards the door and fell into the hall. I stood up immediately and ran after her, but Cara caught my arm outside the drawing room.

'Leave her,' she said as Jenni staggered up the stairs. 'You're the last thing she wants right now. She just needs to cry it off a bit.' She pulled the door closed behind us and smiled. 'How about showing me one of these other rooms?'

Heavy velvet curtains, bronze carvings, ancestral portraits. Wallpaper stripes that matched the deep wine red of the sofa and the cream of the Wilton carpet. A study fit for a king, occupied by a student. Or rather, occupied by two of the student's guests, largely against his wishes. One, torn between compassion for a hurt victim and lust for a fine seducer. The other, leading the way, guiding her mate with soft whispers and firm hands.

Her pace was determined, unrestrained by convention. A fast pace that would normally bring the girl a bad reputation. But Cara had an air that made hesitation seem like the worst kind of Victorian prudery. Was there nothing more to the trick than poised, calculating confidence? The sort of confidence that allows a girl to step out of her silken trousers and still retain her sense of purity; the sort of confidence that makes a man forget everything that exists beyond his striped world.

We lay on that luxurious sofa for what seemed like an infinity. But from the medical record, it was only 11.30 when I heard his voice.

'Ben. Cara. Get up.'

Piers was standing at the door. For some extraordinary reason, he was carrying the flag. Still half-dazed, I thought he was about to give me a lecture on the parallel between patriotism and respect for a host's stake. The idea made me livid.

'Get out of here!' I shouted. 'You had your chance and you screwed it up. Piss off!'

'Ben . . .'

'No! She's made her choice.' I glanced angrily around the room in search of my trousers.

Piers shook his head and walked forward. When he spoke his voice was quiet but strained. 'I'm afraid you have to come with me.'

I looked into his eyes and saw fear. Terror.

He nodded. 'Now.'

The house was strangely still after the tension of the truth games. A cold wind blew through the hallway from the open door. Trails of mud from careless feet criss-crossed the carpet. A weak, flapping sound came from the highest door in the house, as it swung unkindly in the winter night. Outside, the wall of broad and narrow backs was warningly still.

In that grandiose, dark driveway Jenni lay on her side, her pink dress twisted around her waist and her arms stretched out across the gravel. One leg stuck awkwardly sideways, as if trying to reach for the shoe that sulked just out of its reach. A smear of blood darkened her forehead where it rested on the ground.

The group of friends stood silent, waiting for the guilty party to react.

2

Recording No: 11

Date: 16 December   **Time:** 10.45 am

Situation: Veranda of the beach house

Sensory Context: Auditory: Vivaldi (Winter – check for irony, if that's an emotion!); Olfactory: pineapple cocktail; Tactile: sun cream

Cognitive Context: Reading novel, thinking how delicious this life is

Emotional Context: Satisfaction, enjoyment, indulgence

Somatic Response: None

Facial Response: Slight smile

Global Viewpoint: In control

Action Impulse: None

A counter-intuitive but long-standing theory claims it is the body's response to a situation that makes us experience emotion. We grieve because we cry. We feel afraid because our body prepares us for flight. We're happy because we smile. That's the theory.

But I know it's wrong.

Perhaps before that night I could have believed the spiritless suggestion that 'visceral' stimuli were the source of all feeling; that the brightest, the sharpest, the most heart-rending experiences were all determined by changes in blood pressure, pulse and temperature. I could have believed because I hadn't tasted true emotion. I hadn't felt the sudden burst of excitement, passion or anger that crashes through the mind long before the body has a chance to react. I hadn't seen the endless spectrum of emotions, far too diverse for each to be the product of a separate physiological state.

But it didn't take Fieldhead's planning to kill off my emotional innocence. As I stood in the driveway and remembered what I had been doing while she was hesitating alone on that terrace, I seemed to age a thousand years. Opposite emotions often come in sequence, Fieldhead said later. By then I didn't need to be told.

I gazed upwards, uselessly seeking out the tops of the decaying geraniums, two generous storeys above. A wall round the terrace. Must have stood on the garden furniture to get up. Rotting furniture. Might have broken while she was climbing. Would Piers have made her pay? Not after her losses. Anyway, it was rotten. Good furniture left out in the rain. What a waste.

Oh, God.

Piers was tugging at my arm. 'She's breathing,' his urgent whisper told me. 'She's probably OK. It's not that high.' His hands gripping me in unconscious anger, desperate to push any guilt on to me. 'Talk to her, Ben.'

Immediately I was on my knees beside her. 'Jenni, Jenni. I'm so sorry. Jenni.' My voice dropped to a murmur as I grew self-conscious in front of the crowd. No response. Chest moving but face church still. It was too dark to see her pupils when I pulled back her eyelids.

Through my knees I felt the intense cold of the gravel and imagined it biting into her flesh. 'Coats,' I called out. 'We have to cover her. Please . . . Christ, get me some coats!'

My sudden shout awoke the stunned audience from their dreamy stare, and they turned and ran to the hall, bringing back everything they could find. I eased a scarf under her head, careful not to disturb her lower body. Careful not to touch that leg. Head forward, tongue clear, mouth open. Then, finally, the shock of it hit me and I almost collapsed on top of her.

I was vaguely aware of Cara kneeling beside me; vaguely heard her anxious whisper: 'Are you all right?' Behind her was a line of ambiguous faces, fighting off sympathy to evade its partner, guilt. Once friends of a sort, now convenient strangers. We stared at each other, unable to do anything else.

The sound of sirens broke the deadlock. Piers ran to the gate to meet the last guests of the evening. The audience oozed away, loath to be seen staring by the professionals. One stretcher, two blue uniforms, three coats to return. 'Sorry about the blood. I'll pay for the cleaning,' I said.

Max took the coat between finger and thumb. 'Don't worry about it,' he said in an awkward breath.

The corridors of the John Radcliffe were quiet. No one else was having accidents that night. Like the ambulance, the nurses took their time, wheeling the stretcher at stroll-to-the-pub speed, chatting about Christmas presents and nativity plays. Trivia. A quick assessment by the triage nurse, then a no-bubbles injection and a snaking drip into the arm. Anti-inflammatories and all-action painkiller.

'Nothing much we can do until the doctor gets here,' said one nurse cheerfully in reply to my mumbled anxiety.

The stretcher glided through a final pair of doors and one of the nurses detached herself, holding up a kindly hand and pointing me towards a seat in the corridor. Impatiently, I settled into the blue padded plastic and waited.

A telephone rang unanswered behind the closed doors. The caller allowed a two-minute pause, then tried again. A muffled voice answered. The chatty nurse re-emerged.

'Well, the police are here. You'd better go and explain. Floor Two, by the main entrance. Don't admit to anything,' she advised with a smile.

Two officers were waiting in an ice-cold reception. Their faces held unbearably neutral expressions, wearable on any occasion. Even their voices were neutral, no intonation interfering in the calm process of duty.

'Mr Ashurst?'

I'm a student. Don't even pretend you mean the *Mister*.

'We understand that you were the escort of Miss Douglas this evening. Can you tell us what happened?'

Neutral eyes wandered from lipsticked cheek to untied shoelace. A dash of a sneer flickered briefly at the edge of his mouth before the public mask clamped back into place.

'So you didn't see anything at all?'

The second, younger policeman spoke this time, straightening out the meaning with razor-like clarity.

'Or hear anything?'

'Why might she have jumped off the roof?' asked the first.

What can you say to that? She was crazy? She was obsessed? She was upset that I went off with someone else? How vain does that sound? I shook my head.

'So you're not aware of any explanation for a suicide attempt?'

Both neutral expressions were still locked in place, but an almost imperceptible shift had occurred. Tiny muscles had moved around both pairs of eyes. This time there was a pause.

'Where were you when Miss Douglas jumped?'

'Where? Um . . .' I could sense myself feeling – looking – guilty. 'I was downstairs.'

'Where exactly?'

'In the study.'

'Who else was present?'

'Is that relevant?'

'Just answer the question, please, sir.' The policeman's voice was patronizingly patient.

'One of the other guests was present.'

'The name, please.'

I stared at the fragment of hostility in his calm, object-ive eyes. 'Cara. I don't know her surname.'

He wrote the name in his notebook, the pencil moving in slow, careful thrusts. 'And what were you and this Cara doing?'

'What's that got to do with anything?'

'Mr Ashurst, your friend came close to being killed tonight. It is our job to understand why that was the case. You yourself said there was no reason for suicide.'

'I said I didn't know of any. I'm not saying that means someone pushed her.'

There was the smallest pause before he replied. 'Nor are we, sir.' Again that tiny pause. 'But we would suggest you answer the question. Just to avoid any misunderstanding.'

I flushed angrily while telling them. There was just a suggestion of a smile on the younger man's lips. His colleague maintained a perfect mask as he drove the point home.

'But you and Miss Douglas went to the party as a couple?'

I looked down, sick from the pressure of his unspoken judgement. 'I suppose so,' I muttered.

He waited a few moments to let me suffer. 'Thank you, Mr Ashurst,' he said eventually. 'That's very helpful.'

I was mentally drained by the time the doctor arrived. A smiling Sikh – turbaned hope. He disappeared behind the closed doors for a cursory examination and then dispatched the stretcher to various corners of the hospital. First stop was X-ray: skull intact. Next came the CT scan: everything in place, basic concussion, no danger.

'Formalities, really. Fairly predictable results. It's a good sign if a leg is really mashed. You can tell she landed

33

feet first,' he explained. 'Took all the impact below the waist. By the time her head hit the ground, vertical velocity was right down. Only real danger was to her acetabulum and spine, and she was lucky there.'

'What about the leg?'

'Not good, you know. We can pin the femur, but she's also fractured the calcaneum – her heel – and there's nothing we can do there. She won't be able to bear weight on it for about three months. But we'll do our best. Come back in the morning and I'll be able to tell you more.' He picked up the ringing phone. 'I think you have a visitor. Get some sleep. And try and look on the bright side: quite a few students who attempt suicide are successful.'

Cara stood at the entrance, twisting one hand inside the other, her face an agonized emulsion of hope and fear.

'Her head's OK. Her leg's screwed, but her head's OK.'

'Thank God,' she whispered.

That was all we really said that night. She led the way to an ancient MG, and I muttered some brief directions to the flat. Before we reached the little back street off the Iffley Road, we both knew she would come in. When she was sitting in the armchair, a glass of milk in her hand, I knelt beside her and buried my face in her lap. Patiently, silently, she cradled my head and stroked the tension and the guilt away.

'Yes, she's conscious. No, you can't see her. She's just woken up. The doctor has to check her first.'

It was a dark, stormy morning. Droplets of water slithered down each ward pane. The nurse was fiercely efficient with her words and damning with her eyes.

'I suppose you're the young man responsible? Turning idiot girls' heads with your pretty face?'

I didn't reply. I looked at her hands resting on the desk and saw she wore her watch upside down. All the better for taking your pulse, my dear. After a moment she relented.

'Wait over there. I'll call you when he's seen her.'

The hospital was humming with visitors, cleaners and brisk-mannered nurses. The background activity and new-morning optimism made this second wait much less painful than the first. Other visitors smiled at me and offered observations about the weather. A toddler sidled over and gave my knee a secretive tap. Every flash of blonde hair reminded me of the extraordinary girl who'd lain awake beside me most of the night. I found myself smiling just at the thought of her now asleep, the duvet twisted round her body the way I'd left her. I found myself imagining her first smile when I returned at lunchtime to wake her with coffee and a kiss. Inevitably, though, those thoughts brought the guilt back to the surface. When the nurse signalled to me, I snatched an extra breath for courage and picked up my token gift.

Jenni lay in a small, private room, her plastered foot resting on a pillow. White gauze covered her forehead above red-rimmed eyes and puffy cheeks. She was smiling with her mouth, but the rest of her face was tight with embarrassment and apology. Green strings fastened a green gown below her chin. I swallowed and put the flowers on a steel trolley.

'Thanks.'

'I should find something to put them in.'

'The nurse will do it.'

We both looked down during the pause.

'Christ, Jenni, I'm sorry. I –'

'Please don't tell my parents.' She said it in one fast, pre-planned breath, cutting off the end of my apology in her haste.

I stared into her frightened eyes and nodded. She looked round at the flowers, speaking to the wall, making the lie acceptable:

'I told the nurse they were in the Caribbean. No contact number or address. I said they wouldn't be back until after Christmas.'

'OK.'

'I couldn't bear it if they knew.' Her voice was cracking, a damp, nasal tone smothering the words. I looked away from her face. My eyes settled on the plaster. I felt an urge to write messages in felt pen; to force the situation into the familiar.

'How long do you have to stay here?'

'They don't know. A long time. The heel bone was in several fragments . . .' The tone was flat, reporting an incident in another universe. We stared at the plaster for a while. I saw the nurse's face appear at the glass panel in the door.

'Jenni, why . . . ?'

'I'm sorry. It wasn't your fault.'

'But what . . . ?'

'Don't, please.' She looked up at me. 'It's just me. It's my problem. I shouldn't have been so naïve. Can you leave it at that?'

There was a curt rap on the door behind me. I looked back at the glass. The nurse gave a brief signal: visit over. I bent down and kissed one cheek. Jenni waited until I was at the door.

'Are you going to go out with that blonde?' The words were awkward; intonation fluctuating out of control.

'No.' I said it without hesitation. It was the only answer to give.

She smiled painfully before the door opened. 'Thanks.'

Into a different world. I drove fast, looking at my watch for the first time in the hospital car park, knowing I would be late, trying to minimize the reproach. For this last session of the term, he had chosen FREVD – the north Oxford church now converted into a café. I parked illegally and ran up the steps, through the line of crumbling neoclassical pillars and into the cavernous nave. He was sitting at a table in the centre, drinking the finest Arabica on offer and scanning three broadsheets: the young genius enjoying his Saturday morning leisure.

'I'm sorry I'm late,' I said, pulling up a chair beside him.

Dr James Fieldhead looked up from the paper and smiled. 'The FTSE-100 went up 308 points yesterday. I can forgive a little lateness after that.' He stood up, picked up his papers and sauntered over to a table in the apse.

I looked around and guessed he wanted to move away

from the scattered customers at neighbouring tables. Privacy had never previously been a concern to the man who held his tutorials in pubs, trains and punts, but perhaps his views on game theory were even more groundbreaking than usual. I followed him across to the other table.

To my amazement, he stood up again as soon as I reached him, heading this time for a stool at the bar.

'Am I supposed to keep following you?' I called after him.

'You do whatever produces the optimal final outcome for you. First rule of game theory.'

The other customers looked up, curious to hear raised voices on a Saturday morning.

'Well, it's hardly great for me if you keep moving away.'

'That's why I do it. According to your essay there is always a winner and a loser in a game, and what's bad for you must be good for me. Incidentally, did you rush this one?'

'I didn't know we were playing a game.' I felt myself flushing, trying not to show my irritation at this public lesson.

'But of course we are. I make a decision that influences your decision and vice versa. Our actions are inter-dependent. It's a game.'

'It's not much fun.'

Across the nave, Fieldhead chuckled. 'Since when have scientific games been about fun? Games are models of rational interaction, that's all. They're full of surprises and paradoxes, certainly: bound to be with the circular reasoning they require. But fun? The Prisoner's Dilemma game that you described so . . . extensively: how much fun would that be in real life?'

Without waiting for a reply, he stood up and returned to his original table. 'Tell me,' he called to me, 'in terms of seating arrangements, what would be our best strategy for this tutorial?'

'To both sit at the same table.'

'So there is a choice we could both pick where our best interests would be simultaneously served?'

I walked over and sat down beside him. This time he didn't move.

'Your mistake is to assume that every game must be a conflict. You are so concerned with winners and losers, with defecting prisoners, that you ignore a whole array of animal behaviour: straightforward, self-serving cooperation.'

I thought immediately of all those interactions with positive payoffs on both sides – grooming, sex, hunting: cooperative game strategies, evolved through natural selection.

'Even the Prisoner's Dilemma can be played co-operatively, given the right circumstances. Allow me one variation on the basic model and I'll demonstrate.'

Fieldhead stood up and walked over to a nearby table. The solitary student put down his coffee as Fieldhead murmured his request, and then followed him back to the FREVD laboratory. When my opponent was seated opposite me, Fieldhead explained the rules.

'You have a choice: cooperate or defect. If both of you cooperate, you each get five pounds.' Taking out his wallet, he placed two notes in front of us. 'If both of you defect, you each get one pound.' The two coins tumbled out of his magician's hand and landed between the notes. 'However, if one defects and the other cooperates, the bad guy gets seven pounds and the nice guy gets nothing. Standard Prisoner's Dilemma. Understand?'

We both nodded. It was as clear as daylight that both notes would be going back in his wallet. Neither of us wanted to be left with the sucker's non-prize.

'Good. Ben, you'll make the first decision. And by the way,' he casually added, 'you'll be playing this game four times.'

The opponent's eyes flicked up to mine, as if suddenly seeking the collaboration that was forbidden to us. I could see the same thoughts running through his mind. Four times changed everything. Repetition gave an opportunity to prove trust. Repetition made us long-term allies, not one-off unknowns. Repetition gave maximum joint gains through cooperation of £40: so much more than the £8 available through defection. His hand gripped the table edge, as if that alone was preventing him from telling me what to do. I only had to glance at the relaxed smile on Fieldhead's lips to know the outcome.

'Cooperate,' I said. A signal of friendship.

My opponent nodded his approval and smiled. 'Cooperate,' he echoed.

'Congratulations,' said Fieldhead, picking up the notes and handing one to each of us, before reaching into his inexhaustible wallet to replenish the table. My opponent took his money silently, not quite believing his luck.

'Actually, changed my mind,' said Fieldhead suddenly. 'We'll just play one more round. Ben, choose. Quick.'

The shifting conditions were unsettling, but now that we had proven ourselves trustworthy we could once again share the highest overall gain. There was no fear of betrayal now. Fieldhead had made his point, and I had made some money.

'Cooperate,' I said.

But the opponent was shaking his head: half-embarrassed, half-triumphant. 'Defect,' he whispered.

It was almost shocking. I watched Fieldhead hand him seven pounds in real surprise. With an apologetic grin to me he got up, thanked Fieldhead and went back to his table to order a full English breakfast.

'Treacherous bastard,' I said under my breath.

'No,' said Fieldhead. 'Intelligent bastard. He came away richer than you, remember. And he's not trying to make friends with you, so it doesn't matter to him at all that you're left feeling like the sucker you are. Question is: why did he cooperate at first? And why did cooperation break down?'

I tried to sum up my scattered conclusions into the neat rule that Fieldhead sought. 'Repetition. You cooperate if you know you will be involved in future games with the opponent where his trust will be worth more than the short-term gains you would make through not cooperating.'

'Biological example?'

I had to think for a while. 'Cleaner fish. Their clients are evolutionarily selected not to eat them while they clean the parasites out of their mouths because their future services are worth more than the immediate nutrient gain.'

'Exactly. Only when you expect no future productive games with an individual will you cease to cooperate with him. Drop people when they stop being useful.'

My earlier opponent was staring at us curiously. At another table, two older women, perhaps university staff, were working on a crossword together. Co-operation. For what? I leaned back and watched Field-head's green eyes watch mine. Was he trying to provoke me? I knew the scientific truth of what he said, but on a Saturday morning, in a church smelling of coffee and black pudding, it was not a truth I wanted to believe in. I felt like standing up and announcing to this life science prodigy exactly what a certain set of ultra-rational genes had led a first-year girl to do just eleven hours earlier. It was as if Fieldhead used his genius to deny the existence of the normal, mundane, even tragic life that was inflicted on everyone else. Yet even as I resented it, I couldn't help but be enticed into his elegant and articu-late world.

Fieldhead rarely appeared in college. The Senior Common Room had laid down statutes requiring its members to eat a certain number of meals per week in the dining room and fulfil a plethora of duties about the quads, but dusty rules had never been of much interest to Fieldhead. He split his time between the Zoology Department in South Parks Road and a variety of somewhat vague London commitments. Such a casual approach to the institution that paid his salary and picked up many of his research bills would normally have led the college to reconsider his position. But by the age of thirty-six Fieldhead had built up such a legendary reputation in the academic world that, to the dismay of his SCR detractors, he was essentially untouchable.

Great things were expected of James Fieldhead from the moment he took the top first in his year, crowned by his celebrated response to an exam paper on vertebrates. His answer to the typically vague Oxford question, *Women need men like fish need bicycles. Discuss* – which encompassed a wide-ranging discussion of vertebrate reproduction and piscine locomotion – was published as an example of excellence to future candidates. His tutors worked hard to persuade him to stay at Oxford for a PhD, and were consequently disappointed when he bought a backpack and disappeared off to South America. Eight months later, when they had all but written their protégé off, he reappeared in South Parks Road, with long hair and torn clothes. The errant dropout pulled open his backpack to scatter sample cases containing preserved specimens of twenty-eight Amazonian insects previously unknown to science.

The illegally exported goods were removed from the shell of filthy garments that had protected them from officialdom and hastily transferred to the Natural History Museum for classification. Fieldhead then requested the chance to share a few rain forest 'findings' with a number of ecology professors. A week later, after visits to a hairdresser and a clothes shop, he met with a group of eminent but indulgent scientists and proceeded to astonish them with an account of rain forest canopy food webs that radically challenged most previously accepted hypotheses. What he did not mention, but which the less armchair-oriented members of his audience gradually appreciated, was the effort he had made to obtain his data. Fieldhead had climbed 200-foot trees in the middle of virgin rain forest and tied himself to the upper branches for days at a time, in order to observe the complex predator–prey interactions of their elusive fauna.

From that point on, Fieldhead's recognition was assured. But as he brought his unconventional yet astoundingly successful analytical techniques to each new biological field, his status as brilliant young student was quickly converted to that of precocious upstart and dangerous rival in the eyes of the less productive researchers. Gradually he invaded more and more people's turf, but by the time the knives were being unsheathed around him, Fieldhead had published a revolutionary book exploring explanations for human deviancy derived from the animal world. Overnight he became both a serious authority consulted by psychologists and the Home Office, and a pop scientist engaged in debates on fashionable late-night TV programmes. Oxford had no choice but to curb its academic resentment for his premature success and capitalize on his fame. Despite tales of high-speed encounters with the motorway police and a blatant disregard for the scientific protocols of the day, James Fieldhead had become a central pillar of the academic establishment.

The fact that Fieldhead's captivating and seductive charms had more effect on the student population –

particularly the female student population – than on his less pretty but more influential colleagues did not seem to cause him the slightest concern. He cared not at all about the opinions shared of him in Senior Common Rooms and departmental coffee breaks, nor did he show interest in befriending any of the somewhat aged but highly intelligent dons that Oxford had to offer. Instead, it was said – although I still have no idea if the legend is true – that Fieldhead threw regular garden parties throughout the summer, filled with the best and the brightest of London society, who drove down the M40 in a long stream of Porsches and Mercedes. He held these parties on Sunday mornings for two reasons. There was the character challenge to anyone vulnerable to hangovers – which, of course, he was not – to get out of bed and start drinking so soon after the ravages of Saturday night; and it appealed to Fieldhead's sense of humour to be leading a celebration of debauchery just as his neighbours were heading off for the morning service.

What actually went on at these Sunday morning parties, bathed in summer sunlight and lightly dampened by the morning dew, depends on which version you choose to believe. Everyone knows someone who met someone who attended one, for Fieldhead's curiously timed, Londoner-packed drinking sessions were among the favourite targets of Oxford's most adventurous gatecrashing students.

In my favourite version of the story, a focal point of the morning's proceedings was the filling of an expensive pyramid of glasses with champagne. Fieldhead would execute this delicate operation himself, standing on the terrace with the house behind him, all of his guests on the lawn, facing him. If an intruder could time his entry over the walls during the brief moments it took Fieldhead to fill the glasses – so being seen by the host himself, but by none of his guests – then he would be allowed to stay. Judging only by the sounds coming from the garden, the gatecrashers would have to decide the perfect moment to begin their ascent up the wall. Ladders were forbidden in all operations on a point of honour. An even more weakly based rumour claimed that it was Fieldhead himself who – as the supposed founder of the student gatecrashing society – had instituted that particular rule.

Despite the success of his book, no one was quite clear how the academic funded this mythical lavish existence – or even his more-certainly real and rather large house, for that matter – but it was generally assumed that his luck in life had not been limited to his genetic inheritance. Some men just had it all: the alpha males of contemporary society. And within the virtual tribe of Oxford students and dons, Fieldhead's reign looked set to run unchallenged for some time yet.

'Are we playing a game?'

The green eyes flickered, then smiled. 'Certainly. Most tutorials are games. And most good tutors get their optimal outcome. So you have to hope it's not one of your winner–loser games.'

A waitress was hovering near by, perhaps unconsciously drawn, as so many were, to Fieldhead's informed confidence and relaxed style.

'What's your optimal outcome?' I asked.

'Making you a fraction more insightful and less naïve than before.'

'And what are your game choices?'

'Treating you like an idiot who needs other people to stuff conclusions down your throat, or helping you to reach them through Socratic questioning and your own process of induction.'

'And my choices?'

'Reacting well or badly,' he replied.

'What are my payoffs for each outcome?'

'Depends on how much you value your pride.'

'Manipulating me is likely to make me react badly.'

'Only if you let your emotions get involved,' he said. 'Don't. True games should be entirely rational. Natural selection isn't influenced by emotion.'

'I thought you liked emotions.'

'In the right empirical context. And you really should have said yes, by the way. The sensor equipment's just arrived – quite extraordinary. Going to be one of the most exciting experiments of the century.'

'The payoff wasn't right. You played the wrong game.'

'You wanted money?'

I shook my head. 'Not at all. But the effects on my preparation for Finals would have made the payoff negative.'

The green eyes closed for a moment. 'You're right, I should have found someone a little less obsessed with self-measurement to measure.' He called the waitress over and requested fresh coffee. 'But just to show you what you're missing, let's have a little look at emotions in the context of game theory. Think about guilt. In particular, that uncomfortable, unsettling feeling you get when you're considering betraying someone's trust. Why has guilt evolved?'

I stared at him blankly. 'To be honest, I have no idea.'

Fieldhead smiled. 'Worrying, isn't it? You've been through an entire Evolution course and you haven't even stopped to consider the biological explanation for a central feature of your character. You'll have similar problems with the other emotions, I would guess. Don't worry: you're not alone. This whole subject has barely been explored.'

'So what is guilt for?' I asked.

'The repeated Prisoner's Dilemma you played a few minutes ago demonstrated that it is better to cooperate if you're likely to come up against your opponent again in the future. In this simplistic setting it is easy for our brains to cope with that logic. But in the real world we often forget about the future and the repeated games it may bring – we forget that we may have to deal with the same people again, and so we may consider screwing them for maximum short-term payoff. Luckily we have guilt to stop us cashing in like that. Remember how much stronger guilt is when the person you are considering screwing is known to you: or, to put it in more cynical terms, is likely to be around you in the future. Selection has prevented us from destroying our reputation for future games by weighing us down with this apparently self-defeating emotional baggage: tying our hands with something we choose to call morality.

'You can extend this theory to whole communities

and see the repetition of games as taking place with any of a number of players who are in communication with each other. If you screw one player, he will spread the word to all his acquaintances and you have effectively destroyed your cooperative position in future games with all of them. That is why we trust people whom our friends trust, and conversely should be cautious with strangers who have no reputation among our friends.'

I nodded slowly. My head was beginning to hurt. Too much thinking following on too much stress following on too much alcohol.

Fieldhead must have sensed the information overload, because he smiled and spread his hands. 'Let's leave it at that,' he said. 'You've got the idea. Think about the other emotions over Christmas. Love, for example. A most manipulative device. And anger is extremely interesting. But I leave them to you to work out. Just one clue: always view interactions with others through the dispassionate lens of game theory: use backwards induction, like a chess player, to work out what action on your part will induce your opponent to behave in the way that best favours you. Then try to understand how emotions promote those actions. Just as a manipulative child might spend his pocket money on a small present for his father, hoping this apparent token of generosity will earn him a PlayStation for Christmas, so the best game players may appear to act against their own interests to win the highest long-term payoff. Successful game strategies are often counter-intuitive; once you accept that idea, emotions start to make a lot more sense.'

3

Recording No: 14
Date: 16 December   **Time:** 2.00 pm
Situation: Almost asleep, lying on coral island
Sensory Context: All tactile: Cara's hand on my back, hot
    sun, powdery sand
Cognitive Context: Post-coital wanderings
Emotional Context: Contentment, bliss
Somatic Response: Higher sensitivity to tactile stimuli
Facial Response: Broad smile
Global Viewpoint: N/A
Action Impulse: Urge to embrace (resisted – she's asleep)

Jenni didn't mention the jump at all after that first morning. For the next four days I brought grapes and magazines, and we talked about nurses, films and world news: safe neutral topics that allowed us to step around that untouchable crux. At home, Cara mirrored this theme, steering conversations away from serious talk, bathing us in humorous chatter until I began to shrug off the burden of conscience and return to our light-hearted, ivory-turreted world.

Thinking about Cara helped me take my mind off Jenni. After that rocky start to the relationship, I was determined to hold on to this rare catch. She could keep me enthralled for ages just by sitting naked opposite me and laying down strict contact rules: holding my gaze for one minute, allowing me to kiss one part of her body for twenty seconds, then enforced separation again before she would take her turn to kiss me. The tantalizing restraint demanded by this game was almost impossible to bear. But although Cara spent many idle hours in my bed, she was less concerned with the conventional building blocks of romance. I often asked about her background: her family, life at Edinburgh University, her interests. She would offer some morsel in response, but after a few moments would get bored and change the subject. Her own life simply didn't interest her and nor, it seemed from her lack of questions, did mine.

'Edinburgh was all shiny and bright after the Midlands,' was her only comment on university life. 'Lots of fun people with time on their hands to think, drink and leap into bed with each other. We hardly seemed to do any work. It's a miracle I was allowed to stay on.' Then she broke off and started filling in a crossword. 'What's a seven-letter word meaning a game or an insect?'

Each morning I drove to the hospital, leaving Cara to call her lab or climb back into bed, depending on her mood. Her postgraduate genetics project was based on a population of fruit flies that she had left to reproduce over Christmas in the hands of the lab technician. Somehow she had persuaded the man – it had to be a man – to record the genetic diversity of each generation, saving her hours of tedious vacation work. A few words of suggestive gratitude every other day was all he seemed to need.

*

Five days after the party, Cara came to the hospital.

I suppose I had never tried to discuss Jenni's feelings with her. I'd kept the shock of the jump and the excitement of our relationship firmly apart in my mind. I bore my own feelings of guilt and saw no reason to pass them on to Cara. It hadn't occurred to me that she would ever want to visit; that she would get so bored waiting in the flat that her MG would speed over Magdalen Bridge and the glass-panelled door would swing open behind me.

Jenni had been smiling properly for the first time. She'd looked at my latest floral offering with new eyes and sat up to give me a sisterly kiss. Her conversation was more enthusiastic, and for the first time I'd stopped feeling awkward. Then the smile vanished and her eyes narrowed.

'What's she doing here?'

I turned to see Cara wave through the glass and open the door. She hesitated as Jenni shouted the question again.

'Oh hell, Cara,' I said, leaping off the chair. 'Not a good idea.'

She looked at me, a puzzled frown appearing on her face. Instinctively I put my arm round her to lead her back out of the room. That was too much for Jenni.

'You're seeing her, aren't you? You lying shit! You're shagging her every morning before you come here, aren't you?'

I pulled the door shut behind us. The abusive language was audible to everyone in the corridor. A nurse rushed into the room as I led Cara away.

'I'm sorry. I should have told you,' I said. Cara looked round at the curious faces, then back at me. 'She asked if we were having a relationship. I said no – she didn't need to hear the truth. Please don't feel responsible.'

'I wouldn't dream of it. Poor kid, though. Do you think you can come back?'

'I have to. There's no one else.'

'You'd better check with the doctor first. You don't want that happening again.'

When the nurse reappeared, she led us to a distant office where a balding man in a pinstripe suit introduced himself as Dr Williams. He pointed us to chairs, nodding as I explained the background to the outburst.

'Yes, that makes sense,' he said when I had finished. 'I wouldn't normally discuss a patient's case, but you're really going to be too involved in her recovery to leave you in the dark. She's still very distraught about the whole affair. She's going to be all right physically, but I'm more than a little worried about her emotional stability. I had a long chat with her. She's got an awful lot of unpleasantness going on inside.'

'What do you mean?'

'Depression, mainly. Some paranoia, some unhealthy fantasizing.'

But Jenni's not like that, I felt myself thinking. She's an athlete. She loves her work, wants to be a great engineer. She's as normal and as down-to-earth as they come. I had to remind myself that she'd just jumped off a roof.

'Are you sure?' was all I could say, knowing he was right.

'Believe me, I've had a lot of practice identifying these symptoms. I specialize in psychosomatic diseases – medical disorders caused by emotional problems. They've never been very fashionable in England, but I suppose that's the attraction.'

'What kind of disorders?'

'All kinds. Everything from arthritis to heart disease can be caused by chronic emotional imbalance. No one really talks about it, but severe depression or anxiety can double the risk of disease, as well as making recovery much less likely. Stress weakens the immune system; high-frequency anger puts a major strain on the heart. In fact, an angry temperament is a better predictor of premature death than all the fashionable culprits like smoking or cholesterol.'

Cara interrupted: 'You think Jenni's at risk?'

'No, not yet. She's young and healthy still. She has a lot going for her in terms of ambition and determination. Most of the time that keeps her happy. But occasionally she does have a serious problem with depression. It's not uncommon in young women. We frequently see the early stages: self-hatred, intellectual lapses, sleeplessness and inability to enjoy day-to-day pleasures. In her case, it's driven by a strong sense of worthlessness. She's convinced she has no friends and will never find any man who'll even look at her. I'm afraid you were the last straw.' He smiled kindly to soften the statement.

'Will she do anything like that again?'

Dr Williams clasped his hands together. 'You really can't tell. She's retreated inside herself. There's no way to know what she's feeling. That's the main problem with medical psychology: we just can't say what's going on in her head.'

'This happens a lot?' asked Cara.

'There are so many emotion-related problems we see, but because we can't measure feelings, we pretend they're not there. Psychosomatic diseases form just one part of the problem. But even for people who are perfectly healthy, chronic depression can have the most paralysing effects on normal life. We can administer lithium to control it, but we can't check progress except by patient testimony. Until we find some better way to monitor emotions, I'm afraid the medical profession is not going to be able to do much for these people.'

'You went very quiet,' said Cara.

We walked straight back to the car park, avoiding the corridor outside Jenni's room. I had promised the nurse that I'd look in again the following day.

'Don't say you didn't think the same thing.'

She smiled. 'There's more of an incentive when there's an obvious real world application, isn't there?'

'Especially when it's so close to home. Given what I've done to Jenni, there's no way I can just walk away from this.'

Her MG was parked next to my rusting Ford. I opened my door but didn't get in. The moral pressure was almost suffocating. Cara came and stood beside me.

'You know that kind of invention, even if it does work, will take years to be approved for medical use.'

I nodded. 'It's not so much that I can help her directly by doing it. But it would be a kind of spiritual reparation. It would make me feel better about watching her walk around on crutches for months. Christ, she was supposed to be earning an athletics blue next year!'

'Well, if that's how you feel . . . you don't really have a choice, do you?' was all Cara said in reply. Then she smiled and dropped the keys for the MG back in her bag. 'Let's go now,' she suggested, getting into my car. 'Let's go right now. I'm dying to meet him. Is he as gorgeous as they say he is?'

Fieldhead was lying on a leather couch when I showed Cara into the prized corner office that the Zoology Department had finally been forced to award him. I sat in an armchair, accustomed to my tutor's favourite 'thinking position', and waited for him to come down from the clouds. Cara stayed standing, mouth slightly open in wonder as she made inquisitive faces at me. I tried to view Fieldhead with her fresh eyes to imagine her first impressions. The sunburned skin and bleached edges to his dark brown hair – marks of a recent trip to the Okavango delta – gave a rugged look to his otherwise youthful face. Dressed in an immaculately tailored three-piece suit of heavy charcoal wool, his elegance was only heightened by the rakish twist in the purple silk of his tie.

Thirty seconds was too long for Cara to wait. 'Does he often sleep the day away, or has he turned into a cushion since you were last here?'

I smiled to myself as Fieldhead's eyes flicked open and

swung round to search for the disturbance. 'Thank you so much.' His tone was dry sarcasm. 'I was on the point of working out a new model of parasite population dynamics, but now I've lost the thread. It took me two hours to think it up, so I hope you've got something interesting to say.' He turned his gaze from Cara's reddening face and noticed me beside his desk. 'Unlikely, if you're anything to do with him.'

'Well, whatever I say has to be more interesting than tapeworm reproduction.' Cara's fists were lightly clenched and it amused me to see a touch of anger breaking through the cool exterior. She had finally met her match. Fieldhead raised his eyebrows and stared at her, then yawned and turned back to me.

'Interesting response. Who is this girl? Is she free for my little emotions project? It would be quite a revealing insight into the female psyche, don't you think?'

I laughed. 'Absolutely. Her name is Cara. I don't think I need to introduce you, as she seems to have read every paper you've ever written.'

'How kind. It's a pleasure, Cara.' He held out his hand, which she took after a furious glance at me. 'I hope you didn't find them too dull.'

'No . . . I'm, well, fascinated by your approach. I mean, it makes a great change from most of the stuff I have to read.' It was the first time I'd seen her lost for words and I enjoyed every second.

'I made the mistake of telling Cara about your . . . "little emotions project". She thinks I'm mad to have turned it down, so I'm here to eat my words and – if you still need volunteers – find out some more about it.'

Fieldhead blinked. 'The payoff has changed?'

'Something like that.'

He turned and scrutinized Cara. 'Well, if this is your doing, you must have enslaved him. Last time we talked about this, Ben refused point blank.'

She nodded. 'Yes, so he said. But it sounded too interesting to miss. If you need anyone else . . .' she trailed off.

'Thank you. Both for dragging Ben in here and for your own interest. But I'm afraid I only have the resources to use one guinea pig and it has to be someone I know well. However, you could help out by . . . well, let me tell you a bit about it.' He motioned Cara to the other chair and sat back on the couch.

'A few months ago, I was approached by the R&D director of one of the big pharmaceutical companies. We knew each other from a while back when I was involved in sketching out the requirements for an HIV vaccine. They have links with any number of academic institutions to generate research leads, but this time his proposal was somewhat unusual. I'm sure you're aware that new drugs are tested on laboratory animals before being given to humans, to check they're suitable and don't have any lethal side effects. It's an essential step in the development process of pharmaceutical products, and the resulting drugs can be lifesavers for thousands of people. However, sometimes the compounds tested can have unfortunate effects on those animals, and occasionally will paralyse or kill them. As a result, a growing number of individuals who, to be frank, do not know what they are talking about, are making these companies out to be evil profiteers who delight in cruelty to animals. This is causing all sorts of PR problems and making investors nervous. In short, my drug-dealing friend would like to do something about it.

'He has tried educating the public about the importance of his products but that has failed to silence his critics, probably because they are too healthy to appreciate them yet. So now he is trying a different tack and is gambling on a hypothesis that some neurologists believe: namely, that other animals do not experience the same feelings or emotions we do, and consequently do not suffer in the way these people are suggesting. To be specific, while they may share some physical responses, their emotions do not have the same cognitive component as ours. It's an age-old animal rights question that goes back to Bentham in the eighteenth century: "The question is not, Can they reason? nor Can they talk? but Can they suffer?" My executive has asked me to help him find out.

'In the past, emotions have been measured in humans by their physical expression, such as blushing, smiling or accelerating heart rate. Difficult to do in animals, which have totally different responses, and useless for the more subtle emotions that have little – if any – outward expression. The only real solution is to go to the source: to measure the electrical impulses in the brain that generate the experience of emotion.'

Fieldhead stood up and walked over to his desk. He fished around in a drawer and pulled out a matt black object, shaped like a domino but measuring just one inch long. 'This pharmaceutical company has become so interested in the issue that they've already done the hard part. They paid an American firm specializing in high-tech diagnostics four million dollars to develop this gizmo. And the incredible thing is that it seems to work. I give you the world's first miniature emotion sensor.'

I tore my eyes away from the device to glance across at Cara. She seemed mesmerized by Fieldhead's authoritative delivery. Her cool, controlled smile had become eager and excited under the master's spell. I was enchanted by this new side to her.

'The big problem has always been getting access to the brain. Emotions are generated by the limbic system: a collection of structures such as the hippocampus and the amygdala, which lie beneath the cerebral cortex. We know roughly what types of neural impulses are involved, but up until now the only data have come from readings taken during brain surgery, with electrodes inserted directly into the relevant neurones. It has never been possible to measure the neural impulses of someone experiencing a normal set of emotions under everyday conditions. How can you register happiness in someone whose cranium has been opened up?

'But the Americans have now managed to detect, on the surface of the skull, faint electrical signals originating from those impulses using an advanced form of electro-encephalograph technology. As the signal frequencies vary according to neurone type, it is possible to match differing signals to the emotion being experienced. We can even measure intensity: the more rapid the rate of neurone firing, the stronger the signal. All you need is a device capable of registering and recording those signals and a means to interpret the crazy array of data that starts appearing.

'The first sensor they built looked like something out of a sci-fi film. It was a great fruit basket of wires that was fine for reception but a bugger to use. Not exactly portable, so the main emotion they registered was frustration at not being able to act normally. For the designers, miniaturization became critical.' Fieldhead held up the little object in his hand. 'You wouldn't believe the cost of the materials that went into this thing. Even the casing is an alloy invented by NASA. Most of the components inside are made of compounds I've never heard of. But when it's attached to the back of someone's head it picks up those signals beautifully. Then it digitizes them and transmits them up to five metres, to this recorder.' He pulled what looked like a small Walkman off a shelf. 'Simple, isn't it? And now that I've got hold of the gadgetry, Ben, you can see it wouldn't be such a hardship to use, would it?'

I stared at the tiny miracle in his fingers. When Fieldhead had described the system before, I'd envisaged a great block of metal strapped to my head, not this sleek device that looked more like an after-dinner mint. Suddenly, with the equipment in front of me, it all seemed possible.

Cara spoke first: 'But if this high-tech lot invented the thing, why should you be the one to use it?'

'Good question. They have in fact used it quite extensively and they claim they have identified and documented twelve separate emotion-linked sets of signals. Moreover, by repeating the test with different subjects, they've demonstrated consistency in the signals between the subjects when experiencing similar emotions. More importantly to the sponsors, none of these signals is found in non-primate laboratory animals. So you might think the work is done. But you have to remember that these people are a bunch of Californian engineers whom no one has ever heard of. They simply don't have the credibility to deliver the good news to the public.'

'Of course not. But you would.' Gradually the pieces fell into place in my mind. 'With your reputation and high profile, especially after that stuff on human behaviour . . . they want you for your name!'

'Exactly. It annoys me to admit it, but my pharmaceutical friend only wants me to pass on the Americans' message – assuming I get the same results as them. Still, he pays well, and it gives me the opportunity to look into a fascinating subject.'

My mind was still caught up in all the complexities of the proposal. Questions were occurring to me so fast I was in danger of losing track of them. 'But how do you attach the sensor? Do you glue it on? And how do you stimulate the different emotions you want to measure?'

'The first question is easy. You see these little loops on the side of it? We sew it to the skin on the back of the head. It's fairly painless and doesn't leave a scar, but I'm afraid we would have to shave a small patch of hair. Still, yours is sufficiently long that the sensor would be hidden from view.

'As for stimulating the emotions, the Americans did rather dull things like watching sitcoms or playing volleyball, with a few bits of Country & Western music and self-induced pain thrown in to vary the emotional repertoire: the sort of things you would expect from that part of the world. I want to be a bit more adventurous and stimulate more extreme emotional responses, to strengthen the evidence for or against the hypothesis.

'You'll be glad to know that I plan to start with the pleasant emotions, so if you decide to take part I'll only be subjecting you to extreme excitement, happiness, amusement – those sorts of things. The others can come later if the first part works. In the meantime, I've managed to extract a quite substantial budget from the sponsor which will be dedicated to making someone's life as enjoyable as possible for three weeks, at the small price of having a little hair shaved off. In your case, I imagine an exhilarating trip somewhere new would be most effective – with Cara, if she's free. Of course, if you're not interested then I won't press you . . .'

Cara's face had suddenly lit up.

'Where are you thinking of doing this?' I asked.

'No point staying in England: too dull, too grey at this time of year.' Fieldhead strode over to a large map of the world, stapled to the plaster and covered in pencil marks. He gazed at it for a moment, one finger tracing half-forgotten expeditions around Asia and Africa. When he turned back to us he was smiling. 'I've thought of the perfect chap to help us, in the perfect place. How does a beach holiday in Kenya sound to you?'

4

Recording No: 17

Date: 16 December   **Time:** 5.45 pm

Situation: Camel riding along Watamu beach

Sensory Context: Visual: low red sun, Cara in front; Auditory: weird bark/laugh (?); Olfactory: God knows – camel smell – I can't describe it

Cognitive Context: Wondering what the spectators are thinking; T. E. Lawrence; Gary Larson

Emotional Context: Humour, embarrassment

Somatic Response: Slight reddening in cheeks

Facial Response: Laughing

Global Viewpoint: N/A

Action Impulse: Get off and have a long drink

I was born in a small, forgettable Dorset town and spent my childhood under the very ordinary roof of a very ordinary house in the nearest piece of countryside to the local train station. My father had chosen the location to minimize the commuting time to the Whitehall desk he had occupied for almost thirty years. All right, the desk might have been getting a little bigger as his career progressed, but the journey time remained reassuringly constant. Whenever he mentioned his commute, I got the feeling that he was congratulating himself on an investment well made and a lifestyle planned to perfection. Even the timetables had survived privatization and the efficiency consultants almost intact. These things were of crucial importance to my father.

'I think I've found a way to stop the water dripping on to the bathroom window ledge,' he announced to my mother, just fifteen minutes after I'd arrived home for the first time in two months.

'Oh yes?'

'Yes, I think so. I noticed the Leytons have the same moulding on their dormers. But Paul's fitted a rather cunning plastic strip that catches the water and drains it to the side. To the left side, if I remember correctly.'

'Well, I must say, that would be nice,' said my mother. 'To sort that out at last.'

'Yes.'

'It doesn't look too ugly? You know how I love the shape of those dormers.'

'No. I don't think so.'

'I suppose we can always think again if it does.'

Both my parents seemed to have forgotten about me in the excitement of this solution to all their drip problems. I wasn't too bothered by this. The person I'd really come to see was still out. My brother Sammy had been my informal adviser and moral support provider for as long as I could remember. The question of whether I should or shouldn't agree to take part in a mind experiment in Kenya was far better left to him than either parent.

'Mind you, the Leytons had their dormers put in much later,' my mother was saying. 'I wonder if it would work on ours?'

'Oh, I don't see why not,' said my father.

Listening to my parents carrying on their normal Sunday conversation had a soporific effect. The universe was comfortingly small in those quarters, although it was only by escaping to university that I had come to recognize quite how small. Topics of discussion rarely rose above the excitement level of dormer moulding. To her credit, my mother was able to maintain this razor-sharp debate while cooking lunch, loading the dishwasher and laying the table. My father, by contrast, had to stop whatever he was doing if he wanted to say something. There was no unconscious part of his brain that felt comfortable continuing its duties while his mind was elsewhere. Driving with him was a silent business.

'Which route did Sammy take?' I asked, suddenly impatient to move beyond the dormer drama.

My father blinked as if to remind himself of my identity.

'Through the sheep field and round the back of the Burton wood,' said my mother, her hands sunk in a bag of broad beans. Anaemic-green innards were being separated from their shells in preparation for our traditional winter Sunday lunch. 'He set off about an hour ago. If you go down the lane you'll probably meet him coming back.'

'Sammy will know where we could get plastic strips,' muttered my father. 'That can be his project over Christmas.'

I found my brother just past the neighbouring farm. He had been riding along wet woodland tracks, and the legs and belly of his horse were covered in mud. Despite the chill, there were droplets of sweat on his reddened face and his jumper was tied round his waist. When he took off his hat, the hair beneath it remained flattened against the skull, his curls damply collapsed. But his smile was as ready and brilliant as always.

'Finally! Back at last. You're turning into a recluse.' He pulled on the reins and leaped down beside me.

The warmth from the ride was in his skin. 'Recluses live in Dorset,' I said, hugging him back. 'Remember?'

'You're right. I have to get out of here. It's getting harder and harder to get through an evening with the Ps. Wish you'd been here last night to keep me sane.'

'That bad?' I laughed.

'They are definitely getting a lot worse,' he said as he led the way up the lane towards the farm. 'I was stupid enough to mention a small Internet idea that I'm thinking of setting up and they both assumed it must be something to do with porn.'

'Is it?'

'Yes, of course, but don't tell them.' He punched me lightly on the arm. 'You'd love that, wouldn't you? Free subscriptions for friends and family.'

'It would be nice to see a little dirt on the Sammy halo for once,' I said.

'Sorry. Got to disappoint you again. It's just a bulletin board service for virtual clubs.'

'Oh.' I put on my most deflated look.

'I know. Not very sexy, is it?'

'You mean you're not going to make your first million this year?'

'No . . . unless . . .' he grinned, a mock sheepish look in his eyes. 'You haven't . . . you wouldn't have some pictures I could . . . er . . . scan in, have you?'

'That's it. I'm telling.'

'You wouldn't.'

'I would.'

'They'd never forgive me.' He rolled his eyes in terror.

'Too right,' I laughed. 'How was the ride?'

'Wonderful. Great to get out for a bit. You remember that long track on the southern edge of the woods? Jasper took that at the gallop a couple of times. Like we did once ages ago. How long's it been since we rode together?'

'A long time.'

'Listen,' he said, 'when we get to the farm, let's ask Greg if we can hire both horses tomorrow. I've found an amazing new view.'

To one side of the road was a field where Sammy and I had helped plant a small forest of government-subsidized hardwoods. Unimpressive bare sticks were projecting out of pink plastic coats.

'I have to go back to Oxford tomorrow.'

'Oh.' The smile lost out to a frown for just a second. 'I thought you were back for Christmas now. Anyway, what's so urgent that you can't stay a couple of days?'

'That's what I wanted to talk to you about.'

'Shoot,' he said.

I explained about the project and the proposed trip to Kenya. The description of the equipment took me about three times as long as Fieldhead, and Sammy watched me struggle through the technical detail with a mixture of amusement and disbelief in his expression.

'What's the catch?'

'There isn't one,' I said as we reached the farm stables.

'Then why are you asking me? You don't need me to tell you that a free holiday in a beach resort is a good thing.'

'It's just . . . I'm not sure I like the idea of being a guinea pig.'

He picked up a couple of brushes and handed me one. 'Help me with this, will you?' Taking the brush, I began working at the mud on the horse's left flank. Sammy's strokes were neatly efficient, leaving stripes of smooth, clean hair. 'Jasper is really loving this attention. Greg's been neglecting him. Some kind of trouble with his sheep, I think.' He finished off the left hind leg and then, without looking at me, said, 'This girl you're going with. You're not doing the experiment just because you think she wants you to?'

'No! God, why do you say that?'

'I only ask because you said you'd turned it down before you met her. I wondered what made you change your mind.'

'I don't know. Not her.' I wasn't going to start discussing my role in a near suicide. Not even with Sammy. 'I just thought about it a bit more and realized it could be a really important medical advance.'

'Sounds like you're overcomplicating the issue.' Sammy moved round to the other side of the horse and started on the right flank. I could see only his legs below the animal's belly: neatly polished boots, jodhpurs coated in hairs and sweat, knees bending and straightening.

'He's offering you an amazing trip with this girl: I would jump at the chance. What's her name, anyway?'

'Cara.'

'Nice name. Unusual.'

'She is unusual.'

'Tell me about her,' he said.

I hesitated, wondering where to begin. 'She's great,' I said simply.

'I'm sure,' he laughed. 'But can you be a bit more specific?' Then he registered the silence and straightened up, gazing at my expression over the back of the horse. 'She really is great?' he said softly.

'She really is.'

He dropped his brush and walked round to my side. Sammy, too, had once – briefly – known a really great girl. He knew exactly what it meant. 'Tell me about her,' he said, shifting the bridle aside and sitting on a bale of hay.

I sat beside him. As if self-conscious with two sets of eyes now facing him, Jasper began to shuffle around, turning his head away from us.

'She's more alive than anyone I've ever met before,' I said. 'She takes control, but not in a way that weakens everyone else. More like a catalyst – you feel stronger for it. As if she were demonstrating what you *could* be doing. All the usual barriers that you invent for avoiding action, she just shows them for the weak excuses they are and moves beyond them.'

It felt ironic to be describing Cara in those terms, knowing that if she could hear it she would just laugh and tell me to stop wasting time on idle shrink-talk.

'I'm curious,' said Sammy. 'I was expecting you to talk about her background, her looks, what she's doing at Oxford. Most unlike you to get so deep.'

'That's her. The superficial is almost irrelevant. She draws you into herself so quickly that you don't have time to go through all the routine stuff. Her background is straightforward, her looks are incredible, she's doing a PhD in genetics, but none of that matters. What does matter is that sense of awakening, of finally finding reality in life. I feel like I suddenly understand what's going on around me, as if I've just been gently dozing up till now. She has that effect on people.'

'She sounds perfect,' said Sammy, almost reverentially. Then, to bring us both back to ground: 'And great tits too, I bet.'

'Yeah,' I admitted. 'That too.'

Sammy's final piece of advice had been simple: don't mention it to the Ps until you're sure you're going to do it. They won't like the idea so there's no point giving them the opportunity to talk you out of it. After all: emotions, Ben? In this house?

We spent the rest of the day catching each other's eye as our parents launched into one arid topic after another. Sometimes they wanted our contribution, but more often they were content just to chatter between themselves on the perennial issues of fuel prices, the garden and which newspapers to take.

I was peacefully dozing on the sofa that evening when one of those newspapers landed on my chest. It was heavily loaded with colour supplements and excessive business musings, and I started up in surprise. Sammy was sitting opposite me.

'World Affairs section,' he said.

It was a short article, no pictures. But the headline said it all: *Kenyan Coast Thrown into Pre-Election Anarchy as Police Station Burns*.

I stared at it in disbelief.

'Something to think about,' murmured Sammy.

I threw the newspaper on to the desk. The Zoology Department was my first point of call after speeding back from Dorset the next morning.

'You're sending me to a war zone? You're sending *Cara* to a war zone? Are you crazy?'

Fieldhead cast a sleepy eye over the article and then smiled. 'Interesting distinction. I rather suspect she'd be better able to cope than you.' He handed the paper back. 'But you mustn't get carried away by these reports. It's all very isolated. What happens in one part of the country is irrelevant to the rest. When the air force attempted a coup in '82, Nairobi got vaguely concerned but hardly anyone at the coast even noticed.'

'This *is* at the coast.'

'Sure, but it's in Likoni. Other side of Mombasa. Watamu could be a million miles away for all the impact this will have.'

'What about this election? It's at New Year. What happens if the wrong guy gets in and the whole place collapses?'

'Not a chance. They get frightfully worked up before these things, but then accept the result as a *fait accompli*.

Honestly, you shouldn't worry. I was there for the '92 election and everything was calm as a sloth.' He smiled again. 'Really, you should be grateful for the chance to broaden your horizons a little.'

I pointed to the problems in Rwanda, in Ethiopia, Uganda, Sudan, Somalia, in fact almost every other country in the region. But Fieldhead brushed them all aside with equal ease. Eventually I relented in the face of his unflappable optimism, and concentrated on my other worries.

'Piece of cake,' he said breezily, when I asked about the sensor. 'Ana Krugman will do the dirty work. An absolute pro with a needle and thread. You've nothing to worry about. She does this sort of thing all the time.' He smiled at my nervous face. 'The stitches will only last four weeks, but that's more than long enough to get everything we want. After that I'll need about one more day of your time for a debrief and full analysis of all the recordings. You'll be taking notes each time you make a recording, so we can work from those to reconstruct each scene.'

'What sort of notes? I can't see myself scribbling purple prose full of flowery introspective wanderings.'

'Absolutely not. This is supposed to be rigorous science. I'll want to see a date and time to identify the recording – each one will be time stamped when you switch on the machine – and a clear description of the context: what are you doing, seeing, hearing, feeling, tasting and smelling? Then a description of the emotions you experience. What bodily reactions do they cause? What facial expressions? What thoughts or beliefs are going through your mind? How is your outlook on life affected? What actions do the emotions make you want to take?'

I held up my hand. 'You're going too fast. I'm still not sure I should do this. How do I know my brain isn't going to get irradiated by having this thing strapped to my head? If it can transmit data to the recorder, presumably I'm going to have ... what ... radio waves? ... whatever they are, pouring into my skull non-stop for three weeks? Surely that sort of treatment could be carcinogenic?'

'OK, let me explain the equipment a bit more clearly.' Fieldhead picked up the minute sensor and dropped it into my hand. 'The first thing to realize is that the battery in this thing – space age as it is – is fairly limited. It enables the sensor to transmit neural data as radio waves continuously for a couple of months, but only at very low power. To compensate, the receiver in the recorder has to be very sensitive and consequently is worth about a thousand times more than the radio in your stereo. You'll need to make sure that the recorder is within a few feet whenever you use it. The benefit of having such a weak signal is that it will have even less effect on your brain than the standard radio waves that are constantly bombarding us all. So, no problems there.'

I nodded, a little more convinced, but then remembered my other worry. 'Supposing I come back with a bunch of recordings that don't contain any signals. Like a camera film that never wound on properly. How do you know it'll work?'

'You're right. It's time we checked that your brain does

function normally.' Fieldhead picked up the recorder and plugged in a cable. 'Normally, the data would go on to one of these digital tapes, but here we can relay it straight into my computer. Press that thing against the back of your head – move your hair out the way as much as possible – and have a look at this.'

Fieldhead had typed in a password and was opening up an unfamiliar application, its simple design looking out of place against his sophisticated desktop. A logo appeared – a cartoon monkey swinging from the capital S of the engineers' corporate name – followed by a menu of codes. Fieldhead selected F47 and the screen cleared to show a blank graph. He switched on the recorder and wired it up to the computer. Intrigued, I slipped the sensor up against the back of my scalp and held it in place with a fingertip. A sudden burst of movement appeared on the screen, with rapid erratic oscillations being traced along the graph. In a few seconds, these had died away to leave a gently wavering line running along the base of the graph.

'Each person's signal strength is quite different, so what you just saw was the computer adjusting the input to give a more intelligible display.' I nodded, fascinated to see part of my own brain represented on this computer, even if only by a single green line. 'When the software engineers were first designing this program, they had a few problems getting the right sort of base for each emotional signal. The aim was to get volunteers in an emotionally neutral state, measure their signal output and use that level as the baseline for calibrating the computer. They ran into difficulties when they wired up one man off the street to get a baseline for their "excitement" measure. In the calm conditions of the lab, the engineer couldn't understand why the volunteer was producing such intense signals, until he looked up and noticed the man's eyes locked on his and a big erection showing through his beach shorts.'

I started to laugh. 'Well, I promise I won't . . .' I broke off as the line on the screen leaped up the graph, levelled out and then fell back to the base again. 'What the hell was that?'

Smiling proudly, my tutor tapped the screen with his pencil. 'That, sir, is your sense of humour. This graph is the visual representation of one of the frequencies of neural signal coming out of your head. It was the easiest, and the first, to be categorized. As your response to my fictional account of software development shows, the frequency is clearly linked to humour. I'm glad to say you seem to be normal, neurally at least.'

Putting the sensor back on the desk, I watched the line drop to the bottom of the graph and run flat. 'So each of those menu items was a different frequency?'

'Exactly. Many other frequencies are recorded as well, and we're still trying to work out what they all are. Your results will be the main input for those studies. The twelve you saw in the menu are those frequencies that have been reasonably well linked to particular emotions. However, it would be better from an experimental point of view if you didn't know what they are yet. It might influence your notes.'

I stared at the screen, still amazed at the significance of that single upward sweep of the curve: an electronic record laying bare my mind. I felt a shiver as I started to sense the potential of that tiny piece of technology. Up until that moment, it had all been no more than an unlikely theory to me. Now, I was forced to admit the reality of the project. Worries switched from radiation and cosmetics to new fears about what this thing could reveal about me. What private thoughts and hidden secrets would it find?

Fieldhead didn't need any electronics to read my mind. 'Scary, isn't it, when you actually see it work? Makes you wonder what you can think about.' He nodded for me. 'What you have to remember is that these graphs will only show emotional results. It is impossible to determine what was going through your mind from them. If you get turned on by looking at fat men in posing pouches, you could do that quite happily and all I could tell from these data is that you were experiencing high levels of pleasure at the time. The stimulus itself would be a closed book to me.'

'Which is why you need the notes.'

'Exactly. Anything you don't want me to know about, don't record it,' explained Fieldhead. 'But I hope you won't hide too much. Think of me as a doctor or a priest, someone you can talk to in the safe knowledge that I won't pass on anything. That way the data, and your notes, will be much richer.'

I'd run out of fears; exhausted my excuses. It was time to decide. I thought about the two parties planned with Piers and his cronies in far-off parts of the country. I looked out on the bleak, grey field under an even greyer sky. I pictured strained Christmas dinners with ageing relatives. And yes, I confess, I thought about the recurrent, unrelenting guilt and shame every time I visited Jenni's ward. Then I imagined Cara lying on a beach sharing fruit cocktails after an early morning dive. There was no contest.

Cara was in full Kenya mood by the time I got back to the flat, reminding herself out loud to pack a camera. She seemed to have taken it for granted that I would agree to the project, and once I'd kissed her she held out her hand. Three tablets: two proguanil, one chloroquine, she explained. We could have gone for the heavy stuff, but I've heard nasty things about the side effects.

I paused before her excited smile. There was another problem, of course. The question of who would look after Jenni was still unresolved. Although I hadn't been fully forgiven over Cara, I knew I was filling a vital role in providing a basis of familiarity to help her through her recovery – particularly her mental recovery. If she was left alone, I didn't like to think what might happen. The first upper-floor window she came to . . .

Cara was shocked that I hadn't called Jenni's parents. Unconsciously she closed her fist around my pills and dropped it into her lap, berating my lack of responsibility. But I remembered Jenni's frightened plea and stood firm. It took her two hours to persuade me.

Jenni was wearing an earnest expression that spoke of important messages to convey. She was sitting up in bed, her leg lying on top of the sheets, an extra hospital gown

covering the bare flesh above the plaster. The moment
I was seated by her bed she began:

'I think you're trying to prove something to yourself,
Ben.' There was a forceful glow in her eyes. 'Aren't you?'

'Am I?' I felt uncomfortable straight away, but I didn't
want to discourage this new energy. Jenni's conversation
since reaching hospital had been flaccid at best. Except,
of course, for the Cara outburst – if that could be called
conversation. Any progress towards the keen-minded
spirit of before was to be welcomed, even if the subject
matter was disturbing.

'I think you are. It explains a lot about you.'

Remembering the message I'd come to deliver, I wondered if she was right.

'I don't mean you visiting me like this. That's just you
being nice. But all these other things you seem to want
to do. Like going to those wretched parties where everyone is so antagonistic.'

'It's just socializing. That's all.'

'And going out with that girl.'

I felt myself bristling immediately. The hostility in the
remark was undeniable. 'Do we have to go into this
again?' I asked. 'It won't change anything. Besides, what
does seeing Cara prove to anyone?'

She met my stare and shrugged. 'I don't know. You
tell me. You're the one who's screwing her.'

'Look . . .'

'She doesn't love you, Ben.' It came out as a shrill,
unstable plea. A sudden betrayal of the underlying emotion. 'Can't you see that? She's just using you.'

I looked down, unwilling even to answer. It had been

ridiculous to hope she would forget about my budding relationship, or even to pray that her feelings for me would evaporate like a dash of the medical alcohol that scented the room. I should never have come back after that last outburst. The transition was way overdue. I adopted an impersonal tone and broke the news.

'I have to go away.'

She said nothing. In her eyes, a glazed expression appeared. The small flicker of hope that had resurfaced over the last few days seemed to shrivel and die. The flowers were too bright and cheerful, too full of themselves to be placed beside this hurt shadow.

'It's important. It's medical research that can't wait.' It's for you, I couldn't say.

'What about me?' she said. 'I can't face being alone. Endless days of nothing but TV and twittering nurses. I feel so helpless, having to be fed, washed. I need someone to be there for me.'

'Jenni. Your parents . . .'

'No,' she said immediately. 'I told you. I don't want them to know. I'd die of shame if they found out.'

I swallowed and looked down. 'I'm sorry,' I whispered, and opened the door.

As her parents walked in, I turned to wave goodbye. Her face was ashen, shocked eyes locked on mine, contorted mouth paralysed in the motion of cursing my betrayal. The last thing I saw was a bright red felt tip heart on the plaster, just above a mangled, pointlessly mashed heel.

5

Recording No: 21
Date: 17 December   **Time:** 6.30 am
Situation: Water-skiing on Mida creek
Sensory Context: Auditory: racing water, loud engine;
    Visual: dark, mangrove-lined background; Tactile:
    cold
Cognitive Context: Controlling skis, enjoying the rush
Emotional Context: Anticipation, nervousness, then
    excitement
Somatic Response: Butterflies, tense muscles before
    starting
Facial Response: Tense
Global Viewpoint: N/A
Action Impulse: Strong, but can't describe it

Cara was stroking the back of my head. Her fingers
smoothed the surrounding hair over the sensor and ran
down to rest on my neck. I knew from trials with mirrors
that it didn't show, but all the same I was glad for her
reassurances. She brought her lips up to the sensor and
ran her tongue around the edge, slowly caressing my
scalp where the stitches still itched.

'Do you think I can stimulate it directly like this?' she
murmured.

In the aisle seat an overweight American woman, with a face like a pink cauliflower, snorted disapprovingly and moved two rows forward.

'Just don't bite it off,' I whispered to Cara. 'I don't want to have to go back and get it sewn on again.'

The clinic had been a plush but discreet affair, with pleasant staff who appeared to exist solely to put me at my ease, plying me with coffee in an oak-panelled waiting room. I felt as if I was about to have a very expensive face-lift. After a few minutes, a small door behind a façade of fake books opened and Fieldhead walked in with a tall, white-coated woman who introduced herself as Ana.

'So here's the victim.' Her hand was smooth ivory.

Fieldhead just shrugged and grinned. Ana was already running a finger over the back of my head and testing the stretch in the skin. 'Good. You're not too deformed. We should be able to find a nice flat patch.'

The woman led us into another oak-lined room, where various surgical instruments lay around a couch like cocktail accessories in a period drawing room. I climbed on to the couch and settled my face into the pillow. I felt handfuls of hair being pulled back and secured with clips. A pair of scissors worked briefly over a small area of skin at the base of my skull. A damp feeling signalled the shaving cream, followed by Ana's warning about her cutthroat and the slight sting of naked steel on virgin skin. More warnings, and then the twinge as needle entered flesh, almost sideways, to release the numbing fluid. A small pause, then only sensations of pressure as I imagined fingers – probably his – aligning the little piece of Californian wizardry, while other fingers – probably hers – fed the threaded needle through the tiny eyelets along its sides, making brief incursions into my scalp.

It had all been over in ten minutes.

The American with the cauliflower face sneaked back after the stewardesses had served dinner to retrieve her copy of *White Mischief*, careful to avoid eye contact with us. Cara blew a kiss at her retreating perm, then started to read her guidebook. I pulled out the green folder, marked with the Oxford crest, and went through Field-head's instructions once again.

Some of the emotions that you are going to experience will be gold dust to me. It is essential that you keep the recorder with you at all times, primed with new tape and batteries. Be aware that it is very difficult to sustain a particular emotion for a long time. If you find yourself experiencing a reasonably strong emotion, start recording straight away. Otherwise you may miss it. Linked to this is the phenomenon that opposite emotions often come in sequence. So if you experience a period of great happiness, it is likely to be followed by some sort of comedown, possibly even depression. (People very rarely live 'happily ever after'.) This works to our advantage, scientifically, in the sense that you may be able to record a number of less pleasant emotions without going out of your way to achieve them. Please take advantage of any such depression, sadness or irritation that follows the better experiences, and make appropriate notes.

Cara had already discarded the guidebook and was looking aimlessly through the airline magazines.

Unimpressed, she leaned over the aisle and started chatting to the next passenger.

The science of emotions is in its infancy. We are still a long way from knowing how emotions are generated. We don't even really know how to define an emotion. There is obviously a cognitive component – the conscious feeling – but that may be just the tip of the iceberg. The unconscious components that impact our muscular and endocrinal systems are probably far more important, and relate to a range of quite distinct physiological functions. This brings us to the core of the dilemma for neurophysiologists: we talk about emotions as a single concept, and yet in reality they are not a homogeneous group. Some have major visceral components; others are entirely in the mind.

Cara had sent a stewardess to collect some wine, and was busy telling her new friend the garbled trivia she had absorbed from the guidebook. 'You know Kenya was only colonized because of the railway to Uganda? Sort of settled in on the way to Lake Victoria. And Nairobi's only there because they got fed up building the track and took a break . . .'

One way to look at an emotion is as the product of any discrepancy between our expectation and actuality. That is why happiness, love and delight wear off, even if the stimuli that initially caused them are still present. We start to expect what we are getting. When everything happens perfectly in alignment with our expectations (as opposed to our hopes, which may be fulfilled against our expectation, causing happiness) then there is no emotion, except perhaps boredom. To me, this is the most profoundly depressing conclusion, but at least it starts to provide an evolutionary explanation for some of the emotions: they are the body's way of alerting us to an unexpected situation or event. All a bit woolly so far, but we should start to understand much more now that we can measure them.

'. . . and then the whole area became strategically vital in the First World War. The Germans were trying to find the source of the Nile and re-route it south into Tanzania, to kill off Egypt, the Suez Canal and our lifeline to India . . .'

Alan Jackson will be taking care of all your arrangements. He is an old Kenya hand and has been a friend for ten years. He helped me out when I was studying naked mole rats in Tsavo, providing all the logistical support. He is no scientist, but his knowledge of Kenya is second to none and his stories are truly magnificent. You should like him. In any case, he will make sure that everything runs smoothly with your hotel, car, money and any activities that you want to organize. He will meet you at Mombasa airport and get you up to Watamu.

Alan chose your hotel to provide you with as much flexibility as possible. It's a place called Madanzi. You'll be staying in one of their individual beach houses, which are fairly isolated from each other and from the central hotel building. The hotel is very popular with your generation at the coast, so you will be able to choose between the peace and quiet of your beach house or a lively night scene in the main building. I urge you to try some of both, as well as getting around other locations in the area. Diversity of experience is key to this project.

Cara was tugging at my arm. 'Come on. Talk to us. You've done enough homework for tonight.'

Finally, don't become frustrated if you are unable to express the emotions you feel. Just do what you can. As G. K. Chesterton said, 'there are in the soul tints more bewildering, more numberless, and more nameless than the colours of an autumn forest'. Not even a poet could really capture in full what you are going to feel.

'Chas is going to Watamu, too.'

I looked across at the scant bristles that were desperately trying to form a goatee. The hair was lank and greasy.

'All right, mate?' he grunted, a too-chilled grin exposing nicotine-stained teeth that seemed grotesque against the boyish face. A hand was thrust across the aisle. I took it reluctantly, wondering how much of Cara's rambling history he had taken in.

'He says it's the most relaxed part of the coast.'

'Really? Where are you staying?' Don't say Madanzi. Please don't.

'Oh I'll sleep out, I guess. Who needs a roof in Africa, huh?'

'We could give him a lift,' suggested Cara.

I glared at her, unable to be outright rude to this bum. No way, my eyes said.

'Cheers, but I wanna go slowly. I'll take a couple of

days and hitch along the coast. See you there, man,' he added as the lights were dimmed and the in-flight movie started. Thankful for the diversion, I reached for my earphones and closed him out, while the last lights of Italy faded into the blackness of the sea beneath.

Alan Jackson was late. We stood in the early morning sun outside the new international terminal at Mombasa airport, watching the other passengers being herded into white tour-mobiles marked with the names of the characterless hotels that Fieldhead had described along the coast at Nyali and Diani. You don't want to go there, Ben. Forgive my saying so, but it wouldn't be any better than the Med. Far too many obese German *fraus* chatting up beach boys and bagging the sun beds. Jackson suggested Watamu: a much nicer area with just a few small hotels. It's further to go, but well worth the effort, believe me.

We were surrounded by taxi-drivers who half-heartedly approached us every couple of minutes, but retreated at the slightest shake of our heads. The suede bag containing our passports and the recorder lay between my feet. Cauliflower woman panted past, hauling an enormous suitcase. With a glower at us, she got into the most crowded vehicle. As the canned tourists departed, an old Peugeot pulled up to the kerb and Jackson got out.

He was a large man in all dimensions, but didn't carry any fat. He pushed his way through the throng of taxi-drivers and walked straight up to us. Brushing sweat from his thick black eyebrows and pushing damp hair back to display a wide scar across his forehead, he held out an enormous hand.

'You must be Ben. And Cara? Sorry I'm late. The car wouldn't start. It's this damn climate. Just too damp down here at the coast.' He spoke with the slightly clipped drawl of the white Kenyan. Softer and friendlier, it nevertheless bore marked similarities to the South African voices that turned up in various corners of Oxford. Instinctively, Jackson stooped for the two heaviest bags, but I managed to beat him to one of them. He grinned and pointed to the little suede bag. 'Is the gadget in there? I'm looking forward to seeing it. But I suppose we ought to wait until we're in the car.' He cast a suspicious eye over the surrounding crowd. None of them seemed remotely interested in the huge white man with the sweat patches down his back who turned and led us to his Peugeot.

Jackson drove quickly out of the manicured, irrigated gardens of the airport and into urban Black Africa. It was still only eight in the morning, but all along the way groups of people were selling food, carving wooden statues, or mending dilapidated cars. Crowds of pedestrians were spilling on to the road. Bright equatorial light blinded us: the first warning of the immobilizing heat to come. We took the causeway to the island of Mombasa where Jackson ignored road lanes in accordance with local custom and sped past the ranks of election posters that obliterated road signs and every other stationary surface.

'It will take a good hour to get up to Watamu. I'll drive you as far as my place at Kilifi, where I've left your car. I managed to find a hire firm that had a Mercedes

SL. Quite unusual out here and very expensive, but James seemed to think you were worth it. He suggested it might be useful on the excitement front. But for Christ's sake, be careful. The potholes are lethal and there are often Africans wandering around in the middle of the road – especially at night. They're bloody difficult to see in the dark, being non-reflectives.'

Nearing the centre of Mombasa, we began to hear shouting. Angry voices merged with whistles and horns. Jackson frowned and shrugged his shoulders. The noise became louder and as we turned into the next street, we found ourselves facing a wide column of banners and irate faces. Jackson slammed his foot on the brake and threw the car into the side of the road.

'Lock your doors, please,' he muttered. 'Probably best not to look at them. They'll be gone soon.'

The march surged towards us until hot bodies and hot voices surrounded the car. I turned and looked at Cara. She seemed completely unconcerned. A fist struck the roof of the car, and instinctively I glanced round. Wrath-filled eyes stared into mine. The man had KFP painted in red on his white shirt. I turned away quickly.

'Who are they?' I whispered.

'Kenya Freedom Party. New bunch of crazies that got together after the last election. They want to "free" Kenya from its oppressors, apparently. That's us, by the way. All non-blacks. They're giving the Indians a really hard time because they can't stand the fact that they're the ones who keep the country going economically. They've been burning shops and threatening to beat up the Indian traders.'

'Why oppressors?'

'They resent the country's dependence on Western tourism and they resent the affluent lifestyle of the English expatriate community here. The President very sensibly refused them political registration on the grounds of bigotry, and so now with the election coming up they're getting really unpleasant. Keep threatening to shoot a few tourists to show their strength. Make an impression on the world.'

With the bulk of the crowd past the car, Jackson started the engine.

'Great. Thanks,' I said.

He didn't see the connection at first. 'Oh, you don't need to worry. This is a Mombasa problem. Watamu is far too sleepy for this kind of *shauri*.' He pulled out and drove between the remaining stragglers. In the wake of the march, the roads were clear. We quickly reached the bridge to Nyali and the long road north.

Cara sat in the back with one hand resting on my shoulder, a finger occasionally toying with the little black sensor. Neither of us spoke much, as Jackson kept up a running commentary of description and anecdote, only pausing to take a gulp from a bottle of beer. The car sped through mile after mile of sisal farm with the alien, endless rows of spiked succulents broken only by the occasional lone baobab.

'Just say if you want one of these,' offered Jackson as he reached for a new bottle. 'But I suppose it's still only five in the morning for you. Coffee at my place, then. We're almost there.'

I had expected a kind of bushman's shack, perhaps

built of corrugated iron or rough bricks, and adorned with rifles and hunting trophies. Jackson did not seem to fit his elegant white house with its polished stone floors and prints of eagles. Spacious verandas decorated with wicker furniture and overflowing pot plants flanked the building, and as we pulled into the drive, a white-coated house servant appeared. Around the edge of the house, delicate shrubs and flowers spoke of diligent attention from other staff. A small, circular terrace under a Greek dome stood alone and slightly above the house, on a promontory overlooking Kilifi creek. In the centre of the terrace was a table laid for breakfast with jugs of iced juices and baskets of fruit.

'Magic,' whispered Cara as we walked up the grass. 'I've never seen anything like it.'

The seats were spaced along one curved side of the table, and we sat looking out over the cliff, watching the morning fishermen sail across the blue, dazzling sea. It was perfect. Warmth, Cara, beauty, freedom. If this wasn't happiness . . . I reached into the suede bag that lay between us. It felt odd to be making my maiden recording in front of an audience, but Cara nodded and squeezed my hand as I switched on the recorder. Jackson looked across and just smiled. In silence, we sipped mango juice and absorbed this perfect introduction to Africa.

'I'm here quite by chance.' Jackson was replying to Cara's questions about the house. A pair of fish eagles swam lazily overhead, drifting on the air currents forced up by the cliff. The air was growing perceptibly hotter. 'It used to belong to some great friends of mine from my Nairobi days. Peggy and John Asquith. He was a government official in the colonial era. They moved down here when Nai-Robbery started getting too dangerous. Then they got burgled within a year of buying this place and were treated quite roughly in the process. Damned unlucky, as crime isn't usually so much of a problem around here. The police spend most of their time chasing marijuana dealers, as they don't have to worry about many real offences. Anyway, Peggy got fed up with the country after that and they decided to go back to Wiltshire. They couldn't find a buyer quickly so they offered the place to me at half price. As I'd recently had a bad experience in Nairobi, I took it. But I'm certainly not used to this sort of style.' He grinned and refilled our coffee cups.

'What sort of bad experience?' asked Cara, dropping grapefruit segments into her mouth.

'Oh, an attempted burglary. Quite unpleasant, really. I found an anonymous message pushed under my door one day that instructed me to leave the house wide open the following Saturday evening and then disappear. I was to go and stay with a friend, so that a band of thieves could burgle me without any inconvenience to either side. Astonishing, I know, but not unusual in Africa. The note warned me of serious trouble if I informed the police.' Jackson rubbed his neck and allowed a little humour into his face to counter Cara's alarmed expression.

'Well I did what they asked, without telling the police. Instead I had a quiet word with an old friend. He was my driver thirty years ago when I was running hunting expeditions, and is now quite highly placed in the army. He arranged for a few of his troops to drop round on Saturday night – as an exercise, of course. They hid themselves in the bushes around my house and waited. Within an hour, two vans drove up and seven men got out. I think they meant to take everything, even the furniture. They didn't, of course, because the military boys stood up and surprised them. Unfortunately, one of these damn fool villains was stupid enough to loose off a shot at the soldiers, who immediately dropped to the ground and opened fire. They killed every one of the poor buggers, except for one chap who made off into the night.'

The humour had disappeared. 'It doesn't end there, though,' he warned. 'We drove to the local police station to report the incident, the soldiers all in high spirits after their real life engagement. They marched into the station, ready to make their report, only to find a man in the back room pulling on his uniform while sweating buckets and bleeding from a bullet wound in the arm. It didn't take them long to work it out. The man was escorted to a military gaol where I imagine he is probably still waiting for a trial.'

'You must have been all over the papers with a story like that.'

'Not at all. Police corruption is fairly common out here. A lot of them expect to be bought off, and they can get very nasty if you don't play their games. Of course, we don't see the worst of it. If you talk to the local Kenyans, they can tell you stories of police brutality that you really would not believe. The things these people do to each other in the gaols: it's enough to make you sick.'

Jackson stopped, suddenly aware that he was casting a black cloud over our first morning in Paradise. 'Not that you will see anything like that. Three weeks at Watamu will show you how much more there is to life than dear old stone cold England.'

Ten o'clock, and Jackson was getting down to work. On the table were maps, insurance policies, folders of local currency and our hotel reservations. Cara had disappeared with her bags to a bathroom. Ticking off a mental list on his large brown fingers, Jackson was offering cautions, advice, local information and a rehash of Fieldhead's instructions. An old grey cat padded on to the table, yawned and quietly collapsed on top of the banknotes. The gentle patter of a sprinkler drifted in from the lawns below the veranda. We examined the Mercedes – a sleek white vehicle with a black top – and transferred the remaining luggage from the Peugeot. Once again, Jackson traced out the route to Watamu on the map. Straight across the bridge and along the coast road. You can't go wrong: there aren't many alternative routes around here. Just remember to take the Watamu turning, or you'll end up in Malindi and have to speak Italian for the next three weeks.

Cara emerged from the house freshly showered and dressed in a striped top and white shorts, with damp hair lying crumpled over her shoulders. Jackson noticed her bare feet and warned of thorns and parasitic worms, but she just shrugged casually and pulled on her Ray Bans. The great white hunter almost seemed to approve. We thanked him, took one last look at his magnificent view, then lowered the Merc's top and set off for Watamu.

Madanzi was old in Kenyan terms, showing all the signs of its colonial past. White pillars and broad verandas surrounded the main building which housed the reception, restaurant and bar. Everything was open and airy, with only the occasional wall to support the roof. Earthenware pots held succulent green plants with leaves the size and shape of elephants' ears.

A short redhead introduced herself as Kristina and welcomed us by name. She had a *kikoi* hitched up around her thighs, and like Cara she wore nothing on her feet. I began to feel a little overdressed.

Kristina led us down a sandy path towards a line of beach houses, each one screened on either side by a tumbling mass of red and white bougainvillaea. She chose one and guided us round to the front for our first view of the Indian Ocean. The deep blue was as exotic as the sea at Kilifi, but here the slim English yachts were replaced by dhows and squat, brutish deep-sea fishing boats. Great stands of rock protruded from the sea like giants' stepping stones, and in the distance the line of a reef was traced where white water broke over the coral barrier. Along the beach, palm trees were set among dunes hidden beneath thick green creepers. But most striking of all was the beach itself, covered in fine white sand that danced in the wind at each footstep. Far into the distance this shimmering strand separated land and sea, as pure and empty as an undiscovered atoll.

'I've been here ten years and I'm still in love with this view,' said Kristina when she saw our reaction. 'You can never get bored of it.'

'No,' murmured Cara. 'No, I don't think we'll get bored.'

'And there's so much to do here. Great parties on Saturday nights – all the expats drive up from Mombasa. Windsurfing, water-skiing, diving . . .'

'Diving,' said Cara firmly. 'I need to learn. I want to catch up with this guy.' She gave me a playful punch.

'No problem. We have our own dive school and the conditions are perfect right now.' Kristina looked round as the porter arrived with the luggage. 'Come and see your place,' she said.

In the beach house, a spacious front room with pale yellow walls opened on to the veranda and the view to the sea. Between a curved teak bar and a dining table, two sofas stood draped in loose green covers. Above the table, a bookshelf held ancient back numbers of *Country Life* and *Tatler*, rubbing shoulders with a brand-new stereo and a line of compact discs.

'That isn't usually here,' Kristina said. 'Alan brought it over for you. I think he borrowed it off some rich Asian bloke in Mombasa. The CDs are a mixed bunch, but there's some good stuff in there.' She opened a door to the bedroom and showed us how to set up the mosquito net. 'It will normally be done by one of the staff. We don't have telephones in the beach houses I'm afraid, but if you want anything just press the button on the bar and someone will come over. Well, I'll leave you to it. Lunch is in an hour in the restaurant, or you can have it here if you prefer.' She pointed to a menu on the bar, then gave a little wave and was gone.

I took one look around the cool, clean beach house and started pulling off my clothes.

'So, Mr Guinea Pig. How do you like your cage?' said Cara.

'Fantastic. I need a shower.'

'And I need a drink. They've got an amazing selection here.'

I left her hunting through the bar and stood under a freezing jet for ten minutes. By the time I'd found some shorts and walked back into the front room, a row of bottles decorated the top of the bar. I looked around for Cara and found her already asleep on one of the sofas. On the table beside her was a full glass of juice. I sat next to her and looked out over the ocean. The beach was so close, but the slope of the sand left us out of sight to anyone down there. Just a few birds. Gentle waves. The air was cool. A ceiling fan turned slowly above us. So relaxing.

Sleepy.

Somewhere, very close by, a gentle African voice whispered something about food. A soft, pleasant, inquisitive voice. No face. I don't remember replying.

6

Recording No: 26

Date: 17 December   **Time:** 2.00 pm

Situation: Snorkelling in Watamu Marine Park

Sensory Context: Visual: fish, corals, polychaetes – all
stunning colours; Olfactory: salt and rubber

Cognitive Context: Examining fauna, remembering
lectures

Emotional Context: Interest, aesthetic pleasure

Somatic Response: None

Facial Response: Obstructed by mask and snorkel

Global Viewpoint: Engaged, more alive

Action Impulse: Keep looking

She dived like an angel. After a few moments of hesitation
on the descent, Cara was completely at ease. We watched
large fish prowl around us, and when their novelty wore
off we floated upside down or swam on our backs, relish-
ing the three-dimensional freedom that diving brings.
Every now and then, one of the group would spot a
dragonfish or a conger eel, and we would crowd around
to look. The dive leader shone halogen light over blue and
grey corals to convert them into a mass of reds, pinks and
yellows, their real colours freed of the mask imposed by
the heavily filtered light of the depths.

But most of the time, Cara and I kept slightly to one side of the group – checked every few seconds with a glance from the dive leader – exploring our own underwater world. At one point, a manta ray glided past, too distant for the rest of the group to notice, its horned head and massive, avian fins terrifying in their silent motion.

Cara swam for a while beside and slightly ahead of me, allowing me to rest one gloved hand on her buttocks and feel the muscles that powered her fins. She kept her arms under her body, as she had been taught to do, left hand gripping right wrist. When the group stopped to examine one new discovery, I held her back and pulled out my mouthpiece. Without hesitating, she did the same and pressed her mouth against mine to form a beautiful, submarine, watertight kiss. When she replaced her mouthpiece, she blew air through the secondary valve and cleared it like a veteran. Giving a distorted smile, she squeezed her thumb and forefinger together, and turned back to the group.

The morning sun had lulled Cara to sleep by the time the launch drew up against the shore. Casper, the South African instructor, leaped into the tepid shallows with his usual show of energy and yelled for his assistants to carry the equipment ashore. He turned back and gave a good-natured smile to see Cara still collapsed in the back of the boat. As I eased myself down the steps, Casper strode round to the stern and threw two big arms round Cara's waist. With no visible effort, he lifted her out of the boat and swung her on to the shore. Cara smiled weakly in thanks, stumbled a little way up the beach and then crumpled delicately on to the sand.

'Your responsibility once she's on dry land.' He grinned and jumped back into the boat to return her to a deep mooring.

I looked over at the long limbs, still encased in neoprene, and the snakes of blonde hair that lay haphazardly around the novice diver. 'Too bad,' I thought aloud.

I wandered up the beach, shedding my second skin on the way, and dropped on to the sand beside her. She lay on her stomach with her face tilted slightly towards the sun, sand plastered on her forehead.

'Are you breathing?' I tried to sound concerned. Cara smiled and gave a contented sigh, keeping her eyes and mouth closed. I leaned over and gently tugged down the zip on her wetsuit to expose moist skin that had already turned golden. Tiny white hairs stood out among droplets of seawater and I smoothed them away with the palm of my hand, enjoying the warm touch of her back. Little freckles had appeared on her nose, and her hair seemed to have become still lighter. I lay alongside her, resting my cheek against her forehead, and decided to forget Fieldhead for a moment. I'd made enough beach-with-Cara recordings already. I could allow myself a little unrecorded happiness.

Since the first day, when we'd been woken at four o'clock by a quietly curious waiter bearing a tray of tea and cakes, life had been perfect. That evening, we'd chosen dinner in the beach house and watched in awe as waiters laid out a banquet on the table. They left us alone to enjoy the cold seafood and Sancerre on ice until we pressed the bell for coffee. Sitting quietly and listening to the soft crash of sea against shore, we soaked up the heady, liberating atmosphere of our first African night.

When either of us wanted to hire windsurfers, use the tennis courts or eat in the restaurant, the staff treated us with a mixture of fascination and deference, tinged with amusement. Whatever we decided to do, they went out of their way to arrange. I hadn't seen Alan Jackson since our arrival, but his influence seemed to reach everyone from the waiters in the restaurant to Casper in the dive school.

Casper was a powerhouse in a land where lethargy was an accepted virtue. He raced between leading scuba dives, giving lessons in the pool, fixing equipment or fine-tuning the engines on his launch. With his chiselled face permanently fixed in a grin, he thrilled hotel guests with his energy and enthusiasm for life. Born twenty-seven years earlier in Durban, he'd spent all his days on the African coast, leaving his hair bleached and his skin taut bronze. Numerous scars testified to a hazardous lifestyle and inadequate medical facilities. Since leaving school at the age of seventeen, Casper had been working his way up the eastern side of Africa, stopping in any location that offered good diving for as long as it took to grow boring. For me, with a life dominated by centrally heated rooms and other people's expectations, Casper was a revelation.

He had taken up Cara's challenge immediately: a full diving course in just three days. And predictably – irritatingly – she was a natural. Her athlete's body and her confidence in water allowed her to master the basic procedures and emergency exercises in the pool without difficulty. I watched from the side for a while each morning, but mostly used the time to explore the surrounding area. Delightful as Madanzi was, I wanted to see the real Africa.

I found the network of paths on the fourth day, leading off the hotel drive beyond the old gates. Intrigued, I set off down one of them until I was completely surrounded by bush and growing hot from the lack of wind. The vegetation was dense, coarse and dressed in thorns. The complete silence surprised me, and I found that my footsteps on the crumbling coral rock were suddenly very loud. Birds were visible above, playing on wind currents imperceptible on the ground. Nothing moved. Every step just brought more views of endless bush.

With sweat running down my forehead, I stopped at a bend and sat in the shade of a tree. While I was cooling down, I heard sounds of laughter and shrill Swahili floating down the path. I turned my head and saw two men walking towards me, partially screened by the bushes at the bend. The voices grew louder, one man's hilarious story occasionally interrupted by expressions of amusement and disbelief from the other.

When the men were thirty feet away, I recognized the storyteller as one of the waiters who had been so attentive at the beach house over the previous days. Smiling, I rose and stepped into the path to greet him. His reaction was bewildering. Instinctively his hand went to his mouth, and for a moment his eyes opened wide.

I was confused. '*Jambo*,' I offered.

'*Jambo, bwana*.' His voice was hesitant.

There was a brief, embarrassing pause.

'Funny story?' I suggested.

He seemed even more distraught at that. 'It wasn't you I talked,' he said quickly.

So.

'It wasn't English you talked.'

For a moment, he didn't understand. Then his face unwound into a wide beam.

'So you're OK,' I winked, looking more generous than I felt.

'Yes! OK!' He tried to wink back, but blinked instead.

I changed the subject. 'Is there anything to see along here?'

'Yes. My village. I show you!' Feeling safe now, he was grinning enthusiastically.

'Thanks. I'll go and have a look. I'm OK on my own. I'll see you back at the hotel.'

The first drop of irritation. The first cloud in a perfect sky. What did it matter if they talked about us behind our backs, found us amusing, ridiculous? That's the right of service staff throughout the world. Who cared if they thought we were too stiff, too white, too infatuated with each other? Whatever the topic of their conversation, it was nothing to me.

The village lay in a small clearing. Rudimentary huts of wattle and palm leaves stood in a haphazard pattern; the ground was scattered with old tins and coconut husks. A single child sat playing with a toy car, dragging it backwards and forwards through the dust. As I stepped into the clearing, the boy looked round and leaped up. I stopped, not wanting to scare him. Then I realized he had only one leg.

I started forward to help him, but the boy hopped frantically towards the nearest hut and disappeared inside. I walked over, wanting to reassure him, but hesitated when I noticed the KFP poster stuck beside the entrance. In that quiet, rural site, I felt a slight shudder.

Shaking off the memory of the violent march, I stepped up to the entrance. The inside of the hut was dark, and I let my eyes adjust for a few seconds. The boy was crouching in the corner, next to a pile of cooking tins and two unlit paraffin lanterns. But he was not looking at me. I followed his gaze to the other side of the hut. On a low sisal bed a young man was stretched out, staring at me with hostile eyes. Next to the bed lay a gun. A long, angry gun, with a curved ammunition clip. A lone tourist target. A show of strength.

I jerked back immediately, stepping away from the hut, the inflammatory poster filling my view. Then I spun round and ran back along the path, glancing over my shoulder every few seconds. When I reached Madanzi I went straight to Kristina.

'Ben, relax. There are election posters all over the place. There's nothing sinister about someone expressing their political views.'

'He had a gun, for Christ's sake. Alan said the KFP were threatening to shoot tourists.'

'He had a gun. So what? Do you realize how close we are to Somalia? All the refugees used to bring them down here to trade for food. The market price for an AK47 was a hundred shillings: less than one English pound. It probably doesn't even work. If you feel uncomfortable about it, stick to the hotel and the beach.'

Cara's reaction had been typical. She'd immediately wanted to visit the village. Only Casper's easy chatter about wreck diving had distracted her. Suicidal curiosity.

Cara flicked open an eyelid. 'No recording this time?' She shifted a little to slip her shoulders out of the wetsuit.

I shook my head. 'I think we've done this one before, don't you?'

'True. Much as I like lying on the beach, I suppose we're going to have to explore some new areas of your twisted mind fairly soon.'

'Dr Fieldhead will be most grateful for your dedication,' I said.

Cara ignored that, but rolled on to her side, facing me. 'I've got something planned,' she said with one raised eyebrow. 'I wasn't going to tell you. In fact I'm still not going to tell you. Wait and see. Tonight.' She gave a mischievous smile and then rolled back on to her stomach, her face turned away.

With my shoulders starting to burn, I looked around for the sun cream. Casper was ambling towards us, an air cylinder swung over each shoulder. He whistled in a failed attempt to get Cara's attention, then kicked sand over her back. 'Wake up, darling. I want to invite you both to lunch.'

'Ben, if you don't beat the shit out of him for that, you'll never sleep with me again.' Cara still hadn't moved from her collapsed position.

I sat up and winked at Casper's smiling face. 'Sorry,

Cara. I'm afraid he's too big for me. If I do try to beat the shit out of him, I'll never *be able* to sleep with you again. Shall I accept?'

Her head nodded briefly and then lay back in the sand. Casper shifted the cylinders on his shoulders. 'Great. Back of the dive school at one o'clock, then. It's very casual, but you'll probably be glad of that after all the pampering you've had.'

The sun cream was nowhere to be seen.

'I've got to get into the shade for a while,' I said when Casper had gone. 'See you back at the house?'

Cara's responsiveness had evaporated in the heat.

I reached the beach house at the same time as a waiter. The waiter. He was carrying fresh supplies of fruit, ice and mixers to replenish the bar stocks. I couldn't help my nervous curiosity.

'I saw your village,' I started. Neutral territory.

He nodded enthusiastically.

'Do many people live there?'

'Few people.'

'I met a little boy,' I tried. 'With one leg.'

'Yes!' he grinned. All his gestures were a little exaggerated.

'A KFP supporter,' I said, laughing to make it a joke. 'I saw the poster on his house.'

The waiter stopped grinning. He looked nervous. I had to plunge into the painful silence.

'The guy in the hut? Was that his brother?'

'His father.'

So young.

I couldn't stop. I had to keep probing.

'So, do many people support the KFP around here?'

He looked distraught. 'I don't know,' he said eventually. Then his head went down as he thrust the supplies into their places behind the bar. Mixers in the fridge. Ice in the cork-lined bucket. No more conversation.

I smiled a taut goodbye and walked through the bedroom to the shower.

'Ben? Can I have a quick word please?' Kristina's voice was light and friendly as always, but it was the first time she had looked even slightly ruffled.

Cara carried on walking towards the dive school. 'I'll pour you a drink,' she said.

Kristina led me to her office behind the reception. 'I'm sorry about this, I really am,' she started. 'But I just need to get something straight with you.'

I knew what she was about to say, and I felt about fifteen.

'This . . . thing with the KFP. I don't know why, but it's clearly bothering you. Do you want to have a talk about it? I mean, I can tell you more than the staff will, anyway.'

'Look, I'm sorry if I upset that guy. I didn't mean . . .'

'It's not a question of that. You don't need to apologize. It's our problem. But I have to ask you to be understanding here. It's very difficult at the moment, and we're all walking a bit of a tightrope.'

'I just didn't realize he'd get offended.'

'It's difficult for everyone. The election's a sensitive issue anyway, and the KFP is a real hot button at the coast. In a way it's a good thing: it's the first time there's been serious support for a party based on ideology rather than tribalism. It's just tragic that political progress is built from hatred. We're having a hard time with a lot of people. Any white business would around here. But tourism is a big issue for the KFP. And white-owned hotels . . . well . . . it's stretching a lot of loyalties.'

'And most of the staff are KFP?'

'Ben, listen to me. They're good people, all of them. We've been like family for a lot of the local people here. But the speeches that their leader is giving . . . make it hard. The staff are torn. The only way to help them out is to pretend the issue doesn't exist. Until the election is over. Let them get on with their jobs without being reminded of the contradiction.'

Put like that, I had not been exactly discreet. 'Are you worried about them?' I asked.

'No! Not at all. These people are wonderful staff. They're just in a difficult position. And we can't afford any disturbance. We have the local government breathing down our necks, waiting for us to upset people. Honestly, all the problems are with bureaucrats in Mombasa and Malindi. There's no threat here. But if we give those guys in Mombasa an excuse . . . You have to understand, running a business here is very difficult. Please, all I'm asking: enjoy the holiday and don't worry about the politics. That's all I'm asking. OK?'

'Of course,' I nodded. 'I won't think about it again.'

'Great!' she smiled. 'You're having lunch with Casper? Then you must go and join them quick before he has too much time alone with Cara.'

*

108

Damp wetsuits and dripping scuba gear decorated the fence around the plain wooden table behind the school. Casper had ordered a selection from the restaurant and now dished out dressed crab and avocado salad, while Cara filled our glasses from a jug of Pimms.

'So, what do you think, Ben?' Casper asked. 'Have I trained her well?'

'Not bad. Not bad, at all,' I admitted, remembering the ease with which Cara had cleared her mask, and the natural, relaxed movements she'd displayed.

'She did very well,' agreed Casper. 'But Christ, it's been a struggle to teach her anything.'

He laughed and ducked as Cara lashed out at him.

'So you don't reckon she's ready to work here yet?'

The suggestion appealed to her. 'Wouldn't that be great? Spending every day in the sea, and feasting on crab and avocado.'

'Yeah, that's the nice thing about working here. I hardly get paid anything, but the food is wonderful after the rubbish I had to eat in Dar-es-Salaam. They seemed to believe that as I was staff, it would be wrong for me to get the same deal as the guests. They even made us crap in different toilets. Jesus. Madanzi is much more relaxed about everything.'

'What was the rest of the coast like?' I asked.

'Great. I didn't hang around in Mozambique, as the language was too difficult and I used to hear shots most nights, but otherwise I had a good time everywhere.'

'Where was best?' Cara asked.

Casper paused for a moment. 'Difficult to say. Malawi had the nicest people. No diving, of course, but I felt I could trust the locals there. Here I wouldn't leave a regulator on the beach for more than thirty seconds. They nick everything, although God knows what they'd do with that sort of equipment. Probably cut the metal bits off and use the rubber piping to mend a tap.'

Cara nodded. 'Yes, that's just happened to a friend of ours. He's had his backpack stolen.' She turned to me. 'You remember Chas? From the plane? I saw him yesterday.'

I shuddered at the unwelcome memory. Friend of ours? In the perfect surroundings of Madanzi I had quickly forgotten about him.

'I invited him over this afternoon.'

'Cara!'

'Jesus, come on. Don't be so mean. The guy doesn't know anyone here. He's holed up in some miserable guest house, while we're getting all this for free.'

'What happened to "who needs a roof in Africa", then?'

'The guy's just had all his stuff nicked. He's allowed to be a little more edgy now. Be nice. He'll only come for a couple of hours.'

But Chas didn't come. We sat on the veranda with a tray of tea. I put *Aida* on the stereo. What's he going to think when he finds us listening to opera, she asked. That he shouldn't be here, I hoped silently. The afternoon floated by. Tea was replaced by beer. The sun started to fall behind us. Songs of love and triumphant marches gave way to dramatic plotting, recrimination and finally a desperate, melancholic duet. Cara's resistance faded as the music started to reach her. Softly, I described the young Egyptian soldier who loved a palace slave, who betrayed his country for her and was buried alive. The tide came in, bringing gentle waves closer to the beach house. Cara's eyes closed. But the slave girl hid in the tomb so that she could be buried with him. The ultimate sacrifice. We listened to the waves tumble on the shore as the stereo went quiet. Wind rustled around our legs, keeping the mosquitoes away. Cara sighed. Then she stood up.

'Fuck him. Ungrateful bastard. We've got things to do. I'm going to have a shower. Get me a drink will you?'

Dressed in loose cotton trousers and a plain white shirt, she reappeared twenty minutes later. Her hair was braided into a snake that hung over her left shoulder. Outside, the tropical sun had already disappeared. She accepted the whisky sour I had ready and then banished me to the bathroom. On the chair was a set of my clothes: dark chinos and a long-sleeved white shirt. Bemused by this unusual attention, I showered quickly and dressed as she wished. The front room was empty when I returned. A note was lying on the bar: *Start recording. Then get on, and turn right down the beach.*

The recorder sat waiting beside the note, a new tape already inserted. From the discarded wrapper in the ashtray I saw that she had even replaced the batteries. This would be unmissable. I pressed the button and clipped the recorder on to my belt, subconsciously running my hand through wet hair to check the sensor.

The second instruction was too abstruse so I skipped to the third, strolling across the veranda towards the beach.

And then I understood.

Standing to one side of the veranda, his reins attached to a palm tree, his polished saddle and bridle gleaming in the full moon, a horse was waiting patiently for his rider. I laughed out loud as I remembered Cara, tense and alert in trousers and braid. The other horse was nowhere to be seen. I checked the girth and swung up into the saddle.

We trotted down the slope and set off along the beach. The horse was over-excited, perhaps hunting for his companion, and he quickly broke into a canter. I shortened the reins and pressed down with my heels, feeling the iron stirrups hard against my bare feet.

We careered across the bare sands, the noise of the waves almost obliterated by the rush of air past my ears. Riding in the dark without hat or boots was a liberating experience after the staid country outings with my family. I raced past two hotels, one quietly hidden in the shadows, the other brilliantly vulgar in its ostentatious illumination. Guests lounged on the terrace walls of the second, enjoying pre-dinner drinks and gazing with blind eyes out to sea. Beyond the hotels, the land went dark, apart from the few small houses that lay bravely isolated along the coast. All the time my eyes were searching for her silhouette.

When she appeared it was from behind, charging out of the bushes like some ambushing Hun and sweeping past me. My horse needed no encouragement, breaking into a gallop to chase her. Soon both horses were racing along together, hooves throwing up sand in unison.

A large stand of rock loomed up out of the darkness and we swerved into the sea to avoid it. The white fluorescence of the surf became our guide as the beach curved round a point. On this new stretch, the coast was dark except for a single red glow in the distance. On a rocky outcrop a beacon was shining. We raced across the sands towards it, our horses leaping together over a fallen palm tree and daring each other to greater speeds. I begun to make out a line of smaller red lamps that ran diagonally from the beach up to the beacon. Slowing only a little, Cara pointed her horse at the nearest lamp and cantered up a broad, sandy path, bathed in red. Candle flames flickered inside the coloured glass of the lamps, hanging from wooden stakes at fifty-yard intervals. I put all my trust in her judgement and cantered up behind her.

I reached the top of the outcrop just after her and pulled to a halt beneath the tree that held the beacon. A tinted gas lamp, it threw a pool of fiery light over a rug covered in cushions, a basket and a cool box. We both dismounted, throwing our reins around a branch. Then I walked up behind her and ran my face down her damp neck.

When she felt me, Cara whipped round and pressed red lips to mine. Blood had rushed to her cheeks, and tiny beads of sweat lined her skin. Her tongue pushed hard, opening up my mouth and forcing its entry. I kissed her back strongly, driven by the same urgency and roughness of the ride. Her hands raced over my body, pulling at my shirt, running down my trousers. We held each other violently, struggling, fighting to keep balance, bodies pressed together. Cara allowed Fieldhead one more minute, then brought her hand down to my waist and switched off the recorder. She gave way first, and we fell on to the bed of cushions and made love in that small patch of light above the great, dark ocean.

When it was over, Cara pressed her face into my neck and wrapped her arms tightly around me, not letting go even after her taut body had relaxed back on to me. For several minutes I lay watching the night sky, feeling her grip firm against my skin and letting my mind rapidly fall in love with her. Individual stars disappeared temporarily as the black silhouette of a bat flew silently overhead. Once I saw a shooting star, its tail extending so long I shifted in wonder. But I didn't say anything to the girl in my arms. Instead I lay beneath her and dreamed of a life together, where I could tend to her every need and be part of her every thought.

She hadn't moved for some time, and her body was beginning to dry in the gentle breeze. But her face against my neck had become moist; irregular breaths on my skin. It was the first time I had known Cara to cry. She was utterly silent and her body was still. I could feel small tears gather on her eyelashes and scatter down my neck. For once, she seemed vulnerable. All the strong words and confident city humour that she used to build herself up into an invincible force were no longer there.

With the hair pulled back, the skin on Cara's neck was pale red in that light. Gently, I ran my fingers over it, feeling the outline of the vertebrae beneath. I kneaded along the muscles and worked my thumb round to her cheek. The tears had formed a slippery surface and I felt my way slowly up her face, drawing delicate circles on her damp eyelids. With both hands, I lifted her head up and kissed her on the eyes and mouth, savouring the salted vulnerability that made me want to pick her up and carry her home in my arms. I brought my lips to her ear and searched for the right words.

'I haven't felt like this about anyone before. I fell for you the first morning I woke up beside you, but . . .' I hesitated. So difficult to express. '. . . but I didn't know you cared. Now it's as if you're the only person I could ever love.' I paused, looking at the closed, mascara-streaked eyes, and felt my throat go wooden. 'I know you don't like to take this too seriously. But I want to tell you: I'm absolutely serious about you.'

Slowly, painfully, she opened her eyes. Just for a moment, I thought I saw a real and tragic longing there. A look of fear, almost. Then her face grew rigid and her eyes darkened with a look of furious irritation. Pushing against my shoulder, she straightened up and pulled herself off me. Standing naked, glaring down at me.

'Haven't you noticed yet that I'm not interested in that kind of bullshit? I'm still here because I enjoy fucking guys with a reasonable hard-on and a good sense of humour. That's all. If you're about to turn into some obsessed Romeo, then we can finish now. Clear?'

I stared back, shocked by her cruelty but still sure of what I'd seen. 'No,' I said quietly.

'No? What do you mean, no?'

'You were crying, Cara. Don't try and fight that feeling.'

'Feeling?' she spat. 'You think I get laid for the sake of some feeling? Is that what you think?'

'Why are you doing this? You know this isn't real. Why can't you let go of your ego and your comforting tough-girl image for a moment and see that this isn't a threat?'

At that, Cara spun round and grabbed her shirt. Speaking in a low, dangerous voice she let loose her final drops of venom. 'I think you remember me saying I never stay with the same guy for more than a week. Don't think, just because you've lasted a little longer, that the sentiment is any different.'

Picking up her trousers, she walked past me, feet scuffing up the dust by my face. I sensed her mount her horse, heard the clatter of hooves on coral rock as she trotted away. When the sounds had faded, I became vaguely conscious of my nakedness, lit up to any eyes that lurked in the surrounding darkness. But her tirade had drained me of the ability to move. All I could see was her hand angrily knocking the tears from flushed cheeks.

Time was marked only by the occasional appearance of a new shooting star. Gradually, the light above me started to dim. When it flickered and died, it broke the spiral of frustration that had engulfed me and I stood up, noticing stiff muscles and a chilling wind coming off the sea.

I pulled on my clothes and walked to the patient horse.

7

Friday, about 7.00 pm – written 4 hours later.

I'm sorry, but I don't think I can use your forms for some of these. They're just too rigid to explain what I feel. You said emotions often come in opposites, and I think I've just experienced the extreme ends of the spectrum. The bad stuff isn't on tape I'm afraid, but I don't think I'd have been able to write it down, anyway. I'm revisiting this several hours after the event, having been through some serious misery. At least you'll know I'm dedicated to your project: sitting here in the middle of the night, trying to recapture the scene.

I have a suspicion that you knew about the horses. It was utterly exciting and arousing, as I'm sure you planned. The context was unique: darkness, the smell of horses and leather, the sound of hooves and waves battering the sand, and the feel of cold steel and sweating animal. The anticipation was intense. Cara was acting crazily. When I caught up with her, she was very turned on, which of course was further stimulation for me. I think the tape should show what absolute passion looks like. What it won't show is the emotion that I was allowed for a short time afterwards. I think that would have been truly special.

Sunlight was streaming across the veranda when I woke to find Cara sitting on the coffee table. In her eyes, the old carefree, amused look was back.

'You sleep better out here than in bed,' she said, kicking the sofa. 'Maybe I'm just too disturbing for you. Too much stimulation for a decent kip. We should fight more often: you'd get more rest.'

I pushed myself up, straightening the events of the previous evening in my mind. 'Does this mean I'm forgiven?' I had enough sense to put a little humour into my puzzled voice.

Cara laid her head on one side and smiled. 'Maybe just this once.' She leaned forward and dropped a kiss on my cheek. 'Don't be silly; you mustn't take my tantrums seriously. I'd just about forgotten it all by the time I got back here. In fact, I was looking forward to the next session. Most disappointing when you didn't come back.' She winked and leaped to her feet. Reaching one hand behind her, she touched the bell on the bar. 'Breakfast time. Better get up unless you want the whole hotel to know you don't like sleeping with your girl-friend.'

When I came out of the shower, there were voices in the front room. I pulled on a pair of tennis shorts and a loose T-shirt, and rummaged through Cara's beach-bag in search of my sunglasses. I felt a strong need to start the day slowly and had my mind set on the hammock beside the pool. With luck it was off limits to towel-wielding Germans. A couple of hours of swinging gently with a novel seemed a very attractive option. Cara had other ideas.

'Ben, get in here. Great news!' Too impatient to wait for me, she burst into the bedroom. 'Alan's here!'

'Before breakfast?'

Cara stared at me as if I was mad. 'Yes, obviously before breakfast, as it's sitting out there uneaten. So what?'

I shrugged and walked into the front room, hoping there wouldn't be any painful references to the previous evening.

'Morning, Ben. You look exhausted. Fun night?' He gave a crooked smile.

Here we go.

'Yes. And thank you.' I tried to say it sincerely, imagining the amount of effort involved in locating two quality horses in that isolated region.

'You're welcome. It's fun trying to think up amusements for you. I've come to suggest another. May I?' he said, pointing to the pot of coffee on the table.

'Sure.' I collapsed into a chair and reached for a banana. Cara was already spooning scrambled eggs and mushrooms on to a plate, downing glass after glass of guava juice.

'Thank you. I'm not sure if you're interested in what's going on here, but the election effort has really accelerated over the last week. The KFP are making big noises and building themselves up a real head of steam. Today they are holding their main pre-election rally for the Coast Province. All their big cheeses from Nairobi have come down. Thousands of people are expected to turn out. I wondered if you would like to see it.'

'No.' I said it immediately. It sounded ungrateful, but

it was meant only to be a very clear, unqualified response.

Except it was contradicted in the same instant by Cara. 'Definitely!' she said. 'It'll be amazing.'

I looked at her in exasperation. 'Cara, you are really crazy, you know that? You want to be surrounded by thousands of excitable people just as their leaders are inciting them to shoot whites?'

Jackson interrupted before she could reply. 'That's not quite what I had in mind,' he smiled. 'No, I think I'm too old for that kind of close contact sport. I was planning to take an aerial view. I have this little plane . . .'

'Even better!' said Cara. 'Come on, Ben, you can't object to that. Safely out of reach, with a perfect view of everything. Yeah?'

There was no point in fighting. I still didn't like the idea of leaving the protective shell of the hotel on KFP day, but without strong rational arguments I would never get any peace from Cara. I nodded and poured myself some coffee.

We followed Jackson's Peugeot to a tiny dirt airstrip, twenty miles south of Watamu. The gate to the airfield hung open on broken hinges. We drove straight on to the empty runway, racing towards the small plane at the end. Jackson parked by the fuel store, beckoning to us to do the same. Then he wandered over to the plane and started peering into the fuel tanks.

'You should get some interesting material for James. It's really quite exciting, first time.' He smiled proudly at his machine and opened the cowling to check the oil.

'Is there anything we can do to help?' Cara set to

work flicking insect carcasses off the wing. I felt less comfortable about the whole idea now that I had seen the plane. A quick survey of the exterior and cockpit confirmed my worst fears. This aircraft had been built before Da Vinci started sketching. The single propeller appeared delicate enough to snap in my hands. Paint had peeled off large stretches of the fuselage, leaving suspiciously rusty patches. The flight instruments looked prehistoric and the cracked glass on two of them did nothing to calm my nerves.

Jackson squinted at the dipstick, frowned for a second and then shrugged. 'Thank you, but there's nothing else to do. Just hop in, if you would,' he said to Cara. 'Flight performance is pretty terrible in this heat, so I need all the weight as far forward as possible. That means you go in the back, I'm afraid.' He closed the cowling and helped Cara up on to the wing.

'How typical: boys have all the fun,' muttered Cara, gracefully slipping herself over the front seats. 'I suppose you expect me to be the in-flight stewardess as well?'

I climbed into the co-pilot's seat and watched nervously as Jackson ran some perfunctory checks. He tried the radio but discarded his earphones when it failed to work. The engine started on the fifth attempt and, after coughing for a few seconds, settled to a fairly constant hum. I switched the recorder on as Jackson tested the engine power and taxied the plane into position.

'Would you like to try the take-off?' Jackson casually waved at the control stick in front of me. 'It's very easy. All you do is push the throttle in and pull gently back on the column when this dial hits sixty knots.'

I stared at him in disbelief. 'You must be mad! I've never even been in a cockpit before.'

'Honestly, there's nothing to it. Besides, I'll be following you on my controls. If you do something stupid, I'll just take over.'

How reassuring. I handed the recorder back to Cara, then gripped the column.

'Just push the throttle right in and watch that dial,' instructed Jackson. 'I'll be steering us along the runway with my pedals. There's no wind, so when we hit sixty make sure your column is dead centre as you pull it back.'

I did exactly as I was told. Dust rose beneath us as the propeller raced round. The plane rocked and bounced down the airstrip, and I silently urged the speed indicator to rise before we reached the trees at the far end. Finally, the needle crept up to the mark and I brought the column back, fascinated as my effortless actions lifted us off the ground. Jackson's ample hands lay relaxed around his controls. The plane rocked slightly, but then eased into a smooth climb, comfortably missing the perimeter trees.

I felt a sense of enormous achievement in that one action, and turned to share it with Cara. The plane shook violently as I knocked the column round, and Jackson took hold of his controls. 'I'll take it from here, Ace, if you don't mind?'

'Of course. Thanks. That was an incredible sensation.' I started to look around. We were climbing out over the main coast road. On the right lay great swathes of forest, and to the left ran the gleaming ribbon of sand that lined the shore far into the distance. Different colours were appearing in the sea as we gained altitude. Dark blue marked the deep water, black the coral and rocks. Each block of coral was an enormous mass of life stretching for hundreds of yards along the coast. Decorating the whole were the vivid yellows and light blues of the shallows.

Cara gripped my shoulder and pointed, not attempting to compete with the noise of the engine. I looked along her arm and saw a group of windsurfers racing beside the reef. Out to sea, sailing boats and cargo ships looked like toys.

After a few minutes, Jackson pointed out Kilifi. The creek, the bridge, even that beautiful house were clearly laid out beneath us. Beyond, the great sisal plantations formed striped patterns, obliterating the shape of the land.

Just past Mtwapa a dark mass was visible, covering the fields on the coast side of the road for about half a mile. Jackson brought the plane lower and we swept in over the heads of this crowd of thousands. Jackson shouted: 'Should be just about to start.'

Closer to the crowd, it seemed that everyone was wearing white. The effect was like a newsprint photo: black dots and white dots interspersed to create some overall random image. There were gaps between the tightly packed knots of KFP supporters, perhaps to keep slightly different ideologies apart. We only want to deport the Asians. We just hate the whites. We'll kill anyone who reflects so much as a shimmer of light. Even five hundred feet up I could sense the tension and fire down there. I found myself estimating what proportion of the crowd would head north after the rally. What proportion would make it as far as Watamu. What proportion were armed. What proportion would actually go so far as to kill someone for their political leaders.

'Seems thoroughly pointless, doesn't it?' said Jackson. 'They're not even allowed to put up any candidates.'

'Perhaps that's why there's so much interest,' said Cara. 'What's more exciting than the forbidden fruit? Or nut, in this case.'

'It's not interest or excitement. It's anger. These are people who already believed in the message. It made sense to some dark corner of their brains. But it took the ban to really get them going, really build that anger into . . . what was that?' Suddenly his voice was sharp.

'What?'

'Did you hear that noise?'

I shook my head.

'It sounded like shots. Hang on.' He pressed one foot down and pulled the column sideways, rolling the plane on to its wing while he peered out over the crowd. 'Wait . . . Yes. Damn him. There's someone shooting at us down there.'

He brought the column level and angrily pressed in the throttle to lift the plane. We waited, nervous and silent, until we'd climbed a thousand feet.

'Stupid idiot. Thinking he can hit a plane from the ground. But better not to tempt fate. Have we seen enough?'

We turned back up the coast, taking a higher altitude

that allowed us wider panoramas. Then Jackson gestured at the controls in front of me. 'How about learning the basics of flying?'

Cara leaned forward to listen. Jackson started with the dials, describing the function of the artificial horizon, vertical speed indicator and turn and slip indicator. Then, using a Biro as a model plane, he explained the use of the ailerons, rudder and elevator in roll, yaw and pitch. I experimented gingerly until I felt comfortable with the responses to each control. Just as I was starting to think it simple, Jackson set me a challenge.

'If you can keep the plane at the same height and speed, and facing in the same direction for two minutes, I'll let you keep it,' he offered, tapping the altimeter, air speed indicator and direction indicator. Uncertain what I would do with an antiquated light aircraft in Africa, I made a quick review of the gauges. Height: 4,150 feet. Speed: ninety-five knots. Comfortable that following a dead straight coastline would not be a problem, I concentrated on keeping the vertical speed indicator at zero. Within less than a minute, my best efforts had sent the plane into a steep turn that caused us to drop four hundred feet.

Grinning, Jackson brought the aircraft back under control. 'It sounds so simple but it's one of the hardest things to learn. Safe gamble. Try again. No incentive this time.' He took his hands off the column. 'The crucial thing is to look outside. Use the horizon to keep yourself level, and your speed and height won't change. It also gives you a better chance of avoiding other aircraft, if you aren't glued to these dials.'

I fixed my eyes on the horizon, using a dead fly on the windscreen as a point of reference. Whenever the horizon fell below the fly I eased the column forward to bring the plane back level. After two minutes, I had lost just a hundred feet, and the speed was steady. Jackson sat back in his seat and started chatting loudly to Cara. I continued happily, experimenting with gentle turns and level flight until I felt almost in control.

I have heard that most air accidents happen when novice pilots get cocky, usually after about sixty hours of experience. For me, this state of mind came twenty minutes into my flying career. Impatient to try some new manoeuvres, I turned the plane particularly steeply and simultaneously put its nose up, giving an exhilarating sideways climb.

'Uh-uh, don't do that. This plane isn't designed for aerobatics,' Jackson warned. As if to emphasize his words, the engine coughed. I brought the plane level again, but my apology died in my throat as a series of stutters shook the nose. I gripped the controls and we listened anxiously for a recovery. Instead the stutter slowed, the propeller jerking for a few agonizing seconds until the engine died completely. A brief, torturous moment passed before anyone moved. The only sound was the rush of air, and the limp spin of the propeller as the wind caught its blades.

Cara broke the silence. 'Jesus, Ben!' she gasped. 'What have you done?'

'How should I know? What the hell's happening?'

For a moment the great white hunter seemed too amazed – or shocked – to answer. Then he recovered and ran through a mental checklist. 'It could be any number of things. I'll look through them in a second. But the first thing is to keep the plane as high as possible. That way we stay in the air the longest and have the most time to get the engine going again.' He steadied the controls until the plane was gliding straight and level. 'I need your help to fly this thing while I try to find the problem. Just stay calm and hold it at this altitude.'

Reluctantly, I took hold of the column again. Jackson fiddled with the throttle, fuel mixture and primer, and turned the ignition. It didn't take. Muttering expletives, he lowered his head to check the wiring around his knees.

'Just pray that idiot with the gun hasn't gone and shot through something important.'

'But you said . . .'

'I know what I said!'

'You think he could have hit the fuel line?'

'Just fly the damn plane,' he shouted.

I looked down at the altimeter. The needle was falling.

'We're dropping fast,' I called. Cara looked down at the sea and echoed me, her voice shaking.

'Then pull the column back. Put the nose up. It'll give us more lift.'

The sound of the propeller turning uselessly in the wind was terrifying. Jackson was swearing harder now. I pulled back on the column until I couldn't see the ground. The plane levelled out at 2,900 feet, but I could feel it slowing down. The air speed indicator dropped below sixty knots. A green arc extended around the dial as far as fifty. I could guess what it meant.

'We're losing speed badly. Won't we fall out of the sky if we get too slow?'

Jackson swore some more and looked up at the dashboard. He held a dirty wire in each hand. 'Forget the speed. All that matters is staying high. And make sure you keep us level. If one of our wings drops, we've had it.'

I kept the column right back and tried to hold the plane level. With the falling air speed, the ailerons had become almost useless. The controls felt muted and seemed to sag in my hands. Behind me, Cara started shouting as I wrestled the column around in search of balance. Then, suddenly we heard a new sound. A siren.

'Ignore that,' shouted Jackson, as the speed fell to forty-eight knots. 'That's the stall warning, but it allows plenty of leeway. Just don't let the wing drop.'

The plane seemed to stumble slightly sideways and as the needle hit forty-five knots the left wing dropped. It fell away like a rock and pulled the whole plane over on to its side. The nose flipped down, leaving us hanging from our seat straps, staring at the sea. The plane gathered momentum and entered a stomach-wrenching spiral. Cara screamed. We seemed seconds away from smashing into the ocean.

Jackson straightened up immediately. The air speed indicator had shot up beyond the top of the green arc. As the altimeter spun through 2,100 feet, he kicked hard on the rudder and pulled the column back. His right hand dropped to a little red switch between our seats. It was set to OFF. The column came back and the aircraft started to level out. With mounting anger rapidly replacing sheer terror, I knew what would come next. Jackson's fingers flicked the switch to ON. The propeller leaped into life, kick-started by the flow of the wind, as fuel coursed back into the engine's empty veins.

I stared at Jackson's face waiting for the apologetic smile. 'Interesting fucking stunts you pull in the name of science,' I growled above the revived noise of the engine. I could feel the heat in my face as fury welled up inside me.

'At least let me land the plane before you kill me. Or us I should say . . .' Jackson's head twitched backwards and then displayed a very unapologetic smile.

I spun round to Cara. Her panic and terror had been replaced by an amused grin. 'Sorry about that. Alan asked me, and I reckoned you could take it. As you say: "in the name of science".' She leaned forward and planted a pert kiss on my lips before I could pull back. 'Wasn't that the most incredible experience, though?' she said happily. 'I haven't had that kind of rush for years.'

Cara had a way of laughing things off so effectively that eventually you had to give in and laugh with her. Jackson saw me relax back into my seat and offered me the column. I shook my head, but the bridge had been rebuilt.

'Are you saying you were in control all the time?'

'Absolutely. That was a standard training manoeuvre. You stall the plane by killing the engine and keeping the nose up, then put it into a spin. You just saw a textbook recovery. Shouldn't really do it with a passenger in the back, but we tend to break all the rules out here. Incidentally, if your engine cuts for real, the golden rule is to keep speed, not height. Hold the speed at about eighty knots and it keeps you in the air for the longest amount of time.'

I gazed out over the ocean. The calm, flat sea was totally at odds with my state of mind. No one spoke again until we reached the airstrip. But I allowed enough of a smile to put them at ease and confirm that I could take it.

On the way back to Madanzi, Cara noticed a sign to the Paradise Guest House. It had been partly covered by a KFP poster.

'That's where Chas is staying,' she said. 'Let's go and see if he's OK.'

It was not the first time she'd mentioned him that day. His no-show at Madanzi had left her worried. It didn't make sense that he hadn't come. He definitely told her he would. What else would he have to do? Sighing, I turned off down the dirt road to the guest house.

We pulled up outside a low shack with gaudy paint-work and an old Welcome sign. A wrinkled mama sat in the shade of a makeshift parasol. I waited in the car while Cara walked over to the woman. A smile appeared as Cara shook her hand but vanished when she asked about Chas. Didn't come back. Yesterday. Left stuff. She rose and led Cara into the shack.

I turned on the radio, searching for some music. I found one channel. An angry voice was declaiming in Swahili. Election fever was getting intense. I switched him off.

Cara came out of the shack, holding something in each hand. A passport. Traveller's cheques. Stephen Andrew Morely. Chas? But the photo was right. Who leaves without their passport and money? Not even a bum who rejects his own name.

'Put them back.'

'We have to report this.'

'No. You saw what he was like. He's just stoned somewhere. He'll be back when he needs more money. We can look in on Monday, if you want to check.' My voice was distant, unconvinced. My mind was too occupied by the sudden, startling image of a dying youth, chest riddled with nationalistic bullets, a fanatic bent over him, a red-black finger tracing bloody letters on his shirt. KFP. Killed For the Party. Whatever had happened to him, I wanted someone else to find out first.

Cara fixed her stare on me and silently decided which line of attack to use. Her choice, as usual, was extremely effective.

'If you were to go back and tell Jenni that a lonely English guy got into trouble in Africa and you couldn't be bothered to help, what would she think of you?'

'What the hell does it matter?' I said angrily. But she could see she had won. Quietly she stooped over the mama to ask directions to the Watamu police station. I spun the convertible round and waited for her to get in.

The small building was just a few hundred yards down the road. It was painted with cheerful coloured bands, and white stones marked out the drive. An inspector was on duty. Grey curls of hair and a double chin framed a jovial face. He welcomed us with a warm handshake and invited us into his office.

'*Jambo*. Welcome to Kenya. Good holiday?'

We offered him the passport and I felt my hands grip the seat as I waited to hear news of the atrocity. His face grew worried when he saw the photograph.

'He is your friend? Then I am sorry for you.'

'Why? What's happened?' I demanded, too impatiently.

'He has had big problems. Big problems.'

'Is he hurt? What happened?'

The policeman looked surprised. 'No, no. But he is a bad man. He is here. We have arrested him. Drugs.'

'What does that mean?' asked Cara.

'Hmm, yes. Drugs,' he said again.

'Can we see him?'

The inspector shrugged and got up, beckoning for us to follow him. He led the way out the back of the building and walked across a dusty yard to a small, high-windowed block. Chas was in the second cell.

He seemed almost to be expecting us. Cara at least. He smiled up at her and said: 'I wondered how soon you'd work it out. I didn't have any money for a phone-call.'

She immediately stuck her hand through the cell bars and gripped his. 'Are you OK?' she whispered. For an instant I saw in her a flash of that vulnerable look from the night before. It angered me that this dope-head could also stimulate it.

'Yeah. Sure. It's cool. What can they do to an English guy, right?'

'But what happened? Did they catch you buying?' Cara was still holding that wretched, filthy, scum hand.

'Yeah. Bad, huh? Pigs the same everywhere. Can you get me out? I kind of want to get back to the beach.'

'Of course. We'll do everything we can. Do you want us to call your family?'

'No, it's cool. Just, like, get me out, and it'll be cool.' He grinned happily at the thought of more days on the beach, stoned out of his ugly, bristly, brain-free head.

I decided to end the chat. I turned to the inspector. 'What can we do to help him?'

'You must come and register. Then you call your embassy. Then maybe he gets bail.'

I turned and walked firmly back to the office, ignoring Cara's last words of comfort. The inspector pulled out a long, grey form and picked up a stub of pencil. Laboriously he started working down the questions.

'Name?'

'Benjamin Ashurst.'

'Relation to criminal?' Criminal already.

'None.'

'Occupation?'

'Student.'

'Nationality?'

'British.'

'Reason for entry into Kenya?'

'Scientific work.'

The stub of pencil paused. At first I thought he wanted help with the spelling. But when he spoke I realized I had made a big mistake.

'May I see your permit, please?'

I paused, hoping my worry was misplaced. 'My visa?'

'Permit to conduct scientific research in the Republic of Kenya.'

I sat frozen: guilty despite my own personal innocence. Why the hell hadn't Fieldhead got one for me? Did he have one? What was the penalty for not having one? Did we even need one for this kind of experiment? My mind leaped among the different lines I could take. Should I explain what the work was, hoping that it was exempt from the permit rule? I tried to imagine describing emotion science to this policeman and balked at the thought. As Cara walked into the office, I shot her a warning look and decided to bluff it.

'No, no. Not research,' I laughed, unconvincingly. 'Just study. Reading books. We're just here on holiday. Vacation. Christmas holiday.' I smiled as broadly as I could. 'Aren't we, sweetheart?' I added inanely, in some sort of imitation of the stereotype British package couple.

Cara looked at me uncertainly. 'Sure,' she said. 'What about it?'

The inspector ignored her. His earlier good humour was gone. 'You have no permit? That is very bad. You must have a permit to do science here.'

I tried to keep up the smile. 'No, no. Like I said. We're just on holiday. Just a bit of study in books.'

'You bring me the books.'

Without thinking, I closed my eyes in frustration. Where the hell was I going to find textbooks? That gesture decided him.

'We watch. If you do science, you show a permit or you go in there.' He hooked a thumb in the direction of Chas.

I waited for him to add something. But after a moment's silence he got up and went to speak to some colleagues. Cara was mouthing, 'What have you gone and done, you idiot?' I stood up to follow the inspector.

'Is that all? Can we go?'

He gave an impatient brushing motion, which I decided to interpret as consent.

'Come on. Let's just get out of here,' I muttered to Cara.

'What about Chas?'

'He can look after himself. If we hang around here we may end up in there with him. We'll get Kristina to sort him out.' I grabbed her hand and led her firmly to the car. A few yards away, two policemen were sauntering out of the building. We got in and I started the ignition. The two men walked to a patrol car. As soon as we drove off, they followed us.

'No. You have got to be joking,' I said to the mirror. I slammed on the brakes and pulled into the side of the road. The patrol car did the same. For a while, we all sat still in the blistering heat.

'Just outrun them,' said Cara. 'Take us on to the main road and show them what a Merc can do.'

'This isn't fucking funny,' I snarled. 'How are we supposed to do anything with these guys following us everywhere?' I threw the convertible forward and drove the short distance to the hotel. 'What are they going to do? Sleep on the veranda?'

Cara shrugged and put on her shades. 'I'm going to the pool. I want to chill out for a while. Have fun with your guards.'

Getting out of the car, she wandered over to the bar. I slammed the door for effect behind her, then marched past the patrol car to the hotel reception. Kristina looked up with her usual radiant smile.

'Hiya, Ben. Enjoy yourselves with Alan?'

'Uh-huh. Can I use a phone? Somewhere private?' I gestured to my two shadows, languidly propped against their car.

'What's happened?' Her face grew worried. Again I was introducing trouble into her perfect fairy-tale world. 'Have you done something wrong?'

'No, not at all. I just have to clear something up with the guy who's organizing this show.'

'English number?'

I nodded and pulled Fieldhead's card out of my pocket.

'Give me a couple of minutes to get a connection, and I'll put it through to the office.' She pointed me towards the door.

The phone was stained Bakelite; old-fashioned dial with a lock through one of the holes; frayed material on the cord. I let it ring for a tenth of a second.

'James, it's Ben.'

'Ben! How nice to hear from you. Rather thought you were enjoying yourself too much to remember me. How's the weather?'

'Fine. Lovely. Listen . . .'

'Absolutely abysmal here. Wettest day of the year.

Department's almost been washed away, and as it's Saturday I'm the only one here to shore it up.'

'We have a problem.'

There was a pause on the line.

'You've damaged it?' His voice was heavy.

'No. The sensor's fine. But I'm having a little problem with the police. Do we have a permit for this?' Quickly, I explained the situation.

'I thought I told you to go and have fun. What the hell are you doing hanging around police stations, anyway? How's that supposed to add to your enjoyment?'

'It's a long story. We were trying to help someone else. We won't get involved again. But the fact is I've now got two policemen following me around.'

Fieldhead swore. It was the first time I'd heard him do it. 'That is exactly what we don't need. It'll play havoc with your mental patterns. You haven't got any chance of achieving full positive emotions if you're under surveillance.' He was silent for a moment, and I imagined him staring at the ceiling of his office for the solution. 'OK, listen. I didn't bother with the permit because it didn't occur to me that you would come into contact with the police. I've never seen the point of pandering to archaic legal systems when everyone is saved a lot of bother by just avoiding the paperwork. Strictly speaking, you should have one, but there's no way they will work out what the research is from you doing normal holiday stuff. With any luck they'll lose interest after a couple of days and we can get some pure recordings again. Until then, just relax.'

'Fine. But I wish you'd warned me.'

'Yup. Sorry. There it is. One very important thing, though. Don't under any circumstances let them find out about the sensor. If they see it, or even hear about it, they will think themselves quite within their rights to cut it off you and keep it. Do you understand how important this is?'

'Of course. It'll ruin the experiment.'

'Forget the experiment. That sensor took months to build. They don't mass produce them. For the sponsors to have another made will cost about half a million dollars. Just remember it's worth more than the thing it's attached to.'

'Charming.'

'I'm serious. Getting arrested for conducting illegal experiments would be nothing compared to losing that device. You're totally responsible for it. Understand? Totally responsible. You screw up and lose it, your life won't be worth living.'

'Fine, but you're pissing me off even more than the police are. I'm doing you a favour here, and now you're threatening me?'

'OK, sorry. Go and get drunk or something. Just keep that thing secret. Love to Cara. Ciao.'

With the phone humming in my ear, I reached my hand unconsciously round to the sensor and smoothed the hair over it. Disastrous morning.

Kristina walked in. 'Success?'

'Yeah,' I muttered, putting the receiver back.

'Want to tell me what the police are here for?'

I nodded. 'Of course. But just while I'm by the phone, you couldn't place another call for me, could you? I

138

don't know the number, but you could get it from the operator. The John Radcliffe hospital.' I pronounced the name carefully. 'In Oxford.'

'Sure, Ben,' she smiled, disappearing again, not a trace of recrimination over the police presence marring her cheerful aura.

It took her almost ten minutes to get a connection. When she finally put me through, a sprightly Oxfordshire voice answered and warned me that it could take a little while to reach the patient. 'She might be in the middle of a bed bath or something. It always seems to be happening when people call,' she confided. 'Particularly long distance. Anyway, I'll just try her line for you.'

I listened to a few clicks and then a dose of internal hospital static laid quite distinctly over the Kenyan variety. When Jenni answered the phone, she sounded subdued.

'Hi,' I started. 'It's Ben.'

'Don't call me,' she said.

'OK. I just wanted to check how you were.'

'I don't know why you bother.'

The subdued voice had turned scathing. The crime of summoning the parents had not been forgiven.

'Jenni, I really am sorry. But I couldn't just go off and leave you alone.'

'As if you care.'

'How can you say that? You know I do,' I almost shouted, sensing the uselessness of my protestation.

'Your words are always so good,' she cut back. 'So nicely chosen. But so unconvincing when everything you actually do contradicts them.'

'What do you mean?'

'Oh, come on! Think about your excuse for going away. Medical research, didn't you say? Then why are you calling from Kenya?'

I was silenced for a moment. 'How did you . . . ?' But it was easy to guess: Kristina had told the receptionist, who'd been so excited she had to pass it on to the patient. 'I wasn't going to tell you because I knew you'd react like this. But it is medical research, I swear.'

'So you're not just on holiday with the blonde?'

'No!' But even as I said it, I felt a twinge of guilt. What else was this? Could I really cling with such force to that verbal loophole she'd offered: 'just'?

A long silence followed. I felt unwilling to trust my voice to break it without betraying me. Eventually she said my name, quietly and uncertainly.

'I'm here.'

'I'm worried about you.'

'Jenni, please don't go into all that again. I –'

'No, I mean, you being in Kenya right now.'

I hesitated. 'What do you mean?'

'It was on the news last night. The election.'

'Really?' I felt a slight sense of unease return. 'What did they say?'

'It was all about the trouble with that nationalist party. It sounded scary.'

'I don't think it's really anything to worry about. Just a lot of loud electioneering really,' I said, mostly believing it.

Her reaction was surprising. 'Don't keep hiding things from me,' she shouted down the line. 'I saw the pictures.

It looked terrifying. Those people were smashing every-thing in sight. If you get caught up in something like that –'

'Wait a minute,' I interrupted. 'What did you see? What are you talking about?'

'The riots, Ben,' she snapped back. 'We hear about it too, you know. Stop treating me like I'm too unstable to handle bad news.'

'Jenni,' I said quickly. 'What riots? I don't know any-thing about any riots.'

There was another pause. Then Jenni's voice, wanting to believe me but incredulous at the same time: 'How can you not know? They tore up the centre of Nairobi. Broke all the windows and set fire to cars. How can you not know about that? It must be the only thing anyone is talking about there.'

I looked out of the office window across the calm serenity of Madanzi. Cara's supine figure was draped over the tiles beside the pool. A few feet away from her, an American couple were sitting together, reading the same book. The two policemen were still leaning against their car, waiting for me to re-emerge. The only sound was the scuff of Kristina's bare feet on the stone flooring in the reception. It was too peaceful.

'Ben?'

'Yeah.'

'Are you anywhere near anything like that?'

'No, no.' I found myself shaking my head. 'Not at all. I'm in this tourist area. Very quiet.'

'Doing medical research in a tourist area?'

'Yes,' I said, a little too quickly, cursing my mistake.

'It just worked out that way.' So unconvincing. 'Listen, I have to hang up now. It's a really expensive line and it's someone else's phone. I'll try and call again soon, OK?'

'OK.'

'Will you be all right?'

'Yes,' she muttered. 'Ben?'

'Yes?'

'Please do . . .' Her voice folded in on itself. 'Please do call again.'

8

Recording No: 37
Date: 19 December   **Time:** 12.30 pm
Situation: Beside pool, being watched
Sensory Context: Visual: scattered hotel guests and constabulary; Auditory: splashing children in pool; Olfactory: nerves
Cognitive Context: How worried should I be about this?
Emotional Context: Uneasy, uncomfortable, un-everything pleasant
Somatic Response: Slight chill on skin
Facial Response: Occasional frown
Global Viewpoint: Generally a bit pissed off with life, even here in Paradise
Action Impulse: Wait and see

The hotel staff didn't look at all concerned by my new shadows. Two waiters appeared beside the hammock with a jug of fresh orange and suggested a lunch menu. They murmured vague warnings about the one o'clock sun before disappearing to collect the order. Cara, stretched out on the far side of the pool, lifted her head slightly to see them return with trays of seafood, and finally deigned to get up.

We ate in silence for a while, both feeling inhibited

by the presence of the two policemen, sitting on a low wall fifty feet away. And perhaps slightly embarrassed. Fine food, waiter service, sloth, bikinis by the pool: all seemed perfectly natural in front of hotel staff, yet almost insulting when the audience was any other low-paid, working African.

'I should record this,' I muttered. 'Feels awkward. Embarrassing. Fieldhead would love it.'

'Screw Fieldhead,' said Cara. 'The lazy bastard got us into this.'

She stared angrily at the two men. They were leaning back against palm trees. Were their eyes shut? Their posture conveyed one word: apathy. They knew damn well there wasn't a scientific experiment in sight.

'Let's take a boat,' said Cara suddenly. She grabbed my shoulder, already impatient for my agreement. 'Come on. Kristina will find one for us. Let's escape!' And there was that amused smile again, playing, even excited this time.

'Marine biologists.'

'Exactly. It'll give them something to write in their notebooks.'

I looked at her face, all the energy back, a little flushed.

'Let's do it,' I said.

And so we set sail and fled. It wasn't a very appropriate escape module. A little wooden dinghy, an outboard with the power of a sick foal, a sea as calm as an alpine lake. But it felt good. The two policemen sauntered down to the beach in our tracks and settled themselves on a fallen palm trunk. A last look back at their faces: any expression? I creased my eyes against the sun, but couldn't tell at that distance how the black skin was arranged.

It took us less than three minutes to reach the reef – a long, almost unbroken line protecting Turtle Bay from the windy, turbulent Indian Ocean. Except that today there was no wind. We raised the outboard and paddled across the reef, slipping from one millpond to another, much larger millpond. Flashes of coloured fish leaped around beneath us. Strands of seaweed latched on to the keel. One small rock gave the boat one small graze. Then we were over – truly escaped, hanging one hundred feet above a very blue, very distant seabed.

'Here,' said Cara. 'Right here, where you really feel the drop. Let's stop here.'

She tapped the flecks of seawater off her paddle and laid it in the bottom of the dinghy.

'And now?'

She looked at me quizzically, as if surprised that I could be following any train of thought other than her own. 'And now we're free,' she said. With that she leaned back in the bows, dangled one hand over the side, and closed her eyes.

The sense of escape was complete. Madanzi was still visible through the tangle of moored fishing boats; a couple of frustrated windsurfers were flapping their purple and green sails disconsolately near to the shore. But a quick turn of the head and everything man-made was eradicated. I looked out over an infinity of ocean and felt a sense of the millions of living creatures beneath us. Hunting each other, luring unsuspecting prey with decoy body parts, ripping flesh with razor teeth, fighting off rivals. A violent, busy world of half-lit action, unrelenting, unaffected by seasons or weather: continuous struggle. But just above: nothing at all. Not even a ripple to disturb the perfect flatness of our territory. We owned it all. We were utterly free.

I gazed at Cara's outstretched body. It had developed a rich, deep bronze colour, and a thin layer of sweat gave it a luxuriant shine. The urge to touch was compelling. I watched her rising chest stretch at the thin straps of her bikini for a while. Her legs were folded neatly together and resting against the side of the boat. One hand lay, almost as an afterthought, with fingers curled against her left thigh. Small drops of moisture from the cleft of her breasts ran down the line between her abdominal muscles and collected in her navel. The urge became irresistible. As I moved towards her the boat rocked slightly and she opened her eyes.

'Do you ever think what it's like not to be us?' she said.

I stopped in mid-advance, unprepared for her to be following any train of thought other than my own. I looked at her expression, searching for a clue. The mouth was passive, but the eyes were troubled.

'I mean old people, disabled people, starving Africans. How can we just play around like this without ever even thinking about all those millions of people who can't?'

'Well . . . yes, but . . .' I started. I paused. 'What are you talking about?'

'Really. I mean it. I see old people who move around at the speed of a snail. And what if you haven't got any legs at all? We happily run down to the beach, leap into a boat, paddle around. So many people can't even get out of bed without help. What are we doing, lying around here as if everything was perfect?'

I couldn't find an answer that could possibly fit in this whole new dimension of thought that she had unearthed, let alone an answer that would satisfy her. I stared at her face, watching it grow steadily more unsettled and worried.

'And here? Just outside our beautiful, safe sanctuary? How much do the kids get to eat here? Half of them lying sick with malaria, or HIV their parents gave them. Look at us!' she cried.

'Cara . . .'

But instantly her head had jerked up and her expression had changed to one of excitement. 'Oh my God! Look!'

I turned and followed the line of her outstretched arm. Cruising slowly towards us along the ocean side of the reef, leaving a perfect symmetry of ripples behind it, a dark mass protruded two feet out of the water. Cara leaped to her feet, making the dinghy rock violently.

'What is it?' Her voice was nervous.

I stood up, more carefully. The animal's back was flat and wide. Very wide. Behind, a long way behind, the tip of a tail fin protruded occasionally: fish, not mammal. But no dorsal fin.

'It's a whale shark,' I said. 'I'd heard they were big, but I never really imagined it.'

'Do you think it might attack the boat? We could try and paddle back over the reef.'

'God, they teach biology badly in Edinburgh,' I laughed. 'Whale sharks don't have teeth. They're the largest fish in the world, and built entirely out of plankton.'

She gazed doubtfully at the oncoming hulk. 'That thing is a filter feeder?'

'Yes.'

The animal was only sixty feet away now. It must have measured at least half of that length.

'You're sure?'

'Definitely.'

Cara smiled. The whale shark had chosen a course between the boat and the reef.

'Then what are you waiting for?'

She stepped up on to the seat, and without a thought for the old, the disabled or the starving Africans, she dived into the ocean.

I stared in disbelief after the girl who could change her emotions so quickly. Real fear to utter confidence and even a little teasing in a matter of seconds. The shark was close enough now to see the white spots dotted across its black skin. The moment Cara hit the water it stopped finning, but its bulk kept it moving.

I knew she was right, that it was an unmissable experience. That even if we lost the boat we could swim to the reef and stand there until someone came to rescue us. That we had been scuba diving in the same ocean, so there was no logical reason to fear its inhabitants now. That whale sharks are known to be friendly to humans. And I also knew that she hadn't bothered to think any of those thoughts. That she was just much more impetuous, more carefree, more alive than me. I tore off my shirt and leaped in after her.

In the brief moment that my weight carried me underwater, I saw the flank of the whale shark beside me and sensed the absolute mass of the animal as it glided slowly past. When I surfaced, Cara shouted back to me in excitement, then dropped her head into the water and swam fast towards the side of the shark. I followed quickly, and through the turbulent water saw her reach out and grip its lateral fin. She looked like an awkward child beside this graceful giant, and I waited for the fish to flick itself free of its irritating burden. But instead it seemed to respond as if to a gentle nudge and began to pick up speed. Cara relaxed her arms and allowed herself to be carried forward, holding her breath as both mount and rider disappeared into the gloom.

Anxiously, I swam back to the boat and pulled myself up in time to watch the fish curve round in an arc that brought it slowly back towards me. It was gliding again, Cara's extra resistance hardly slowing it at all. As it drew level with the boat, I saw Cara let go and swim to the surface, gasping for breath.

'Wasn't that incredible!' she said as the whale shark dropped below the surface.

I helped her into the boat. Definitely not an activity for the old or infirm. But I couldn't spoil her mood by reminding her of her recent words.

'I'm stunned,' I said. 'I'm very impressed you did that.'

'Really?' she asked, suddenly girl-like, suddenly interested in a lover's opinion.

I nodded, lightly brushing the drops off her shoulder.

Her hair was drawn tautly back by the water, showing a perfect forehead split by two almost nervous creases. Then she smiled and let her body lean against me. Little drops of water clung to lips that clung to mine.

The cruel words of the previous evening were completely forgotten. 'Thank you,' she murmured, her eyes bright with happiness. 'Thank you, my love.' It was as if she had been reborn.

Saturday night brought the Mombasa party crowd to Madanzi. These expats were mostly in their late teens and early twenties, and all seemed glamorous in a rough sort of way. The men wore chinos and light shirts, while the girls were in *kikois* with bikinis or tight shorts under crop tops. Those on holiday from British universities were paler than the permanent residents, but they brought a cosmopolitan touch that added spice to the crowd. Cara and I sat on a low wall, drinking margaritas while we watched them pile out of Land Cruisers and beaten-up Toyotas. Within half an hour, the place was full.

For a while we felt invaded. In the space of a week, Madanzi had become our territory. Now, suddenly, new owners with an older claim had arrived. Easygoing owners, forming a gang that excluded us. Old acquaintances and friends swapped kisses and bear hugs. Everyone knew everyone. Cara sat listening to the music, her face set in a sulk, while I fetched the third round of margaritas. But by the time I returned, all was happiness and smiles again. Casper was by her side.

'Ben, good to see you.' He gave a warm grin, and

pumped my hand. 'I was just telling Cara off for being antisocial. This is going to be a great night: last Saturday before Christmas. Let's eat?' Without waiting for a reply, Casper grabbed Cara by the hand and headed for the laden sideboard.

'How's your day been?' he asked when I joined them.

'Interesting. No – worrying. I just heard about the riots in Nairobi.'

'Ya, bad business, heh? Let's hope they don't come here.' He flashed a wide grin at us and turned to more important matters. 'We missed you down at the dive school. I heard you took off in that dream machine of yours for the whole morning.'

'Yeah, it was fun,' I replied, not wanting to go into the details. Memories of the police station were still making me feel uncomfortable. Our shadows had patiently waited for us to return from our boat trip, checked the dinghy for fish or seawater samples, and then got into their car and left. Cara had already suggested a bet on whether they would return the next day. I was trying not to think about it.

'We'll be back at the school tomorrow,' said Cara.

Casper piled king prawns and crab salad on to Cara's plate before filling his own. 'Sundays, the dive's in the afternoon, you know? It gives us time to dctox after the night before. Believe me, there is nothing like diving to make your hangover worse. Have you tried the oysters here?'

Cara grimaced and refused. I remembered the delicacy from a dinner with Piers and looked around for them.

'They keep them on ice, out the back. It's far too hot

to leave them lying around here,' explained Casper. He signalled to one of the waiters. 'When you get them, come and meet some of the town kids,' he said over his shoulder, guiding Cara to a table outside.

My oysters caused a stir among Casper's friends. 'You didn't say there were oysters!' shouted one man, leaping up and racing back to the buffet. He was followed by two others who threw me a quick greeting on the way. Two girls were left; they shrugged at each other and then introduced themselves.

'It's the aphrodisiac thing. It makes them feel more virile,' said the one called Leo. 'Christ knows they need it.' She laughed loudly with her friend. 'Michelle and I are forever trying to send them off to impotency clinics.'

I smiled nervously, and swallowed the oysters. The taste was obliterated by loud dance music and the discussion of the creatures' powers. Cara kicked me under the table, amused at my discomfort. I turned to Michelle and asked how often she came to Madanzi. She had a pair of gentle, grey eyes.

'Hey, good line!' yelled Leo from across the table. 'Say, do you come h–'

'Shut it, Leo,' shouted Michelle. To me, she said in a softer voice, 'Leo is on very good form tonight. It can get a little irritating. She's been locked up in Aberystwyth studying British seaweed for two months and so now she's a little over-excited to be back.'

Michelle's deep tan and sun-bleached hair suggested she had definitely not been locked up anywhere further north than Egypt. Her East African accent was particularly marked, and she spoke in a quiet but easygoing way. As we chatted, I found my eyes wandering over her strong face and tropical figure. Why do men lust over one woman at the very moment of falling in love with another? Cara, busy describing our aerial adventure to Casper, could not have been less interested.

'You're not studying in Britain, then?' I asked, feeling slightly boring in this high-spirited group. The oyster-hunters had returned and were engaged in a machismo test, holding their fingers over candles. Leo, one of the main contenders, was frantically trying to get Casper involved.

'No,' Michelle smiled shyly. 'I'm not really smart enough for that stuff. I skipped uni and decided to work as a graphics designer in Mombasa. It's not a great career opportunity, but I like being here all year round. I don't think I could face winter in Newcastle like these guys. They call me a Ken-chick, can you imagine?' She raised her eyes to the stars and gave a quiet laugh.

'Where did you learn graphics design?'

'Oh, nowhere really.' Michelle leaned back and casually rested one foot on the lower strut of my chair. Her *kikoi* fell away to expose a toned brown thigh. A silver bracelet hung around her ankle. 'I always used to sketch when I was a kid, up-country. Then we moved to the South Coast and I started drawing fish. One of Dad's friends saw them and offered me a job at his agency on the spot.'

One of the oyster-hunters leaned across to Leo. 'How about getting some grass in?' he yelled above the music.

'Don't be stupid,' Leo yelled back. 'You know the police are getting serious about that shit. Kristina said they busted a tourist just yesterday. They're not playing around any more.'

'Who gives a shit? We're all going to get knifed in our beds by the KFP any day now, so what does it matter?'

The music was growing louder. People were wandering towards the dance floor. Two oyster-hunters recognized a favourite track and raced off, pulling Leo after them and shouting the words. As if to distract me, Michelle started describing some of the characters around us.

'The guy in the purple shirt is Danny. We call him Desperate Dan, as he's always hanging around hotels, looking for fresh young tourists – preferably American girls. One year he spent so long staking out a girl at Diani Reef that the hotel manager gave him a brush and told him he could only stay if he swept the sand off the terraces.'

'And did he?'

'Sure. The poor guy cleaned the whole area around her beach bed, but never had the courage to talk to her. After three days, she tipped him, kissed him on the cheek, and left for the airport. He was gutted for a week.' She picked up a new bottle of beer. 'The stunning girl by the palm tree who all the boys are avoiding is Jessica. She got so pissed off with their attention that she started telling people she had seven black lovers. One for each day of the week. What really put them off was when she announced she was looking for an eighth, as an extra for Saturdays, but wasn't sure whether to make it another guy or to try a girl this time. The boys around here can be so gullible sometimes.'

I looked over in admiration. It was amusing to see grown men torn between approaching her and running away. Unconsciously, I took a sip from Michelle's glass. I saw Cara frown and walk round the table. Her voice was relaxed, but it carried an edge: 'I see you two are getting far too intimate. I'm going to have to break you up, I'm afraid. Ben, come and dance with me.' Flashing a slightly offensive smile at Michelle, she led me into the throng.

The DJ was playing a standard collection of tracks that could have been found in any number of London dives. The main difference was the temperature. A fresh breeze blew in from the sea and aired the dance floor, keeping the conditions far more pleasant than in most city clubs.

At first we danced together, but Cara's lithe movements soon attracted the attention of the nearby oyster-hunters. Within a few minutes the circle grew to include several unknown punters. Casper and Leo joined us, turning the dancing into the piss-taking variety, with everyone sending up old moves from the past. One of the punters was flirting outrageously with Leo, but her supposed boyfriend was too busy with a redhead to notice. Casper started sending Cara into jive spins that had her colliding with other dancers and laughing apologies at them. Increasingly irked by Casper's friendliness with Cara, I headed for the bar.

Pushing through the crowd, I bumped into Michelle, who was bopping with Desperate Dan. The purple shirt was half open to expose thick black hair that glistened under the coloured lights. Very appropriate. He seemed intent on trying his luck with Michelle, who had a strained smile on her face. Relieved to have the excuse to move on, she threw her arms round my neck and carried on bopping, taking me with her. Desperate Dan looked heart-broken and for a moment I felt sorry for him. But Michelle's enthusiasm was overpowering and soon we were pounding the dance floor with all our energy. Even some of the black guys looked quite impressed.

Finally we stumbled out of the morass of bodies, picked up two beers at the bar and went outside to cool down. Michelle had taken off her white shirt to leave only a bikini top and a film of sweat. Under the moon her body was a delicious pale amber. She walked over to a table and dropped her bag on it. I ran the bottle of ice-cold Tusker down my face.

'That's what I need on my back,' she teased.

I walked over and rolled the bottle slowly between her shoulder blades, unable to resist following with my hand over the moist brown skin.

'Delicious. How about the front?'

I hesitated. Sensing it, Michelle twisted round and pressed her stomach against the bottle. I moved it gently back and forwards, but kept my right hand by my side. Watching me with a calmly amused expression, Michelle brought her own bottle up and rolled it across her breasts.

'Now it's time to down these,' said Michelle, threading her arm through mine so that we drank with our elbows locked together. She spilled some of her beer, and it ran in two narrow streams into the bikini top. She started laughing. 'Wait, wait! There's a better one: much more fun.'

We unlinked our elbows and Michelle positioned my arm round her neck, before mirroring it with hers. Our efforts to drink from the bottles over each other's shoulders pressed us close together and had Michelle laughing again. She was more successful in reaching her bottle, and took a big gulp, which she transferred to my mouth as a consolation prize. I swallowed quickly but her lips remained pressed to mine and I could feel her tongue exploring my mouth. I pulled reluctantly away, shaking my head.

Michelle just laughed. 'What are you scared of? We Ken-chicks are quite harmless, I promise. I only have three black lovers at a time . . .'

I smiled unconvincingly. 'Thank you. But I really don't want to.'

'Of course you do. You think I can't feel it? See, it's still there.'

I stepped back, pulling her hand off my trousers. 'Don't you know I'm going out with Cara? I'm not going to cheat on her.'

'Man, why not? Everyone does it quite openly around here. Anyway, how about looking at your angel now? How long do you think it's going to be before she's inside Caspernova's wetsuit?'

I spun round. Through a gap in the dance-floor crowd I could see Cara locked into a Latin clinch with the instructor, who seemed to know as much about lambada as lifejackets. Each had a leg wedged between the thighs of the other and together they were moving erotically from side to side. Around them, some of the other dancers had stopped to watch. I felt sick.

'That's bullshit. Cara wouldn't do that.'

'Well, then, she'll be the first in a long line to turn him down. Apparently his conquests litter the east coast of Africa. They say that's why he has to keep moving. I'm still waiting for him to ask me.'

I stared at her provocative smile for a moment, pure anger forming in my chest, then turned and ran towards the dance floor. Pushing myself through the crowd, I felt a cigarette burn my hand and heard people laugh as I stumbled past. In the middle of the floor, Cara and Casper were demonstrating more steps to a small but enthusiastic set of spectators. I walked straight up to Cara and pulled her by the hand. She let go of Casper and followed me through the dancers until we were out of sight behind the back wall of the bar. I stopped and stared at her, feeling the blood surge in my cheeks and trying to detect guilt in her face.

Cara looked at me mildly, concern coupled with a hint of amusement showing around her eyes. 'That probably wasn't the best way to make friends with the guy whose job it is to keep us alive down there.' She said it softly, without any trace of cruelty or sarcasm.

'Jesus, Cara, you were just about fucking him on the dance floor. Why the hell should I want to make friends with him?'

'This is jealousy? Oh, Ben. Don't you know you have nothing to worry about?' Her eyes were wide and totally sincere. Her mouth and forehead tightened in a pained expression. 'Look, I'm sorry, but I used to do a lot of

Latin dancing and you hardly ever find anyone who can lead properly. I really didn't expect you to mind. You should know that I'm not interested in anyone else, let alone a beach boy.' Gently she stroked my cheek and put her arm round my neck. 'I thought you felt totally secure about me. You have every reason to, I promise.'

My anger vanished; my indignation collapsed. I rested my face against her neck. 'Thank you,' I mumbled. 'I'm sorry for the scene.'

'Don't worry about it,' she replied. 'Just believe in me a bit. I admit I said some harsh stuff last night, but you know I didn't mean any of it.' She looked into my eyes to check I was convinced and then went back to her light, playful tone. 'Anyway, wasn't it you who was getting off with someone else tonight?' I froze. She smiled into my guilty face. 'That's what Leo was saying just before you pitched up. Don't worry; I put it down to a bit of drunken friskiness. I trust you too much to believe you wanted anything more from her.'

I felt wretched. As we walked back to the beach house, with the sounds of the party fading behind us, Cara's light chatter jarred against my misery. I had assumed wrongly and accused unjustly, while all the time Cara knew about and accepted my own weak behaviour. Like the kindest nurse she read the shame in my eyes and led me to the veranda where she kissed me softly until the calm returned. But even in bed, as we made love to the sound of a distant disco thud, my mind could not let go. Eventually Cara paused and looked up.

'What's wrong, lover? Don't tell me I'm not good enough now that you've tasted that Kenyan beauty?'

I flushed and looked away. 'It's not that. I just feel so bad about what happened.'

She grinned and rolled on to her side next to me. 'That was nothing,' she said. 'Surely you've done far worse things than that?'

I nodded. 'Of course, but that's hardly going to make this any better.'

'Sure it is. You just have to think about the worst thing you've done and this whole business will become irrelevant. And please don't start talking about Jenni – I'm not in the mood.'

She lay with her cheek resting on my shoulder, eyes half-closed. And of course she knew at once that there was something bad, a secret that I'd never confessed to anyone.

Cara's limbs shifted around me. 'Well? What was it?'

I laughed nervously. 'Oh, you don't want to hear. It was just something . . . a mistake I made that I'd rather just forget about.'

'Come on. It'll help to talk it through.'

'I don't particularly want everyone to know.'

I felt her body stiffen and knew I'd said the wrong thing.

'First, you think I'm about to sleep around, and now you can't trust me with a secret?' Her voice was hurt and angry. 'What kind of relationship is this, exactly, Ben?'

'I don't know what kind of relationship it is. Not after last night.'

In the silence that followed, Cara's body unbunched and her hands sought out my face. Her voice, when she eventually spoke, was a tiny shadow of her earlier confidence. 'Please, Ben. Be patient. I'm just very . . . confused, at the moment. I'm not used to this. Any of this. None of it's happening the way I expected it to happen. It's really difficult for me to know what to think. Can you understand that?'

And suddenly I had a terrible longing to share that secret with her. To hear someone I loved forgive me, on behalf of someone who could never know the truth. To bind her closer still to me with this admission of weakness, of unintentional destruction. It was the first time I'd ever voiced it aloud. Yet the act of sharing made its sour memory and more recent thoughts of betrayal recede into the background. Nothing was important but the present. The girl I loved brought her lips to my ear and her tender, reassuring whispers made me love her a little more. I breathed out slowly into the soft, silent darkness and tasted perfect happiness.

It would last for just two hours.

9

Recording No: 23

Date: 17 December   **Time:** 10.30 am

Situation: By pool, watching Cara's diving lesson

Sensory Context: Visual: beautiful girlfriend and (also rather beautiful) instructor; Auditory: his professional spiel

Cognitive Context: Thinking how great she looks; slightly annoyed that instructor feels the need to handle her so much

Emotional Context: Pride, bit of jealousy/irritation

Somatic Response: None

Facial Response: Firm

Global Viewpoint: None

Action Impulse: Jump in and do the teaching myself

When I woke, the darkness had become sour and my stomach was a living, churning creature inside me. I pulled myself out of bed and stumbled to the bathroom. Closing the door, I groped for the light switch. A spasm had me doubled up before I found it. By the light of the moon, I vomited into the loo. My breathless retching brought Cara through the door, rubbing her eyes as she turned on the light.

'What's wrong? Are you ill?'

I threw up again. 'Those damn oysters,' I groaned. 'I felt dodgy when we got back. They probably left them lying around too long.'

Cara was in a sympathetic but sleepily impractical mood, dropping a 'Poor boy' and 'Oh, darling' between retches, while patting me on the back. To be fair, there was nothing much she could do as no medication would have stayed down long enough to have effect. After a few minutes I sent her back to bed. She wandered around for a little while longer, bringing cushions and bottles of mineral water into the bathroom, then yawned and gratefully went to sleep.

As the pain grew worse, the diarrhoea started. Although there was nothing left inside me, I continued to retch and the spasms in my gut intensified. Each one seemed to rip at my intestines, leaving me gasping for air. Several spasms later, I was getting scared. No bug had had this sort of effect on me before. I started to think about the terrifying symptoms of the more virulent exotic parasites I'd studied.

In England, I would have headed for Accident & Emergency. But it was 3.30 on a Sunday morning in Africa, and I was an hour away from the nearest hospital. Travelling on bumpy roads in the middle of the night, in search of some nurse's choice of a cure seemed an infinitely more dangerous option. I decided to sit it out.

After a while, there didn't seem any point crouching in the bathroom. I could suffer in more comfortable surroundings. I took a bottle of water and wandered out into the night. The beach was empty except for one couple, presumably left over from the party, slumped together under a *kikoi*.

I eased myself into a hollow in the sand. The spasms were less frequent and less intense now, but a dull ache had appeared in their place. I tried to think of something else and settled for the stars, joining them up to form new constellations of my own. Only the Southern Cross so clearly deserved its name that I left it alone. Other stars turned into aeroplanes, beds, scuba tanks, Cara, Jackson, Fieldhead . . . until gradually I was in a dream. As I lay dying in a hospital bed, Fieldhead was complaining that my illness had infected his sensor and was threatening to sue me for half a million dollars. Casper and Jackson stood at the bottom of the bed accusing each other of giving me altitude sickness and the bends. Cara just lay by my side with an adoring smile on her face and said I could be ill as often as I liked – she would still love me all the same.

I woke with a stiff neck and aches in my back that mirrored the constant pain from my gut. With the spasms over, I tried drinking some of the water. The Southern Cross had sunk towards the horizon, taking my blanket of planes, scuba tanks and faces with it. I picked myself up and walked back into the house. Cara's body was sprawled diagonally across the bed. Gently, I bent her legs up and rolled her over, feeling a rough complaint from my stomach as I moved. One more gulp of water and I collapsed on to the sheets to resume my dream.

*

Cara's morning wake-up routine was more tender than usual, and when she saw my condition she decided to let me lie in.

'I don't know what you were up to during the night, but you've brought half the beach in here with you.' I blinked and looked at the sand on the sheets as she smiled. 'Never mind. I'll ask the staff to leave you alone this morning. We can clean it up later.'

I focused on my watch. It was just after eleven o'clock. 'What are you going to do?' I asked.

'A little sunbathing, then lunch.' I winced and Cara gave an apologetic grin. 'Sorry. I won't have it anywhere near you. Then this afternoon, we can have that dive if you feel up to it.'

I shook my head violently.

'Well anyway, if you need me I'll be right outside on the veranda. Oh, and the police are back. They're sitting by the bougainvillaea.' She rubbed some oil haphazardly over her body, gave me a kiss and sauntered outside with her sunglasses and an old *Tatler*. Strains of Alanis Morissette filtered in through the door as I drifted off again.

I slept a heavy, dreamless sleep, and when I finally dragged myself into the main room there was a note on the bar.

Wow, you must have been tired! I couldn't wait any longer – the boat leaves in five minutes. We'll be back at 4 pm. Get some fresh air if you can. See you soon!

It was 2.45 and definitely time to get up. A fruit basket lay on the bar, but I still couldn't face any food. Feeling cold from the bug, I had a shower and dressed in slacks, a long-sleeved shirt and espadrilles. Then I took Cara's advice and set out along the beach. A single policeman detached himself from a palm tree and wandered along behind me.

I stopped and gave a little wave to my tail. This time he was close enough for me to see the scowl. I frowned and walked a few steps towards him.

'You don't need to worry about me today. I'm sick,' I said, touching my stomach and pointing my thumb down.

The policeman said nothing. He had a large frame, and folds of skin around his face. His blue shirt was unbuttoned. Sunday afternoon relaxation of discipline. Underneath was a white T-shirt. I read the lettering. KFP. I looked up at the malignant face, then turned and walked quickly on.

Some way past the hotel, the sun and exercise made me feel unwell again, and I sat down in the thin shade of a casuarina tree. My policeman, ever vigilant in case I should start measuring seaweed density, slumped down a hundred yards away. A gentle breeze cooled me, and I decided to collapse for the rest of the day. I wanted to read but couldn't be bothered to fetch a book, so I simply gazed out at the ocean. In the distance, a speck grew larger and turned into a motor launch. A few people wandered past, but most of the beach was empty. Down by the sea, a young African was peddling carvings to a sceptical French girl.

The motor launch drew closer and turned into Casper's boat. I looked at my watch. They were coming back half an hour early. Evidently I hadn't missed much if they had abandoned the dive so quickly. The carvings seller had moved on to an American youth. He seemed delighted and was producing wads of shillings. I turned to watch the launch draw up at Madanzi. I could just make out Casper as he hoisted some cylinders with his boatmen and strode up the shore. Cara was easier to identify from her slim figure and snakes of blonde hair. There was no one else on board. I felt a slight uneasiness return.

'Hey man, I ask you no feel good?'

I looked up and saw the carvings seller standing a few feet away. He was grinning wildly. I gave a tired smile, polite but not encouraging further conversation.

'What's the matter man? You need a doctor? We have very good doctor here,' he informed me proudly.

'No, I'm fine. I just feel a little weak.'

'Aahhh, OK!' He laughed loud, producing a noise that grated in those quiet surroundings. 'You just need a littol pick-m'up, yes?'

I nodded faintly, praying he would go away.

'Something to make you happy, yes?'

I wasn't really listening to him.

'Something to make you very happy!'

As I started to get up, he bent down and stopped me with one hand.

'I have something for you. Make you happy.' He reached into the bottom of his satchel and produced a crudely shaped carving of a monkey. 'Ha ha. Make you feel very happy. Inside. You see,' he promised, gesturing at the artefact.

The last thing I needed was some sort of spiritual nut,

trying to cleanse me 'inside' with a charmed idol. 'No, thank you. I'll be fine,' I assured him.

'Is very good,' he promised. 'Only one thousand shillings.' A thousand shillings for that piece of . . . ?

'I don't have any money with me.'

'This is my price. Now you say your price. We bargain.'

'I said, I do not have any money here.' I spoke each word loudly and separately, attracting a stare from the policeman.

The seller looked disappointed. Then his grin returned as he found a generous compromise. 'No problem. *Hakuna matata.* You keep this one. If you like, you come back for more. I am here always.'

I could see my shadow getting up and walking along the beach towards us. I was irritated by the seller's persistence, but there was no point causing him trouble with the police. I agreed quickly and took the carving. It was surprisingly light.

'OK, man!' The seller threw our hands into a compli-cated shake, and promised to see me the next day. 'Like Michael Jackson, yes?' He stuck a pair of mirrored aviator glasses over his eyes and seemed ecstatic with pleasure when I nodded. He gave a quick 'Yeah!' and turned to leave.

Perhaps because of my own weak condition, I was astonished at his speed. The seller took one look at the policeman advancing towards us, dropped the satchel beside me, and started sprinting down the beach. The policeman took a few steps, but soon realized he was no match for the younger, fitter man. I watched in horror as he struggled with the strap over his revolver. But by the time he had the gun up, the seller was out of range.

The policeman swore and trotted over to me, dangling the gun by his side.

'Look, he wasn't really bothering me . . .'

He ignored me and leaned down to grab the carving from my hand. Eyeing me with distrust, he held the gun by its barrel and brought the handle down on the little monkey. It split neatly in two. From inside each section fell little black, waxy lumps.

Astonished, I forgot to protest at first. The policeman put the broken carving and its contents in his pocket, then picked up the satchel. Hauling me to my feet, he began marching me back up the beach. I started speaking very fast.

'Wait! What have I done? I haven't done anything! The guy just gave me a carving. I didn't know there was anything in it. What is that? Drugs? I don't even use drugs. Are you listening to me?' I could hear my voice rising to a shrill yell as panic filled me. Posters at the airport had promised ten years just for possession. Already, images of disease-ridden gaols in the middle of an African jungle were filling my mind.

'You can't arrest me: I haven't done anything! Ask anyone at Madanzi. I never touch drugs! I'm not like that other guy!' I screamed. The policeman ignored me.

I tried to think fast. The situation was terrifying. I could be dragged off to some prison without anyone ever knowing where I had gone. 'Wait. At least let me talk to someone. At least let me tell my girlfriend. My wife. She's at the hotel. Then I'll be quiet.' He loosened his grip on my arm and motioned me towards Madanzi, still without a word.

I almost ran to the beach house but found it still empty. Before the policeman could change his mind, I set off for the dive school. He marched heavily behind me, sending the sand flying with his combat boots. His patience was wearing thin. The door to the dive school was closed and for a terrible moment I imagined some nightmare in which Cara and Casper had driven off for the afternoon. But the instructor's jeep was still parked outside, and the door to the school wasn't locked.

I walked into an empty office, and heard muffled sounds coming from the equipment room. I pulled open the heavy door and time stopped. Cara lay naked on a pile of wetsuits, her head stretched back and her hands gripping bunches of neoprene. Casper knelt astride her, driving rhythmically into her and running his face over her breasts.

I remember taking in every detail of the scene. Salt had crystallized on their bodies, leaving tiny white traces over their tans. Cara's nails had drawn new marks on the instructor's back, bright red beside the dark scars. Her heavy breathing sounded grotesque. The smell of neoprene permeated everything.

It felt like an age before Cara saw me.

'Shit!' she said. Casper froze and looked round. As the policeman appeared beside me, she shouted: 'What the fuck?!'

Her voice broke my trance and something snapped inside me. In the split second that followed, Casper shot up to block me and the policeman locked his arms around my body. Before my murderous fists could reach them, he was hauling me out into the daylight. He dragged me down to the beach, and marched me along the shore. Cara came running out naked after us, but the policeman waved his revolver at her and Casper pulled her back into the dive school.

We reached a dirt road: the local access to the beach. A rusting patrol car was parked under a tree. A second policeman was asleep in the back. My mind was still racing between anger, shock and humiliation. How could she do that? How could she even . . . ? The policeman gave me a shove. Obediently, I got into the car.

This time the police station seemed a dismal place, with a few sticks of rotting furniture under burnt-out light bulbs and a cracked, stained ceiling. After some cursory administration in an office marked 'O/C Crime', I was escorted to the back of the building. A door opened into a cell containing four sullen and grimy men, beads of perspiration shining brightly on their black skin. The policeman nodded.

I sat on the concrete bench as far away from the others as possible, trying to ignore the overpowering smell of stale sweat and urine. They were completely silent. There was only one thing to think about.

While I was revisiting the scene in the dive school for the hundredth time, building up pure hatred for Casper and that bitch, I heard Kristina's voice outside. She was speaking in rapid Swahili to my captor. They were arguing: her language was verbose and frantic, his answers quiet, monosyllabic statements of fact. Finally, bored with the conversation, he opened the door and waved her in.

'Jesus, Ben, are you all right in here?' she started. She gazed around the confines of the cell in dismay. Then she turned back to me and said, 'God, what a bloody disaster. Corporal Kamau says he caught you buying drugs. What the hell do you think you were doing? Don't you know how seriously they take that around here?'

I described the hollow carving, described my innocence.

Kristina nodded. 'Yeah, a lot of the dealers hide their stash in wooden –'

'To be honest, I don't give a shit what they do,' I said. 'This will all blow over as soon as I can find a reasonable officer who understands English. I just can't fucking believe Cara would do that to me.'

Kristina grabbed my arm. 'I don't think you're listening to me. You're in a lot of trouble. You were found in possession, and that's all the courts care about. Your claiming you didn't know what was in the carving won't get you anywhere. Anyway, who's going to believe the guy just gave away a thousand shillings' worth of drugs?'

That hadn't occurred to me. I felt the panic return. 'He's probably found it's good for creating repeat business with tourists. If we can get him picked up, he can at least confirm that bit, and say I didn't actually ask for drugs . . .' Hopeless optimism.

'Ben, Ben! He's gone. Probably disappeared to Mombasa. He saw your arrest or, if he didn't, he heard all about it in the village. He's not going to show up on the beach again for a long time.' Kristina lit a cigarette in agitation, took a long draw, and offered it to me. For a moment I was tempted to start. 'No, your best chance is with Alan. He can pull a lot of strings. I've already called him. He's speaking with the High Commissioner to get the British support, and then he'll come straight down to see you.'

For the first time I saw the facts of the case from the police point of view. Even in my panic, I could understand the logic of Kristina's fear.

She squeezed my arm and whispered, 'I'm really sorry about Cara. You have to concentrate on the charge, but I know that bit hurts like hell. If it's any consolation, this isn't the first time Casper has done this – broken in on a perfect match. He's just really . . . persuasive: good looking, charming, charismatic; and very physical.' I stared silently at the filthy floor. I did not particularly want to hear about the instructor's qualities.

'We had one guest leave her husband for him on the fourth day of their holiday. He dumped her within a week. I keep threatening to dismiss him, and this time he really is out. The trouble is, he'll just go and carry on somewhere else.'

Kristina lit another cigarette and hesitated. 'Look,' she said, 'I want you to know that Cara is in pieces over this. She desperately wanted to come, but she didn't think you'd ever want to speak to her again.' She stood up as the corporal shouted something, and held my eye for a moment. 'I really hope you guys can get it back together. It was beautiful to see.' She gave what was meant to be an encouraging smile, and then turned to Corporal Kamau. After a brief exchange, she came back.

'They may transfer you to Shimo-La-Tewa prison. It's not a nice place, but at least it's not too far away. Alan will come and see you there soon. I've asked Corporal Kamau to go with you. In fact, I've bribed him very heavily to stay at the prison and keep an eye on you. He's grumpy and uncommunicative, but we know him well and he will make sure you don't get treated too roughly. Just keep your head down, don't provoke anyone and you'll be fine.'

'But he's a KFP supporter. What if –'

'He's a policeman. Damn, Ben, his politics are irrelevant! Stop getting so paranoid about the KFP. He's the best protection we can get you until Alan fixes something.'

I nodded reluctantly and she patted my arm. 'Is there anything you want me to say to Cara?' she asked. But she must have seen my face darken into a scowl because after a couple of seconds she gave a nervous wave and left.

In the fifteen minutes after Kristina had gone, I began to get very scared. I was in a system that was totally out of my control. I was carrying half a million dollars' worth of equipment that would be discovered the moment they decided to check me for head lice or shave off my hair. And I was in Africa.

Against this mental backdrop, the word 'bail' was held out to me like a life raft.

'Mr Ashurst again.'

Mister Ashurst. Again. The inspector had summoned me to his office and offered me the same chair.

'Yes.'

'No science experiments,' he smiled.

'No.'

'We watched you carefully.'

'I know.'

'But you are here again.'

'Yes.'

I was growing exasperated, but the inspector seemed to want to lay the foundation in a calm, explicit fashion.

'We can give you bail,' he said, picking up an envelope. He opened it and took out a bundle of notes.

I saw the Madanzi logo in the top left-hand corner of the envelope. Thank you, Kristina! He licked his thumb and counted the notes very slowly, twice through.

'There is fifteen thousand shillings.'

He waited for me to say something. Was I supposed to check too?

'It is enough for bail.'

I gave a sigh of relief. All over. Let the sponsors' lawyer take it from here. I could go back to Madanzi for a change of clothes and a long drink. Cara could go hang. I was going to finish the project alone.

'Great,' I said. 'What do we need to do?'

He looked down at the table for a moment. 'You see. If I give you something, I need something, too.'

I silenced the Western morality building up inside me. 'How much?'

The inspector shook his head. 'No. I want to help you. So you must help me.'

I waited in silence.

'Your friend. Mr Morely. You work with him, yes?'

'Chas? No. I've only met him once.'

'But you work with him on these . . .' he searched his vocabulary for the correct term, '. . . irregal substances.'

'No! I already said: I'm innocent! I have nothing to do with drugs, and I have no idea what he was involved in.'

'But my friend,' he said, with a slightly embarrassed smile, 'you bought drugs while we watched. Just like Mr Morely. You export together?'

'I have nothing to do with him!' Already, my voice was getting louder and louder as indignation at being associated with Chas kicked in.

The inspector shuffled some report papers around his desk and fidgeted with a desk toy – some kind of paper-clip holder shaped like a boat.

'Here in Kenya, we don't like trouble,' he said. 'We like to help each other.' There was a long pause, painful for me, pensive for him. 'If you tell us you were working with Mr Morely to buy drugs then we are happy. You have bail, you sleep well tonight, you eat prawns again. He stays here because we know he is a bad man. You are a good man. You go home.'

I could feel the most awful sense of what was to come. I stared at this bargain-maker with dread settling in my disturbed stomach. There was no way an innocent man would make such a confession. But a guilty man . . .

'I swear to you. I have nothing to do with Mr Morely. You can call him in here and we can both tell you together.'

The inspector twisted a finger in his ear. 'Yes. Maybe I must speak to Mr Morely. But I think it is better if you are not here.' He picked up the shillings and stuffed them back in the Madanzi envelope. 'If you do not want bail, perhaps these can be used for someone else.'

'You can't do that,' I said, feeling like an ant crawling uphill as a torrent crashes down towards it. 'You can't offer him bail with my money.'

But the inspector was already standing up and calling in Swahili to the police in the reception. Corporal Kamau walked in and led me back to the cells. As we reached the block, another policeman was opening the door to let Chas out of his cell. When he appeared, I had about fifteen seconds.

'Chas, they're going to ask you to confess to a lie in return for bail,' I shouted at the surprised dope-head. 'Don't confess anything! It's a trick to try and get us both put away for years. I haven't said anything to them; you don't have to either.' Corporal Kamau gave me a rough push into the cell before the other prisoner could reply. Through the high window, I watched as he was led in to take my place in the confession room.

They were in there for just ten minutes. Did he have any kind of internal struggle at all? Did he even once consider doing the right thing? When the door opened, he walked out into the yard alone. In his hand was a little plastic bag – his few belongings, perhaps. He looked around in disbelief, then stared at the cells. From that distance it was hard to tell, but I thought I saw him give a little helpless shrug. I opened my lungs and screamed at him across the yard. But with another form-less gesture he had turned and was shuffling out on to the main road.

A few moments later, the inspector came to show me

the indictment and announce my transfer to Shimo-La-Tewa prison.

At six o'clock I was handcuffed and led to a sealed van. The two small windows were painted over and the only light came from an electric bulb. Corporal Kamau sat opposite me, staring into my face. The angry scowl never relented. Neither of us spoke. Eventually I closed my eyes to shut him out.

Most of the journey was along the straight coast road. I guessed we were travelling south towards Mombasa. I imagined passing the same villages, the Coca-Cola signs, the fruit stalls that we had pointed out from the convertible. I thought I felt us cross the bridge and then drop into the dip near Jackson's house at Kilifi. Then I gave up guessing, and let my mind drift back to Cara.

Treacherous Cara. I weighed up the title and decided it fitted her well. I cursed myself for leaving her alone with her instructor every morning; for not believing Michelle's warning, or rather, for letting Cara dispel it. What an actress she had been. I almost choked when I remembered the remorse I had felt at her performance. And yet Kristina talked of getting it back together – as if Cara's behaviour was no more than, as Cara would say, uncontrolled friskiness. My aching gut, forgotten over the course of the afternoon, was joined by a leaden feeling in my stomach when I thought of our life together before this nightmare.

After about an hour, the van slowed for some speed bumps, turned right and then stopped. I heard a gate being drawn back. The driver moved forward at a snail's pace. Finally he braked and reversed round a corner, then switched the engine off. Corporal Kamau got up and threw open the door.

It was dark outside. Floodlights illuminated the concrete ground and the faded grey paintwork on the steel door that faced us. I had never felt so alone in my life.

A guard appeared and unlocked the door, pushing me through into a thin passageway smelling of sewers. A single dim bulb hung from the ceiling. The passage contained nine metal doors, four on either side and one at the end. Each one had a small grille at head height and, as we walked between them, a dark face appeared at each. When we reached the end cell, the guard held the door open and watched me enter. His face was devoid of interest as he removed the handcuffs. Then the door was pulled shut and silence settled around me.

The light coming through the grille was just sufficient to make out the bare shape of the cell. It had no windows, and the walls were covered in a decaying, crumbling cement. It was about four feet wide, and barely long enough to hold the mattress. Years of body odour were embedded in its foam. In the corner stood a bucket. Thankfully, it was empty. I sat back on the mattress and waited for Jackson.

I have endured long, dark, nervous waits before. On a school cadet exercise, I pulled the short straw and had to guard a checkpoint for the whole night, under constant threat of attack. To pass the time, I led my mind on a complete review of every place I had ever been, building up a mental catalogue of my life's experience. During a sailing trip with Sammy, we were forced to stay at sea for a night and settled for two four-hour shifts. I kept my mind off imaginary rocks and unlit ships by dreaming up a perfect private island, complete with orchards, three swimming pools and a windmill. Before I had thrashed out the final details of the artwork in the house, it was dawn. But each time, I had known that the waiting would end.

Now, unable to sleep with so many questions and fears in my head, I did not have that luxury. I had no sense of time: they had already taken my watch. But as the hours passed, my hope of seeing the door flung open and Jackson appear faded. I fought to distract my mind, to avoid dwelling on criminal charges and Cara's betrayal. But I couldn't concentrate on dreams of private islands. Nothing could keep my mind away from her.

As a concession to the inevitable, I tried to think only of the good times, sketching out each day we had spent together, exaggerating the best parts and skimming over the rest. I built fantasies around her, partly sexual but mostly involving normal university life: Cara drinking in the bar after a day's work at the lab; Cara sitting on Port Meadow with a picnic; Cara helping me through Finals and being there to celebrate at the end; Cara stretched out in a punt with a glass of Pimms in her hand; Cara naked with an instructor on a pile of neoprene.

I shook violently as my dreams were shattered by the recollection of that scene. Swiftly, fantasy dragged my mind into uncharted territory. I began to imagine what else they had done together, what had happened after I left, what they were doing at that precise moment. I saw

Cara's long fingers tracing sensual curves down the scars on his back; her lips, engorged and rubber-flavoured from the mouthpiece, plucking kisses from his sinewy shoulders. I felt warm skin move over warm skin, and the touch of his hands on her neck. I could taste the salt that she licked from his nipples, from his concave stomach, from his waistline; her chin resting for a moment against his groin as she gave one last teasing smile. And when it was over, an uncharacteristic cigarette, as a final betrayal of a dying image, and conspiratorial laughter at the blundering appearance of a sick cuckold.

I have no idea when I fell asleep. Time had lost all meaning. A loud slam was the next thing I remember, and it woke me immediately. I stood up to look through the grille. The guard was opening the cells one by one and dropping a tin bowl in each. The sight of those shiny dishes made me realize how hungry I was. My last food had been on Saturday night – however long ago that was – and most of that had come up again. But when my door opened, the bowl held nothing but water. I drank it in one gulp and called 'Food!' after the guard. There was no reaction from the grey-uniformed back.

When the guard reached the last cell, the prisoner inside started shouting in fast, angry Swahili. I watched as the guard stiffened and began shouting back. Faces appeared at each of the grilles. The exchange grew louder and more vitriolic, until the prisoner was suddenly silent. After a few more angry words, the guard opened the door to place the container inside the cell. As soon as the lock was drawn back, the prisoner gave a loud yell, kicked the door open and leaped at the guard. A large man with dreadlocks flying around his face, he threw the guard against the opposite cell, sending the bowl flying down the passage. It ricocheted off my door as the two men struggled, lost balance, and crashed down on to the concrete floor. I watched in amazement as they grappled on the floor, raining punches and kicks down on each other.

The main door flew open. A new guard ran in and stunned the rebel with a blow from a baton. For a moment there was complete silence. Then the first guard stood up, scowled at us and rubbed his face. With a sharp instruction to his colleague he stormed out.

We stared silently at the crumpled figure on the floor. He did not even try to get up but held his hands to his head, moaning softly. The baton lingered as a warning, two feet above his face. When the first guard returned he held a bright red pot. It contained a folded rag, grey-white as if torn off an old sheet. The shiny colour of the pot looked so out of place in that grey passageway that for a few seconds I just stared at it blankly. Then I heard the gasp from the other prisoners.

In an instant, the casual sense of security that had allowed me to wallow in misery over Cara vanished. As my gaze moved to the guard's right hand and found it firmly clenched around the handle of a machete, all the rules that I had unconsciously assumed disintegrated. I stopped breathing when the guards forced the prisoner to lay his left hand flat on the floor. I wanted to shout, to make them stop, hesitate, anything. But terror of involvement held me back.

I tried to turn my head away, to sink my face into the rank mattress and suck anaesthetizing gulps of its filth into my lungs to block out the barbarity. Instead, I found myself pressing my face into the grille, transfixed by the impending atrocity and straining to see what was happening. When it came, it came quickly and the man's screams reverberated around the cells. The sound was of vocal cords stretched beyond their natural limits, ripping in sympathetic agony for the maimed. After they had thrown the prisoner back in his cell, clutching the rag to his hand, the guards collected up the four black pieces off the floor and dropped them into the red pot. Together, they walked out with their trophies and locked us in with the aching screams of their victim. And then the dim, inadequate, pathetic, lone passage bulb went out.

Darkness. Pure black everything. No walls, no bucket, no mattress: I was suspended in space; battered by the sound of the tortured man; reeling from the shock of the atrocity; unable to displace that grotesque image; robbed of the simplest piece of reality to cling to by the flick of a switch. The blade rose and fell, rose and fell, tearing into the prisoner's flesh, into my flesh, my arm, my face.

And I screamed. Half-crazed by the act, floundering against invisible walls, sensing guards everywhere, I screamed so hard the sound drowned out the other man's cries. As the legions of blades surrounded me, I closed my eyes and ran.

And I think I must really have tried to run, because I came to sprawled across the cell with a throbbing pain in my head. I felt a foot nudge my calf and turned over to see the guard standing above me. I cringed back against the wall in automatic terror.

He blinked at my reaction, then opened his lips wide in an attempt at a smile. 'You ask for food,' he said, and indicated a bland-looking stew on the floor in front of me. It was watery, with small morsels of meat in it, and it tasted foul, but my stomach was crying out to be fed. As I ate, the guard became increasingly merry until he was chuckling happily to himself.

'What's so funny?' I asked, trying to use a meek, placatory tone.

'Good?' he asked, nodding at the stew.

I decided to play it safe and lie. 'Yes,' I nodded.

At this the guard laughed hysterically, rolling his eyes and clapping his hands. Then he looked at me and pointed at his fingers, gesturing at the stew with his head. I was still half-dazed and didn't immediately understand. I stared at the pot, noticing its shiny red surface for the first time. In horror, my eyes flew to the guard's shadowy face, desperately searching for some sign that it wasn't true. He was nodding happily and waggling his fingers. Instantly I vomited into the bucket. Then I was gagging – almost suffocating in disgust. Wave after wave of nausea and revulsion flooded through me, while the guard scooped up the pot, refilled my water container, and walked off.

When I could breathe again, I gargled half the water, spat it through the grille, and drank the rest. Somehow it stayed down, although my body was shivering violently. Visions of the atrocity kept racing through my mind. I would have begged to be able to think of anything else, even Cara. But my commotion had woken the injured man, and his groans filled the air.

IO

Recording No: 1

Date: 14 December   **Time:** 9.00 am

Situation: Breakfast at Alan's house

Sensory Context: Visual: stunning view of sea, bright bright light; Auditory: fish eagles, wind in the trees; Olfactory: mango juice, grapefruit

Cognitive Context: This is the most wonderful country in the world

Emotional Context: Pure happiness

Somatic Response: Warmth (or is that the sun?)

Facial Response: Smiling

Global Viewpoint: I want to stay here for years

Action Impulse: Lie back and think of Kenya

I stood for an age with my face pressed against the grille, the rusty iron lattice digging into my nose and chin. Outside in the passage was air. Not clean, fresh air, but worlds better than the vomit-laden stench that enveloped me. And there was light. The guard had left that feeble, wonderful bulb glowing, and I gazed into it, taking comfort from its familiar, English shape. Each dimly lit crack in the grey cement on the walls was a solid feature to store away for retrieval if the passage went dark again.

Then there were the other prisoners. At five of the grilles, dark faces were visible and a low whisper of Swahili flowed between them. At first I ignored them, in shocked retreat from all humanity. Only my physical, visible anchors were trustworthy: the bulb, the cracks, the grille that bit into my face. But gradually the gentle hum of their voices and the soft, constant glow of the bulb brought a sort of calm and I found myself needing to talk.

I whispered to the nearest inmate, 'Hey, do you speak English?'

His face registered a look of surprise, and he quickly withdrew into the darkness of his cell. I felt hurt that he was unwilling to extend the prison camaraderie to me. I turned to the next one and called softly. His face disappeared as well. One by one, the other men stood away from their grilles as I tried to make contact. I felt as if I'd been kicked in the stomach. There was nothing I wanted to say, but suddenly I had to talk to someone. I had a desperate need for sympathy, shared suffering, something human.

I started to get angry with them. 'What's the matter with you all?' My eyes flew from grille to grille, finding only darkness. I guessed that eight pairs of eyes were staring back, but no one answered me.

'Jesus, why can't you speak to me? You all speak English, don't you? It's your official damn national language!' My voice broke into a shout. 'Please, I have to talk to someone!'

I was cut off by the sound of bolts being drawn back. The main door opened and the guard appeared. Bright

sunlight poured in, blinding me. Immediately, I understood their silence and knew I'd made a huge mistake. I
had broken some terrible noise rule. Hastily I looked to
his hands for a machete, and relaxed slightly when I saw
them empty. But I knew I would be punished in one
way or other. I wondered how much he would hurt me,
and tried to prepare myself for the pain. Then another
figure appeared behind him.

Against the sunlight the man was a silhouette, but the
bulk in his shoulders was instantly recognizable. I almost
collapsed with relief to see Jackson march towards me,
growling at the guard to unlock my cell. The man
scurried forward to insert a key, and I stepped back to
let my saviour in.

'Ben, the first thing I'm going to say to you is that I
can't get you out,' he started. 'Not yet, anyway.' Sniffing
the air, he stared at the bucket. 'What a damn mess
you've made.' His eyes told me I was not built of the
right stuff if I was going to puke at a little spell in prison.

'But I can't stay here! Can't I get out on bail? This
place is horrific!'

'Not a chance. They say you refused to cooperate
with the police in Watamu and they have a signed
testimony of your guilt by some friend of yours.'

'He's not a friend! He only signed that because they
offered him bail in return.'

'As you say. But now it seems he's taken off. Skipped
bail. He's probably hiding in Mombasa. It just makes
you look even guiltier. Believe me, I've spent the whole
night finding out about all this. Officially, you have to
stay here until the trial.' Jackson stuck his hands in his

pockets and stared at me angrily. 'It was a damn stupid thing to do. This is not a place to get involved in narcotics.'

'But I didn't do anything,' I protested. 'I had no idea there were drugs in . . .'

'Listen, I don't want to hear it. Kristina told me what you said, and I'll tell you now, that's bullshit. Those dealers don't give their merchandise away for free. I've seen too many young smart-arses from England think that they can bend the law because they're white in a third-world country. So have the police. They're dying to make an example of you.'

Jackson let this warning hang in the air. His face was set in a grim, hostile glare. I started to repeat my innocence, but his look cut me dead.

Jackson changed tack. 'You're also causing enormous problems for the High Commissioner. He's having to tell London that *another* of Her Majesty's subjects has embarrassed her in the Commonwealth. It's a serious diplomatic problem at the moment, with the KFP campaigning to kick the British out. The last thing the President needs is a showcase tourist flouting his laws. And there's absolutely no way, in the current political climate, he can sanction special treatment for British criminals. It would be political suicide. The High Commissioner is in such an awkward position, he's inclined to let you rot.

'I've appealed on your behalf, asking him to intervene. He may agree to put pressure on the police to keep you in better conditions, but he will not interfere in the process of law.'

I closed my eyes and tried to calm my voice. When I

spoke, it was half steady. 'But surely, if James Fieldhead talks to him and explains why I'm here, it would be different.'

'To be totally blunt, I don't think you have the right to expect anything of James. He has spent months preparing this project, only to have you screw it up. He was livid when I called him. He's also very worried that we're going to lose that sensor in the process. You will have embarrassed him in front of the university and his sponsors, and damaged his reputation.' Jackson hesitated, and then stuck out his jaw. 'In fact, I find it astonishing that you had the audacity to dabble in drugs while he was paying for your luxury holiday. I am personally very angry at seeing my efforts wasted, and my investment has been nothing compared to his.'

I felt utterly squashed, small as an ant. My innocence became irrelevant. Jackson's fury, coming so soon after the horrors I had witnessed, left me feeling genuinely guilty.

'What can I do?' I muttered.

'Nothing much, except sit tight,' he answered. 'The High Commissioner may ask for you to be transferred to a better prison, where you can at least talk and read, and use a lavatory.' He looked down at the bucket in disgust. 'Otherwise, we can only wait for the trial. There is a lawyer that the High Commission uses for cases like this, but your family will have to foot the bill. The Foreign Office has called them, by the way.'

I felt the shame rise at the thought of my parents hearing the news. I hadn't believed it would reach this point. I pictured them sitting in shock at the breakfast table in Dorset, shaking their heads at my deviancy. The crime would not be an easy one to accept in those quarters. I wondered which would concern them most – my fate in an African gaol, or the embarrassment of having their son arrested on a drugs charge. It had been bad enough when Sammy turned up on the doorstep with that letter from the headmaster in his hand. I tried to imagine how they would react this time.

'I've got to go now,' said Jackson. 'The first priority is to get that sensor off your head before they tear it off and send it to Nairobi as a trophy. Make damn sure no one sees it, and I'll try to come back in a few hours with a doctor and a scalpel.' He rapped on the door. 'I'll get the guard to clear this out,' he said, pointing at the bucket. 'Is there anything you need?'

'Food,' I answered instantly. 'I haven't eaten since Saturday.' Jackson nodded and shouted to the guard, who picked up the bucket and walked out. As Jackson followed, I called after him. 'When will the trial be?'

'No idea. Of the last two cases, one took six weeks and the other five months to come to court. Yours could be anywhere in between, depending on the backlog.'

I was stunned. I had assumed I could be clearing my name within a week, and flying home within two. Now my course and even Finals were in jeopardy. Jackson was almost outside when I called him again. 'And if they convict me?'

'Oh, that's easier. Possession always gets ten years here.' There was not a drop of compassion or tact in his voice.

I gasped. 'Surely they must make exceptions?'

'Never have yet.' And then he was gone.

I sat back on the mattress and stared at the wall. All hope that I had held had been ripped away. My certainty that Jackson would sort everything out; my belief that justice would prevail immediately; my prayer that I would be out of the cell before any other horrors took place; my assumption that I would be back in England before term started: all lay shattered after Jackson's blunt and hurtful words.

But Jackson had influence, I told myself. He would be able to pull the right levers. He was exaggerating the dangers, only because he wanted to keep my expectations down. He didn't actually think I would be convicted. All he was really worried about was the possibility of the guards taking the sensor.

Oh, God.

I replayed that last thought. *All he was really worried about was the possibility of the guards taking the sensor.* That could be true in a very different sense. What if all he cared about was retrieving the sensor? I had half a million dollars' worth of equipment sewn on to my scalp that Fieldhead desperately wanted back. Jackson was being attentive now, but if they both thought I was guilty and both were furious with me for it . . . just how much help should I expect when they had their precious sensor safe and sound? Neither of them would lose anything if I stayed in prison for ten years. Both had unjust but compelling reasons to want me punished. Did I really have any allies out there?

I rocked forward with my head over my knees, a new sense of resignation swamping me. There were two options: cooperate in salvaging the sensor or make sure they couldn't get it until I was freed. A game. Just as with Chas and his confession, I heard Fieldhead's words in the near-empty nave: *Since when have games been about fun?* I forced myself to concentrate. Interdependent actions. Their options: high effort or low effort to get me released. And high meant the full resources of the sponsor. It could make a huge difference.

If I handed over the sensor when Jackson reappeared, that was it. He could decide to wash his hands of me at any time. But if I was to hold on to it, should I make the deal explicit? How angry would that make him? I couldn't decide how to handle the rough-edged Kenyan. What was clear was the importance of that sensor. If I wanted to use it as a bargaining chip, I had to keep it hidden.

The door opened and my hand rushed up to smooth the hair over the back of my head. The guard entered with an angry sneer on his lips. Jackson had upset him. Although the man had obeyed the barked instruction, he was furious at being ordered about in his own domain. The other inmates had listened to the demands and seen the guard docilely pick up the bucket. Jackson obviously had some influence at the prison, if not enough to get me into a better cell. But the guard must have resented this demonstration of a greater power in front of his subjects and chosen to take out his aggression on me.

He threw the bucket into the corner and held a cane above me as I sat on the mattress. With a nasty smile, he brought the tip down in front of my face, and held the point to my neck for a few seconds. I waited for the beating I knew would come. But instead he stepped outside and reappeared with a flat bowl full of white paste. In his menacing way, he was still obeying Jackson.

The guard placed the bowl on the floor in front of me and closed his feet round it so that it was wedged firmly between his boots. I did not even try to shift it. He started to chuckle again. There was no spoon, so I put my hand down between his feet to scoop up some of the paste. Immediately the cane crashed down on my arm, and I jerked back, my eyes watering at the sting.

'No hands,' ordered the guard, waving his cane in warning.

I stared at him in disbelief. The man was determined to wring enough humiliation out of me to compensate for Jackson's lack of diplomacy. I had to eat, so I did what he wanted and lowered my face between his stained boots to lap at the food. My cheeks were burning with the degradation I felt, as I pictured his view of me: kneeling in front of him, eating like a dog. I tried to concentrate on the food, sucking it up as fast as possible, but I hadn't finished before I heard the wet rasp of his throat and felt a soft glutinous mass land on the back of my head. I forced myself to lick up every last bit of the paste, and was about to retreat to the security of the corner when I felt the tip of the cane press down on my head. I allowed it to push my face into the empty plate. The extra humiliation was irrelevant. I was suddenly very nervous. I could feel the tip of the cane moving slightly on the back of my skull. It was too close. Any second he would find it.

The guard gave an ugly laugh at the thought of my face pressed into the slime of paste and saliva. Then the cane slipped. It didn't move far. The tip caught against the edge of the sensor and I felt a wrench as the stitches pulled at my scalp. Instantly I heard a grunt of surprise and the cane dropped to the floor. Fingers came down to pull my hair aside. For a few seconds, I didn't move. Then I rocked back and pressed myself into the corner, denying him any further examination. The guard looked at me uncertainly, trying to imagine what the strange device could be. Then he picked up his cane.

'I take later,' he scowled.

The moment he left, the light went out again.

Even before the images returned, I was terrified. The blackness alone was overwhelming. Immediately, I felt the blades reappear. I sensed bodies all around me, ill defined but all the more threatening for their nebulous forms. I forced myself to lie down, face buried in the coarse, fetid foam of the mattress, seeking maximum physical contact with reality. Again and again the film in my mind replayed the scene, each time a little faster, a little more graphically. I longed to knock myself out again, but couldn't get up. Instead, I gripped the mattress with clawed fingers and fought for control of my mind.

Everything I tried to picture was too remote, too unreal in that cell. Oxford did not exist, snow did not exist, even Watamu beach did not exist. My subconscious rebelled at the effort and flew back to a dimly lit passage containing torturers of grotesque form. When I could take no more, I opened my mouth and screamed into the mattress. The brutal, bestial noise shook me free of the images for a few moments. I stared blindly at the mattress and turned my thoughts to the one memory that was close enough and powerful enough to sustain.

It wasn't a pleasant memory, but it was the only way to stop the nightmare coming back. On that last night with her, I had lain in darkness and confessed my secret to Cara. Now I wanted to confess it again and again; repeat it a million times if necessary; not stop until the light came back and the knives went away . . .

'It's about my brother.'

She breathes out slowly and rolls over. 'You didn't say you had a brother.' She flicks out the light and lies still beside me. We listen to the stark thud of a bass that has lost its melody somewhere in the cool breeze along the way.

'I didn't think you were particularly interested in the rest of my life.'

'Well, now I am.' Cara is turning, twisting her head beside me. Through the darkness I sense her indignation. She is still suffering the uncertainty of undefined feelings. 'Tell me about him.'

'Sammy? He's two years younger than me. The perfect brother: generous, intelligent, on exactly the same wavelength as me. We're different characters but we understand each other completely. We were at school together – a little boarding school in Devon. I didn't much like it, but having Sammy around made it a lot more fun. We were quite unusual – older and younger brother hanging out together as much as with our friends – but I think we always enjoyed each other's company more than anyone else's.'

'So what happened?'

I find her back and caress the nape of her neck, imagining the tiny bleached hairs folding beneath my touch. 'It was after I left. Sammy was just going into his last year: getting ready for A-levels, Oxford interviews. He was a prefect and captain of the cricket team.' The perfect all-rounder. A touch lightly built, but otherwise ideal schoolboy hero stuff. 'I went down at the beginning of that year to play in the old boys' football team: just a bit of fun away from Oxford; hook up with my friends. Took Sammy out for a pizza before the game. All I remember was the expression on his face. I'd never seen him so happy. And this is a guy who's always cheerful. Of course it turned out that he was in love, or whatever you want to call it.' There is no reaction from Cara. It hadn't been an overly subtle reference. 'Anyway, it wasn't one of the sixth-formers. Sammy had gone and fallen for a new cook – French, young. I think it was her first job. She barely spoke English. But clearly very charming and just as infatuated with Sammy as he was with her. They'd been meeting secretly for four weeks. I was really happy for him. She was his first serious girlfriend and it transformed him. God, he was over the moon! He could hardly get the pizza down he was so busy describing her.

'I kept thinking about it during the match. Such great news. Sammy was on the touchline, supporting me, even though half his friends were playing on the school side. It didn't matter, of course: it was a friendly game and they beat us anyway. Afterwards, Sammy had to go off to finish some homework, so I wandered back to the changing rooms with an old friend from my year. We got to the showers ahead of everyone else, and were deep in memoryland when I mentioned Sammy. Obviously he had to keep his relationship secret, but I knew I could trust Andrew not to repeat it to anyone else. You know how sometimes you just have to share news with someone?'

Cara nods silently. The pain of the story is worse than I'd imagined.

'So anyway, I told him my little brother was seeing this French chick – isn't that great – and the funniest part is that she works here – as a cook. We were both laughing about it until I heard this tapping sound and realized there was someone else in the room. Just behind a row of lockers. I walked round and found this guy sitting there, listening to every word. Just sitting there, tapping the lumps of mud off his football boots, listening to all the details of my brother's secret. I knew roughly who he was: a bit of a loser who didn't really fit in with anyone else. Of course, I immediately asked him not to repeat what he'd heard. He didn't say anything. Kept tapping away, watching the clods of mud fall to the floor. The rest of the players started arriving. I don't know what he would have done if I'd left it at that, but for some stupid reason I threatened him. I suppose I was nervous and that made me aggressive. Anyway, I threatened him the way I would have done a couple of years earlier when I was one of the top dogs and he was just reaching puberty. I can't even remember the threat – some crude schoolboy effort. All I remember was him levering the last pieces of mud off his boots with his fingernail, then his smug grin as he told me my threats didn't count for shit any more. And of course he was right. What's more, I'd given his vindictive, petty mind an extra reason to use his knowledge.'

'He told everyone?'

'No,' I reply. 'No, he didn't want everyone hating him for grassing on a popular prefect. He wasn't stupid. He just left an anonymous note for the headmaster. Very simple, very effective. They called in the girl immediately and she was so frightened – young, new to the job, in a foreign country – she broke down and told them everything.'

'What happened to your brother?'

'What always happens in repressed boarding schools when the staff get too friendly with the pupils. Both were kicked out. The girl lost her job and ran back to France, too ashamed even to say goodbye to Sammy. He was asked to leave the following day. No more prefect, no more captain of cricket. Just a couple of suitcases and a one-way train ticket.'

'Jesus,' Cara murmurs. 'The bastards.'

'He had to prepare for his A-levels at home, and – not surprisingly – screwed them up. Destroyed his chances of getting into Oxford. He'd never wanted to go anywhere else.'

'Ben. Look,' she whispers. 'It's not your fault. You can't blame yourself because some little shit grassed.' I feel her hand brush against my cheek, the touch of a body-warm silver bracelet between our skins.

'You're wrong. It's absolutely my fault. I might as well have shopped him myself. He even made me swear in the pizza place not to tell anyone. But within a couple of hours, I'd broken my promise.'

'Come on. I'm sure he doesn't blame you.'

'No. He doesn't. For the simple reason that he doesn't know. I just couldn't admit it. When he came back home he was cursing "the arsehole that did this". That was just it – he didn't know who'd grassed. He hadn't told anyone except me. And obviously there was no way I could possibly be responsible . . .' I laugh bitterly, '. . . so someone must have seen them together somewhere. That's what he said. He spent weeks trying to work out who'd done it. Who'd killed his academic dream and destroyed his relationship. I tried to stay out of it, but he kept asking me my opinion. Each time he talked about it there was this mad glare in his eyes. It scared me, I have to say.' Cara stops stroking and lays her hand firmly over my cheek. Already I can feel my throat harden around the words.

'So I gave an opinion built on lies. And over time the lies mounted up. Once or twice I wanted to admit what had happened. But by then I'd lied so often, and let him go deceived for so long, that it was too late. It would undermine too much, would destroy the best friendship I have.'

For a long time we lie silent. I remember his brave face a month after the exam results came out, as he opened the Oxford envelope, fingers already shaking from the premonition that its tiny size gave. And I remember most of all his words, which even in my state of absolute confession I cannot bring myself to repeat to Cara: 'Don't worry,' he muttered, barely holding back the tears as the rejection slip fell on to the table. 'It really doesn't matter. I'm just sorry we can't be together any more.' An unsteady, strained smile. 'I've gone and let you down this time, Ben.'

Facing ten years in gaol, the memory of those not-quite tears left my head exploding with fury and remorse. What had I done? My brother's life screwed up by one careless conversation. Perhaps this was God's justice. My own life shortened by ten years – if the verdict went against me – and all because I'd been in the wrong place at the wrong time. Such simple things I would miss: the walks with Sammy, the arguments, the understanding. And instead I would be faced with that guard or some similar creature for a decade.

That guard, when he returned, was carrying a penknife.

I was almost reconciled to the blackness by the time the passage bulb came back on. I had managed to distract myself with thoughts of Sammy, and the continuing dark was a welcome stasis. While nothing changed, nothing truly bad could happen. When the light snapped on I felt all my muscles tense.

It was a red Swiss Army model, its shape difficult to make out in the half-light of the cell, but its purpose immediately clear. I pushed myself back against the wall.

The guard studied me with interest, then selected a blade. He beckoned with his fingers.

'Come,' he said.

I shook my head, wondering if resistance would make

him give up or just heighten his interest. The moment he had that sensor, I had lost my best ticket out. Jackson would reappear with the doctor, scream at me for my stupidity, then storm out, perhaps for ever. Half a million dollars. A big enough loss to turn Fieldhead firmly against me. I couldn't let him take it.

'Come,' he repeated, leaning forward with his other hand and pulling at my arm. I shook him off immediately. That made him angry. His hand darted forward again. I leaped to my feet.

'No!' I shouted. 'No!' What was the penalty for refusing to cooperate? I knew I couldn't touch him. That any violence from me could easily lead to that terrible punishment.

He dropped the knife – blade still open – into his breast pocket. Then he used both his hands to grip me. His strength was surprising. In an instant, my face was pressed against the wall and his hand was pushing my hair up.

'No!' I shouted again, pushing backwards, pulling myself free. The sound of my voice was too loud. He didn't like it. In his eyes I read real malice.

During the brief standoff, we heard a knock on the outer door.

The guard stared at me a moment longer, then locked my cell behind him and went to open the door. I heard voices, a small argument in Swahili. Then footsteps coming back to my cell.

The door opened and Corporal Kamau walked in. He brought with him a halogen lamp and a piece of paper. The lamp was dazzling after so much darkness and it threw eerie patterns up the walls. He handed the paper to me and spoke in English for the first time.

'Sign,' he said, tapping the bottom of the sheet and handing me a chewed ballpoint.

I took the pen. The paper was yellow and stiff. Below a crest, the message was in heavy print. It was devastating.

I declare that I, Benjamin Robert Ashurst, of the United Kingdom, purchased 2 ounces of cannabis resin at 3.45 pm on Sunday, 20 December, on Watamu beach. I am aware that this is a crime in the Republic of Kenya, punishable by a prison sentence of ten years. I wish to apologize publicly and fully to His Excellency, the President of the Republic of Kenya and to the whole glorious country for my abuse of their generous hospitality.

I looked round at the corporal. 'I'm not going to sign this,' I gasped. 'It's not true. I've told you it's not true!'

Not a flicker of expression appeared on his face. He simply repeated his order: 'Sign.'

'No!' I was indignant. 'Do you think I'm stupid? This is an admission of guilt. If I sign this, I stay here for ten years, don't I?'

The policeman sighed. 'It will save time,' he explained in slow, clear English.

'Save time?' I screamed at his unblinking scowl. 'I should do ten years to save you the effort of going to court? No!'

He picked up the paper and pen from the floor where I had thrown them. 'You must sign. Please, do it now.'

'Why are you doing this? Is this for the KFP? Are you trying to get me convicted just as the elections are happening?'

He continued to hold out the paper. I could feel my voice getting desperate, strained. 'It's not going to help anything,' I pleaded. 'Getting me convicted isn't going to win you the election.' He ignored my words completely.

'Listen to me. For the last time, that statement is not true. I will not sign it. If you have a problem with that we can call my lawyer,' I finished bravely.

'This is very simple,' he said, as to a child. He called to the guard and then held out the paper. 'You do not need a lawyer because you do not have a choice. I recommend you sign now.'

I turned my back on him as the guard marched in. Corporal Kamau muttered something to him and then stepped back. A second later, I was on the floor, feeling a stabbing pain in the back of my legs where the guard had kicked them. The guard hauled me flat so that I was lying on my stomach, my legs crumpled up against the wall. He held me down with a boot between my shoulder blades while Corporal Kamau placed the pen and paper on the floor by my right hand. When I ignored it, he stepped outside. In the brief moment that he was gone, the guard stamped hard, winding me so that I had to suck air and dust from the floor into my lungs. Corporal Kamau walked back in. He held the bloodstained machete in his hand.

My reaction was instantaneous; animalistic. I screamed, producing a sound I'd never heard before, that rang shrill and long around the tiny cell. I screamed until I ran out of breath, and even then kept screaming as I gasped for air. The guard gripped my left arm and forced my hand to lie flat on the cement floor, holding it down with his other foot.

Corporal Kamau looked on impassively until my hand was pinned in position. Then he crouched in front of me and gestured with the machete to the paper by my right hand. 'You have three minutes,' he said, quietly. He did not bother to check his watch.

The guard was bracing himself against the low ceiling and I couldn't shift him, however hard I struggled. Instead, his pressure on my chest became stronger each time I moved, until I was fighting for breath.

'Please! Please!' I screamed. Corporal Kamau ignored me completely. 'Don't make me waste my life here!'

Both men were silent.

There was nothing I could do. Gradually, my resistance was worn down. Unable to think, I lay gulping air and sobbing violently at the injustice and cruelty of the man.

Four fingers against ten years of life. Rational choices were beyond me. But I knew I couldn't let that machete cut into my flesh, slice through the bone, destroy my hand. Pitifully, tearfully, I reached for the pen and signed my confession.

Above me, the guard chuckled quietly and stepped away from me. Corporal Kamau scooped up his fabrication without a word. I didn't lift my face off the floor. I could only suffer the self-hating, soul-destroying emotions that raced through my head, as I faced up to the sentence I had signed.

'And what exactly are you feeling now? That's what I would really like to know.'

I knew instantly that Corporal Kamau was not the speaker. My head jerked up. Beside the open door, the corporal's khaki trousers and polished boots had been replaced by a pair of light slacks and suede lace-ups.

For a moment I thought it was the High Commissioner, arrived one minute too late. But as I pushed myself off the floor, I stared into my tutor's face in amazement. 'You! Here?'

'Yes, yes,' he answered amiably but hurriedly. 'While it's still fresh, tell me quickly what you're feeling – or were, thirty seconds ago.'

He even had a notepad out and a pencil poised. I stared at him in total confusion. After a few moments, he realized I was incapable of analysis, and murmured, 'Oh well, let's hope your memory is good.' He helped me to my feet and handed me a stool that the guard seemed to have conjured up from nowhere. He sat on another, and the guard slouched against the wall behind me.

'Nightmare's over, Ben. You can calm your troubled mind and start to forget the whole thing, while basking in the enormous gratitude of the scientific community in general, and my client in particular. The material is first-class. You've done magnificently!'

Understanding sank in fast. Instinctively, I touched the back of my head to check the sensor that had lain forgotten throughout that last ordeal.

'Oh, Jesus,' I whispered. Fieldhead stayed silent, a mild grin on his face as he let me think it through.

'Where is it?' I asked quietly, my eyes searching the walls and ceiling.

'Francis?' Fieldhead looked up at the guard.

Francis pulled out his penknife and leaned over to the wall between us. Carefully, he scraped away an uneven flake of paint to expose a small black object the size of a pencil.

'The advantage here was that you weren't going any-where, so we didn't need to use a full-size recorder. Just this little receptor, with a wire running into my computer next door. We didn't need any tapes, so we recorded the whole time. There's simply acres of data to analyse,' Fieldhead concluded happily.

'And the arrest?'

'Well, clearly there we needed a mobile unit – it was in the satchel that the beach seller dropped beside you. Was it good? I'd love to have been there.'

I ignored his question. 'They're all actors?'

'Well, not really. Joseph – Corporal Kamau that is – and Francis are professionals, and so was the prisoner with the big part. Who does still have all his body parts, in case that's been worrying you. They rehearsed that bit for days to make it look realistic.' I winced at the memory. 'The other prisoners really are inmates here, although they normally have much better quarters. This is the isolation block and it's generally empty. We steril-ized it completely, by the way.'

'How thoughtful.'

'Otherwise, the rest are just normal people helping out for a laugh: the Watamu police have been wonderful; Alan and Kristina, of course; Chas to build credibility for the arrest; and the beach seller, whom we all thought was absolutely marvellous.'

My mind had calmed down and was starting to catch up with events. 'Can we speak privately for a moment?'

'Well, actually, no. Sorry. Much as I hope you will see all this in retrospect as a wonderful exercise in science, I'm slightly concerned about your immediate reactions. Francis is just sticking around to keep me alive while your head is still at boiling point.' He scratched his nose.

'You see, I have another confession to make, which you may not already have guessed. Casper was also on the team, and I'm afraid I asked him to try a bit of a foul shot. Wasn't at all sure it would reach the goal but . . . well, as it turned out, it did. Good for the project as the timing was spot-on and it neatly complemented the earlier stuff. But not so great for you.' Once again, I found myself staring at him, astonished. 'Still, think of it like this – if she went off with someone else that quickly, she wasn't right for you. Doesn't deserve you.'

He had the grace to look a little ashamed. I started rising out of my seat and immediately felt Francis holding me back. I dug my fingernails into my palm. 'What else don't I know?'

Fieldhead looked amused. 'Oh, lots, really. Although most of it you could work out for yourself. In fact, as your tutor, I'm rather disappointed that you didn't. After Alan gave you a preview in that delightful little aeroplane of his, you ought really to have been a little suspicious of the train of disasters that followed. Good thing you weren't, of course.

'After all, food poisoning, arrest and betrayal – all within twenty-four hours? But, God, we got some good material. Dear Michelle – isn't she a sweetheart? Honestly, Ben. No disrespect intended, but when was the last time such an attractive girl did all the hard work to pull you, without you lifting a finger? She was wired, you know. You'll love seeing the conflict of emotions that was going on in your head when you turned her down. Bet you wish you hadn't now,' he added with a laugh, and then looked slightly guilty.

'I'm sorry. I shouldn't make fun of what you've been through. Don't think I'm ungrateful. I really do appreciate everything that you've endured. None of it was gratuitous, I promise. I kept the unpleasantness to the bare minimum necessary to obtain everything we wanted. I apologize for it all, but believe me: none of it was wasted.

'Take the food poisoning, for example. Your whole house was wired. I captured everything until you went out on to the beach.' I looked up sharply. He nodded. 'You have to understand that getting you to make recordings was really just part of the deception. The bulk of the data comes from my fixed wires and from mobiles carried by people like Joseph and Michelle. Your material is only really useful for the notes you kept.

'The trouble is that emotions are easily distorted. This is something the Americans never allowed for, and is consequently why their product is near useless. Just the simple knowledge that you are recording yourself is enough to change the way you feel. I know you probably thought you were doing perfect science, but I'm afraid the only times your recordings were really pure was when you forgot about them. The flying stunt and the horse ride are the best ones. All that endless dull stuff, lying on beaches, is too contaminated by thoughts of me.' He grinned at the idea.

Fieldhead took stock of his jumbled account and then continued. 'Back to the food poisoning. Nasty, I know, but I absolutely had to understand the emotions associated with pain. In a way, that was the central thesis, if you remember. Again, I'm slightly surprised you never guessed I would try it on you. When the Americans measured pain, all they got was a sort of "nobility in the face of unpleasant duty" coming through. It's a waste of time unless the victim is unaware of the test. Your reactions, dominated by fear, demonstrate how far off the mark they were.

'I chose food poisoning because I didn't want to give you any lasting injuries. The strain of bacteria that I poured over those oysters is known to produce severe but temporary pain, without ever causing any real danger to the victim. You *are* fully recovered by now?'

'You were here all the time? What about that time I called you in England?'

'*Thought* you called me in England. I was about a hundred yards away, halfway through a delicious lobster thermidor.'

'Wettest day of the year?'

'Was, actually. I'd checked, in case you did.'

'How did you set it all up so fast?' I asked.

'Oh, I didn't at all. It took months to sort out.' He nodded at my incomprehension and explained, 'I'd made all the arrangements in Watamu by September, and was just waiting for a suitable guinea pig. You see, it was the perfect location. Enough elements on both sides of the equation to build up absolute Paradise and total Hell, at least for an uninformed English boy with exaggerated ideas about African prisons.

'The election troubles had us worried for a while, until we worked out how to exploit them. Your obsession with the dangers of the KFP was very useful, and of course we played up to that. Alan was crucial to the whole exercise, spinning you stories about evil policemen, and using his contacts to build the charade at the hotel and borrow a section of the prison. And there's one more consideration. Should you get bitter about this, we are not in the EU or any developed country where you might be able to kick up a fuss. The police here are all buddies of Alan's, so if you complained they would just buy you a beer and send you on your way.'

His smile had a confident finality about it – a sense of *fait accompli*, as if nothing I could do would interfere with his plans.

'You know I won't let this lie,' I said. 'Not when you sent Casper after Cara, and put me through all this.' I didn't make the threat, but we both knew how easily academic reputations were ruined.

'I realize that you are longing to gouge my eyes out, or do whatever legal equivalent is available back in England. But I hope you will come to appreciate how little good it will do you when you've thought it over. To encourage you to do so, I should add that you will find a significant improvement in your financial position at home, which I hope will positively colour your memories.'

'What do you mean?'

'Think of it like this. My sponsors wanted to make a deal with someone. That person would spend forty-eight hours in hell – that's all it's been since the poisoning – and for their troubles they would be paid £5,000 in tax-free cash. Not a bad hourly wage. The only trouble was, the individual couldn't know about the deal. So, as your tutor, I accepted for you. I took the liberty of checking your wallet at Madanzi, and your bank details are already in their hands.'

'The money is supposed to keep me quiet?'

'Absolutely. Amazingly versatile stuff.'

'I'm not interested in your bribes.'

Fieldhead raised an eyebrow, but he didn't seem surprised.

'No, well, carrots don't always work with unimaginatively righteous people. So OK, here's the stick.' He held out a typed sheet of paper. 'I only have your word for it, of course, but it did sound like you wouldn't want this reaching your brother.'

His smile was still strong, but the edges had become taut and his eyes had lost their earlier warmth. I read the first line and felt sick. What had felt like safe pillow talk was black and white confession in transcript.

'I was planning to send him a copy of the tape as well. It might cheer him up a bit to hear the remorse in your voice.'

I stared at him in fury. 'You bugged the beach house?'

'I bugged everything that didn't move. After all, where

you have an emotions recorder you may as well have a little audio too.'

A great swell of anger was flooding through me. My head felt ready to explode. 'And even after you listened in to every word, every feeling between Cara and me, you still went ahead and destroyed us.'

'Yes, well . . .' He gave a vague wave with one hand.

'No! Absolutely fucking no!' I yelled. 'I am not going to be pushed into submission like this. I am not going to let you bribe and blackmail your way out of this. I am damn well going to make you pay!'

I was already on my feet, my fists bunched, when Francis threw his arms around me and pulled me back down. Fieldhead didn't move at all. He left a long silence after my outburst.

'I'm going to tell you why your threat doesn't worry me. And I'm going to base my belief on two assumptions. That you're smart enough to act in your own best interest. And smart enough to resist being manipulated. Because you are still being manipulated. Not by me now, but by your emotions.

'One of the main functions of anger is to convince others of our intentions. You'll remember from game theory that a threat must be credible to influence an opponent. If future threats are to be effective, current threats must not be shown up as bluffs. Anger must be followed – when necessary – by action, for it to remain credible.'

'I can't believe you're trying to lecture me now,' I snarled.

Fieldhead continued as if he hadn't heard me. 'Your

anger is designed to make me believe you will carry through your threat. And it is very believable. Trouble is, we're not playing a game any more. I'm out of options. I've chosen my course. There's now no reason for you to demonstrate a credible threat because there's nothing I can do to change what's happened. All that's left of the game is your choice of reaction, and if you're sensible you will make that choice based on the payoff to you. Clearly, your rational choice now is to take the money and avoid the ugly scene with your brother. But your anger – selected to preserve its credibility for future games – is putting enormous pressure on you to strike back. Emotion is distorting your reason.

'It is not intelligent for you to fight me, Ben. You will lose a lot and you will gain nothing of substance. You will simply have shown yourself to be passion's slave. You do not need to give in to manipulation by a stone-age force. You know what's going on. You know the payoffs. Fight it!'

I watched him lay out his arguments with a kind of horrified fascination. This was the same man who had instructed an actor to threaten me with a machete just a short while earlier. I could still smell the scent of terror in the air and sense the animal reflexes that had taken hold of me. Fieldhead's armchair persuasion techniques belonged to a different world.

'And if you need emotional ammunition to fight emotional pressure,' he was saying, 'think of what this project has achieved. It is a turning point in science. That gadget stuck to your head has made it possible to do some of the most groundbreaking research since Watson and

Crick. This isn't about drug companies, or beach holidays, or relationships. It is far, far more important. The knowledge you've helped me build up will revolutionize the mind sciences, and lead to any number of psychiatric breakthroughs. It's more important than any of this.'

I heard every word, but none of it made the slightest impression on the stone-age force inside me. Fieldhead could see I wasn't convinced.

'Emotion science is the ultimate art. Think about what we have. You have been through almost every colour of the emotional rainbow, and it's all recorded. Happiness, humour, joy, excitement, lust, contentment, relaxation, even love perhaps. Then terror with Alan, scorn with Chas, jealousy with Michelle, discomfort and fear after the poisoning. Then, finally, here: surprise, loneliness, horror, hope, desolation, revulsion, disgust, humiliation, sadness, anguish, shame and self-hatred. I've probably missed a few, but the list is amply comprehensive as it is. Every one registers as a different frequency or combination of frequencies. I am starting to distinguish simple and complex emotions; seeing similarities in frequencies that explain why some emotions are coupled with others. It's extremely exciting material.'

I began to understand the magnitude of his work. But more than that, I was stunned at Fieldhead's planning capability. To have achieved such results in so great a diversity of emotions was truly impressive. He had been a virtuoso conductor, leading me through more emotional variations than most people see in a year. And yet, despite all his explanations and justifications, I knew I had to hit back.

If I was passion's slave, so be it. Material payoffs meant nothing after such an intensely psychological experience. Everything was in the mind. Everything was in the emotion. Anger demanded, fury ordered. I had to hit back.

But I had learned one thing from the last hour: Fieldhead's intelligence and imagination were unbeatable. If he knew I was still determined to blow away his reputation, he would keep finding transcripts or similar devices to stop me in my tracks. I couldn't fight him head on. My only chance was surprise. And that is why finally, after an hour of scowling, I forced a smile. Feigned commitment.

'Well done,' I said quietly.

For a moment, the great man was silenced. He almost couldn't believe his application of cool logic could have worked so quickly.

'You mean that?'

'Yes. Well done. I suppose I never really appreciated what it was all about. I'm still angry inside, but . . . in a way, I'm almost proud as well. To have been *the* subject.'

Francis let out a small sigh and leaned back against the wall. Fieldhead grinned and picked up the transcript, tearing it down the centre. 'Thank you,' he said. 'That is exactly how I hoped you'd feel.'

For a few moments there didn't seem to be anything else to say. He beamed at me. I half-beamed at him. Francis probably double-beamed at both of us. Then Fieldhead stood up.

'Come on. Let's get out of here. There are hot showers round the corner. We brought all your clothes round.

Why don't you have a shave and clean up, and then come and take a look at the data? Your plane's not until late tonight and I've got some serious question marks I could use your help with.'

Painful cooperation. Revisiting the nightmare. Revisiting happiness and love with Cara. But essential if I was going to make my deception anything like as effective as his. 'Sure,' I nodded. 'It'd be interesting to see.'

The outside door was wide open, afternoon sunshine pouring into the isolation block. All the cells were empty – the curtain had come down and the extras had gone home, leaving the director and principal actors to mull over the performance.

I looked for the first time around the prison that had held me in such fear for a night and a day. In the sunshine it looked a friendly place, with palm trees scattered around a dusty exercise ground, and inmates chatting together in groups. One of the groups saw me and waved. I took them to be my silent companions, and waved back, because I did not have the heart to shun them.

Francis took me to a shower block and left me with my bags. He was all good cheer, wanting to discuss the experience in detail and get feedback on his performance. I parroted 'No hard feelings' back to him, but didn't quite match his enthusiasm. I couldn't resent him, even though I was longing to stick my fist in his face for what he'd done. At the end of the day, they were not his lines.

PART TWO

One of the most important things to realize about systems of animal communication is that they are not systems for the dissemination of the truth. An animal selected to signal to another animal may be selected to convey correct information, misinformation, or both.

Robert Trivers
– *Social Evolution*, 1985

11

'We've put you in business class. Thought you could use the sleep. I'm afraid I can't join you as I've got a bit of clearing up to do here. Might even fit in a few days' holiday. Been getting awfully jealous of all your frolicking.' He grinned at the road. Fieldhead had commandeered the Mercedes and was speeding across Nyali Bridge. Darkness denied me a last proper look at Africa.

'Cara flew back yesterday evening,' he said, pursuing the theme remorselessly. 'Said she'd call in Oxford. Up to you, of course, but I wouldn't waste my breath answering. Definitely unreliable. Not your type.'

With great strength of mind I stuck to my cooperative façade, resisting the temptation to introduce a little brutal violence into his perfectly cerebral world. How did he dare to say that? Halfway down a back street, Fieldhead pulled into the side and got out of the car.

'I know it doesn't look great,' he said, indicating a decaying Arabic house, 'but it's hardly a difficult operation.' On the door, a small plastic panel announced Dr Ramesh Patel, General Doctor of Medicine. One chair, one bright light, one scalpel. Fifteen minutes later, we were back in the car and the half-million dollar sensor was resting in Fieldhead's breast pocket. I rubbed the fine growth of fur on the back of my head.

'There. No more manipulation. If you get arrested now, I promise it's nothing to do with me,' smiled Fieldhead.

If you get arrested, I hope it has a lot to do with me, I thought in return.

At Mombasa airport, a long queue of people stretched out behind a single operational check-in desk for the 23.05 flight to Heathrow. I took one look at the slow-moving torment and wilted. But Fieldhead ignored the queue, leading me instead to a small airline office, where an official greeted him and took my ticket. Within two minutes I was checked in and ready to board.

'So. How about a quick drink?'

I shook my head.

'Sure. Right. Probably easier if I just send you on your way and be off? You going straight back to Oxford?'

'Yes.'

'Good. Get some rest. Oh . . . I nearly forgot.'

Fieldhead walked over to the car, opened the boot, and came back carrying an enormous parcel.

'Just to say a big personal thank you, beyond the cash in the bank. We all think you were wonderful.'

Resting the parcel on the ground, he handed me a card. On the front was a mounted photograph of Madanzi with the grinning faces of all the cast: Kristina, Jackson, the inspector, Chas, Joseph, Francis, the beach seller, Michelle. Casper was tactfully missing. Inside, above the array of signatures: *We hope you don't hate us too much – come back anytime, you lovely guy!*

'Michelle wrote that,' smiled Fieldhead. Then he

hoisted the parcel. 'And this is from me, to help you see everything with a good sense of humour.'

He passed it across, a nervous look on his face as if he were worried I might not approve of this peace-making effort. Careful not to show too much enthusiasm, I pulled off the low-grade wrapping paper and stared at the carving. The same monkey, swollen to three feet and several kilograms, stared back at me. Only this time, the detail was more intricate, the workmanship much cleaner, the choice of wood much more expensive. Really, he was sick.

'I had it made by a Watamu craftsman out of a local hardwood called *mbambakofi*. He spent a week carving it. Then the women in his village oiled it repeatedly over a further three weeks. It's even been blessed by their holy man. So if you decide to keep it, you'll have a piece of the area to remember it by. I hope you will.'

Somehow, to reject it now would have been to tread all over the spirits of those hard-working Kenyans. I muttered something vague and thrust the carving under one arm. Fieldhead held out his hand. One more forced gesture of friendship. I shook hands briefly, then turned and walked to the gate.

So strong was the effect of Fieldhead's gestures, it was not until the plane had taken off that I began to think again about the extent of his manipulation. Everything. Everything I'd seen had been artificial. Everything! I thought about the desperate pleas in the police station, the Prisoner's Dilemma, the psychological torment of that atrocity. How could he possibly do all that to me and then fob me off with some wooden monkey? I gazed angrily up at the overhead locker where his inadequate token lay sandwiched between other people's duty-free bottles. Wasn't that the biggest insult of all? The moment he returned I would take it back to him.

But then what? Would that be the end? Dr James Fieldhead does it again with honours? I couldn't let him get away with it. I had to hit back. Fine, he had the transcript – a smart move and a lucky chance for him. But I could hurt him in one area while still holding something else in reserve as a counter against his own threat. Such easy targets: Oxford position, sponsor relationship, public image, personal reputation.

And what about Cara? Before it had been black and white: she was a whore who I would never speak to again. Was that still true, given the effort he'd put into seducing her? Would those first roots of love that I'd felt – that I knew she'd felt, even as she'd shrunk away from admitting it – be hardy enough to survive such a crippling blow? Did I even want them to?

Betrayal. An impossible crime to evaluate. Both of them, in their different ways, were guilty of it. Cara had betrayed my love, but Fieldhead had done something worse: he'd betrayed my trust. And yet just as Cara had been provoked in her betrayal by a scarred sun god, Fieldhead too had his excuses. Teflon-coated, cast-iron excuses: in the name of Science – that god of our times. For priests such as Fieldhead, no deception, no manipulation, no psychological torture was a step too far in service of its hallowed shrine. All that mattered was the Truth, the answer that would glorify his name for generations to come. And if a young apprentice had his trust abused in the process, so be it.

But then, why was I even thinking like that, imagining that Fieldhead had ever worried about trade-offs? What kind of bastard throws an innocent boy into a pitch-black cell and terrifies him with spectres of infinite gaol sentences? This was not a man who'd spent a second worrying about the morality of what he was doing, let alone the suffering that he was causing. All his attention was – and always had been – focused very firmly on the academic prize, never on the victim. That was about to change.

Choosing me was a mistake, James. You think you can win me over with logical argument, with your talk of scientific advance. Yet these are totally powerless when every feeling in my body is screaming for revenge. You once told me that emotions sometimes short-circuit the cool, logical reasoning of the neocortex. Massive emotional overload. Temporary effect only, you said.

Don't count on it.

You reap what you sow, James. I will take you apart. I will finish you for what you did to me in that cell; for what you made Cara do. I will tear down your throne, I will rip out your clinical heart, crush your ambitions. And I will not stop; I will not let go until everything you value has been destroyed.

'Are you all right?'

I looked at the passenger next to me. He had little round glasses and an overweight but kindly face. He was in his fifties and wore a plain white shirt and red sunburn.

He smiled and gestured at my hands. I looked down and saw knuckles white from gripping the armrests. Every muscle in me was taut.

'It really is a very reliable airline, you know,' he said. 'And it's one of their newer planes.'

I forced a smile and relaxed each muscle, one by one.

'That's the spirit. It does seem an awful shame to undo all the good work that a couple of weeks lying in the sun can do for you. Are you in insurance, then?'

'What?' I said, confused. 'Er . . . no.'

'Just a guess. Young face but very bright, I thought. I can always tell when someone's very bright. And of course insurance is the trendy profession for young, bright people these days, isn't it?'

'Um, is it?'

'You'd probably rather not talk about work in the middle of your holidays, eh? Did you have a nice time? I always think it's better to travel alone, isn't it? Stops you being a tourist and really lets you get into the local culture. I always think of myself as a traveller, not a tourist. I'm sure you've found the same thing. You look like the sort of person who really understands the human side of foreigners.'

I caught a passing steward and ordered two whiskies. Around us, the rest of the passengers were already asleep.

'But we all have to come back for Christmas, don't we?' he said. 'Run back home to our loved ones. Mine are all older than me, I'm glad to say. I never did get married. How about yourself ? Are you married?'

'No.'

'Terribly sensible, I say. Don't you? My name is David,' he added, holding out his hand. 'From St Albans. I'm in insurance. I must say you look better already. Best thing with these flights is just to sit back and relax.'

I nodded silently. There was a pause while I emptied the miniatures into a glass and swallowed the contents in one gulp.

'Super monkey, by the way. Wish I'd known you could get them. I was looking for something similar myself.'

'It was made specially.'

'Oh, I see. Well, that explains it. When I asked for monkey carvings in Mombasa, they said they were very bad luck and they didn't make them. But I suppose you can always find some fellow.'

I nodded again, then very pointedly turned off my reading light and reclined my seat.

'Good night, then,' said David.

It wouldn't be. There was no chance I would sleep. But at least I could shut out the idiotic conversation of this lonely holidaymaker. It was tempting just to give him the monkey, but then he'd insist on my address to send me something in return. Besides, I wanted to use it as a poignant part of the revenge I was planning. If Fieldhead liked misplaced symbolism then I would provide it. Perhaps leave it on his desk after that damaging denouncement, its belly cut open and drugs pouring out . . .

And as my mind filled with that fantasy picture, somewhere over Khartoum, where the White Nile meets the Blue Nile, I suddenly had a terrifying thought.

My eyes flew open and my back jerked straight. No. Just no. No way.

Monkey carvings are very bad luck.

I stood up and flung open the overhead locker, pulling the carving out, almost sending bottles of Smirnoff flying around the cabin. David was looking at me intently. I could see the next inane question forming on his lips, so I gripped the carving and marched through the darkened cabin to the toilets. Inside, I locked the door and pressed my body against it as I held the statue up to the light.

The craftsmanship was superb. There was no obvious groove this time. After the sanding and oiling, the hairline crack was almost invisible. But it was there – a neat, microscopic belt around an overweight primate.

Breathing fast, I set the base of the statue on the floor and leaned it at an angle so that the head rested against the wall. I stood still for a moment, trying to detect movement outside the cubicle. All I could hear was the rush of air and noise of the engines. I braced myself against the door, lifted my foot and brought it crashing down on the monkey's belly.

There was a popping sound as the glue gave way and the two halves slid to the floor. Heavy, swollen plastic packets fell from each end. I gave an involuntary, terrified gasp.

What the hell was he doing? Trying to make me experience panic again? Instinctively, I ran my fingers over the back of my head. No sensor. It had to be real. My shaking hands tugged at the packets still lodged inside the carving. Layer after layer. A treasure trove of white powder. Ranks of packets, tightly wedged in, every cubic millimetre used. Now my whole face was trembling. Industrially sealed. Piled up around my feet. Thirty, perhaps forty of them. Kilograms of the stuff. Jesus!

Panic took over quickly. It seemed that at any moment I would be pushed aside as cabin staff burst in and handcuffed me before turning the plane back to Mombasa and handing me over to the real Corporal Kamau. I was staring at one of the most illegal cargoes imaginable. And it was scattered all over the floor of a toilet cubicle.

Get rid of it! my brain was shouting at me. Get rid of it quick! Frantically I raised the lid of the toilet and broke open the first packet. The white powder scattered over my hands and shirt cuffs, clouds of it settled on the seat and on the floor. The rest hit the metal base of the toilet with a thump. Another packet, and another. Then flush. Blue industrial goo swirled out into the snowy scene, drawing expensive patterns on the stainless steel. Most of the powder was carried away. I picked up the next packet.

What was he doing? What was he doing? Jesus, kilos of hard drugs. Cocaine? What? Kilos! How much was that worth? I flushed another batch away, my breath becoming more and more ragged. I kept knocking the carving pieces against the side of the cubicle, producing sharp noises that sounded like explosions to me.

How much? How valuable is this? In London? Millions. So much of the stuff. Was he a drug dealer? Why me? Why had he given it to me? I suddenly stopped and stared at myself in the mirror. The clean-shaven, neat young man in his newly pressed clothes and his earnest but exhausted expression. The man walks calmly, ignorantly through the green channel, his giant carving proudly tucked under one arm. The perfect picture of well-bred innocence. The perfect courier.

Get rid of it! Quick! I had almost lost control of my muscles, and white powder was flying everywhere as I tried to rip open more packets. Slow down! Don't panic! Just . . . get . . . rid of it.

But how was he planning to get it back? *You going straight back to Oxford?* Such a casual question. Was he going to come and visit me? Ask for his gift back? Even steal it? The flat. Just off the Iffley Road. Where else would I leave a three-foot monkey? A quick break-in. A couple of other minor thefts to make it realistic. Cargo salvaged.

Get rid of it! A burst of powder shot up as I cut into the next packet. I turned away and buried my mouth and nose in my shirt-sleeve. How strong was this stuff? What would it do to me if I inhaled it? I counted to twenty then turned and emptied the rest of the packet.

How many times had I answered that question? *Did you pack everything yourself?* Well, yes, everything except the contents of this surprisingly heavy giant monkey. As for that, your guess is as good as mine, your honour. But never mind, it's a gift from a very authoritative guy, so I'll just carry on without questioning it.

But why would he do it? Why jeopardize the emotions work – in fact his whole career – for money? Surely he didn't need it that badly. Were those fabulous garden parties real? Had they left him with debts he couldn't afford? Or perhaps he had other expensive tastes. Drugs? For personal use? I laughed out loud at the thought, but stopped as soon as I heard the noise echo around the cubicle. It focused my attention and I picked up the next packets, slitting them open with my keys and sending another hundred thousand pounds into the sewage system.

Why did he need to do it? Academics aren't supposed to want money. They want publications, offices, tenure, chairs, society recognition, discoveries. And then? When they have all that by the age of thirty-six? What then? When they have spent half their research careers rubbing shoulders with the industrial elite who sponsor their work, what then? Do they turn to money as the final temptation? Why not? The more I thought about him, the more I realized that Fieldhead belonged very little to the dusty old world of Oxford where those rules applied. The truth was, until I walked into that cubicle, I knew nothing about the real Dr James Fieldhead at all.

Trying to bring my shaking hands and my breathing under control, I poured the final packets into the bowl and stuffed the empty bags into the used towel receptacle. I kept pushing the flush button until there was no sign of powder left. Then I ran hot water over both my hands, soaking the cuffs of the shirt, rubbing everything over and over with soap. I used wet towels on the floor and seat, knowing there was no chance of eradicating everything, but desperate to leave no visual sign of the powder. I looked at myself in the mirror and saw the face of a frightened fugitive. I threw hot water over it, flushed the toilet one last time, and opened the door.

I jumped immediately.

'Are you OK?' asked David. 'You were gone so long, I came to see if you were OK.'

'Fine, thank you. Really. Fine.' I pushed past him and walked back to my seat, clutching the monkey together as best I could. What strange activities he must get up to with African carvings, I could see him thinking. I shut my eyes and tried to settle down.

What the hell was Fieldhead doing?

12

The garish Christmas lights decorating Oxford's main streets did nothing to brighten the winter gloom that met me on my return. Raw, dazzling Africa was a thousand years away. But after the horrors of the isolation block, there was something vaguely comforting in the crowds of shoppers searching desperately for those last-minute presents.

On the first morning back, I wandered for hours through the streets, just to be outside, surrounded by straightforward, harmless people. No sadistic guards, no drug-trafficking scientists. I gazed at families, the excited faces of expectant children, soft-drink advertisements; anything and everything not associated with prison. Lively, colourful sights that kept the torturous memories at bay. But nothing could stop the dreams.

I spent a broken first night waking every two hours. Images of machetes and visions of infinite gaol sentences filled my dreams. When I first woke, I found myself in total darkness and the instinctive terror came back. I lunged for the lamp, dislodged it, and heard it smash on the floor. Panicked, I ran to the door and crouched naked in the moonlit living room until the images had gone.

The bed still carried Cara's scent. I changed the sheets, but her presence simply merged with the dreams until she was the one bolting the cell door and wielding the machete. There was no message on the answer phone, no note on the doormat. For hours, I sat by the phone, convinced that she would ring that minute. How could she not? Did I really mean nothing to her? In my mind, I rehearsed the cruel responses I would give. I saw her begging for forgiveness, suffering terrible guilt as I rejected her, leaving her only enough hope to keep begging.

On the second day, I went out looking for her. She had never taken me to her flat or given me a number. I wandered up and down the High Street and the Cornmarket, checking every blonde in sight. I looked in the coffee shops, the pubs, the college bars. I drove around the city centre, searching for the little red MG. I checked the residential streets: Jericho, Cowley, Summertown, hoping to find the car lying under an open window. Finally, at seven o'clock that evening, I gave up.

The lights were on in the kitchen and living room when I got back to the flat. One of my flatmates had returned. I hesitated on the doorstep, not knowing how to deal with him. The idea of cheerful holiday chatter was nauseating.

Then I realized what he was playing. The desperate, tragic melody of Aida's final words to Radamès as they face death together, sealed alive inside a tomb, flowed out of the living room. I closed the door and stood still, my eyes locked tightly shut, listening to the sorrowful words. *O Earth, farewell – farewell, valley of tears, dream of joy vanished into sorrow. Heaven opens to us, our wandering souls fly to the light of eternal day.*

'I have my own copy now,' I heard her say through my mind's image of the subterranean despair. I had already given her face to Aida, so it seemed almost natural to hear her voice blend with the music. When I opened my eyes, she was standing in front of me, one hand twisting awkwardly in the other. Her face, tear-stained and black-smudged, looked more beautiful than ever.

'I'll understand if you just want me to go.' She held out the key I'd given her.

I looked down at the carpet, gazing intently at a small dark burn from one of Philip's cigarettes. He was always forgetting to find an ashtray before he sat down, and would prop his burning fag ends on the edge of the table.

'I know it's impossible to defend what happened,' she said. 'There's no way you could *not* hate me after what I did.'

She was sobbing gently, her words merging together. I was silent, unable to tell her how badly I'd missed her, how much I wanted her just to kiss me and tell me it had been a mistake.

Cara took my silence as confirmation. 'I'd better go.'

She looked wretched, and if I'd been closer I would have thrown my arms around her. But the cigarette burn formed an insurmountable barrier between us. My inaction decided her. She looked up at me once more, and stumbled to the door. With her piteous expression searing into my brain, I spun round, still unable to speak.

Cara had the door open by the time she finally delivered the message that she'd waited all afternoon to tell me. 'Making you hate me was so . . . I was so stupid! That guy . . . it was just the whole exotic thing . . . the tan, the scars . . . the physical life. Jesus, the diving instructor! What a terrible cliché.' She was shaking her head in silent, tragic astonishment. 'Something just went click inside me and the next moment he was kissing me. It meant nothing at all. I've just never not responded to that kind of instinct before. Can you understand that? I've never had a reason to resist before . . .' she trailed off, tears running down her cheeks. 'Then we started and I immediately knew it was a mistake. But I didn't know how to tell him to stop. When I saw your face in the dive school and knew you would never speak to me again, I felt as if I'd thrown my life away. Just . . . thrown it away . . .' Then she was gone, bolting into the night.

The sudden silence jarred me into action, and I wrenched open the door, racing into the road after her. I saw her disappear round a corner and sprinted in her tracks. She was standing beside the old MG and rummaging in her bag for her keys. As I approached, the bag slipped out of her shaking fingers and the contents spilled into the gutter. Crouching in the dark and fumbling for her keys, she looked small and defenceless.

I dropped down beside her, lifted her face up and kissed her. She threw her arms around my shoulders and squeezed tightly. A shipwreck survivor's urge to cling to safety. We knelt on the pavement, Cara sobbing into my shoulder, for an age.

'I'm so sorry,' she whispered.

'I know.'

'Oh, Ben.'

Eventually the sobbing diminished, and she lifted her beautiful, quivering face towards me.

'Thank you for not hating me,' she murmured.

'Don't thank me too much. I haven't exactly been loving you, the last few days.'

She nodded weakly and looked down at the mess of lipsticks, address book, keys and mobile phone beside us. I dusted down the bag and helped her replace her belongings. A red handkerchief was still tucked inside. I pulled it out and handed it to her.

'I just hope you'll be able to forgive me,' she said, reaching down for her bag.

'I'm trying my best.'

I put my arm round her shoulders and guided her towards the flat. There was nothing else to say. Everything was in the mind. The beginning of a long process of recovery that might or might not save a fatally wounded relationship. Once inside, Cara led the way to the bedroom. I knew she was right: that any chance of salvaging the past could only come through physical contact. That was our nature. No words. Just a quiet, half-shy undressing, a world away from the violence of that rock above the sea. Hesitantly, and very gently, we made love. When we had finished we lay with our faces pressed together, a small kiss every few minutes to reassure ourselves.

We ate simply. A plate of spaghetti, pesto sauce. A bottle of wine. No conversation. All through the meal we exchanged nervous glances, like first-night teenagers. So much trust to be rebuilt. She slipped away to clean her face of the smudged mascara. As I washed the dishes I found my hands were trembling.

I walked back into the living room. Cara was staring at the sofa as if it was an alien object. She looked up at me, her face distraught.

'I can't just sit here and make polite conversation,' she sobbed. My dressing gown was far too large for her. Wrapped almost twice round at the waist. Feet barely visible. 'Oh God, Ben.'

When she turned out the lights, I felt the prison fear resurface, but she held my hand tightly in hers and led me back to bed, breathing soft words to calm me.

'It's over,' she murmured. 'I know they did something terrible to you, but it's over now.'

The mattress beneath my back felt soft and protective. Cara's arm lay across my chest. All over. Calm, quiet, safe. I felt myself slipping too easily back into the old trust.

'We have to . . .' I began.

'I know.' She shifted her head a little closer to mine. 'I know.'

Invisible lines joining two hurt minds.

'I don't want to go through every detail. But we have to talk about it,' I said. 'Otherwise, it will always be there.'

'It'll always be there whatever we do, Ben. When I'm sixty I'll still regret what I did.'

'It wasn't . . . you know, he put so much effort into making you do that.'

'It doesn't make any difference.'

'It does to me.'

'Ben.' She kissed my shoulder once, twice, a third time. 'You don't have to say this. I just have to live with it, and that's all right. Really, it's all right.'

'I don't want you to . . .'

'I must. It was me that did this to you. Not James Fieldhead.'

'Cara.'

'You can't blame him for my actions.'

'I damn well can!' My voice made her flinch. 'He went too far. Way too far. He had me screaming on the floor of a prison cell with a fucking knife over my fingers, just so that some pharmaceutical company can feel better about torturing kittens. And . . .'

'Ben, please don't do this. It's over.'

'No, Cara! It's not over.' I sat up and stared down at her dark form. 'He made me think I was going to lose my fingers. Do you understand what I'm telling you? He had a guard standing on my back and a knife over my fingers. You can't see it, can you?'

'I can see it. But it was for a scientific cause. With time . . .'

'Bullshit! You think I'm just going to forget about it? What about the drugs?'

'Ben, what are you –'

'He tried to make me carry a stack of drugs back to England for him.'

'What!?' Now Cara was sitting up as well.

'He gave me a carving at the airport. Full of some kind of powder. You think I'm just going to forget he did that?'

'I don't –'

'Kilos of the stuff. It was unbelievable.'

'Ben.' She was gripping my arm, fingers digging into the muscles. 'What did you do with it?'

'I found it on the plane. It went down the loo.'

'Oh, Jesus!' Suddenly her hand was at her mouth. I tried to see her expression in the darkness.

'What? You think I was going to bring it through Customs and give it back to him?'

'Ben, listen to me. Listen to me!' she shouted. 'This is serious. You said kilos of powder? Then this is fucking serious. Do you understand what I'm saying?'

But I stayed silent. Her voice was terrifying.

'You think he's just going to say, "Oh well, never mind" when he finds out what you've done?'

'He can say the Lord's Prayer for all I care.'

'This isn't some little game, Ben. Don't you see that? He's going to try and get it back, and when he finds out . . .'

'Yeah? What?'

'Stop being like that! Wake up, will you? Try to understand what kind of person does something like that.'

'I know what kind of person he is.'

'Oh, really? And have you updated your opinion since you opened the carving? You don't have the slightest idea! Giving you that cargo was a crazy thing to do. He's not sane, Ben. You don't know what he might do to you. You have to get away from here.'

'You want me to run away? Are you serious?'

Her hands were gripping me again. Tighter and tighter. 'Listen to me, you idiot! He will go nuts when he finds out. He could . . . do anything. At least give him a chance to calm down before you see him again. Please, Ben, you don't want to be there when he explodes.'

I left a pause; let the air go silent again. 'But I do,' I said quietly. 'That's exactly what I want. Just once. Just once to see him lose his mind with rage.'

'Ben . . .' She dropped back on to the bed, pulling me down beside her.

'It's very simple, really. He's spent a week fucking around with my emotions. It'll be payment in kind.'

'It's too dangerous.'

'It's nothing after what I've been through.'

'Please, Ben, I couldn't bear it if . . . I . . .' She stopped and rolled over, facing the wall. 'Do you remember that time in the marine park? Just with snorkels. When I was happily floating and feeding the fish? And you swam up behind me and bit my leg. I was so annoyed to be caught out, even for a second. To be tricked. Even for the tiny second when I believed it really was some dangerous fish.'

I dropped a finger on to the back of her neck and traced the length of her spine.

'I thought about that so much on Sunday. After they'd taken you away. Strange, huh?'

She twisted back again, and I knew – even in the dark – that there were fresh tears in her eyes. All the cruel, hateful things I'd thought about her that afternoon. A small, shivering form, crouched in a lonely beach house. So unjust.

'It was such a gentle bite. You don't make a very good fish,' she choked. 'And your mouth must have been full of seawater. That got me most of all. That you would swallow enough salt to feel ill, just to give me a love bite. And all I could do was kick you away with my fin.'

I could feel her breathing on my cheek. Soft, warm currents. Grazing, moistening, loving. Something her diving instructor would never have felt. Misty breezes, given life by the blood that lay closest to her heart. Now regular and peaceful, now hesitant, as if doubt had bruised her again, or some new memory had stirred old feelings. I imagined an entire conversation, with no language but breathing. Harsh, brutal, angry breathing; questioning, forgetful breathing; deep, throaty, lustful breathing; soft, silent, adoring breathing: the most honest language born out of the most basic, crucial act. The best chance we had to rebuild something out of the ruins of that earlier, innocent relationship . . .

Then a small, blunt object shattered a small, brittle pane of glass, and immediately I was on my feet.

'What was that?' whispered Cara.

'It's him,' I muttered grimly, picking up my dressing gown. 'Whatever happens, keep out of this. Just stay in bed.'

I ignored her frightened face and eased open the bedroom door. Across the living room, what remained of the window was opening. With a shock, I realized it wasn't Fieldhead.

In sudden terror, I cursed my stupidity. Why on earth had I assumed he was operating alone? A multi-million pound drugs haul? What kind of partners might he have for that? What kind of hardened individuals were needed to distribute kilos of highly illegal powder? Suddenly I realized what a mistake I had made. On the table stood an empty monkey. At the window stood possibly one of the most dangerous and violent criminals in the country. What revenge might he exact when he opened the carving and found out my secret?

I had to seize the initiative. I picked up the wine bottle from the table and threw on the lights, ready to charge at the intruder before he could pull out a weapon. The man turned instantly, blinking in surprise. Dressed in black, his shoulders square and his back straight, he seemed taller now. The bristles were gone; the hair was cut short and brushed back. His face was dominated by a sense of purpose. Quite a metamorphosis.

'Hello, Stephen Andrew.'

Chas nodded brusquely. 'You're not supposed to be here. The flat's been dark for an hour. How early do you go to bed?'

'If you'd bothered to stick around in prison, you'd have found out,' I growled.

We looked at each other warily for a moment.

'James wanted me to find out a little about you from your flat. For your psychological profile.'

'You could have knocked. I'd have been happy to give you a guided tour.'

'Just little things,' he said, logical flow straining in his brain. 'How you fold your clothes, what you eat . . . your taste in music, whether you squeeze your tooth-paste from the middle or the end. I don't know. It's a bit odd, but he said it was important.'

'Do you make a habit of breaking into other people's houses?'

Chas gazed around him, shaking his head. Then abruptly he sat down in the armchair. He stared at the bottle. 'Are you going to put that thing down?'

'How about playing fuckwits in African police stations?'

'No.'

'Then what do you normally do?'

'I . . . I'm a student. At London University.'

'Studying emotions, of course?'

He nodded carefully. 'I heard about James and the project. I said I'd like to help. He asked me to play a drop-out backpacker.'

It was so hopeless. Every twitch of his face was a perfect lie detector. I decided to put him out of his misery.

'What's a limbic system?'

He looked at me blankly.

'Come on. You study emotions. You should know. What's a limbic system?'

He got up. 'I'd better go,' he said, walking towards the door.

'What about visceral stimulation of emotions? What's your opinion on that?' I shouted at his back.

He said nothing. His hand was on the lock.

'And you can tell him I looked inside.'

He paused and glanced round, his eyes dropping immediately to the monkey. I suddenly realized how controlled he'd been up to that point. 'What do you mean?' he said, looking up again quickly.

'I looked inside.'

Chas said nothing. He stared at me for a moment,

then opened the door and whistled. A moment later, James Fieldhead walked in.

I went straight to the carving and sat beside it.

'There's something terribly ungenerous about giving someone a present and then stealing it back,' I said. 'You weren't planning to do that, were you?'

Fieldhead stood for a moment at the door, examining the scene. His expression was unreadable. He walked over to the table and sat opposite me, peeling off his gloves and removing his scarf.

'Too damned curious. Just too damned curious.'

'What the hell did you think you were doing?' I demanded.

The green eyes gazed across the table at me. I wondered what kind of game he was trying to orchestrate. Chas remained standing: the dope-head turned hard-man.

'We both know what I was doing.'

'You must've been out of your mind.'

'Not at all,' he said. 'One of my sanest moments, in fact.'

'Then you're a lunatic.'

'Because I transport drugs?'

'Because you transport drugs.'

'At the risk of upsetting your conservative roots, may I ask what your concern is with the world's second most valuable area of international trade?'

'The minor things like illegality, damage to social fabric, health problems, that sort of thing.'

'And yet you ignore all the great benefits it has to offer.'

I scowled at his assured smile. 'Benefits.'

'Benefits. For everyone.' Fieldhead paused for a moment as if to gather together his mental lecture notes. 'The substance in that carving, like any other renewable, sun-created product, comes from a crop. The only difference is that this crop is grown solely in the third world and consumed mainly in the first world. It has an enormous, insatiable and unquashable demand. People have always and will always want drugs. For those interested in risk, the business of drug distribution is one of the few wild frontiers left in this life. In all of these ways, it brings great benefits.

'By conveying drugs between Asia and Europe – via Africa in this case – I am channelling large amounts of hard currency into some of the most poverty-stricken corners of the globe. I am providing borderline farmers with a market that allows them to bring home to their families a hundred times what their neighbours can earn from tobacco or rice. I am also bringing a good quality, reliable product to the thousands of people in this country who – however harshly you may judge them – find that their dull, tedious lives are immensely enhanced with a dash of oriental magic. Enough of the altruism. I am, of course, doing this for me. Aside from the money, I find teasing the system in one of the most paranoia-inducing areas of law to be incredibly stimulating. It does for me what the contents of that ugly creature do for consumers. And I'd say I'm getting pretty good at it. Wouldn't you?'

I gave him a sincere nod of agreement. 'Oh, absolutely. The carving was a brilliant idea. Hiding the cargo by making it so prominent was inspired.' I could see Field-head beginning to smile. 'In fact, the whole arrangement was so neat that it seems almost sad it had to fail.'

The smile disappeared. 'Why should it fail just because you know about it?'

'To be honest, that's quite an important factor right now,' I said, tapping the monkey.

The room seemed to become colder in the silence that followed. Chas shifted his weight from one foot to the other. I glanced at the bedroom door, wondering if Cara could feel the tension.

'Please don't imagine you are in control of this situation, Ben.' There was an icy stare in Fieldhead's eyes. 'You may have a few lingering memories of Stephen in his former incarnation. I warn you not to be misled by them. If you underestimate him now, you could get hurt.'

'That's not quite what I meant. What happened to your subtlety?'

He sighed. 'Look, I accept you want a cut. Fine, we'll give you a cut.'

'That might be a bit difficult.'

'No problem. There's a lot to go around.'

I smiled patiently. 'As I said, it might be difficult, unless you can sieve it out of a few hundred litres of airline sewage.'

It was the most delicious reaction. His mouth half-opened; his eyes widened. Then his teeth came together as he lunged forward. The carving fell apart and Field-head stared in absolute fury at the empty hollow.

'Not true,' he yelled. 'You've hidden it somewhere.

Not even you would be stupid enough to throw away seven and a half million pounds.'

'You used me, James. I could have gone to real prison.'

His head jerked round to Chas. 'Look for it. He's hiding it somewhere.' A red vein had appeared on his neck. Severe emotion, leading to high blood pressure. He pointed an irate finger at me. 'You think you have the first idea how to sell those kind of goods on your own? Innocent country boy like you?'

'It's gone, James. Gone. I found it on the plane. It never even got as far as Customs.'

'Jesus!' he roared. 'Seven and a half million! Do you have even the smallest, tiniest idea how long this has taken to organize? Huh? You stupid, puritanical imbecile! How could you throw it away?'

'You put the project at risk. You should never have done that. If I'd been caught, everything would have fallen apart.'

'The project?' A strange look of surprise immediately replaced the anger in his eyes.

'Your sponsors would have found out. No one would have touched that work if you'd been implicated in a drugs offence.'

Fieldhead sat back in his chair and stared at me. 'You mean you haven't even worked it out?' he said slowly. 'You honestly, really are too stupid to see the obvious?'

Now it was my turn to look surprised. 'Are you saying they were involved?'

For the first time since the news of the lost drugs, Fieldhead smiled. It was ugly and overstretched. 'You are a total moron, you know that?'

'But the sponsors . . .'

'There are no fucking sponsors! You've been sitting there in full knowledge of that cargo for almost two days and you still believe there actually was an emotions project?'

I must have forgotten to breathe. A few moments of silent astonishment and then I was coughing furiously.

'What are you saying?' I managed to whisper eventually.

'I'm saying, as you put it, I used you. Completely. You were only ever the courier. A nice, clean, sincere boy without a shred of interesting deviancy to raise a Customs officer's suspicions.'

'But the project . . .' I said. 'The gaol . . .'

'. . . was the best strategy I could think of to leave you utterly disoriented and confused. The whole point was to ensure you would accept a giant, unfamiliar object and carry it on to an international flight.'

'You mean . . .'

'And it served the purpose beautifully. There was no way you were going to start questioning that ridiculous carving only five hours after being threatened with a machete and a ten-year sentence in an African gaol.'

'What about the . . .' I hesitated, '. . . recordings?'

Fieldhead shook his head. 'You're not getting this, are you? There are no recordings. There is no emotion-recording technology. That priceless sensor is sitting in a Mombasa airport flowerbed. It's an empty box.'

'But all those people: Alan, Casper, the police . . .'

'Oh sure, they all believed in the project. Kept happy with a small scattering of shillings. Originally we were just going to chuck you in gaol for a night, but Alan and Kristina got very enthusiastic and creative. They made the whole thing more complex than was necessary for my purposes. But as I couldn't very well say I didn't need the extra emotions material I had to let it grow larger and larger. Besides, it was an amusing intellectual challenge to control it all.'

At last a spark of anger broke through my bafflement. 'You found destroying my relationship an amusing intellectual challenge?'

'Oh, for God's sake. You're not still worried about that slut are you?'

'I was in love with her!'

'Of course you were.' He gave a cold laugh. 'And doubtless she was equally in love with you, before I messed everything up.'

When I thought of that frightened, shivering girl on the other side of the bedroom door, a cold fury swept over me.

'You're not fit to teach,' I said. 'I'm going to take this to the vice-chancellor and make sure you never fill another teaching post again.'

There was a sudden silence. When Fieldhead spoke, the dark smile was back.

'What exactly are you planning to tell him?'

'The truth.'

He laughed out loud. 'The truth,' he mimicked. 'Run me through the truth, a moment, will you?'

'You deal in drugs and set your students up as unwitting couriers. I think that's simple enough for most people to understand.'

'Or, to rephrase it,' he offered, 'an exemplary Oxford tutor organized a pantomime in Africa – which no one will admit to – so as to have a student transport drugs – which no longer exist – back to his criminal UK operation – the details of which are unknown. Be serious. Why the hell would anyone believe a story like that? You'll be laughed out of every cobwebbed office that you try to tell it in. It's just not credible.'

And with a sinking heart, I remembered that first party game where I had dared to speak a truth that was just not credible. I saw a vision of deans and masters and proctors and the vice-chancellor all raising their hands to the question *Who thinks Ben is lying?*

Fieldhead stood up, beckoning to Chas. 'Don't even bother,' he said to me. 'You'll only hurt yourself.' He picked up his gloves and scarf, and the two of them walked to the door. He looked back at me one last time. 'You stupid . . .' He was shaking his head as he walked out.

I sat with my empty monkey and listened to the car drive away.

All for nothing. All of that pain and fear, without even the consolation of scientific advance as justification. Casper sent like a shark after my lover – for what? Just to add that little extra bit of spice to the fiction within the fiction. Disoriented and confused. Willing to accept that oversized monkey and carry it on to an international flight. And for that I had been forced to contemplate a machete slicing through my hand.

Fieldhead's voice still lingered in my ears. His self-righteous discussion of the merits of drug trafficking had made me feel sick to watch him. The guiding star had proved to be a shabby forgery: sixty watts behind a pierced black cloth. What was worse was the knowledge that he had chosen the forgery over the natural brilliance. A man with a capacity for greatness but a penchant for sleaze. An insult to every hard-working but mediocre researcher.

The bedroom door cracked open and Cara's face peered through, pale and shaking.

'Have they gone?' she whispered.

'Yes.' I pulled out the chair beside me and she sat down. She was fully dressed again, as if she'd been expecting to have to flee the house, or rush in to my defence.

'Thank God. I was so scared for you.'

I would have laughed if I hadn't still been seething. 'He's a biologist. That's all,' I said quietly.

'I know. I was just so . . . I'm sorry I can't be stronger about this.'

'You're allowed to give in, now and then.'

'It's not quite me though, is it?' she said.

'No.'

'No. Right. Pull yourself together, Cara.' She sat up straight and pressed her hands against her face, working them up and down for a moment. Then she stared at me, her eyes angry. 'I heard all that. You wouldn't think someone like that could be such a shit.'

'All for nothing. That's what really pisses me off. And you know, he's the kind of guy who would have really enjoyed doing it to us.'

'I know. After you'd come into the dive school, he

appeared and started laughing. And Casper started laughing too. And he threw me my clothes and told me he couldn't have hoped for a better slut if he'd prayed. I've never felt so . . .'

I visualized the scene, heard Fieldhead's laugh as he congratulated his stud actor and gazed in amusement at my naked, deceiving, deceived lover.

'I never quite realized what he was like,' I said. 'I've always had this image of James that I could respect. Worship, almost. I just ignored the rumours, put them down to petty jealousy.'

'What rumours?'

'That he wasn't the ideal genius I thought he was. That he was just a cynical bastard. That he liked screwing other people – enjoyed their suffering. *Schadenfreude*, isn't that what it's called? One emotion, at least, that he didn't get out of me.'

Cara was looking pale. She dropped her gaze and stared at the table. 'Don't talk about him any more,' she said. 'It's horrible.'

'OK.' I stroked her arm and kissed the back of her neck, feeling hair still tangled from the bed brushing my cheek.

'I feel ill just thinking about him.' She shivered slightly and entwined her arm in mine. 'It's left a vile taste in my mouth.'

'I know what you mean.'

She nodded softly, her eyes still cast down. Then some connection formed in her brain and she looked up at me. I felt the enquiry in her stare, the uncertainty, the search for a double meaning in my words. As if to clear away the doubts, Cara got up and poured herself a glass of water. She added two ice cubes and stood at the door to the living room, staring pensively at the furniture.

'How do you really feel about me?' she asked eventually, all sense of the earlier anxious fear replaced by a dry resignation.

'What do you mean?'

'I mean I'm not going to lead you into answers I want. I don't want to hear you just being kind, confronted by a sobbing wreck. You were very sweet to me when you found me here: very forgiving. But that's your nature. It doesn't mean it's the truth.' She was watching me carefully. 'I've been unfaithful to you, plain and simple. Left a vile taste in your mouth. Sometimes that never goes away. It's unfair on both of us if you don't say what you're really thinking.'

'To be honest, I don't know what I think.'

There was the briefest movement at her throat, and her eyelids blinked once, slowly. But her expression never changed. She just met my gaze and whispered, 'That's what I guessed.'

Silently she put down the glass and reached for her coat.

'What are you doing?'

Cara's face was still calm, but her hand trembled slightly as she picked up the coat. She gave a small, regretful smile but said nothing.

'What are you doing? Are you leaving? Just because I'm still trying to understand things, you're leaving?'

'I'm sorry I came to see you. I knew it was a mistake, but I just . . . I just hoped it might work out.'

My hand closed on her arm. 'It will work out,' I said, standing up, urgency in my voice.

'Please, Ben. It's better this way.'

'No! No, it's a fucking disaster this way!'

For a moment we were both staring into each other's eyes, our faces just inches apart. The perfect situation for the screen hero to press his lips against the leading lady's and make her see the true depths of his love through violent, passionate contact. Reality didn't allow it. Cara's gaze, simultaneously tender and forbidding, warned me away.

'It's died, Ben. I killed it the day I let him touch me underwater. Let him kiss me in the boat. Believe me, I love you more right now than I've ever loved any man. But even feeling like I do, I can't hide the fact that we're finished.'

I was shaking my head, gripping her hard around the forearm. 'You're over-reacting. This is insane!'

Cara gave me that pained smile once more, then leaned forward and kissed me on the cheek. 'You'll see I'm right. Really you will. It hurts badly now – for me as well – but you'll find the memory fades quickly.'

'You don't know me at all, do you?' I cut back. 'Every time I see you in the Zoology Department, I'm going to fall apart inside.'

'No,' she whispered. 'That won't happen. I won't be staying in Oxford. It's too . . .' She pulled herself gently free of my grip. 'I don't belong here. I never did.' Her head dropped forward for a moment, then she twisted round and walked over to the door.

'Where will you go?' I called.

But she just smiled and pulled open the door. 'Good-bye, Ben,' she said. And three hours after walking back into my life, the girl I loved was gone for ever.

13

It's hard to say exactly when I reached my lowest state of despair, but that night I must have come close. Admittedly, I was still under the impression that it was just one man who had done all these things to me. Believing I understood my world, I could still enjoy the illusion of control – at least control of myself. Those foundations of my sanity had not yet collapsed. But the loss of Cara, coming so soon after the discovery of Fieldhead's fraud, left me almost paralysed with misery and frustration.

When the spirit falls that far, any human support is welcome, even when it comes from another shattered mind. By 3 am I had decided to visit Jenni the moment visiting hours permitted. She'd asked me to call again. That was enough of an excuse.

When I arrived at the ward, the same nurse was on duty and she scowled to see me. Did she blame me for calling Mr Douglas? Or was it just my long absence that incensed her? Of course: the tan. Off enjoying himself in the sun while the poor lassie's stuck here, she would tell the other nurses. I dropped my gaze and followed her down the corridor.

Jenni had been moved to a new room. No more privacy: there were five other beds, three of them occupied. Perhaps that was a good sign. Safe to bring back into the community. The white plaster had turned into a smudge of coloured ink. Writing and pictures in multiple hands. The Douglas family had mobilized the troops. Two of them sat on the edge of the bed, chattering about Christmas game shows. I waited in the corridor until they had left.

'You can come in now.'

I stuck my head round the door and summoned up a smile. 'I didn't think you'd seen me.'

She watched me as I bent to kiss her cheek. 'Nice tan.'

'Thanks.'

'Must have been fun medical research.' Her voice marched firmly along a single tone. No emotion, no interest, no life.

'Really, it was.' I felt myself redden. 'Tropical diseases.' I gestured at my face. 'Couldn't help getting burned.'

'Fine.'

I gazed at the pale cheeks, the scar on the forehead. There was no blame in her eyes any more. There was nothing.

'So, how's life been here?'

A distant shudder in one eye. But her voice remained dead as she answered the thoughtless question.

'I haven't been able to leave this bed for three weeks. I scream in agony every time they move me. I'm hoisted into the air twice a day while they change the sheets. I have inadequate plastic containers shoved under me whenever I need to go to the loo. I have bedsores all over my back from not being able to move. Every night, a nurse wakes me up to give me a sleeping pill and then allows me about four hours' sleep before she decides it's daytime. Each morning, trains of giggling medical students come in here and suddenly go all silent and apologetic when they remember what a head-case I am. I lie here and watch children in the corridor, insanely jealous that they can move around. The constant noise is exhausting. And by the way, I've been through some of the worst, worst pain it can be possible to feel. Life is horrible.'

I looked down. Her stare was relentless.

'How's the leg?'

'Fine. Gradually withering away.'

'And the heel?'

'As good as it's going to get. I won't run again.'

No regret visible. I fought to hold back the pitying words.

'When do you get out of here? Must be soon, now.'

'Next week. I'll be going straight back to college.'

'Great!' I said. 'Then as soon as you're back, I'm going to take you out to dinner. We'll go to that Italian place on North Parade.'

There was absolutely no reaction. I waited, feeling hurt. Eventually she spoke:

'Are you still going out with her?'

'No,' I said. 'All over.'

She stared up at me, a slight sigh her first human reaction. 'That's it, then. You lied the first time I asked you about her. You lied about not telling my parents. And now you're lying again. Don't bother about dinner. I'd rather jump off a roof.'

'No! It's the truth. We're finished.'

'Sorry. You're just not believable any more. Dream

couples like you two simply don't split up after a few weeks. Better get back to her. I'm sure she's more interested in seeing you than I am.' With that, her eyes closed and I was shut off.

'Jenni . . .'

But there was no reaction. I stood there for a few moments, trying to find better words, then walked quickly out of the hospital. I sat in the car park for an hour. Around me, visitors unlucky enough to have relatives in hospital over Christmas came and went. Every few moments I would start the engine, resolving to drive to London and drink myself under the first table I could find. Then I would pull out the key and sit with it dangling over my knees, wedged between my thumb and the steering wheel. Finally, I moved.

'I just want you to know what's happened to me,' I said loudly as I marched back into the ward, attracting bewildered stares from the other patients. 'I have been poisoned; I have been thrown into the worst kind of African gaol. I have been betrayed and used, and everything I believed in has been torn apart. I will not have you make me feel guilty!'

She looked at me in astonishment. Well, good. Some kind of human reaction, at least. Then she looked around her. I followed her gaze, seeing the intense fascination on the faces of the grannies in the other beds. Quickly, I drew the curtains around her and lowered my voice.

'The truth is, yes, I have been on holiday with Cara. Sorry. There's no way I can stand here and defend my taste in women. But it's also true that we're finished. And it hurts like hell. I've been through the worst experiences of my life, and if you've got the time I would really like to tell you about it.'

And she smiled. Uncertain, timid, but it was still that warm, generous, utterly real smile that was her most serious weakness, and right now my greatest comfort.

'I've got time,' she said.

I sat down beside her, put my hand on hers and told her everything.

When I had finished there was no reaction. For about a minute, she just stared at me.

Then she said, 'You're crazy.'

'Crazy?'

'You're crazy and you're extremely gullible to believe a set-up like that.'

I felt my face stiffen. 'You don't know what it was like in there,' I breathed. 'You don't have a fucking clue what it felt like to be totally alone, face ten years in that pit, and hear the screams of that man. When they threatened to do the same to me, I was so far gone I couldn't even feel my fingers to check they were still there. Those images are with me for life,' I warned, 'so don't tell me I'm gullible.'

Jenni was shaking her head. 'I'm not talking about that. I mean the drugs story.'

'What?'

'Tell me again why you don't just go and report him for drug trafficking?'

'No one's going to believe a story like that.'

'Then why do you?'

I stared at her in confusion. Somehow her face seemed much stronger now. 'What are you trying to say? That it didn't happen? I was there. It did. It would be crazy to say it didn't happen.'

'Did you try the drugs?'

'Of course not!'

'Do you know for sure that the sensor was a dummy?'

'No, but . . .'

'Ben, think about it. Why did he put you through that whole circus?'

'I already said: to get me really disoriented and confused, so that when he handed me that cargo I wouldn't question it.'

'Disoriented and confused? Is that all? Is there no other, simpler way he could get you disoriented and confused? How about sending you on a project in the game parks and arranging for you to break down and be stuck there overnight? Or if he's got so much power with the authorities, why not just get you arrested full stop? How would you feel if you were delivered to the airport immediately after either of those? Disoriented? Confused?'

I couldn't reply. I could only nod. So many other, much, much easier ways.

'This emotion measurement is so extraordinary that it must be true. Don't you see that?' She was almost pressing herself out of bed now. 'All this other stuff with the drugs: it's hardly creative. Anyone could make that up. But what kind of nutter would build a major smuggling plan based on such an extraordinary concept as emotion measurement?'

'But why?' I muttered. 'Why would he do this? Why deny it all?'

'Why else? He doesn't want you to believe the technology actually exists. He's used you so badly that you hate him. You could do anything to hurt him. If the sensor is a secret, he has to stop you from spreading the word. What better way to do that than send you off on another wild-goose chase?'

'But to paint himself as a drug dealer? Isn't that a bit of an extreme goose chase?'

'Not at all. What does he care what you think? You're not going to tell anyone anything – it's not credible. And he's left you with the idea that you've hurt him badly. He's probably counting on you dropping it at that.'

'How could he know I'd look inside?'

'Hasn't he proved himself pretty good at manipulating your actions? He's bound to have had someone on the plane.'

And immediately I thought of David. *Super monkey.* Drawing attention to it. Standing outside the cubicle. What would have come next? A request to look it over? *Have you seen? There's a crack round the middle. Must be hollow. Quite heavy though, isn't it?*

I stared at her in confusion. 'Why the hell is it so secret?' I whispered.

A twisted, terrifying cover-up. But why? What was so important about this innovation? Why was Fieldhead so energetically trying to mislead me? The stunt with the powder – where might that have gone? If British Customs officers had got involved it would have created a real mess. What was at stake that could drive him to such measures?

Jenni let her body collapse back against the pillows.

'Nope. Can't help you there.' She gazed at the curtains around us, her voice taking a distant, harsher tone, as if she'd suddenly grown tired of the game. 'If you wait a couple of weeks, I'll hobble around and ask a few questions for you. Not that you'll want a cripple hanging about. Like this, I'm going to be even more of a social millstone than ever before.'

'Jenni.' I laid my hand on her shoulder. 'Please don't. You know I'm sorry. You don't need to try and make me feel worse than I do.'

'I know.' She'd closed her eyes.

There were small traces of mascara on her eyelashes. They only helped to make her face look paler than ever. I heard the beginning of a sob.

'The doctors tell me the femur will be even stronger when it's healed. The bonding at the break does that. Toughens it.' She looked up at me and gave a small, choked laugh. 'Should be useful, now I can't use my foot properly. Every time I lose my balance I'll know I've got this nice strong bone to fall on. Comforting, huh?'

The tears were flowing freely now. I rubbed her shoulder in a hopeless attempt to comfort her.

'If only the same were true up here,' she said, weakly gesturing at her temple. 'If only that got stronger every time it was broken. Think how strong I'd be then. Take on all those bastards. None of them would have a chance. None of those smooth shits with their sports cars and their clever little jibes and their beautiful hair and designer French make-up. They wouldn't know what hit them. They wouldn't . . .' Her words disappeared behind her hands, pressed hard against her face. 'None of them.'

A reedy, nasal voice pierced the curtain. 'Forget about them, dear. They're not worth it,' it advised. I pulled the curtain back an inch and found an indignant face staring at me. 'You tell her,' said the old lady from the next bed.

Jenni had opened her eyes. 'But then maybe I do get stronger,' she said, more softly. I let the curtain fall back in place. 'Maybe I'd have cracked up a long time ago, otherwise. Instead, I just lose something each time . . .'

She gripped my hand for a moment. A hard, purging grip. 'Go on,' she said eventually. 'Get out of here. You've got things to do.'

I watched her force a smile and felt my own tears just seconds away. I bent down quickly and kissed her cheek. 'Thank you.'

'Just get him.'

I began my search in the Psychology Department library. It was unfamiliar territory, but the few remaining occupants paid me no attention. Two men were poring over the same huge textbook, their heads so close together that a small movement by one would have knocked the other out. Behind them, an older woman was slumped in a chair, her eyes closed, a half-eaten sandwich on the desk in front of her. I walked past them to the stack of journals, scanning all the relevant issues from the last five years, hoping to find some reference to emotion measurement.

There was nothing.

Even in these waters, emotions research of any kind was scarce. Only one British name cropped up on a

265

regular basis. In the absence of a definitive guide to emotion measurement, the advice of an expert would be the next best thing. I wrote down Professor Anthony Carrington's details and called the University of York.

'Well, no, I mean, I'm afraid he'll be at home until the New Year,' said the lowest paid receptionist on the university campus.

'Can you let me know his telephone number? It's quite urgent,' I said, wondering why I thought that.

'It's not really allowed for us to give out personal information on the faculty. Oh dear, you say it's urgent?' She hummed a bit more, then said, 'I really can't decide this myself. Let me have your number.'

At home, I leafed through the Carrington articles I'd copied in the library. Experimental psychology. 'Rat' psychology. Pages and pages of tedious experiments. Electric shocks, monetary rewards, film footage – the methodology seemed so dry after Fieldhead's creativity. But scattered among the inconclusive data was the occasional gem of insight. He was clearly a man who had spent many years thinking about the subject.

At four o'clock, the phone rang. 'I think it's OK,' said the lowest paid receptionist on campus. 'I left a message for my superior and she hasn't rung back, so that must mean it's OK. Don't you think?'

'Definitely,' I breathed.

'Here you are then. Have you got a pen?'

I thanked her quickly and hung up. Professor Carrington's home phone rang eight times.

'Carrington.'

I bit my lip and tried to keep the lie steady.

'Hello. Please excuse my calling you at home. My name is Benjamin Ashurst.'

'Yes?' The voice was wary, sounded old.

'I'm ringing because I understand you're an expert on emotion psychology, and I desperately need some help on my thesis. I'm calling from Oxford University.'

'Good God!' There was a brief chuckle on the end of the line. 'I heard you lot work hard but I never realized it was this extreme.'

'Excuse me?'

'Well, I mean, Christmas Eve of all days! I wish my students were that dedicated.'

Christmas Eve. I had lost all track of time.

'I . . . Well, I've got to a fascinating part in the thesis. It's much more interesting than Christmas TV.'

'Good for you,' he laughed kindly. 'What can I do for you?'

'Well, it's a bit complicated. I was wondering if I could come and see you. Perhaps after Christmas?'

'That'll be tricky. I'm going on holiday to the Caribbean. I'm flying on Boxing Day. I'll be away for two weeks, I'm afraid. But after that you're welcome to come and see me in York.'

Two weeks. Too long. I couldn't sit here not knowing for two weeks. I had to have an answer.

'I'm afraid that will be too late.' I took a deep breath. 'Professor Carrington, I know it's a lot for a stranger to ask, but you couldn't spare me half an hour tomorrow, could you?'

There was silence on the line. I had gone too far. His voice carried a real edge of surprise. 'I don't mean to sound prying, but . . . don't you have a family to go to?'

I nodded pointlessly and thought of Sammy. I knew my mother wouldn't miss me, except perhaps to help with serving the Brussels sprouts. But Sammy . . .

'It's very important to me,' was all I said.

Professor Carrington sighed audibly down the phone. 'How can I discourage such enthusiasm?' he said. 'But you know I'm in Northumberland? Do you have a car?' He gave me the directions. 'Why don't you try and arrive directly after the Queen's Speech? You can listen to it on your car radio,' he said quickly. 'At least we'll be sure to have finished lunch by then, and my grand-children will probably be glued to the television for the rest of the day.'

'Thank you, Professor, thank you!' I said. 'Happy Christmas.'

I was terrified of being late. I pulled myself out of bed at four in the morning to begin the long drive north. Happy Christmas. The ancient Ford's heating system took an age to get going, and the radio seemed incapable of picking up any stations. But there was no problem with speed. On empty, early, Christmas morning motorways, I put my foot down and ate up the miles.

Of course, I arrived far too early. The house was a lonely, two-storey affair, nestled between the hills and surrounded by fields full of sheep. A handkerchief of forgotten garden had been carved out of the neighbour-ing farm and tentatively defended with a two-strand wire fence. There were no trees in sight. Christmas Day had started grey and bleak, and had got steadily worse. I drove a little beyond the house and pulled into a lay-by. Checking my watch, I settled back and tried to catch up on some sleep. But anticipation kept me nervous and on edge. Reception was terrible, and when the Queen finally began to speak I made out one word in three. I allowed her a few minutes to retire at the end, then switched on the engine and turned the car around.

Professor Carrington came to the door in an old kitchen apron. He was tall, thin and slightly bent, wide bushy eyebrows compensating for the thinning white hair. He had a gentle face, with deep furrows etched around his mouth and eyes.

'Happy Christmas, Benjamin,' he smiled.

I shook his hand and followed him in.

The front door led straight into a stone-floored kitchen, where a large central table was covered in dirty plates, glasses and serving dishes. Bedraggled streamers bogged down in congealed gravy crept over the edges of the plates. Paper chains, roughly painted by a child's hand, hung between wooden beams. In a room next door, the theme tune of a Bond film was playing.

'Can I offer you a cup of tea? No? How about some mulled wine, then? You have come a long way.'

I nodded gratefully. He picked up a cup and ladled some of the thick red liquid out of a saucepan.

'It's gone cold, I'm afraid. I'll just pop it in the micro-wave for a moment.' He looked embarrassed to have to rely on such unnatural technology. The bell went and he handed me the bubbling drink.

'Would you mind awfully if I carry on washing up a bit? I promise I'll stop if we need to look anything up.

My son and his wife had a bit of a row over lunch, so I've sent them off for a walk in the fields. It would be lovely to have made an impression on all this before they get back.' He gestured hopelessly at the Augean heap.

'Of course. Let me help,' I said, picking up the first stack of plates and carrying them over to the sink.

'That's terribly kind of you. Quite unnecessary, but terribly kind.' He started running the taps. 'So tell me, what are you researching?'

It seemed safest to use the truth as much as possible. I took a quick breath and began. 'It started with a friend of mine who suffers from serious emotional disorders. She's had real medical problems, but her case is only half taken seriously. All the doctors tend to look the other way, and I was told it was almost impossible to do any thing because of the difficulty of measuring emotions.'

Professor Carrington was nodding sadly. 'Impossibility, in fact. They never like to move unless they can monitor everything, it's true. I've spent most of my life trying to get emotions taken seriously, but without graphs and tables of data it's really no good. No good at all. How is she coping, your friend?'

'Um. Not so bad at the moment. But it comes and goes.' Professor Carrington was gazing at the window, so I dropped the plates into the water and started washing. 'Anyway, it seemed to me that if emotions are generated by neural impulses, it should be possible to find some way to detect those impulses without opening up the skull, just as we can detect a heart-beat without opening up the chest.'

'That's a rather golden dream, don't you think?'

'Possibly, but who would have predicted radio waves? Or aeroplanes? Or telephones? We can't know whether the possibility is there until we look for it.'

He was shaking his head. 'You know, I'm a psychologist. If this is what your thesis is about, you've come to the wrong man. I can't help you at all if your questions are neurological. I'm afraid you've made a rather long trip for nothing.'

'Professor Carrington.' I put down the dish I was washing and turned to face him. 'What I need is an argument. A reason to pursue this research. If there is a solution out there, I'm prepared to work years to find it. But I need funding. I need university support and corporate backing. Otherwise, there's no hope. What I need is an application – a sound justification for researching emotion measurement. You understand emotions. What can they tell us?'

He looked puzzled. 'Well . . . Well . . . So much. After all, we're largely made up of emotions. Reason hardly gets a look in for most of our decisions. If we can understand emotions, we can understand what we are. Why we are. It's almost like reaching into the core of our being.'

'Yes, but what about measurement? How can measurement of emotions help?'

'Really so many ways. You could almost re-run every experiment there has ever been in human psychology, trying to understand how emotional variation affects the results. Learning, for example. All those experiments we've done on learning. I'm afraid all the variables they were studying were basically irrelevant. Emotional well-being seems so central to learning, I'm sure all of their results were really driven by the emotional states of the individuals. Oh, and intra-group cooperation. Just think of it! How much more we would understand cooperation, game theory, so many experiments, if only we knew the emotional context of the individuals.'

'And once we have that knowledge,' I prompted him. 'How can we use it?'

'Use it? I don't think I understand.' He looked genuinely troubled. 'I'm terribly sorry, but I don't really think in terms of using knowledge. For me, it is enough that knowledge exists. To know something is to be happy. And to know something more about emotions, well, to me that is an end in itself.'

I knew what I was about to say was badly timed. That it was totally out of place in this house, on this day, with this man. But I couldn't turn away without making my question unambiguous.

'What I really meant is: do you think there are any commercial applications to be had from measuring emotions? Besides whatever could be gleaned out of the health service. Is there anything people would pay money for that measuring emotions would enable?'

Before I had finished, I knew it was useless. He looked at me with confused apology in his eyes and shook his head. 'I just . . . don't really think like that,' he said. 'I wouldn't know where to begin.'

The wonders of the English university system. The system that could allow a talented man to grow old in the blissful pursuit of pure, inapplicable knowledge. No need to justify his work. All that was required was a steady outflow of learned papers and a lasting zeal within. Exactly the kind of academic I was glad to have avoided in Fieldhead. It was almost impossible to hide my disappointment.

'Well, thank you,' I began, resting the last dish of the pile on the drying rack. 'I wonder, is there anyone else who . . .'

'I'm sorry. It's just not a topic I've ever come across. Maybe in America . . .' he trailed off, no doubt equally disappointed in me. The keen young Oxford boy who couldn't think of any better way to spend Christmas Day than researching emotions: all he was actually after was money.

I put on a crooked smile. He was probably an expert at detecting artificial emotions, but it was the best I could do. He looked for a moment at the rest of the washing up, then remembered himself and muttered something about my having a long journey. He shook my hand at the porch. Then there was a call from the next room. He gave a little sigh and closed the door.

I sat in the car cursing my ridiculous expectations. Why should a psychologist be able to provide a recipe for making money? Why should he have any better idea than I what would possess an Oxford tutor to stuff a monkey with harmless white powder and then break into an occupied flat? What kind of instant answer was I looking for?

As I was about to turn the key, the front door opened again. Professor Carrington looked almost disappointed to see me still there. He walked slowly over to the car as I wound down the window.

'I hardly like to say this, as it's not a very pleasant thought. But your question made me think about other scientific discoveries and the commercial applications that followed. I mean, on several occasions, pure knowledge about biological substances and systems has turned out to have commercial applications. Insulin, antibodies, genes, parasite ecology, what have you. After all, in each case, knowledge about the biology has allowed us to manufacture or manipulate it.'

I breathed out slowly, trying to stop my mind from racing ahead. He continued, almost regretfully.

'And I suppose if you can find the technology to measure emotions, it probably wouldn't be too difficult to turn it inside out and start dictating emotions, would it? Actually generate the neural impulses. It's a horrid idea, but you were looking for commercial applications and, I mean, Mao would have bought it, wouldn't he?'

'Thank you,' I murmured, too stunned to say anything else.

'Well, I'm sorry I couldn't be any more use than that. I don't suppose you'll seriously want to propose it in your thesis.' He stepped back and waved. 'Have a safe trip. And good luck.'

I reversed out of the gate and drove back to the motorway on automatic pilot. Turn it inside out. Stick a little black box on the back of the head and dictate emotions. Laugh now. Cry now. Be compliant now. My God. That was a secret worth keeping.

14

Paranoid ideas. But nothing is impossible when the strong are given the opportunity to become stronger. And emotion control was one hell of an opportunity. How much easier government would be if all citizens were in a permanent state of happiness. Everyone kept contented, no one questioning authority.

Would the black box be necessary? Could the technology be taken one step further, with broadcast impulses moderating the emotional status of entire groups at the flick of a switch? So many routes that might lead. Broadcasting negative emotions? Spreading fear, panic? In combat, as the enemy advances, simply fill them with terror. Victory without bloodshed.

A red light appeared on the dashboard. Petrol tank nearly empty. I realized I hadn't noticed a single detail of the drive for two hours. I forced myself to concentrate on the signposts and found a service station within a few miles. The pumps were decked out in tinsel and cheap plastic holly.

Calm down. Be sensible about this. Forget dictators and generals. There were plenty of real possibilities out there. Smaller groups – psychopaths, schizophrenics: after all, the Americans performed lobotomies on thousands of them in the forties. If they were prepared to cut out pieces of someone's brain, then using a gadget like this would lose them no sleep at all. Permanent calm; stasis where once there had been unpredictable danger. How different was a little emotion-controller from the electronic tags that were being fitted to criminals? If the Home Office could consider locking a radio transmitter on to an individual's ankle, then why not attach a calming device to the back of the head? It could even be quite an attractive deal: ten years less in prison for a little black box under your hair – no pain, and we can adjust it to make you enjoy life more than everyone else. So the controlled might even volunteer.

I found myself driving straight past the turnoff for Oxford. Concentrate. I took the next exit and fought my way through a network of villages and rural lanes. Warm family glows behind every ground-floor window. Natural happiness.

Who else would have an interest in controlling other people's emotions? Business? Of course. Why not? Who wouldn't work better if they were constantly feeling enthusiastic? Whole lines of factory workers, acres of open-plan office staff, battalions of cleaners. Efficiency gains everywhere. But go one better. Companies that depend on staff personality to satisfy their customers. Airlines, leisure companies, telephone sales organizations – thousands and thousands of people. Unable to oppose the new orders from Head Office. You don't like it? You don't want to give our customers the best possible experience? You can collect your P45 on the way out.

Any major corporation could be behind the research. A few million dollars would be a small price to pay for a

276

smiling, eager workforce. A workforce obliged to put on emotion controllers every morning if they wanted to keep their jobs. And would they object? Why not go along with a project that produced permanent happiness? How much more pleasant the average job would be if joyous impulses were drip-fed into the brain all day long. What was wrong with that?

I struggled with that question for the rest of Christmas Day. The flat was empty, damp, depressing. No amount of logical argument could stop me from recoiling at the idea of mass mind-control. Yet it was impossible to deny the incredible advantage for any company that could pull it off.

I broke open a pack of beers. Bitter Christmas. Dull grey winter England. The one certainty in technology was dispersion. Any useful advance would not stay in one company's hands for long. A few years for the sponsor to make a reasonable return, then the patent would disappear, the espionage would start, and emotion control would be everywhere. And how did that make me feel? The first recorded music must have been viewed in the same way by the great performers, who saw no threat in those initial, poor quality offerings. But with a little foresight, the utter dominance of recorded sound over live performance could have been predicted.

Emotion control: an unstoppable advance, making redundant a beautiful, natural phenomenon, yet too convenient to be opposed. I could see future generations looking back and wondering why anyone should be concerned about replacing detrimental, unpredictable natural feelings with controllable, performance-enhancing artificial emotion.

The ghost of Christmas Future.

It was Boxing Day and I was starving. No food other than a grease-laden service-station burger in twenty-four hours. The fridge was empty, so I drove straight to the nearest supermarket, filled a basket with reduced-price Christmas specialities and suddenly found myself face-to-face with Ripper.

He seemed embarrassed to be seen in such a mundane location, but recovered quickly.

'Ben, you old devil, what are you doing back among the dreaming spires? Not still stuffing the cranium, I hope?'

'No, not at all,' I smiled. His loud drawl was not well suited to public places. Heads turned every time he opened his mouth. 'It's a long story. How about you?'

'Oh, uninspired by the parents. Piers called me yesterday and we both agreed to flee back here,' he said. 'Rather fortuitous to bump into you, actually. You ought to know, Piers is still a touch miffed about that move of yours on his girl. You might want to wander round and smooth the man's feathers.'

I nodded, feeling myself slipping back into the old please-Piers routine.

'Tell you what. How about coming back to his place for brunch? I'm looking for smoked salmon for the scrambled eggs, but I can't seem to find it anywhere.'

*

Piers scowled when I appeared in the kitchen. For almost a month, he had been wallowing in fury at my disgraceful behaviour. He was not a man who believed in the healing power of time.

'I got dumped, anyway,' was the first thing I said.

Piers pretended to ignore the statement, but there was a visible brightening in his eyes.

'Fine. Happy Christmas and all that. What are you doing here?'

'Caught him provisioning in Sainsbury's,' said Ripper. 'Decided to bring him in for trial.'

Piers sniffed. He was unshaven and seemed fatter around the cheeks than before. 'Um. Well, the more the merrier. Why aren't you in Dorset?'

'It's Sammy's turn for duty this year,' I said. 'You remember Sammy?'

Again, I had hit a good note. On one of his brief visits to Oxford, my younger brother had been as seduced as I was in the beginning by Piers' exotic lifestyle. Piers had enjoyed the one-night hero-worship from a second Ashurst and liked to be reminded of it.

'Then what have you been doing?' he asked, his voice a little mellower.

I started to search for some plausible, vague story, to conceal the terrifying reality of the prison cell and emotion control. But none came to mind, and suddenly I couldn't be bothered to lie. What did it matter if Fieldhead's dirty secrets were known? If Carrington's manipulation theory was correct, I was going to make everything public anyway. Why not offer a sneak preview of the conspiracy to test the solidity of my logic? And what

279

better way to regain Piers' friendship than to tell him of my suffering?

'I've had quite an odd holiday,' I began. 'You remember that brain sensor you wouldn't believe in?'

And for twenty minutes I held their attention while the coffee brewed and the eggs scrambled. I talked about Kenya, the prison, the carving. I described the project in intricate detail. I lowered my eyes and told them about Cara: on the beach, crying above the dark sea, falling in love – then being snatched away. Somehow brunch was prepared while four eyes stared at me. And after twenty minutes, Piers pulled out his wallet and solemnly handed me eight pounds.

'That includes the two you should have won off me,' he said.

I tried not to laugh.

'Old man, you've been taken up the backside,' said Ripper. 'Definitely calls for a little tit-for-tat, I'd say.'

'Pointless,' said Piers. 'What can Ben do? It's too one-sided.'

I was surprised. Although I agreed with Piers, I'd never known him be cautious on an issue that didn't directly threaten him before.

'You're probably right. But I've got no idea what's going on here. Before I can decide what to do, I have to know who is funding this and what it's for. I need information.'

I felt a bizarre pride at this calmness and maturity. No mention of fury, of blind anger at Fieldhead, the man who had twisted me around the most convoluted little finger in the history of deceivers, the man who had torn apart a beautiful relationship and planted enough seeds of distrust and fear to ensure it could not be rekindled. I didn't even hint at the fantasies of brutal revenge that I imagined hourly. Since Professor Carrington's parting suggestion had reframed the project in a new, dark light, Fieldhead had taken on a whole extra dimension of evil. In the absence of other faces to blame, his now carried the burden of all my grievances and all of my imagination's most terrifying predictions for the future. But even my most restrained suggestion did not meet Piers' approval.

'Why bother? Just drop it,' he said. 'Who cares what company or government agency is funding it? There's nothing you can do about it. You'll only depress yourself.'

'Disagree, old chap,' started Ripper. 'Ben could . . .'

But Piers cut him off with a word and a glare. His pride was so mulish that even alternative points of view were unacceptable. Worse, his strength of opinion was starting to make me doubt my own resolve. How tempting it was just to forget it all, to go skulking back to Dorset and sink myself in a world of my mother's cooking and Sammy's enthusiastic marches across the countryside. And in that fresh, lonely air, sort my life out enough to come back in better shape and try to begin again. Sensible logic, but it didn't work.

'I have to know,' I said quietly, surprising myself with my determination. 'Even if I do nothing else, I have to know.'

Piers shrugged and shifted in his seat so that his body was turned slightly away. As usual, subtlety was not enough for him and he picked up a newspaper to make his point. For a couple of minutes we sat in silence; Piers pretending to read, Ripper and I picking at the remains of the brunch. It was disheartening, to say the least.

Ripper caught the look on my face and muttered: 'Anything I can do?'

'Yes,' I said gratefully. 'Yes, there is. Can you type?'

Once again I was betraying the host. Hardly criminal, on either occasion, but the sense of Piers' displeasure hung over me as we sat in that striped study, just like before. Only this time there was no naked seducer to distract me.

'Everything I need to know is on Fieldhead's computer.'

'You're sure?' asked Ripper.

I nodded. 'He's the most technologically advanced guy in the whole Department. Everything he's written will be stored there.'

'And you can get to the computer?'

'I'll find a way. The difficulty is the password. Even when the machine is turned on it locks itself after a few minutes of inactivity. I'm going to go and see him this afternoon – demand a transfer to another tutor. I'll watch as he opens up his computer. I've seen him type in his password before. He does it fast, but I'm sure he doesn't bother to hide it. I want to learn how to read that password from the keys he hits. I'll have one chance, so I need to get good at this.' I nodded at the PC on Piers' desk.

Ripper nodded. 'OK, it could work. But what makes you think Fieldhead will be in his office on Boxing Day?'

'He'll be there. He's got some pretty special data to analyse.' I smiled grimly at the thought of my brain waves being washed, scrubbed and sorted on the great man's computer.

'All right, let's get going. We'll start with slow typing, and then speed up. It could be a random series of letters, or a word backwards, so we'll try that as you improve.' In the excitement of an actual goal he had temporarily lost his verbal ornamentation. He held his hands over the keyboard. 'Obviously, with his hands in the way, you won't be able to see half the letters, so you have to know instinctively what the movement of each finger means. For example, what's this?'

He curved the third finger on his left hand down while ensuring all the nearby letters were covered.

'C,' I said.

'Good. Let's hope he uses standard typing technique, or you're screwed. Here comes the first one.'

Ripper's fingers tapped out a word at a moderate speed. 'Castle,' I said. He nodded and tried another. 'Fishing.'

'Double letters could be a little tricky to spot so keep your eye out for those. How about this one?'

Gradually, imperceptibly, Ripper picked up the speed. Piers looked in and scowled, then walked off without saying a word. As the morning dragged on, punctuated only by hourly coffee breaks, Ripper managed to overcome some of the tedium of the task by producing funny, dirty or outrageous words. At one point I realized he was forming a sentence about me, and deliberately misinterpreted the final, insulting word in the sequence.

When he was comfortable that I could manage normal words at high speeds, we moved on to the inventions. 'Spankletrice,' I laughed, 'angireophasy.' Finally they became unpronounceable and I had to concentrate hard to recite the random collections of letters. I knew Ripper was satisfied when I started spelling his final offering. 'G-O-O-D-L-U . . .'

'Thanks,' I said.

Fieldhead was astonished to see me walk through his doorway. 'Well, well, well. Back for more sparring?'

Secrecy. Feigned ignorance. Remember you're supposed to believe he's a drug-dealer. Acted fury masking real anger. The only way to win.

'Don't even start with that,' I warned. 'I am very close to fucking exploding over you.'

'Then why don't you take your sweet little volcano elsewhere?' he suggested nastily.

'Why don't you ever let yourself drop control of the situation for a moment? How about just listening?'

'Fine. But at least try to make it interesting, this time.' He sat back in his chair, inviting the speech. My body felt tense, just from being in his presence. Acting was easy, after all.

'What you did disgusts me. I don't want anything more to do with you.'

'Thrilling.'

'No more tutorials.'

'What a loss to my intellectual stimulation that will be,' he sneered.

'Christ, keep your arrogant remarks to yourself, for

once! You think, of all the people on this planet, I am at all impressed by anything you say?'

'The naïve acceptance is thankfully less dominant in you than before, certainly.'

'What a service you've done me.'

'Actually, I suspect I probably have. You were always rather a damp sort of fish.'

'And you were always a gutter drug-dealer.'

'Where's your sense of discretion? Even on Boxing Day, I'd thank you not to shout that around this department.'

'That you value so highly.'

'We all need our covers. And you'd be surprised, there is the odd interesting bit of research that still pops out from the statues around here.'

Every angle allowed him a touch of superiority. The comparisons, implicit or not, floated around him, adding little touches of brilliance to his intellectual halo. And he loved the acting. The drugs pretence was the greatest challenge for him, keeping his one-upmanship in the face of every social value. And encouraging me to despise him; he loved that best of all.

'Well I want to transfer to one of the statues. I want a new tutor.'

'Splendid idea. I was wondering how I could get rid of you without hurting your feelings.'

'Hurting feelings is your speciality. Or have you forgotten that role already?'

'Not at all. It was tremendous fun. Do you have anyone in mind?'

'Godfrey.'

Fieldhead gave a scornful laugh. 'Very suitable. Safe, straightforward, awfully reactionary. Just like you. One of the most retarded minds in science, but that shouldn't make any difference to the quality of your learning.'

I ignored the predictable response. Even in mid-performance, he seemed a little resentful of my choice – a professor who stood for all the values that Fieldhead rejected. 'And I want the transfer request to leave me shining,' I said.

'Oh, you're always shining – in your own mediocre way. That's what's so sickening about you.'

'This is what I want you to write,' I began.

'Little demanding, aren't you?'

'You're not in a position to deny small requests from me. I might just start shouting out those incredible truths,' I said, trying to tighten the muscles in my face still more.

Fieldhead smiled ironically and picked up a sheet of paper.

'No, I want it typed,' I said. 'And three signed copies.'

Wearily, Fieldhead turned towards the computer. I moved forward just in time to see his hands come up to the keyboard. I bit my lip and focused all of my energy on following those fingers as, for an instant, they let out their secret.

Tap-Tap-Tap-Tap. It was absurdly easy – only four letters; two of them the same.

c-a-r-a

My teeth bit hard into my lip to see her name spelt out by someone who had no right to use it. I almost cried out, but some instinct kept me silent. My face must have gone chalk white. Fieldhead never saw it. He remained facing the screen, opening up a word-processing application and finding a letter template from among his files. The movement of his fingers had been second nature to him, and he was deaf to the story that it told.

'Well?' He turned round to prompt me.

'I . . . er . . . just something short. From early confidence to this weak stammer. But Fieldhead just waited patiently. I could not think of a single word for the letter as my brain struggled to throw up all the questions and implications of that name. Were they lovers? Had they always been lovers? Could he really have manipulated me in such entirety? Had she been wired too? Had it all been a game to her, to coax the maximum amount of emotional variation out of me? What sort of girl would do such a thing? What sort of man would ask it of her?

'Look, I know you can't write a decent essay, but do you really need so much time to plan a letter?'

'Um, something like, "Dear Professor Godfrey, Due to my growing research commitments, I am finding it impossible to take so many students for tutorials."'

I stopped in a daze. So many things were becoming clear. There was Michelle, whose primary purpose was to make Cara's betrayal seem credible; the collusion between Cara and Jackson, the timing of which had always puzzled me; the fact that so many of the emotions relied on having a partner, and yet Fieldhead had not specifically sought a couple; the crucial role Cara had played in getting me involved with the police. And finally, that tearful reunion in my flat, just long enough to control my movements and evaluate my credulity while the final deception was acted out.

'And then . . .' I tried weakly, my voice cracking. 'And then, something about, um, "Could I ask you to take on one of my more gifted students", um, "excellent record so far", or "one of the few students who seem genuinely interested in the subject", I don't know, something like that.'

Fieldhead was staring at me, an amused grin delighting in my illiteracy. 'I think you'd better let me phrase it,' he said. 'I've got the gist of what you want.'

I nodded, fury just a breath away. Casper was nothing to this. Betrayal, betrayal, and more betrayal. What had Fieldhead said the morning after he'd set me up with her? *We trust people whom our friends trust and should be cautious with strangers who have no reputation with our friends.* Who, after all, had known anything about Cara?

It seemed ridiculous to wait for the irrelevant letter. All my instincts told me to run out of that room and retreat to Dorset for the rest of the academic year. But I couldn't just give in. I scanned the table beside me for something to read, to disguise my agitation while I waited. A stack of journals. An electronic personal organizer. An address.

I stared at the device. Fieldhead was still facing the computer. With luck he might not turn round for a minute. I snatched up the organizer and flipped it open. An address book button, but no entry under her surname. I tried typing Cara. On the first letter, an address appeared. *C. 84 Dawson Road, Summertown.* An address.

I slipped the organizer back into place beside the journals. Fieldhead was turning to the printer. Three copies. Three signatures. What you had in mind? Swift departure and no pleasantries. *84 Dawson Road.*

It was dark as I left the Zoology Department. I decided to hold back until the morning. This needed daylight. Besides, the last thing I wanted was Fieldhead appearing five minutes after I got there. Painfully, I imagined the two of them together. Lover and lover. Genius and beauty. Who had the upper hand? He with his mind games, or she with her forceful energy?

Once again, the betrayed innocent. In my head, Fieldhead's words took on a new meaning: 'Honestly Ben. No disrespect intended, but when was the last time such an attractive girl did all the hard work to pull you without you lifting a finger?' Silently, belatedly, I answered the question. 'That time your girlfriend did.'

The sky was still dark when I forced myself out of bed, gulped scalding coffee and set off towards Summertown and Dawson Road. Two lines of small terraced houses behind neatly clipped, leafless trees. The MG was sitting right outside number 84. I parked on the opposite side of the street and waited.

She was dressed in red jeans and a long black overcoat, a light polo neck showing beneath tied-back hair. Stepping purposefully out of the house at twenty minutes past ten, she crossed to the MG.

'Allow me,' I said, from behind her. She spun round and stared in astonishment as I smiled and gestured her towards the passenger seat. 'Well, you've seen how well

I drive sports cars. Surely you wouldn't deny me a go in this beauty?'

'What are you doing here?' Her eyes were flickering from side to side, resting on me for a fraction of a second at a time, before skipping off to check the empty street in each direction. 'How did you find me?'

'You don't look very pleased to see me.'

'No, I . . . how did you find me?'

'By looking for you. Shall I drive?'

She nodded dumbly and handed me the keys. Her face showed apprehension and shock, but she walked round to the passenger side and stepped in. I started the car and set off down the road.

'So, where would you like me to take you? The lab, perhaps? No, stupid of me. Of course not. How about Port Meadow for some ecological studies? I do still believe you're a biologist, you know.'

'What are you talking about?' Her voice was strained, nervous.

'Well, it does seem odd that you kept dialling the wrong number for your own lab. My bill is itemized, of course. Maybe I was just too distracting? I am curious, though. What on earth did you keep bothering James about? Particularly before you'd even met him?'

My bluff worked. She jerked round to face me, and then hesitated. 'He called me almost as soon as I'd met you. Said he'd heard I was your new girlfriend, and asked me to help persuade you.'

'That's odd,' I observed innocently. 'Didn't he mind when he found out you were cheating on him? I imagine I would get quite upset if you cheated on me.'

This time she just froze, facing straight ahead. 'I told him not to tell you,' she whispered.

'That you were actually *his* girlfriend? Why would you do that? Surely you weren't embarrassed about screwing three different men in the space of a week?' I kept my tone airy and uninterested.

'I just didn't want you to know,' she muttered.

I looked round. She was staring at the dashboard. The little MG was freezing cold, but she made no attempt to warm herself as I turned out towards the meadow. The road ended in a small car park: a few square feet of decaying tarmac, carved from one corner of that great expanse of grass and river. An old wooden fence separated the two, keeping the cars out, the livestock in. In the distance a kite played over the meadow, its strings invisible, its owner enraptured.

'I know this isn't about drugs,' I said, throwing away all my secret cards in one impulsive move. 'I know the carving was full of talcum powder or something; that I was supposed to find it.' Cara's face was rigid. 'I think I even understand why the emotions research is so secret.' Turning off the engine, I opened the door and stepped out into the winter sunshine. 'The one thing I don't understand is you.'

I walked through the gate, following the path towards the river. After a few minutes, Cara joined me. We stood in silence for a long time, firmly apart, watching swans gliding over the shallows. Icicles had formed at the edge of the water, their tops glistening as they melted in the sun. There were no eights anywhere. Christmas had finally brought peace to this little section of the Thames.

'I'm sorry.'

'I doubt it.'

'What do you want me to say, then?'

'How about just telling me what's been going on? That would be a start.'

'You know it all . . .' She shook her head, looking down. 'What's the point?'

'I'd like to hear you say it. I'd like to hear the way you justify it.' We were still facing the river, still not looking at each other. 'Maybe it will help me understand what kind of a creature you are.'

'Do you have to be like that?' Her voice was half apologetic, half indignant. I ignored it, fixing my eyes on the red progression of the kite.

'Let's take a small example. How exactly do you feel about what you did the day I was arrested?'

'It . . .' She brought her lips together and let out a slow breath. 'It was important.'

'Important.'

'To the experiment. Jealousy.'

'Oh, of course. The experiment. The sensor,' I murmured casually. Lulling her into a sense of security. Then shouting at her: 'The sensor that wasn't even fucking attached when you came back to my flat. When you made love to me again. When you made me love you again!'

Cara was defiant. Recognizing her guilt and struggling to hide it. 'Look, I just did what James told me to do, OK? He wanted me there for the break-in to . . . well, he said, to "manage" you. I had to make sure you stayed at home all evening and then get you in the bedroom with the lights off. So that they could pretend they thought you were out.'

'Why? Why bother with the whole charade?'

'He was afraid you'd try and wreck the emotions work after all that stuff he did to you. He thought you'd probably hit out at the sponsors and he was trying to protect them – letting you think they didn't exist, that everything was just a hoax to make you carry drugs for him. He wasn't too worried if you attacked him, but he didn't want to cause them any problems.'

'Very noble. Who are the sponsors?'

'I don't know. What difference does it make?'

'It would save me some time if you could give me a name.' I met her gaze, my anger controlled but visible. 'But it doesn't matter. I'll find them anyway.'

'What do you want with the sponsors? I thought it was me you were angry with.'

'It is. I feel a lot more than anger towards the people who paid for all this.'

'Then you're over-reacting,' she said. 'They're just some faceless company. They've got nothing against you personally. It's just business to them. It's ludicrous to wage war against a balance sheet.'

'You're lecturing me on what I should be feeling? You? Let me tell you something, Cara. You've probably already consigned what happened in Kenya to some tidy corner of your distant memory, secure in the knowledge that you can tuck yourself up beside your genius boy-friend every night, free – after your clever "it hurts for me as well" break-up – of that tedious adolescent you had to fuck for a couple of weeks. But I'm still living that nightmare.' I paused, lowered my voice. 'And I can still hear you say you loved me. Still. Nothing goes away for me.'

'I'm sorry,' she whispered.

'Forget about it,' I said roughly. 'You aren't nearly as significant as you think you are. Do you honestly imagine they stick someone in an African gaol every other day? This is big, OK? Got that? Whoever did this has got such a huge agenda that suddenly the thought of driving some boy to the brink of insanity doesn't seem so unreasonable after all. Hey, fuck it, let's screw with his mind, the big picture's worth it.'

'Ben . . .' The muscles in Cara's face and neck had become taut with anxiety.

'No, listen to me, Cara. If you had one ounce of human understanding, you'd see perfectly well that I can't just drop this. So why don't you run off back to your lover and tell him his business pals are going to be splattered all over the newspapers the moment I find their name. Mental torture, buying the services of a foreign police force, poisoning: should make quite a story on the front pages.' I let the image sink in for a moment before adding the final ingredient: 'Particularly when the whole project is aimed at making mind control a reality. The tabloids will love that one.'

The silence that followed seemed interminable. The kite dodged back and forth, tugging furiously at its strings. I watched it complete an almost perfect figure of eight, coming undone only on the final curve, victim of a sudden downdraught. As the flimsy device crashed into the meadow, I turned and found tears on Cara's cheeks;

tears that I hadn't expected. The image I had formed of her overnight was one of cold, uncaring malice. A chip off the Fieldhead block. It hadn't occurred to me that my anger would actually cause her any emotion other than amusement.

'I'm upsetting you?' I asked harshly. 'Oh, I'm so sorry.'

Cara reached into her pockets, searching for a handkerchief. When she couldn't find one, I very deliberately didn't offer my own. She looked at me once, almost hurt, and then ran her fingers over her cheeks to clear away the tears.

'You've got me wrong,' she said finally, very very softly.

'No, I got you wrong before. Hardly surprising, given the amount of effort you put into leading me down your darkly beautiful, enigmatic garden path. In fact, tell me – the enigma thing, was that your idea or his? Because well done, really. The perfect amount of variability and mystery to keep a guy interested.'

'Everything was his idea.'

Cara had closed her eyes. I turned to face her, willing her to look up and laugh at me. To make it easier to hate her. There was a small silver locket around her neck. A photo of him? A piece of his hair?

'Why did you do it?' I asked softly.

'Because James asked me to do it. Because I was so overwhelmed by him that I couldn't say no.'

'Couldn't? Or didn't want to?'

'He was so convincing, Ben; you know how he is.' She opened her eyes and looked at me shyly. 'You know how he can argue anything he likes. The research sounded so important. I was just a . . . just a little girl, really. I only had a basic degree – no different from thousands of others. I was nothing. Yet suddenly, God, this guy, this genius that we'd all read about, suddenly he was interested in me. Do you understand what that's like for a girl?'

She was half smiling, a timid glance now and then to check my reaction.

'I mean, I was at his feet the moment he spoke to me. I would have done anything, really anything. He talked about his work as if he was interested in my opinion. I can't tell you how amazing that was: to have Dr Field-head asking *me* advice. I was . . . I was too blinded to see it was just a quick way to get an impressionable student into bed.'

'I don't think you're in a position to criticize others for tricking people into bed.'

She looked down again, the smile disappearing. 'I've said I'm sorry.'

'Sorry implies regret.'

'I do regret it,' she said immediately, dark spots appearing on her cheeks. 'I regret it more than anything I've ever done. Can't you see that?'

'You've forgotten how to be convincing. It's not credible to say you regret something you planned so carefully.'

'I told you, it was him that planned everything.'

'Getting yourself invited to a party with the sole intention of seducing one of the guests? Sounds fairly premeditated to me.'

'How can you condemn me when you don't even know what happened?' she shot back.

'Let's hear it, then,' I sighed. 'What happened?'

But she looked away again, focusing her gaze on the resurrected kite. It was like a neutral arbitrator, drawing our vicious feelings away from each other. Cara's voice turned distant, questioning.

'What were you thinking when you walked through the surf with me, that first morning in Watamu? When we went and stood on the headland and looked over the ocean.' Cara had pulled her hand out of her pocket and was holding it awkwardly at waist height, as if daring herself to touch me with it. 'When we saw the sun low over the ocean for the first time?'

'I can't remember.'

'Were you thinking of me?'

'No.' Every opportunity, I had to attack her. It made me feel disgusted with myself.

'Then what about that time we went out to that island? About the third day. You remember, we waded out at low tide and found a little beach on the far side. Away from everyone. And you built a sandcastle for me. You called it Castle Cara. With little battlements, and buttresses, and some pile of sand in the middle that you said was my private bedroom. For my very private love affair with my favourite knight.'

'It was stupid.'

'It wasn't stupid. What were you thinking?'

'It was stupid,' I said angrily. 'It was stupid, we had sex, you went to sleep. That's all.'

'What were you thinking?'

'If I'd been thinking, I wouldn't have been there.'

'All right, what were you feeling?'

'What does it matter, Cara? What do you care?'

Softly she slipped her hand into the crook of my arm. 'I think you began to love me there. You wrote *contentment, bliss* in your notes. But I think that is where you began to love me.'

'Go to hell.' I pulled myself free of her grip.

'Yes,' she said, dropping her hand back in her pocket. 'Perhaps I should. Because I repaid your love with contempt. Utter contempt that I'd felt for you right from the beginning. Did you ever sense it? You shouldn't have, because I was working very hard to hide it. But that's what was driving me forward, right up to that ride along the beach.'

'Contempt?'

'It's true. Don't look at me as if I'm mad. You think I'd do the things I did to you without being badly provoked? Whatever you may think of me now, I'm not some slut who goes about screwing up people's lives for the fun of it.'

'Wait a minute,' I said angrily. '*I* provoked *you*?'

'You're not listening to me, are you? I told you James planned everything. And I mean everything. He made me so disgusted by you, I walked into that party loathing everything you and your friends represented, even before I'd met you. People with swollen egos who couldn't think of any more intelligent way to spend their time than playing drunken truth games and persecuting lonely girls.'

'Don't group me with them.'

'Why not? You've been trying to do it yourself for the last two years.'

I stood frozen, cut to the bone by the truth. Then her expression softened. 'I know you're different,' she said quietly. 'I know that now. But I had to discover it during the time we spent in Kenya. James had spent so long brainwashing me that for the first couple of weeks I just dismissed all the contradicting signs as flukes or – even worse – a superficial veneer.'

'Why would he bother to make you despise me?'

'How many times do I have to say it? He planned everything. With such a close relationship – even a fake relationship – he knew there was a danger I might start to fall for you. A danger that I might not be able to go through with everything. From his point of view it was better to tell me all sorts of lies about the man I had to seduce. Like he's totally self-centred. Like he's an intellectual snob. Like he enjoys other people's suffering. What's the word again?'

'*Schadenfreude*,' I whispered.

'That's it. I think he knew it, too. You gave me quite a shock when you turned the description back on him. I'd already decided to leave him by then, but that clinched it.'

'You're leaving him?'

She gazed at me wonderingly, shaking her head as if in disbelief. 'You still think you're the only one who got hurt here, don't you?'

'You're saying you had a bad time in Kenya? Got hurt? What was it? Sunburn? A mosquito bite? Or did you just find the whole deception thing a touch boring?'

Cara didn't answer. Her head was moving slightly, as if to escape my words. Half twisting her body away from me, she closed herself to me, locking out the reality that I was forcing upon her. 'You've got me wrong,' she said again.

And then, silence.

A group of unshaven men walked past us, on their way to The Perch. Their laughter carried back to us on the wind. Cara's hands were sunk deep in her coat pockets, her arms drawn close against her, pressing the thick, warming material to her sides.

'I don't think you'll understand this,' she muttered eventually. 'I don't really know how to explain it without sounding fatuous. But it's almost worse to be manipulated when you know all the time – and are *supposed to know* – what is being done to you.'

I was about to shoot her down once more, when something in her tone made me hesitate. Perhaps it was the sound of unqualified confession being wrenched from a guilty soul. Perhaps it was bottom-of-the-barrel despair.

'He loves me. I know he does. And yet he loves his work more: enough to sacrifice me for it. He never said as much, but he didn't hide it.' She dabbed her fingers to her eyes again. 'The ridiculous thing is that I have never loved him. But because of who he was, because of what he was doing, I couldn't resist him. So much so that he had me volunteering to do things I hated. And when I hesitated, he always found some way to convince me, some button to push. I've never known anyone like him before. I'd only really thought of boyfriends in terms of sex, yet here was a man who was so brilliant, so eloquent that he offered something more. Fascination. There was nothing romantic about it. But because he was different, because I had never before allowed myself a relationship based at all on the mind, he had this terrible hold over me.'

One of the pub-goers came running back. A misplaced wallet perhaps. He gave an embarrassed smile.

'You know, he showed me the readings from that night above the ocean. Taken from a recorder hidden beside the cushions. A little purple line he called F111 appeared on the screen, soaring above the others. He told me what it meant and laughed at it.' Her teeth came together in unconscious fury. 'Laughed at it! I thought it was the most beautiful thing I'd ever seen.'

'Am I supposed to understand this?'

One strand of hair had come loose in the wind and was blowing around her temples.

'And then the next night, there it was again, while we lay in bed after the party. Solid, strong. Unwavering.'

'If you're trying to ridicule me by reminding me of my feelings for you, it's too late. Your boyfriend has already done it – much more efficiently.'

'No.' She shook her head. 'No, that's not what I'm trying to do. But I think you're right. It is too late.' Arms pressed tightly against her sides, Cara hunched her shoulders and stared disconsolately at the swans. 'I've pushed you to the stage where you don't even want to hear what I am saying.'

Denied view of her eyes, I had no idea what she was thinking. Only her body language – the huddled smallness of her posture, the occasional shiver – gave clues. I found myself staring at the nape of her neck, remembering it salt-encrusted and inviting, longing to read in it some kind of communication.

When my fingers touched the hair on the back of her head, I think it surprised me as much as her. The skull beneath my hand twitched forward fractionally, but she let me reach further round – nudging her cheekbone – to guide her face back towards me.

'Talk to me,' I said, when we had looked at each other for a few moments.

She studied my face, dried traces of tears beneath her eyes, shaking her head slightly. 'The trouble with acting,' she said at last, 'is that you're so busy lying and faking and generally fooling everyone – including yourself – that when suddenly a truth appears in that great mountain of deceit, it's pretty much impossible to see it.'

Just occasionally, an entire, silent conversation can take place in an instant. An agreement, a coming together of the unillusioned. As her arms reached around me, I dropped my face against her shoulder and felt the waves of exhaustion and relief flood through me. Exhilaration fought with resignation. I gripped hard, desperate to test the solidity of the girl beneath the discarded mask.

'Let me help you,' she whispered. 'Whatever it is you want to do, let me do it with you.'

'Yes.'

'I want to help. Somehow make up for what I did to you.'

'You will. Just by being there.'

She nodded, rubbing her cheek against mine. 'More

than that. Let me do the hard work. Just ask and I'll do it.'

'Stop it.' I lifted her head up and ran my fingers over her lips. 'Don't start martyring yourself. We'll do it together, as partners.'

'Yes. OK,' she said, kissing my fingers with almost desperate zeal. 'As partners.'

And it seemed to make sense. If anything real was to come from this, it made sense that it should be born from the ruins of Fieldhead's tower of lies and hidden motives. Two minds, cleansed by determination to find the truth.

'I've felt so guilty for so long,' she whispered. 'Every lie, every false emotion has come back to haunt me. Right back to the party. Right back to that hospital set-up.'

'Shh,' I murmured. 'Don't think about it. Let it . . .' Then a sudden blast of freezing air seemed to run down my back. 'What hospital set-up?'

She hesitated. 'That, um . . .' She looked down. 'We had to convince you to do the project.'

'What do you mean?' My defences already rising in expectation of new betrayal. 'You had nothing to do with that.'

She shook her head, still not looking at me. Then she seemed to make a decision. 'You remember I made you go and see Dr Williams at the hospital? He . . . he's a friend of James. All that stuff about needing to measure emotions . . . James said it's always easier to influence someone's decision if they don't know they're being influenced.'

Fresh conspiracy. Where would it end? The theatre now seemed limitless. A medical doctor. Supposedly the most trustworthy of all professions. Just another actor in Fieldhead's cast spouting lies to direct a conscientious, guilt-stricken boy to do the right thing for a suicidal friend. Limitless theatre.

The next moment I had pulled myself away and was staring in astonished fury at Cara.

'The whole thing!' I shouted. 'You mean the whole thing!' I was appalled. I was scarcely able to piece it all together. 'The whole thing,' I whispered, unable to believe it.

'Ben, wait,' she called, as I turned and started racing towards the road. 'Ben!'

I leaped over the fence and pulled open the door of the MG. Cara was running towards me, shouting. The ignition started first time, and I threw the car into reverse, spinning it round. Cara had stopped at the gate, her voice drowned out by the engine. I jammed my foot down and sped off towards Headington.

Oxford's streets were still deserted. The MG took the hill in top gear and a minute later I was running into the John Radcliffe. The ward was as busy as always. Anxious relatives still filled the seats, and efficient nurses still marched from room to room. Only one thing was different: where once a broken, twisted leg had supposedly lain, now there was nothing. An empty bed. I gazed at the frightened looks on the faces of the other patients and took my wrathful face away.

15

In the short time it took to reach her college – our college – I tried to piece together the events of that night. What had I actually seen? I thought of the machete chopping away four fingers before my eyes. Such skilful stage-management. What had I actually seen? A flapping door, a lifeless figure, a hitched dress, a touch of blood. Melo-dramatic props. And a leg uncomfortably twisted out to one side. Impossibly twisted? Not necessarily. What had I actually seen? No jump. No impact. Just another fine piece of theatre. Then cut to a hospital where doctors were in league with the maestro, and a girl lay with costume plaster around one foot.

That pitiful girl. I had felt such terror that night. Lying awake for hours, racked by visions of lifelong paraly-sis, amputation, prosthetic legs. Such guilt. The sheer psychological burden. All just to make me say yes.

I left the MG right outside the Lodge and ran through the quads. Her room was in the modern block, specially constructed to take the new waves of female freshers. A concrete security bunker that desecrated the Renaissance architecture around it. I ran up the stairs and banged on the door. No response.

'How could you!?' I shouted at nothing. 'How could you!?'

Suddenly exhausted at the sheer extent of the

deception, I slumped down against the door and tried to clear my mind. It was swimming with fragments of that night. I saw Fieldhead standing outside the house, helping her to arrange her dress, dabbing her forehead with paint, all the time smiling at the thought of his girlfriend seducing the guinea pig only a few feet away.

Jenni and Cara. And the link. It was so obvious, but after Jenni I felt nothing at the logical conclusion. Good friend Piers: pimp to the unwary, assistant to outdoor theatre directors. The man who arranged for me to meet the seducer, the man who waited until Jenni was properly in place before summoning the innocent to view the exhibit. The man who called the fake ambulance and briefed the rest of the party. Were they all acting too? What did it matter?

And then after Christmas, when the final deception had been enacted and the director wanted feedback, a chance interception in a supermarket and an invitation to brunch. Piers, eager to discover what I believed, then quick to dispel plans for revenge. Don't even bother trying to find out what it's all about, he had advised. Just forget the whole thing. Traitors everywhere.

My flow was interrupted by the appearance of a Spanish cleaner. Feet in Sunday slippers, long white stockings.

'Did you call?'

'Yes,' I began, scrambling to my feet. 'I'm looking for Jenni.'

When my eyes met hers, I saw her expression change. The edges of her mouth drew in. Sudden glances at my hands. I looked down and saw my fists were clenched.

'She's not here,' she said quickly.

'Can you open the door? It's important.'

She was about to refuse, then bit her lip. Her eyes were very nervous now. A key appeared in her hand.

'Thank you.'

The room was utterly empty. No sheets on the bed. No toothbrush by the sink. No clothes, no books, no bottle of fruit-flavoured drink concentrate. No crutches.

Did she even exist? Was she actually a student? Had she been planted to work on my mind just as surely over a long period as Cara had in a few hours? If the Kenyan theatre was being prepared back in August, why not the British one as well?

The cleaner stayed outside the room, watching me, but half-turned towards the stairs.

'Thank you,' I muttered again. She stepped back as I passed.

Already I knew what I would find on the next stage. The door locked, the BMW departed, even the flag removed. Piers was not a guy to hang around and apologize. If I was lucky there might be some telltale trace. Or perhaps a clue deliberately left to confuse me still further. Nothing was beyond Fieldhead's imagination, and Piers would have been only too glad to help.

But as I tore up the lane towards his house, I saw the dash of red and blue fluttering proudly over the roof terrace. Another bend, and a line of cars came into view. An open gate bade me welcome to the unexpected. I squeezed the MG into the last corner of the driveway and walked to the door.

No one answered my knock, laughter and shouts

drowning it out immediately. I turned the handle and let myself in. Traces of mud still lurked in the carpet. Travel bags and small suitcases lined the hallway. Three dinner jackets hung in crinkled plastic sleeves on the coat rack. A red silk gown lay doubled over a walnut side-table. Beneath it were two cases of trademark-orange Veuve Clicquot.

The noise was coming from the dining room. Not somewhere I had ever known used before. Piers, for all his grandeur, normally preferred to eat at the kitchen table. The dining room made this a special event. The double white doors swung open at the softest touch, and I stared at the crowd of suddenly silent Bacchanalians.

Thirteen people sat around the broad, white-clothed slab of table. Every face was turned towards me. The centre of the table was a trophy line-up of empty bottles: Gewürztraminer, Mouton Cadet, Stella Artois, Cockburn's, Veuve Clicquot, Absolut – a hideous cocktail of excess. A sea of glasses and the remains of a cold-platter lunch lay scattered around this central display. The tablecloth was decorated with splashes of red wine, piles of coffee grounds, a pair of stockings.

Somewhere, someone giggled.

My head whipped round to find the source of the noise. Sal, Max, Ripper, Duncan, all of them there; Rachel, Charlotte, quite a few others I'd never seen before. Faces were starting to broaden; the grins appearing all round the table.

'He actually came,' said a voice, scorn mixing with amusement.

'Outstanding.' The speaker was slumped low in his

chair, a trickle of port staining his collar. In another life he was an ex-treasurer of the Union. Fired for incompetence.

'What a performance. What a show!' Glutinous irony from Max. He pulled out a mobile and selected a number.

'Don't listen to him,' said Sal. 'You did so well, Ben. He's just jealous.'

In the pause that followed, I stared at each of the people I thought I knew. They all looked different. Undoubtedly drunk. But that wasn't unusual. It was something else.

'What was that epithet you came up with for Ben?' Rachel called out to Charlotte.

'That's too mean,' said Charlotte.

Rachel laughed. 'Too mean? You're one to talk.'

'At least let him get his breath back. Can't you see the poor boy's in shock? I mean, this must be – mustn't it? – a really terrible shock.' She swept her arm wide over the table.

Rachel stared at me curiously. 'Ben, darling, you don't look well. And you haven't said a word yet.'

As if on cue, their heads jerked up once more, placing me in the spotlight of attention. Total silence for almost a minute.

'What about Arezzo?' called a short, grey-faced guy at the end of the table. His belly was visible beneath an untucked, partly unbuttoned shirt. A creased corduroy waistcoat added to the air of shabbiness that he seemed to cultivate.

'Yeah, I think there's one in Arezzo,' said Duncan, pronouncing the name as only an English-speaker could. 'Maybe two.'

'The church.'

'Right. But falling apart. The best are in Sansepolcro. That's where he lived.'

'Uh-uh. It was Urbino,' said the corduroy waistcoat.

'Bullshit. He was from Tuscany.' Duncan was getting annoyed.

'Guys!' shouted Charlotte. 'Who cares where he was from? It's a name, so it doesn't count anyway.' She turned to Max. 'You can't use names – you have to drink.'

Max shook his head. A shot-glass of clear liquid stood in front of him, but he ignored it. 'I didn't mean the artist. I meant the clown.'

Duncan looked up in surprise. 'There's a clown called Piero? Is he famous?'

'It's not a person. The word means clown. You know: those ones with white faces.'

'Never heard of it.'

'Ignorant fool.'

'OK, I take your word for it. Let's start the clock again. Now.'

The ex-treasurer stirred a little and said, 'O. Orifice.'

'No!' said Max triumphantly. 'It ends in a *t*, not an *o*. Pierrot, with a *t*. Got you,' he said. 'Drink.'

The ex-treasurer picked up his shot-glass, drained it, and reached for the Absolut.

'I smell a foul,' said Ripper suddenly. 'Correct me if I'm wrong, old chap, but that word sounds distinctly foreign. You're not trying to introduce some vulgar French term, are you?'

'It's no more French than lieutenant. It'll be in the dictionary.'

'No comparison. Lieutenant has been solidly angli-cized. Your word, however . . .' Ripper looked up to where I still stood by the door, too astonished by the scene to do anything else. He seemed to notice me for the first time. 'Sweetheart, I must say you've given a new meaning to being fashionably late,' he said, unsmiling, his words slurring. 'Nothing remains but the cheese.'

'Cheese,' laughed Sal.

'And grapes.'

'I have mustard,' called the corduroy waistcoat.

'Mustard and cheese!' shouted Sal. 'You're in luck!' She stood up, gripping the edge of the table. 'And wine! We have wine!'

'We have wine!' chorused Max, also standing. In one perfectly fluid movement, he snatched up his glass and threw the contents in my face.

Absolute silence.

I lifted one hand to my eyes and wiped away the beads of liquid clinging to my eyelashes. Max was still standing, frozen like a stone, glass gripped between fingers and palm.

'Shame,' said Rachel. 'He hasn't even had a chance to apologize yet.'

She stretched her hands behind her head and yawned.

'What for?' My voice seemed alien, stretched thinner and older than normal.

'What for?' She lit a cigarette and waved it towards me in an impatient gesture. 'You're late, Ben. You're very late. Bad form. Apologize to Piers.'

I looked around, confused. No one else seemed to have noticed the absence of the host. One chair was empty. In front of it, a blue china plate bore a half-eaten mixture of ham, coleslaw and Branston pickle. The champagne flute was full.

'Where is he?'

Rachel looked genuinely surprised. She turned towards the head of the table and then waved her cigarette again. 'Oh shit, right, I forgot. He had to leave.'

'Where did he go?'

But Rachel had turned to Ripper and was unbuttoning his sleeve. She balanced her cigarette between his fingers.

'Rachel, where did he go?'

To be completely ignored in front of an audience of thirteen would be an unsettling experience at any time. Following on from the extraordinary behaviour of Max, it pushed my already stretched temper over the edge. Rachel had started licking Ripper's wrist.

'Fucking answer me!'

The shout produced a reaction in about half of them. The rest were too far gone to notice. Rachel jumped slightly, then moved her tongue further up Ripper's arm. Ripper himself had collapsed back in his chair, eyes closed and mouth loosely open. Every few seconds, Rachel stopped licking and took a drag on the cigarette lodged between his fingers.

'I'll tell you,' said Charlotte, standing up and beckoning me. 'I'll tell you if you'll tell me.'

'What?'

'Things.' She smiled and cleared the table around her seat. 'Come here.'

I walked over and she waved me into her chair, her movements sober. Then she lifted herself on to the table and stood among the glasses. 'We're all dying to know,' she said.

'What?'

Charlotte was wearing blue jeans, pressed into creases, and black loafers. She made a point of strutting somewhat as she walked down the table. Two glasses toppled over as she passed. She bent down towards Duncan, her face parodying curious innocence.

'What do you want to know?' she whispered to him.

'What she was like in bed,' he muttered straight back.

Charlotte smiled and crouched over Ripper. 'What do you want to know?' she whispered again.

'What she was like on the beach.'

Charlotte straightened up, brought her heels together and looked over her shoulder to where Max still stood. 'What do you want to know, Max-man?'

'What she was like on a deserted rock, under a red, red light, above a black, black ocean.'

I felt the breath leave my lungs. Everything was known. The most intimate moment, catalyst to a frenzied outbreak of laughter. Strange faces bellowing shrieks of delight. My cheeks grew molten red. Charlotte marched back towards me, a broad smile on her lips, and sat on the edge of the table, one foot resting on each arm of my chair.

'So, Ben, what was she like?' she asked.

'Go screw yourself.'

'Right here?' She brought her hands down to her groin, an inquisitive grin on her face. 'Would you like to do it for me?'

'Where's Piers?'

'What was she like? What did she do for you?'

'Where's Piers?'

'He'll be back soon. What was she like? Was she dirty? Did she make you –'

'I'm not playing your games.'

Charlotte leaned back and gazed down the table. 'Hear that?' she said. Someone started laughing. 'It's not a game, Ben.' She paused and lowered her voice. 'Unless, perhaps, everything is a game.'

She said it lightly, but the possible meanings stampeded through my mind. I stared around the knowing crowd and began to feel claustrophobic.

'So, back to the interesting stuff. We feel we have a right to know. I mean, you walked in here last time and treated the place like a car dealership: selected the shiniest, tackiest model you could find and traded in your old, faithful rust bucket.'

'I wasn't in a relationship with Jenni.'

'Of course not, darling. But your face when she dropped off the roof . . .' Her laughter was jerking, apologetic, as if she simply couldn't help it. To me, it was obscene.

'So you knew?' I said as softly as I could, denying her the pleasure of my anger.

'Knew?' She gazed at me solemnly, all laughter gone. Then she smiled. 'Understatement of the year, sweetie.'

And with that, all those who were still conscious joined in the laughter and I suddenly knew what it felt like to be utterly, totally humiliated.

No one could think of anything else to say. I sat still, feeling trapped, unwilling to push against Charlotte's legs to make my escape. She was gazing at the wall, apparently oblivious to me. It seemed almost pointless to run away. All those eyes had already watched me spend an evening jumping through their hoops. They'd probably even seen a videotape of my shaming credulity in Kenya. What did it matter if I looked ridiculous again?

'Did Piers organize it all?' I asked.

'Yes,' said Charlotte, still looking over my head. 'Of course he did. It's his house.'

'I'm talking about that night.'

'Oh . . . that,' she sighed and closed her eyes, bringing her legs up on to the table and crossing them in front of her.

'Come on, Charlotte. I deserve the truth.'

It was a delayed reaction, but when her eyes opened she grew animated again. 'Deserve it? Why? What have you done to deserve it?'

'You know what I've been through.'

She laughed again. 'Poor darling. All right. The truth. But you have to earn it. First we get to ask you questions. Then, when we're finished, it'll be your turn.'

I swallowed and nodded silently.

'Who wants to go first?' she called out, still watching me.

'Me!' called Sal. 'Ben, are you circumcised?'

I said nothing, for some reason expecting Charlotte to arbitrate, to ridicule the question. But she just carried on staring at me.

'Yes,' I replied eventually.

'How many segments are there in an earthworm?' said Duncan.

315

'What?'

'How many?'

'I don't know. What does it matter?'

'Aren't you supposed to be a biologist? They obviously teach you very badly.'

I stared at him in shock. Where did that come from? An innocent remark? No way. It was too close to my own words to Cara. His face was a blank.

'Hey, Ben, here's a good one,' said Max. 'What's the worst thing that's ever happened to you? Oh! Sorry, we've had that one before, haven't we? Some crap about being locked in the dark. Nothing new to, er, report . . . is there?'

His mouth was an infuriating smirk. Everyone colluding. Everyone in the know. Everyone except me. Had they scripted that whole truth game? Was this all just some weird entertainment for the depraved? Fieldhead, Cara, Piers, Max, Charlotte . . . the whole lot? Just toying with me? Perhaps the technology really didn't exist. *Perhaps everything is a game.*

I stood up abruptly and walked towards the door.

'Hold it, Ben, you haven't answered the question.' Max stepped forward to intercept me.

'Don't let him leave,' shrieked Rachel.

Somehow the ex-treasurer pulled himself to his feet and I found two large men between me and the doors. I looked round. Rachel was already at the door to the kitchen, turning a key. Ripper and Duncan were standing. Only the small huddle of comatose people around the corduroy waistcoat seemed unable to move.

I took it all in. A split second and I understood.

316

Absurd conversations about Renaissance art, ridiculous questions, long pauses. Time.

They were using up time.

Max calling someone the moment I arrived.

Don't let him leave.

Delay.

Perhaps everything is a game. Or perhaps that was just another way to pass a few, vital seconds. An open-ended question or two. A little confusion. A diversion to Italy. Anything. Just keep him there.

Where was Piers? Why had he left in the middle of lunch? Summoned to help find me? *He's dangerous, volatile. He's running around the hospital, scaring patients. He's working it out as we speak. The project is in jeopardy. We have to act.*

How much time did they need? How long would it take for him . . . them . . . whoever it was . . . to get here?

Rachel already had the key in her pocket. I looked once more at the two men standing in front of the double doors and made up my mind. I measured the distance, took three running steps, and kicked the kitchen door open.

The sound of metal lock tearing through wooden frame was unbearably loud in that sudden silence. The door whipped back and struck the wall of the kitchen, sending bottles of vinegar and olive oil tumbling off a shelf and crashing to the floor. Shards of glass skimmed across the tiles, reaching into the dining room and rebounding off the skirting board. Spilt oil formed a slick that covered half the kitchen floor, edging its way under the cabinets and forcing me to leap high to avoid it. When the shouting began all I heard was pure noise: not a single word was recognizable to me any more.

The men reacted by instinct rather than logic. Just as I'd hoped. They raced after me, past the broken lock, forgetting that my escape route lay the other side of the double doors. I ran out of the kitchen and down the hallway, slamming the front door behind me. The sound of its heavy wood striking the frame gave a sense of reassuring barricade. By the time they had it open, I was in the MG and reversing out of the drive.

It took less than ten minutes to reach my flat. I went straight to my bedroom. Clothes first: wherever I was going, I would need clothes. Young men turning up unannounced at guest houses with an MG but not even a spare pair of socks fall under immediate suspicion. Anonymous clothes: respectable but worn, in neutral colours and standard designs. A razor, a toothbrush; then proof. I had to have some kind of proof.

The empty monkey carving still stood on the table. Hardly a smoking gun, but it was a start. I scooped it up, together with the card from Michelle, and threw it into my travel bag. Perhaps the craftsman could be traced, a photograph of a reputable scientist recognized. At the very least, it showed a connection with Kenya. I had no expectation of supporting testimonies from any one at Madanzi. If it came to that.

I rummaged around the bedside table and found the red handkerchief that Cara had used on the night of the break-in. The unsavoury nature of the evidence was irrelevant to me. If Cara chose to deny knowledge of me, at least I had that.

Because the terrifying thing was, there were no other physical remnants at all. Fieldhead had been careful to remove all instructions, all notes, all material relating to the experiment from my possessions before returning them scrubbed and clean at the gaol. Phone records would mean nothing without the conversations. And by the time I was safely hidden somewhere, telling the whole outrageous story to disbelieving police officers, any files or other incriminating evidence in Fieldhead's possession would have been irretrievably hidden.

Gathering up the only other two items I could think of – a photo of Jenni and the boarding ticket from my return flight – I sealed my paltry collection of evidence in the travel bag and dived into Philip's room. He once told me he kept an emergency credit card in his desk. I felt quite justified in borrowing it. Reaching to the back of his top drawer I found the little piece of magic plastic, dropped it in my pocket, and picked up one of his coats. Anonymity was everything now. A different look, a different source of cash. Anything to stop Fieldhead finding me before the police had decided to believe me. I picked up the travel bag and headed for the door.

Those few seconds were of crucial importance. If I hadn't paused to turn off the light in my bedroom, I would have walked straight into his arms. Instead, when Piers rang the doorbell, I froze.

'Ben?' he called, almost immediately. 'Ben? Are you there?'

Gingerly, I pulled my bag off my shoulder and slipped into the bedroom, drawing the door almost closed.

'Ben? Are you all right? It's me, Piers.' There was a quick rattle at the door handle.

Through the crack in the door I watched his outline appear briefly by the living room window, heard the crunch of gravel under his feet, saw his hand reach for the cardboard panel in the window. No need to break the glass this time. I looked round at the bedroom window, wondering how quickly I could find the key and get it open. The reason for having window locks at the back of the flat but not the front had always escaped me. Right now it was serving me particularly badly.

Piers did not attempt to dislodge the cardboard panel. His fingers brushed lightly over it, testing the deceptive resistance offered by the few pieces of Scotch tape on the inside, then withdrew. Turning for a moment, he spoke in a low voice over his shoulder. Then he bent down and pressed the edge of his hand against the glass, peering in beneath it.

'Ben? It's Piers,' he repeated. 'Come on out.'

I closed my eyes, waiting for the tear of Scotch tape and the sound of the window catch opening from the outside for the second time. Who it was didn't matter. None of them was known to me. All strangers. Footfalls on the carpet, the bedroom door opening, rough hands on my shoulders. Cursing me, breaking me. Abduction.

But it didn't happen. Piers' feet scuffed once more through the gravel and I opened my eyes to see him out in the road, just for a second, before he disappeared from the little rectangle of vision the window allowed. And seeing him walk away, I let go of my lungs and took great bites of air, feeling the pulse in my neck racing for the first time.

When my breathing was under control, I picked up the travel bag and looked through the letterbox. The street was empty. In front of the MG was a small blue Nissan, parked so close that the sports car could only move backwards. It was either careless or clever. An untimely example of bad citizenship or a neat delaying tactic. I strained to see further round, but the edges of the letterbox blocked my view.

Then a man appeared on the pavement. He wore a baseball cap and tennis shoes, a thick green coat turned up against the cold. His face meant nothing to me. But when he drew alongside the MG, he stopped and bent over it. From where I knelt, staring through the letterbox, all I could see was his back. The meaning was clear. There would be no escape from the flat. The game had gone too far.

It is a terrible thing to realize finally that you are trapped. When steel walls form all around, and there is nothing left to do but wait for their decision. Their retribution. Knowing that the opportunity to escape was there. That it was lost in the space of a few minutes.

Just a matter of time before they came. Who would Fieldhead send? Piers? Chas? It could be anyone. Friend or enemy. Anyone who could neutralize the threat.

The flat grew smaller by the hour. Footsteps in the street became more ominous. The dark settled heavily over the outside world, leaving me even more petrified. Black spots on the wall turned into microphones, cameras, emotion recorders. Electronics everywhere. Hidden in the phone, under the furniture, between the books. I brought the whole lot down. Standing in a mire of scattered chairs and papers, I screamed at the watchers I knew were out there.

Fieldhead, of course. Cara on his knee. Her arm round Piers, his hand in Jenni's. She, impossible to miss, completely reinvented: make-up, hair swept to one side, an alluring dress. Who else? Ripper, the whole crowd? Corduroy waistcoat? Of course. Every one of them wearing a knowing smile, calmly relaxed, pleasantly amused, watching a fellow human self-destruct. Watching him tear his flat apart until nothing is left standing. Waiting until he collapses to the floor, sobbing in terror at his own madness.

By the time the triple knock sounded on the front door, I was resigned to the worst. Unable to do otherwise, I slowly pulled myself off the floor and walked to the door. But however much I tried to prepare myself for Fieldhead's next move, there was simply no way I could accept the lengths to which he had now gone. On the doorstep, smiling his sincere smile, holding out his small, white hand, shaping his lips for a festive, long-lost greeting, stood my only, my trustworthy, my own flesh and blood, loving brother.

16

The greeting died, the smile vanished from his eyes, even the hand fell back to his side.

'Oh my God,' whispered Sammy.

I couldn't speak. He stared at me in dismay, unconsciously took a step back. I turned away from him, collapsing into a chair. 'No, no, no!'

'Ben?' His voice was hesitant. 'Ben? What happened?'

He was staring at the broken window, the mess of books, the up-ended furniture. His wide, childlike eyes turned towards me.

'You've been burgled. Oh God, are you OK? Were you here?' He ran towards me and put an arm round my shoulder.

I convulsed under his touch and flung off the arm. 'You of all people! How could you do it?'

He stood still for a moment, shocked by my violence. 'Do what?' he said in a small voice. 'What have I done?'

'How did he persuade you? Did he say he was trying to help me? Or did he tell you it was for the greater good?'

'Ben . . .' He had moved back towards the door. 'Ben, it's me. Sammy. You're frightening me.'

I knew my face must have been black as the night. 'Why are you here?' I demanded.

'To see you,' he said, a slightly indignant reproach creeping into his voice. 'It's Christmas.'

'Why are you here?' I screamed, standing up and bunching my fists. 'I'm supposed to be in Kenya. I never called. No one knows I'm in the country! Why are you here?'

But I knew why he was there. Piers had the number. Piers had worked his influence on Sammy before. A quick summons, another seductive man-to-man chat, this time with Fieldhead. Your brother's in rather a tight spot. Would you be able to help us out?

'Ben.' He was shaking his head. 'John Ryclough saw you in the High Street. You know. Mum's friend. We tried to call you. I . . . I wanted to check you're OK. What's happened?'

'That's all? Check I'm OK and then leave? So go,' I said coldly. 'You've seen I'm fine. You can get in your car and run back to Mummy.'

He looked away, his gaze falling on the nearest pile of books. Automatically he started picking them up and stacking them on the bookshelf.

'Can't you come home for a bit? It's Christmas. We're worried about you.'

And there it was. The message he'd been sent to give: unsubtle, ill disguised. He just didn't have the acting talent of a Cara or a Fieldhead. He didn't know how to spin the irrelevance out long enough until the innocent was sufficiently trusting to accept the real message, casually slipped into the dialogue several pages through the script. Take him back to Dorset, Sammy. Get him back home. He's got mixed up in some awkward business.

Wants to stir up trouble. Best if he's with his family for a while; gets back into that conservative routine. Tranquillity. Rationality. Country life. A couple of weeks like that should calm him down. And Sammy, thanks – you're really doing him a big favour, you know.

I waited until he had set the books in order and had brought his eyes back to mine. 'I think you'd better get out now,' I said.

'But I've just got here! How have I upset you?'

'Now, Sammy.'

'At least say what I've done,' he pleaded.

'I don't know what James Fieldhead told you. Why you got involved. But what you don't seem to understand is that you're doing serious damage here. Last warning, Sammy: stop trying to meddle in what you don't understand, and get out.'

'OK, OK! I'll go,' he said. He turned towards the door. 'But I don't know what's upset you, or what I'm supposed to have done. And I certainly don't know anyone called James Fieldhead.'

I had remained calm. I had endured the insult, the tragedy of family betrayal, without losing control. But now, a single statement – a statement that could only be a lie – penetrated that calm and touched a nerve deep inside my limbic system. My own brother denying the most obvious truth of all.

The anger poured back, fists tensed, lungs filled. I took one furious step towards him and I cursed my brother with the loudest, meanest words I could find.

But almost before the tirade was over, I had my arms around him, adding confusion to confusion, mixing apologies with explanations that neither of us understood.

'It's OK,' he said softly. 'Tell me.'

Sammy spent the rest of the evening straightening out the flat. He found a screwdriver and fixed the phone. He called home with neutral words that were perfectly chosen to soothe our mother's nerves. Then he cooked some food. Frozen chicken and frozen vegetables: I can't remember what it tasted like. After my third nervous stare at the broken window, he sighed and pulled a whisky bottle out of the cupboard.

'Drink,' he ordered.

'I have something to tell you.'

'You've told me plenty for one day. Now drink.'

I took the glass from his hand and drained it. Immediately he refilled it.

'Sammy,' I said quietly. 'Listen to me. If I don't tell you now, I'll talk myself out of it. Just like I have for the last year.'

I saw him frown and forced myself to continue. The guilt of accusing my own brother had bitten so deeply into my conscience that suddenly I had to wipe the slate clean, even of that earlier crime. Whatever the consequences. I just couldn't carry on deceiving him.

'Oh,' was all he said when I'd told him why. Why he'd lost his first love. Why he'd been kicked out of school. Why he didn't have a university place.

'I'm so sorry.'

He nodded, slowly rubbing his neck. 'Yeah. I can see that.' He leaned back, smiling faintly. 'You know, it's funny: I've often thought you were holding something back. Not telling me what was on your mind. I never pushed you, because I knew you'd talk about it when you were ready. But I had no idea you were suffering unnecessarily on my account.'

'What do you mean?'

'What do I mean? Step back and think about it for a moment. All you did was chat to a close friend. You had no idea anyone was eavesdropping: it was a perfectly innocent mistake. Yet you've been castigating yourself relentlessly for months because of it.'

'It's my fault you didn't get into Oxford.'

He grinned. 'And? What's so great about Oxford? I should thank you I've been spared that miserable, reactionary old people's home. Look what it's done to you! I've found a million things I'd rather do than go to university. Even if I'd got a place I probably would have turned it down.'

I found myself left silenced by my brother's stupendous generosity. It didn't matter how much truth there was in his words. All that counted was the softly laughing, loving glow in his eyes as he raised his own glass.

'To misguided emotions?' he suggested.

'We'll start with your college,' said Sammy at breakfast. 'Find out if they know about Jenni. If that doesn't work, we'll call her parents and see if they'll admit anything.'

I nodded, feeling the hangover dig its talons into my brain. That was if the people I had called to the hospital were her parents. The porters at the Lodge had given me a number. A man had answered. Two individuals had presented themselves at the John Radcliffe. Who could say who they were?

Sammy raised his eyebrows at the MG. The last thing that worried me was Cara's mobility. 'I'll take it back this afternoon,' I promised. Shouldn't be too painful: keys through the letterbox and then a quick getaway in my own car.

At the Lodge, one junior porter was on duty. His black suit and bowler hat were perfectly arranged, despite the virtual absence of residents to appreciate them.

'Miss Douglas?' he replied. 'Oh yes, she's here, poor love. Broken her leg, she has, so we've moved her to a ground-floor room. Only been out of hospital a week.'

I stared at him in surprise as he rattled off the room number from his list. Sammy nudged me.

'Looks like you may have got this one wrong, too,' he whispered.

I shook my head. 'We'll see,' I said rigidly. 'I wouldn't be surprised if Fieldhead . . .'

But at that moment I heard his voice. Loud, confident, and coming towards the Lodge: 'It really is a smart move for you to form a relationship with the Zoology Department at this point in time,' Fieldhead was saying. 'True, we're still at the stage of begging cap-in-hand for funds from business, but the balance of power is definitely changing. Business is rapidly waking up to the extraordinary amount of useful research being conducted in the life sciences, beyond the obvious fields like genetics and parasitology. Hold on a moment. I just have to pop in here.'

'It's him,' I whispered urgently to Sammy. I turned

and faced the row of pigeonholes in the far corner of the room, determined not to be seen as the two men walked into the Lodge.

'Take evolution, for example. The more enlightened members of the business community are starting to realize that commerce is just another system, like any of the eco-systems we see in nature. It has its competitors, its predators, its changing environment and its cyclical patterns. Businesses evolve just like any natural species through a process of internal mutation, cross-fertilization and natural – or rather financial – selection.' He had reached the junior porter. 'The key to the wine cellar, please. Thank you. Great, successful businesses collapse and die because the environment changes around them and they are too complex to adapt, while the smaller, meaner enterprises – newsagents, brothels – survive for ever. Just like dinosaurs becoming extinct while the little rodents they had looked down on made it through to the Quaternary.'

Fieldhead was back outside the Lodge. I turned round. Sammy was gone.

'Of course, business will plunder our accumulated knowledge without paying for it, in the usual way, but I think more and more companies will come to appreciate the value of an evolutionist's mind in planning their long-term strategies . . . Yes? What is it?'

A note of irritation had interrupted the charming of a new corporate client. Then I heard Sammy's voice.

'I'm terribly sorry to bother you, but are you Dr Fieldhead? I mean . . . *the* Dr Fieldhead?'

What on earth . . . ?

'Yes.'

I could hear the delighted, teenage smile in Sammy's voice. 'Oh, that's so cool! I never dreamed I'd actually meet you. I mean, I've seen your photograph, but . . . I mean, I'm hoping to apply here to read biology.'

The crazy idiot! What was he trying to do?

'Splendid. Now if you'll excuse –'

'It's so great to meet you. I've heard so much about you. That cool emotions stuff you're doing.'

I couldn't believe he had just said that. Neither could Fieldhead.

'What?' To give him credit, his voice was level, if a little strained.

'Yeah. It sounds amazing. Who was it, some girl was telling me about it at the Zoology Department. I can't remember her name. Blonde. Working with fruit flies.'

'Curious.' Fieldhead's tone had recovered its amused calm. 'My reputation appears to be growing without any effort on my part these days. Emotions, you said? Shame it wasn't some serious field, or I'd be happy to take credit for it. But I'm afraid if you're after soft nonsense like that, you'd better go next door to Psychology.'

There was an uncomfortable pause. Then I heard Sammy's cheerful voice again, completely unfazed. 'Sure! Anyway, thanks for stopping. It's so cool to meet you. I can't wait to tell my teachers. Goodbye!'

When I was sure Fieldhead had gone, I walked outside. Sammy was standing there waiting for me, a big smile across his face.

'What the fuck do you think you were doing?' I said.

'Checking to see if my brother had gone completely mad.'

'Excuse me?'

'Ben, I'm sorry, but you've been acting very strangely. Admit it. It's not normal to ransack your own flat and accuse your brother of treachery. Nor is it normal to jump at the slightest noise behind you or refuse to go out into the street until someone else has checked it for dangerous scientists. And it's certainly very odd to start screaming in your sleep. So you understand why I could be a little doubtful about your stories.'

'And now?' I glared at him.

'Now I'm not. Dr Fieldhead's response was very cool, but his eyes gave him away. Definite shock when I mentioned emotions, so my guess is you're right. If he's that concerned to keep it secret, it's got to be pretty serious.'

'I'm glad you believe me at last.'

'Well, I'm still not sure I believe everything. This girl with the broken leg, for example. That is going too far.'

'Oh, really? Let's find out, shall we?'

'Calm, Ben, calm. I'm just trying to help.'

But how could he help when he didn't know? Sammy had never experienced the efforts Fieldhead was willing to make to deceive. Spinning tales to the porters was nothing. And as we walked through the quads towards her new room, I realized it was his only possible move. My impetuous assumption that Jenni had been withdrawn from the stage underestimated Fieldhead. What possible explanation could he have given? Why does a student suddenly leave Oxford? There was no way she could simply disappear in mid-action. To protect the deception, a gradual recovery was essential. Then what? A decision to take some time off for mental recuperation? A few exchanged letters? *Dear Ben, Things are getting better. I'm feeling much more confident about myself. Life doesn't seem so bad any more. But I don't think I'm going to come back to Oxford. There are just too many negative memories. I've applied to a university in Australia. I think it would do me good to move to a new environment. Of course, I'll still write.* But eventually the contact would be dropped, as the project fell into the distant past. And the creation that was Jenni would be no more.

To think of her progressively dropping me was too much. The guilt and the shame, the terror of the jump, the visits, the coaxing, the trust. A bright red felt-tip heart on the plaster, just above a mangled, pointlessly mashed heel. A fully functioning, temporarily restrained, artfully disguised heel.

The betrayal.

I marched into her room without knocking, the full force of anger back and crying for blood. She was dressed in a short tartan skirt and black jumper. On her feet were black loafers. On her legs were dark tights. No plaster. In her hands was a sheaf of papers. In her eyes were surprise and shock. She was standing by the bed. She was standing.

'Ben . . .' Both brother and fraud spoke the word at the same time.

Already my fists were clenched.

'God damn you! Don't you realize how much I worried about you? Don't you realize that this . . . this

332

went too far? Unforgivable? That no one could ever deserve it? Can't you see?'

Then she smiled. It was a tiny smile, barely moving her mouth, but it was enough. I crossed the room in two paces and brought my palm crashing into the side of her face.

As Sammy shouted behind me, Jenni shuddered under the force of the blow, lost balance and fell backwards on to the bed. And as she fell, she twisted desperately sideways, taking the impact on her right leg.

'Ben, no!' Sammy's voice was taut with shock. 'No!'

My head jerked round to see him holding a pair of crutches. More props? With a terrified girl sobbing on the bed, a kind of nascent horror started to grip me as I realized the enormity, the obscenity, of what I had just done. Frantically I dropped down and grabbed the material on her left leg with both hands, ripping the tights from thigh to heel. That pointlessly mangled heel.

A great white scar ran across the skin where the knives had cut. Bruised flesh everywhere. Lines of incision, points of sewing. As much proof as I needed.

I heard myself crying out apology, over and over again, my face pressed against that torn-up leg. I felt her fingers grip my hair, my skull. Jenni calling my name, voice breaking, tears coming. Sammy's voice, faltering in the background, then gone. My eyes ground tightly shut. My head lifted by strong hands.

I let her wet face drop against mine. Nothing more. Just touch. Closed eyes. Cognitive collapse. Contact.

When I looked around a long time later, Sammy had

disappeared. The door was still open. I don't know how much he watched.

We spent the afternoon walking along a frosted river-bank. Sammy had taken one look at my face, as I came back from Jenni's room, and prescribed three hours of therapeutic exposure to the elements. We spoke very little at first, my brother content to wait until I'd worked my way through the confused mess in my head before nudging me towards future plans. After so many intense hours believing that Fieldhead's tentacles were all around, it was almost impossible to dispel my paranoia. His solid, silent presence beside me was the best anchor in sanity I could have hoped for. Only when he saw a good clean anger resurfacing on my face did he start to speak:

'Are you back?'

'I'm back.'

'Thank God for that,' he said, smiling gently. 'I was beginning to think I'd have to do it all myself.'

'Hey, watch it,' I smiled back. 'I'm the one who got screwed here. Don't even think about denying me the satisfaction I'm due.'

And so, at four o'clock that afternoon, we began to plan the first offensive. By six, we were installed in the Zoology Department library, waiting for Fieldhead to go home.

The night security guard sat facing a minute television screen, his feet on the desk and his hands clasped over greased white hair. The Department was almost empty.

Every few moments he hummed a fragment of the Broadway musical he was watching. From where I knelt, behind the reception desk, there was a clear view of the long, shallow cupboard above his head. A hoarse chuckle emerged from the security room as some forgotten gag unfolded on the screen.

When the first crash came, there was no reaction from the guard. It echoed loud through the empty ground floor, but the man knew there were still people in the building. He whistled another few bars of the tune. At the second noise, his head twitched round a fraction, as if examining the calendar on his wall would explain why an unidentified biologist was slamming doors.

Then there were two slams in succession. The guard let out an exasperated sigh and lifted his feet off the desk. He picked up a small black pendant with a red button, which he stuffed into his breast pocket. Then he strolled round the corner towards the main lecture theatre.

I leaped up and ran to the cupboard. There were two more slams, muffled this time. Sammy had moved through the darkened lecture theatre and was at the far door. The keys were in neat, brass rows, each representing one floor. Room numbers were painted on the chipboard below each key. A click announced the guard's arrival at the lecture theatre. He would turn at any moment now. Fieldhead's key had the room number faintly scratched on the brass. The empty space where it had hung seemed painfully obvious in that mass of shiny metal. On impulse, I moved the key below on to the bare hook, before dashing down the corridor towards the lifts.

Sammy was waiting in the darkened coffee area, beneath the benign painted gaze of Charles Darwin.

'OK?' he murmured.

'Fine. Good slamming.'

He grinned and followed me towards Fieldhead's office. 'This is fantastic,' he said. 'An entire science department to ourselves. We've got to make the most of it; enjoy it while we're here. Perhaps one of these labs is open?'

'Sammy . . .'

'I've always wanted to play with locusts.'

'Don't even think about it.'

'Or perhaps frogs. Do you still cut up frogs? You know, like in ET? Bung 'em into a glass jar with chloro-formed cotton wool?'

'No! Sammy, for God's sake . . .'

We reached Fieldhead's door. The key slid in easily. Sammy sauntered along the passageway, checking the dark strips under each of the nearby doors. Inside the office, I closed the blinds, then turned on the desk light and placed it on the floor. Sammy reappeared, pulling the door closed behind him.

'Gloves. Damn, why didn't I think of gloves?' he whispered, examining my precautions. 'All I've ever wanted was to be a jewel thief that people could respect and I slip up on a detail like that. Bugger! Sorry. You're going to have to type with your knuckles.'

'Have you finished?' I switched the computer on and entered her name.

'Moment of truth. Is Piers a treacherous devil or just the shallow snob we know and love? Aha!' he cried as the desktop appeared. 'Another one in the clear. It's almost disappointing when the legions of imaginary enemies start fading away, isn't it?'

'Don't push it,' I warned. It *was* almost disappointing. Perhaps I'd secretly wanted an excuse to loathe Piers. But his innocence was clear. There was no way Fieldhead would have left his password unchanged after a word from my supposed friend.

'Sorry,' murmured Sammy. 'Just trying to get you in the mood. Get the old Ben humour back. Perhaps we could veg out afterwards with a marathon comedy video session instead? You know, all your old favourites? The Carry On films . . . Mr Bean? . . . Jesus!' he said. For a moment he was silenced. I too was staring at the name on the screen. 'You're kidding,' he muttered at last.

It had taken precisely forty seconds to discover the identity of Fieldhead's sponsor.

'They're not small.'

'No,' I agreed. 'They're not small.'

'I'm pretty sure my stereo –'

'Yeah, look, Sammy, a lot of people's stereos are made by Sato. I don't think yours is really the critical focus here.'

He looked aggrieved. 'It's an awesome stereo.'

'I know it's an awesome stereo. I gave it to you, remember?' I said. 'Would you mind if we concentrate on this for the moment?'

'Terribly sorry . . . Concentrate . . . Come on, see if there's anything else there.'

'If you'll give me a chance . . .'

The icon named *Sato* yielded three folders. I clicked

on *Accounts*. The first page was titled *Expenses*. We scanned the list of items.

'Must have been a nice hotel,' remarked Sammy.

All the details of the experiment were laid out in neat chronological order. Below that came a long list of minor UK expenses. I switched to the second page: *Fees*.

Cara, Joseph, Francis, Kristina, Jackson, Michelle, Casper, Chas – each one had an entry. But the figures beside their names were dwarfed by what came next. Instalments 1 and 2 were in the *Received* column. The remaining four numbers were marked *Due*, with different dates beside each. Forget drug runs. Fieldhead was about to get seriously, legitimately rich.

'Wow! If only I'd known biology was that well rewarded,' said Sammy.

'But why the hell was it worth so much to them? What do they want emotion data for?' I clicked on *Letters* and opened the first document. It was dated 25 March.

Dear Mr Miyazawa,

   I most enjoyed meeting you yesterday, and would like to thank you for an excellent lunch. I am delighted to hear of your interest in emotion science, and flattered by your invitation.

   I look forward to meeting Mr Jerome, next week.

The next was equally uninformative.

Dear Mr Miyazawa,

   Thank you for arranging the meeting with Mr Jerome. I was extremely impressed by the technical innovation

achieved. Clearly the device is not yet ready for field tests,
but the laboratory results are excellent and Mr Jerome is con-
fident that the miniaturization is on track for completion by
October.

I will, therefore, begin looking for possible subjects and
will sketch out an experimental programme.

We scanned the next four letters. The tone was becoming more informal, but the content remained sparse. They had clearly said all the interesting stuff face-to-face.

'No wonder your tutor's considered a genius,' Sammy complained. 'He writes so few words you feel he must be hiding an enormous amount of knowledge up his sleeve. Doesn't help us much though, does it? So far we know he can spell – -*ion* words at least – and that's about it. Hard to prove a conspiracy with just an -*ion* or two.'

I stared at him, shaking my head. 'Why do I get the feeling you're not taking this seriously?'

'Would it help if I blacked my face and put a penlight between my teeth?' he asked. 'Come on, Ben, look at us. We're nicely brought up young boys from Dorset. Yet somehow you've managed to talk me into breaking and entering. I have to laugh to stop myself from crying at the shame of it,' he grinned.

'If only your mother could see you now,' I muttered, turning to the filing cabinet. 'Miyazawa's letters to James might have more.' But even before I tried them, I knew the drawers would be locked.

'That's one key Security probably don't have.'

I nodded. 'Anyway, we don't want to try our luck

with that guy again. He's got some kind of alarm button he carries. Probably linked straight to the police, after those animal rights bomb threats we got last term. He might get jittery if you go slamming doors again.'

The next letter was dated 18 June.

Dear Mr Miyazawa,

I think I've found our man! Ben Ashurst – he's an undergraduate student of mine. You were perhaps looking for someone older, but I believe he may be perfect. He's straightforward enough and sufficiently credulous to accept the scenario we have selected. Best of all, he's rather emotionally repressed, so we should see some impressive swings when we implement the main stimuli.

I enclose a psychological profile of the subject.

'Let's have a look at that . . .'

'No way.' I was not amused by the judgement and I let him see it.

He shrugged and turned back to the screen. The remaining letters dealt with the arrangements for the project. None of them explained it. By the time we reached the final letter, we had given up hope.

It was dated 24 December.

Dear Mr Miyazawa,

Excellent news. The results are far better than we expected. Our subject swallowed everything, and I am now in the process of cataloguing his overexercised mind. I can guarantee that we have an almost perfect portfolio for use in Phase 2.

*I look forward to sharing the initial results with you at
the Dorchester on 29 December. Shall we say 4 pm?*

Sammy looked round at me, a questioning gleam in
his eyes. 'That's tomorrow,' he said.

'It's an opportunity,' I conceded.

'It's more than an opportunity.'

'If I could get there before Fieldhead . . .'

'You could spin a story . . . just get him to say a few
words . . . you never know what he might admit to.'

'Right. What story?'

'We'll work on that,' said Sammy. 'Come on, we've
found what we wanted. Let's get out of here.'

'Wait. I want to copy some of this.'

'Fine. But get on with it. I'm going to the loo. Back in
a moment.'

Sammy opened the door and stepped out. In an
instant, he had lunged back inside.

'Someone's coming!' He eased the door closed and
turned the key silently. 'What the hell's anyone doing
here at night? At Christmas?'

'Did they see you?'

'No. I just heard a man's footsteps. He's coming down
the next passage.'

'Then there's no problem,' I whispered calmly. 'Just
stay still until he's gone past.'

We stood motionless, listening. Echoing footsteps
were moving closer. The hum of the computer suddenly
seemed too loud. It was making Sammy nervous. I could
see him glancing towards the door, an uncertain look
filling his eyes.

'He'll notice,' he whispered.

'No, he won't. Just stay still.'

'He'll hear it, I'm telling you.'

The next moment, he'd killed the computer at the mains and was reaching for the lamp.

'No! Wait!' I mouthed, turning frantically to the blinds. But before I found the strings, the light went out.

Total darkness. The blind strings and the moonlight they controlled could have been in a different country.

A swarm of screeching metal blades diving towards my face.

I froze, trying to focus on the footsteps, trying to keep hold of my mind. Sammy's breathing adding to the shapes around me. A dark cellar in Dorset. A dark cell in Africa. Think lights. Think warmth.

The howl of a thousand tortured souls – their limbs hacked off, lying on the floor around them.

I felt my breathing quicken. Then real noise as my breaths caught the tops of my vocal cords.

As the footsteps reached us, a hand stretched out of the darkness and clamped down over my mouth. I twisted away in terror, my chest racing to suck in air. The footsteps seemed deafening.

Again the hand reached out, and this time my whole body was seized. I doubled up, straining to get away, losing balance. Still gripped from behind, I crashed down and felt the wind knocked out of my lungs by the weight on my back.

Gasping for breath, I heard Sammy whisper violently in my ear: 'Shut up, for Christ's sake! Shut up! Please shut up!'

The footsteps had stopped.

My head was pressed into the floor and Sammy's hand was locked over my mouth. Two tentative steps back towards the door. There were tears in my eyes from the strain of breathing under his weight.

'James?'

The voice was hesitant. A man. Soft, but very, very loud to us. A gentle knock.

'James? Is that you?'

My breathing was shallow and fast; sharp little bites of air that sounded like rifle shots.

The handle moved. The lock rattled.

'Who's in there?'

His voice was nervous now. It carried an edge.

'I know there's someone in there. Open the door,' he commanded. The voice belonged to one of the senior lecturers. He was starting to get angry.

'For goodness' sake! Open this door.'

Sammy sensed my breathing quieten and relaxed his grip. Hot sweat dripped across my face under his hand. The man rattled the door again.

'We'll see about this!' Angry footsteps retraced their earlier path up the corridor.

'Where's he going?' whispered Sammy.

'His room. To call Security. It's about fifty yards along the next corridor.'

'Then he could be back in no time. We've got to get out now.' He rolled off me and turned on the light. 'What happened to you?'

'I'm sorry. It's the darkness.' I switched the computer on.

'No! We don't have time for this!'

'I want those letters. I'll be quick.'

But the screen flashed up a new message: 'Incorrectly shut down. Scanning disks for errors.'

'Not now. Come on, not now!' I muttered.

'That's it. We've got to go.'

We both heard the sound of a door opening in the next corridor.

'Wait.' I pressed my hands flat over the keyboard, hitting every key. Something worked. The scan aborted and the password box reappeared. 'Cara Cara Cara, dammit, Cara!'

Sammy edged the door open. I jammed a disk into the drive and opened the *Sato* folder.

'This is taking too long,' whispered Sammy. He had his head out the door, listening for the footsteps to come back.

'I've got to get this. It's the only record there is.'

I copied the letters on to the disk, waiting agonizing seconds for the process to finish. Then a door closed along the corridor.

'He's coming back. Turn it off now!'

'I'm coming.' I ejected the disk. 'No, wait. Just one more file.'

'Now!'

To have any chance against Sato, I had to understand them. I inserted a new disk, copied the document called *Company Profile*, closed the folders and shut down the computer. Sammy had the light switched off, the blinds open, and was holding the key in the door. Clutching my disks, I raced out and down the stairs. Sammy locked the office, then ran after me. There were more footsteps on the lower floor. Immediately, we ducked into a shadowy laboratory. The security guard marched past, his right hand swinging the pendant.

'I'd love to see their faces when they open that door,' whispered Sammy, relief creeping into his voice.

'They won't be able to. They've got the wrong key.'

Running into the empty security room, I hung Fieldhead's key on the upper of the two bare hooks. The guard would be confused. He would curse himself for selecting the wrong hook. But nothing would be said to Fieldhead.

We slipped quietly out of the side door, and disappeared into the night.

17

A victory at last. We had a corporate name, an individual name, and an appointment in London to crash. For the first time, Fieldhead had lost the initiative. After weeks of being his puppet, moving exactly as he wanted me to move, I had finally done something unpredictable.

The Sato profile was two pages long and it made for confusing reading. Sato, it seemed, was not a company at all but an association of companies called a *keiretsu*. Each company – or *kaisha* – was linked to the others by trading agreements, cross-holdings of stock, management exchange programmes; in short, every kind of informal or formal network device that could be employed to favour those within the *keiretsu* at the expense of everyone else. It even had a separate holding company that controlled the bulk of the *kaisha* stock and managed the group policies and trading practices.

Still more impressive was the list of activities in which Sato *kaisha* were involved: they manufactured everything from aeroplanes to hi-fis, industrial chemicals to domestic heating systems. The main five *kaisha* alone employed 57,000 people. Annual turnover for the whole *keiretsu* was so enormous I couldn't begin to get my head around the number of zeros after the yen sign. This was a corporate giant of quite unbelievable stature.

'So who is this Mr Miyazawa?' wondered Sammy.

'No idea. Presumably part of the holding company. Any way we can find out?'

'Give me a moment.' Sammy was seated in front of Philip's PC, flicking through the copied files. 'Does this thing have a modem?'

'Um, yes, I think so. If you mean does Philip generate huge phone bills without having a girlfriend, yes he does. Oh, and he often spends long periods in here with the door closed, coming out complaining of a sore wrist and a fear of going blind . . . so yeah, he's probably doing a lot of surfing.'

Sammy grinned and rummaged behind the computer, finding a cable that he unwound into the living room and plugged into the phone socket. Within seconds he had dialled into a service provider, located Philip's browser and started a search for Sato Holdings' web site. It appeared at the top of a list of Sato references that stretched to 1,728,912 items.

I brought a plate of tacos through from the kitchen and looked over his shoulder.

'Any luck?'

'Well, he's in the annual report.'

'Any clues from his position?'

'Oh yes.' There was a triumphant smile on Sammy's lips.

'What is he then?'

'Human Resources Director for the holding company.'

'You're joking,' I whispered, staring at the photograph of the middle-aged man above Sammy's finger. 'So I was right. Jesus.'

'They actually want to use it on their workforce.'

Sammy shook his head. 'It could only happen in Japan, huh?'

'Even there, it's almost impossible to believe it could work.'

Sammy started opening up links from the home page to each of the *kaisha*. 'Here, I'll print off all these. You'll need to understand everything the group does if you're going to see this guy.' He shook his head. 'It really is scary, isn't it?'

There was nothing else to say.

The early morning mist hung silent over Dawson Road. My car still stood opposite Cara's house. I parked the MG a hundred yards away and went to drop the key through the letterbox.

The moment I reached it, the door opened. She was wearing a dressing gown, her golden hair loose over one shoulder. She smiled a kind of double smile – hesitant at first, then broader, as if she was trying to force herself back into her old ways.

'Hello,' she said brightly. 'I hoped you'd come back. You're just in time for breakfast. Well, just in time for whatever you like, in fact. What'll it be? Eggs sunny side up? All-over body massage? Fifty "Hail Bens" from a penitent Cara? Or shall we just collapse on the bed together?'

'I'm sorry I took your car.'

'God, don't worry about it. Hang on to it if you like. I think I almost managed to hot-wire that loveable old heap of yours. But I'm not really cut out for engine work. I need a man around the house,' she said with a wink. 'So was that yes to the eggs? The coffee's ready but you'll have to wait a moment if you want bacon. We can start with fruit. I have a sudden urge to be fed strawberries by a delicious love god, but you must promise to use your mouth.'

I held out the key but stayed where I was.

'Will you come in? Please?' Suddenly she had turned serious. Her eyes were wide under a furrowed brow.

'No.'

'He's not here. You know I'm not seeing him any more.'

'Then I'm sorry.'

She gave an exasperated sigh. 'I don't want you to be sorry!'

I shrugged my shoulders and turned to go. She reached out and caught my hand. 'Ben . . . It's not as though . . .' But she didn't know what else to say. I pulled my hand away.

'What's changed?' she asked. 'Why do we have to throw it away?'

'I didn't know "it" was worth the script it was written on.'

'Ben, please!' Her head was bowed. I looked away. Just a few steps to the car. But turning back to say goodbye, I found her eyes red and pleading.

'Cara . . .'

'Can't you see beyond the script?' she said suddenly. 'Don't you realize the script ended in Kenya? When I came to your flat I came because I loved you. Yes, James wanted me there for his burglary farce. But why do you think I agreed to do it?' She was shaking now, sobbing freely. 'You know we can make this work – it was so clear on the meadow.' Her dressing gown had slipped open, leaving only a thin nightshirt between her and the icy December air. 'Why should it be different now?'

I had to leave soon or else risk falling back under the spell of those tragic eyes. At the end of the hallway was a slice of kitchen. It was surprisingly neat. She saw my eyes evading hers and stepped out on to the pavement. Freezing stone under her bare feet. Such a simple gesture, but it almost broke my resolve.

'Look, I have to go.' My voice was rough, almost failing me.

No, she mouthed, shaking her head sadly.

I spun away, angry with her for my own reaction.

'This is me, Ben,' she called out as I walked across the road. 'This is all there is. No strings to him. Just what you see. It's all there is, Ben.'

I got into my car and slammed the door. The old longing fought with bitter experience. I started the engine and fled the temptation.

At three o'clock that afternoon, Marble Arch was awash with activity. Streams of post-Christmas bargain-hunters, their arms laden with fashionable branded bags, were heading for the tube or desperately hailing cabs. Tempers, already frayed by the demands of family Christmas, were giving way on every side. The Oxford bus dropped me right in the thick of it, and I hurried down Park Lane to meet a man who might or might not have received a message and might or might not have decided to grant its request.

Inside the Dorchester Hotel, a polite crush of guests, staff, late lunchers and early drinkers mirrored the chaos outside. At reception I asked for Mr Miyazawa, feeling like a child interrupting a formal dinner-party: a novice in a world of rules he doesn't understand. The receptionist placed a call and announced my arrival. She gave an almost imperceptible signal and a bellboy appeared beside me.

'Sixth floor,' she smiled.

I followed the immaculate tailoring into a lift. On the sixth floor, the bellboy indicated the direction, then trusted me to find the remains of the route. I knocked on the heavy door and practised a smile.

Mr Miyazawa was wearing a three-piece, grey pin-stripe suit. His cuffs and collar were white; the rest of his shirt, blue. Both tie and tiepin were discreet but expensive. His glasses were metal-framed. In his manner and appearance, he was the perfect corporate father figure – the ideal man to solve the emotional problems of his grateful workers. But behind the trustworthy image, his soft eyes gave a hint of ruthlessness.

'It is an honour,' he said carefully, a little bow turning his eyes to the ground. His hand emerged to meet mine.

'Thank you. And for me.'

'No, no,' he smiled. 'I know you have endured much. Truly, it is an honour to be able to thank you myself.'

'Well . . .' I had no idea what the correct formalities for such a meeting were. 'I'm sorry you'll get the story twice. Did Dr Fieldhead explain why I couldn't come at four with him?'

'I did not speak to Dr Fieldhead. I understand from his

message that you must travel.' His English was carefully pronounced, giving a clear but over-emphasized meaning to each word. 'It is not inconvenient. I am happy we are able to meet after all.' He smiled, a slight drop of the head the only external proof of his embarrassment.

'Oh. You mean the drugs story? Really, it was not necessary.' I felt myself matching my phrasing to his, eliminating contractions to follow the same verbal contours. 'I am really glad to know something useful is coming out of the project. If it had just been about pharmaceutical public relations, I might have been a little unhappy about the . . . about some of the arrangements,' I admitted, sensing a direct referral to the forced confession would be out of place. 'But it all seems worth it now.'

Mr Miyazawa only nodded. The sparkle in his eyes congratulated me on the maturity of my tact. My flatmate's charcoal suit was perfect for the occasion. Opening impressions had been made.

'Can I offer you tea?' suggested Mr Miyazawa.

His tone was so soothing, so courteous, it was impossible not to like him. He stepped across to the bar and poured two cups from a silver pot. Tea freshly delivered at 2.55 for the all-forgiving young hero of the project.

'I dislike winter,' he said, with barely a murmur of a pause as he slipped into this opening conversation gambit. 'I do not object to the cold, you know. That I am used to. It is the bareness of the trees. My temperament is much improved when I see leaves. Do you know why?'

I shook my head, taking the cup he held out, bemused

by this curious admission and the question that followed. His tone gave the impression that Mr Miyazawa was inviting me into his confidence, despite the banality of the weakness. Perhaps that was the secret of managing people. He motioned me towards one of the over-padded armchairs, taking the other himself.

'When I was young, my favourite game was to catch the leaves that fell in autumn. There was a superstition among my family and neighbours: each leaf you caught allowed you a day of good luck for the following year.'

'We have the same,' I said, smiling at the shared culture. 'But we get a whole month for each leaf.'

'Then I would not have enjoyed growing up here. For me the end was catching the leaf. The good luck was only the excuse. With your rules, I would have had to stop after twelve.' He chuckled. 'Even 365 was not enough for me. When I had a full set, I always caught some more for my family. More excuses.'

I glanced around the room, trying to relax into this unhurried conversation. Clearly, immediate discussion of the project objectives would be unwelcome. Mr Miyazawa's briefcase lay open on the desk, its rich, dark leather clashing slightly with the upholstery of the chair beside it. There was no laptop, no mobile phone or other sign of modern business gadgetry: just a Montblanc pen resting on the pure-white, unblemished blotter.

'That is why I dislike winter,' he concluded. 'No more leaves to catch for almost a year. A genuine sentiment in my childhood that has persisted irrationally many years after I caught my last leaf.'

'A good enough reason,' I replied. Then, keeping the

subject abstract: 'Your English is extremely fluent. Have you lived in this country?'

'No. I have never lived in the United Kingdom. But I did spend two years in Sydney as General Manager of Sato Electronics Australia. It was important to me that language should not be an obstacle between me and the local management. I spent considerable time learning correct grammar and pronunciation.'

It occurred to me that he hadn't thanked me for the compliment. Perhaps he was too used to the admiration of English-speakers, themselves unused to such linguistic competence in their own race or among the Japanese. 'How did you find Australia?' I asked.

'I think the Australian culture is difficult for Japanese people to penetrate,' he said. 'They are very welcoming to Asian races, much more so than the United States. But they choose to welcome us by inflicting on us the rites that we do not understand and cannot enjoy. I think in the end they did not like me. Or perhaps they did not dislike me; rather they found me amusing at good times and embarrassing at bad times. Some of the managers invited my family to their houses, which was kind of them. But the tradition of barbecues and eating while standing is not one with which we felt comfortable. Moreover, my wife was somewhat distressed when the Australian ladies – out of kindness I am sure – coerced her into joining them on the beach and drinking beer. Apparently some of the conversation was . . . unfortunate in its taste.'

Mr Miyazawa's face had darkened a little. His eyes were not angry, but nor did they contain that cheerful glint that memories of catching leaves had evoked. I remained silent, curious to see where this reference would lead the executive. But he must have sensed his own mood – subtle as it was – and decided it was not the one to share with a young English stranger. Instead, he rose to his feet and gestured to my empty cup.

'Would you like some more?'

'Thank you.'

While he was bent over the tea tray, I stole a glance at my watch. Time was moving fast. Fieldhead would be arriving in just over half an hour for his appointment with his paymaster. I tried to imagine his face if he were to get here early and find me still present. The surprise and anger would be worth a good deal to see. But it would also kill any chance of getting further information out of this man. And so far I'd only heard about leaves and Aussies.

'How did you come to work for Sato?' It was the most delicate way I could find to steer the conversation in the right direction.

Mr Miyazawa handed me my tea and walked to the window, gazing out over the park. 'My father had three sons. More than was necessary to look after his small farm. I was the youngest, so I had to find work elsewhere. The Sato Group owned the only factory in the nearest town. It made spare parts for farm equipment: I felt at home there. Many of my friends from the school were also working there. None of us came from families with enough money to pay for university education, so operating machinery on a production line was quite acceptable to us.'

'It's a big jump from the factory floor to com- missioning emotion-controlling devices,' I said as casu- ally as I could, probing the possibility in a way I hoped I could excuse if I was wrong.

But Mr Miyazawa did not react particularly to the suggestion. 'Yes,' he agreed. 'But it has been also a long time. And there were many steps on the ladder to get here. I have . . . how do you say? Earned my stripes?'

'I'm sure,' I said. 'And of course, you must have an excellent perspective of what it's like to work at the bottom of the company: very useful for an HR director.'

He nodded, smiling again, but careful to retain the air of humble hard worker, even as the conversation turned to his current exalted position. 'I spent five years on the production line, and I grew to love the work and my comrades more than anything else in life.'

'Well, that's what I find confusing,' I said. 'Given how close your ties are to the workforce, why do you want to inflict this . . . this device on them? Why do you want to take away their natural emotions and replace them with something artificial?'

Immediately, Mr Miyazawa's smile disappeared and he jerked his shoulders back like an animal threatened by a snake. I hadn't intended to sound so confrontational, but the executive clearly read my words that way.

'You misunderstand,' he began, apparently pained at the injustice. 'This is a wonderful breakthrough, for the workers most especially. It gives them a way to fulfil their duties happily and pleasantly; free of the boredom or anxiety that plagues many in the factories. It is pre- cisely because I have worked for so many years on the production line that I value the invention – and the project that you were part of – so highly. Perhaps, without experience of factories, you cannot understand this.'

I nodded, displaying my most serious air, but internally I was already celebrating. I had confirmation. There was no question about the goal now. The only uncertainty was the motivation. Altruistic concern for the blue-collared did not ring true.

'So this is entirely for the sake of the workforce?'

'Of course.'

'Have they been consulted?'

'It is still too early. We do not want to raise hopes in case the technology does not succeed.'

'What if they don't want it?' I asked.

'That is not possible,' he said. There was no dictatorial arrogance in his voice, but neither was there any uncertainty. The workers would want what they were told to want. End of story.

'How are you going to attach the . . . um . . . devices?' I asked.

'The transmission units have a bio-polyerene base. It is possible to graft it into the flesh.'

'Permanently?' I said, my surprise making my response a little too sharp.

He nodded. 'It will be a sign of status that will give them much pride. They will bear the mark of a great *keiretsu*.'

I swallowed, trying to imagine thousands of compliant Japanese workers lining up for surgery. The image was too distasteful for words. It seemed astonishing that this leader of men could give such placid consideration to the plan. Was it simply an objective calculation on behalf of the employees? Happiness every day in return for a small foreign object lodged at the back of the skull: denying the user the chance to have a bad day, walk around in a grump, curse people for just being there.

'It's costing you millions of dollars,' I said petulantly. 'Are you really telling me there is no material benefit to the company? To the shareholders?'

It is curious the way the emotions work. I had arrived at the hotel determined to be polite and charming to this man. He had not offended me in any way, nor threatened or intimidated me. He had offered me nothing but hospitality and pleasing anecdotes. Yet the manner in which he related the plans for his employees' mental manipulation so shocked me that suddenly I was directly challenging him.

Quite reasonably, he was upset. 'It is difficult for you to understand the bond between employer and employee in Japan. There is no equivalent in the West.'

'And the shareholders . . . ?' I persisted.

Mr Miyazawa sighed and looked down. I was being offensive, by his standards, and I knew it. But I was determined to get an answer. Eventually, he gave me one: 'There will be a benefit to shareholders. Yes.'

'More happiness means higher productivity?'

'That, of course, and . . .' He stopped himself.

'. . . and what?'

'The productivity gains will be the most significant. We are expecting improvements at all manned points in our manufacturing plants if positive emotions can be continuously maintained. We will have fewer stoppages, fewer quality rejections, fewer delays, fewer disputes, fewer bottlenecks caused by difficult staff. It is very important now. The younger workers have less patience than before. They are too influenced by America.' He bowed his head in apology for this slur on the Western world.

'And what else?'

'What else?'

'You said there was another benefit to the shareholders. Are you going to start laying off people, once productivity increases?'

Mr Miyazawa looked genuinely shocked. 'We would never do that,' he said firmly. 'We are too much of a family to do that. Sato *kaisha* are like fathers to their employees. That is how we inspire the loyalty that is missing in this country. That is why our workers sing the Sato song with pride, and every one of them wears the Sato pin.' He paused and indicated the small disc on his buttonhole.

'It might be slightly different if it was welded to their heads.'

'Please, Mr Ashurst . . .'

I ignored the aggrieved tone in his voice, refusing to be thrown off the scent. 'You still haven't told me what this great benefit will be.'

Mr Miyazawa closed his eyes and sighed. For a moment, I thought he was going to throw me out. But when he looked at me again, his eyes were forgiving.

'The fact that I am going to tell you what you so urgently wish to know is a sign of the immense gratitude that I and the Sato Group feel towards you,' he said. 'It is on the understanding that you will be discreet with your knowledge, remembering that knowledge of this kind can be used as a club to destroy the progress of a great organization.'

He stared at me, as if seeking some kind of reassurance that I understood his plea, then continued. 'The emotions project is expensive. Very expensive. Some years ago that would not have mattered. We would have recognized the immediate benefits to the workforce and the long-term productivity benefits to the shareholders, and that would have been sufficient justification to make the investment. The Sato Group, like other *keiretsu*, had its own bank, which owned much of the *kaisha* stock and provided most of their credit. In that time, such investments would not have been questioned.

'Today it is different. Throughout Japan, the financial position of the banks has been severely weakened. As a result, many of the banks from different *keiretsu* have merged and restructured, diversifying their lending profile and effectively severing themselves from their *keiretsu* roots. Sato Bank did the same. We tried to avoid too much dilution of control by buying the Sato stock they owned through a holding company. It was the only way to hold the *keiretsu* together without the bank. Regrettably, in order to finance the stock purchase, we were obliged to invite a number of external investors to take an equity position in Sato Holdings.

'Since then, our decisions have been hampered by three major shareholders who care nothing for the culture of the group but who have acquired sufficient stock to demand positions on the board. For them, long-term productivity gains are too distant. And so for them, we have had to agree to implement a wage reduction once the emotion control is in place.'

I blinked. 'What?'

'A wage reduction.' There was a strange modulation in his voice. I was so shocked by what he said that I hardly noticed the odd way in which he said it.

'You're going to use the units to reduce salaries?'

'That is correct,' he said, his voice recovering its previous shape. 'We are exchanging happiness for wages. Our workers will have less need of money when they are happy.'

In my astonishment, I had lost my calm. 'You might be in for an unpleasant shock when they all decide to leave.'

He did not like to contradict me directly, preferring instead to provide more information to show me my error. 'The *kaisha* in Japan is not an ordinary company. It is . . . an institution, a society of brothers and sisters striving towards a shared destiny. This is true for all the *kaisha* of the major *keiretsu*: Matsushita, Sumitomo, Mitsubishi – all are of this nature. And our people are dedicated to the *kaisha*. We have a saying, "The people are the walls, the people are the moat, the people are the castle." Nowhere is this more true than in the Sato Group.'

'And when the castle stands up and marches off to work for a less manipulative company, what will Sato do?'

'Japan is not like this country. There is no labour market for older people. Most workers are recruited from school or college and stay with the same company for life. As I have stayed with Sato. There is nowhere else for them to go.'

'What about the trade unions? They would never allow a wage cut.'

'We do not have trade unions. Our employees are organized in an enterprise union. It is also loyal to the *keiretsu*. It is fully supportive of all board decisions, including wage reductions. In the past, they have been necessary during difficult economic conditions to avoid redundancies. There is a precedent.'

'How much?'

'We expect to implement a phased reduction of both wages and bonuses over eighteen months of forty-seven per cent in real terms.'

'Forty-seven per cent!' I stared at him in amazement. 'How do you expect them to live on that?'

'Most of our workers live in company dormitories or on company housing estates. Japanese people do not concern themselves with housing as Europeans do. Our employees receive subsidized meals and transport. They have sports facilities at the factories. They have less need of money than European workers.'

'And their families?'

'Other things . . . they will find they do not need them so much when they have our transmissions.'

'Not need their families? You're crazy!' I tried to imagine this man running a Human Resources Department. His cool barbarity was awesome. 'They'll leave in floods.'

'No. I do not think so.' He smiled a less amiable smile.

'If anyone shows desire to leave us, well, there are ways of using your other material. We can arrange for them to think life without our transmissions is too unpleasant to contemplate.'

'What does that mean?' I breathed.

'They will think the unit is inactive when they are in their homes. We will transmit unhappiness and fear during the evenings and nights, only allowing them happiness in the workplace. We will make them think they are dependent on artificial emotion.'

'What!?'

This time the change of accent was blatant. 'I said, we'll make them think they're dependent on artificial emotion.'

I stared at the man opposite me. His smile had broadened to very un-executive proportions. His formal posture had turned into a slouch. His jacket hung open. The skin colour and bone structure were right, but I knew that accent was not from Japan. Somewhere in south London was my best guess.

'What is this?' I whispered.

'He wanted to answer that himself.' Pure south London, now. The man grinned and pulled an envelope from his jacket pocket.

I tore it open and pulled out the letter.

It was everything I should have expected and had never even imagined.

Dear Ben,

Please forgive the exhibition. As you can see, I am rather addicted to the theatre now. Before you do anything rash, remember that the gentleman with you is a professional actor and therefore not deserving of your characteristic rage. Take it out on me when you come back to Oxford.

I looked up to see the 'gentleman' holding out a laminated ID. Takeshi Otoya. The Anglo-Asian Perform-ance Agency. AAPA. Valid for life. Still grinning.

First, allow me to congratulate you on your intelligence. I am impressed both that you saw through my deception with the carving and that you had the wit to tease my password out of me. Very smart. I am glad that you will not go to your grave thinking your (ex-)tutor a drug-dealer, even if the loose ends are now not as neatly tied as they might have been.

Second, I regret that you had to find out about Cara, especially through the blunt medium of a keyboard. Believe me, her role was essential to the project, but I had hoped that you would suffer no more pain with her than the rather graceless exit she made from your flat (and, as you have come to appreciate, from your life). You will by now be aware of the service your friend Piers has done me. Unfortu-nately, he was a little slow in transmitting your intentions to me. I was informed in time to adjust the contents of my hard disk before your nocturnal visit, but not quickly enough to change my password to something less revealing. Sorry.

So, why the charade? Think of it as a gentle lesson in power. Information is power in this game, and as you are no doubt realizing, your information is extremely unreliable. Your friend Piers explained your rather extraordinary theories about my sponsors' intentions and I'm afraid I just couldn't resist playing them back to you. I fully understand your quest for the truth, and I am genuinely sorry that I cannot share it with you. All I can say is that it is much more palatable than you seem to imagine, but commercial pressures demand secrecy for a few years. Please accept this statement in good faith and put aside your detective work.

There are no threats. Neither my sponsors nor I are interested in making life difficult for you. We are all extremely grateful to you, as you can imagine. However, if you persist in digging you will find there are no more leads. No appointments in London hotels. No references to Phase 2. No indiscreet Japanese directors. No names of evil corporations. No unguarded computers. Even if you should miraculously track down Cara and charm her into revealing all, you will see I have been careful to keep her in the dark. There is no one else. There is nothing else. And once you have searched for a few weeks, you will realize that the exhaustive removal of all fingerprints from the crime scene meets the standards of precision with which I have arranged the rest of the project.

Please excuse the vagueness of this letter. In itself it is a fingerprint of a kind and I am concerned to make it as smudged as possible. I wish you a Merry Christmas and hope you will be able to relax a little now. If you would like to reconsider your earlier decision about transferring to another tutor – given that that was part of your keyboard gambit – I would be delighted to have you back. It has been a pleasure.

Yours, with my very best wishes,
    James

I looked up at the actor. He had ruffled his hair forward and removed his tie and glasses. He could have been any Japanese man in the street.

I gave a cold nod. 'It was a good likeness. I saw a photo of him.'

'Not really,' he said. 'He's pretty different. But we all look the same, right?' He raised the glasses. 'It doesn't take much.'

I looked around the suite. 'Nice stage.'

'I have to be out of here by six.'

I nodded. 'Enjoy it,' I said, turning abruptly. As I walked through the doorway, he was heading for the bar.

18

Fieldhead was badly mistaken if he believed that his gratuitous new move would put me off. *Manipulating me is likely to make me react badly.* That was a warning he had casually ignored. My characteristic rage grew steadily stronger on the way back to Oxford. Just one lead, that was all I needed. One name to give me something I could use.

But even with my mind leaping to the next course of action, I couldn't help thinking again of Cara. He didn't know I'd seen her. The letter made that clear. He didn't know I had found her home. *84 Dawson Road.* And if he didn't know, it meant that she really had left him. Really was being sincere. Really was hoping . . .

'Well?' said Sammy.

'You won't believe it.'

'Was it all true?'

'No. It was all fake.'

He looked at me in confusion. Wearily, I explained the latest in the long series of amusements that my ex-tutor had seen fit to indulge in, describing the fluid transition from reason to madness in the actor's speech.

'So that's it then,' he said, when he'd read the letter. 'He's won.'

'No! I'm not just going to drop this now,' I said. 'This has just made me more angry.'

Sammy sat down in one of the armchairs. 'You know,' he started hesitantly, 'sometimes it's best just to let go.' He looked down, expecting a furious reaction. But before I could say anything, the phone rang. It was a shock to hear that sound penetrate the still seclusion of the flat. I picked up the receiver.

'Yes?'

'That you, Ben?' asked Fieldhead. 'Are you safe to talk to? Takeshi said you were looking a little explosive.'

'What do you want?'

'Well, it's more a question of what you want, actually. Thought you might like a little chance to work off some aggression on me.'

'I'm fine, thank you,' I said coldly.

'Oh, I'm sure you are. Nevertheless, it would be useful, don't you think, if we saw each other in the flesh? Now that everything's straightened out – a little anyway – I thought it might be good to check there wasn't any bad blood left.'

No bad blood! But I remembered that lead I didn't have and brought my anger under control. Just one clue. There was nowhere else to look.

'All right,' I muttered. 'When?'

'How about tomorrow morning? OK? Great. Let's meet at the Department. Come in warm sports clothes and tennis shoes.'

'Tennis shoes?'

'Yes. I have a new game I'd like to try.'

We walked the short distance to the outdoor tennis court in silence. Fieldhead didn't attempt to initiate conversation and I kept my eyes locked on the path. At the gate he struggled with the rusting padlock, then handed me a racket and walked over to the sagging net.

'A little higher than normal for this, I think,' he muttered, winding the handle and raising the net. I began to stretch my muscles, still looking away.

'I really don't know how this game will go, so this is a genuine test,' he said. 'Richard Dawkins came up with it the other day and reckoned it might have some useful biological application, but for now let's forget about that.' He threw a clutch of balls over the net. 'Basic rule of the game: we count the number of strikes in each rally and the winner of the rally receives that number of points. We both therefore have an incentive to keep the rally going, but ultimately we both want to play the winning shot. The challenge is to anticipate your opponent's defection from cooperation so that you can defect just before he does. Of course, as in any repeated game, your actions in one rally will influence his actions in the next. We'll play exactly thirty rallies and alternate service. The object of the game is to maximize the number of points you have – not necessarily to get more points than the other player. It is therefore effectively a cooperative game, although spiced by the increasing temptation to indulge in uncooperative behaviour as rallies get long. Is that clear?'

I nodded.

'Assuming we are both excellent tennis players, the maximum score that fully uncooperative behaviour will yield is 15 each. That is the result if we both serve aces every time. Of course if we choose to serve more gently, we both have the potential to reach much higher scores. Shall I start?'

I walked to the baseline and adjusted my grip on the racket. A cold wind was blowing across the fields. Icicles hung from the fencing. Fieldhead grinned once and served. The ball landed neatly in the centre of the service box then bounced slowly up towards me. I hit it calmly, placing it in front of his racket.

'Good. Two,' he called, as he returned the ball. 'Don't worry about the counting, by the way. I'll take care of that.'

I caught the ball on the volley and sent it straight back to him.

'Do you mind if we chatter a bit?' he asked. 'It doesn't put you off?'

'No.'

'Excellent,' he said, catching the ball on his backhand. 'How are you feeling?'

'Pissed off.'

'That'll fade away.'

'Is that so?'

Fieldhead smiled. 'You know, I once came across a variation on the Creation story,' he said. 'Would you like to hear it?'

I gave no response, keeping my eyes on the ball.

'A village elder in Zimbabwe told it. No idea how he got hold of it, as it certainly wasn't a local favourite. But I've found it useful in all sorts of non-religious ways since then.'

Fieldhead moved slightly further back to increase the distance between us and slow the rate of the rally. 'It begins in Paradise, of course, although his description was delightfully different. Paradise, Zimbabwe-style, is dominated by water and cows. There's everything else as well: abundant fruit, creepers, sunshine, predators and prey frolicking together in the usual way, but the scene is heavy with large, fertile, warm milk producing cows. Waterfalls everywhere. Lovely big rivers with nothing remotely grey-green or greasy about them. Rock pools, cool streams: water in every possible form.

'And then there is the proto-man – let's call him Adam for the sake of simplicity. Like his biblical equivalent, Adam is exquisitely happy and only requires the companionship of a woman to complete his perfect existence. God, true to the original, obliges, and woman is created. The story only diverges from ours when it comes to Adam's downfall. In this version, there is no serpent and there is no Tree of Good and Evil.

'Adam is already curious, already questioning. He must have been a scientist at heart, because whenever he looked around him and saw the wonders of Paradise and the beauty of Eve he couldn't stop asking himself How? And then later, Why? For a while, he kept his curiosity under control. But no amount of nectar and love could take Adam's mind off the questions of Paradise. How had God done it? And why had God done it?

'So eventually he called out to God, and put the questions to him. And God told him to forget such pointless concerns and concentrate on enjoying the good life that he had been given. "Look at the symmetry of the blossom," God told him. "Marvel at the iridescence of the kingfisher, and do not worry yourself with the how or the why."

'But Adam could not resist the urge to know the truth. And finally, after enduring the same questions for many years, God told him. "How? It is simple. Everything around you is made of the same mud. I have forged it into different shapes and colours, it is true, but if you melt it all down you will see that everything is made of mud." And Adam looked around him and no longer saw beauty or richness, but merely pieces of mud in different shapes. Even the first woman, Eve, was no more to him now than a lump of earth.

'In his misery Adam realized his mistake, but still he had to persist. "Then why?" he demanded of God. "Why have you created Paradise?" And God looked down and spoke to him for the last time, destroying as he did all hope of future contentment: "Why? Adam, there is no why. Or rather, there is, but it is meaningless. Why did I create you and all of Paradise? Because I had nothing better to do at the time."'

My returns had been becoming more and more forceful as I listened to this nonsense. 'Is that supposed to be a parable for me? Teach me that I shouldn't keep investigating your sordid dealings?'

'Perhaps.'

'Well, congratulations,' I said icily. 'That's the first time I've heard anyone compare themselves to God.'

'It's just a story, Ben. Even if I did believe in God, I'd still use it. I'm just trying to show you that we often make ourselves more unhappy if we keep trying to uncover everything.'

'Amazingly hypocritical sermon, given your profession,' I spat back. 'Besides, I wouldn't liken your manipulative games to Paradise. Not by a long way.'

I brought up my racket a fraction faster and a fraction off-centre, slicing the ball so that it bounced just inside his tramline and flew into the fence.

'Your rally,' he announced. 'Fifty-eight points to you. Question is, did you do that on purpose? Should I now punish you by trying to win the next rally immediately, or should I continue to cooperate on the assumption that you screwed up? Difficult to tell,' he grinned. 'What makes this game fun is the uncertainty of intention resulting from our less-than-perfect tennis ability. You can defect and pretend that you were trying to cooperate. At least, the first few times . . .'

I served a medium-strength ball. Fieldhead made no attempt to win with it.

'You're bound to be pissed off,' he said. 'But you should be glad that the employee manipulation stuff was nonsense. Interesting idea, though. Think how different the world could be if a central body controlled all our emotions.'

'I've already thought about it.'

'Yes,' he agreed, running a little to get the ball. 'But your ideas were probably fairly superficial. I'm talking about total eradication of emotions. Think of that. It would completely change all the rules of life. The final victory of Reason over Emotion. The world could be run so much more efficiently. Get everyone working at what they were good at rather than what they just felt like doing. We could even manage the

373

population properly: cull the aged, prohibit reproduction by the genetically impaired, perhaps organize human breeding programmes to generate superior genetic profiles. All without anyone objecting on sentimental grounds.

'Of course, the downside would be the loss of motivation. We would still act rationally to protect our interests, but the nature of those interests would have changed completely. Without emotions, we would no longer have any interest in entertainment, relationships, prestige, discovery or self-actualization – all the things that normally drive our activities. In fact, we wouldn't even care if we lived or died, because the very act of caring is emotion-driven. So all the interests to do with survival – shelter, food, self-defence – would disappear. Hard to imagine what would interest us at all, really,' he decided. 'How's that for a tennis-court conclusion? "Life becomes pointless without emotion."'

I smashed the ball on the volley so that it bounced at his feet and flew off the court.

'Your rally, twenty-one points. Now I know you're doing it on purpose,' he said.

His next serve was an ace.

'Over to you. Think carefully.'

My attempt at a vicious, point-winning serve hit the net both times.

'Neither virtuous, nor skilled,' smiled Fieldhead. 'You lose before both God and Darwin. It seems to be up to me to get you back on the straight and narrow.' Again his serve shot past me.

This time I paused for a moment, as if contemplating

the righteous path, before driving the ball with all my force into the box so that it flew past his back.

'Oh dear. Are we going to get locked into a mutually destructive sequence of non-cooperation?' he asked. 'It hardly seems right when there are twenty-four more rallies to go.'

Fieldhead knocked the ball gently over the net so that it bounced straight on to my racket. I hit a drop shot and the ball skimmed over the net, then fell to the ground.

'Why are you doing this?' said Fieldhead. 'You just get two points for that. Didn't you recognize my gentle serve as a gesture of cooperation?'

'You're looking for logical, unemotional thinking,' I growled. 'You've made me incapable of that.' My first service went into the net. My second was no less forceful and bounced straight past his leg.

'You're not still thinking about that monkey, are you?'

'What?' I stopped still and stared at him.

'That monkey carving on the aeroplane. You're not still sore about that, are you? I really am sorry about putting you through all that, but I had to try and give you the impression that the emotions technology was fake. A drugs story was the best alternative explanation I could think up. Look, nothing bad would have happened to you. The passenger sitting next to you was a friend of mine. If you hadn't got rid of the powder, he would have taken care of it before the plane landed.'

But I had seen a different monkey appear in my imagination. A cartoon monkey. A logo, flashing up briefly on a computer screen. Over three weeks ago. Too briefly to be a hoax. A cartoon monkey. A name. A lead.

'No, I . . .' I looked across the net at the puzzled genius and smiled. 'I have to go now,' I said and dropped his racket to the ground.

'I've got a lead!' I said immediately. 'I've got a name.'

Sammy was sitting at the table, reading a novel. He looked up and held out a letter.

'It came a few moments ago,' he said weakly. 'I didn't see who brought it.'

I took the plain blue envelope. Her writing. He looked worried, a little embarrassed. Perhaps he'd caught a glimpse of her through the window.

Ben,

You didn't let me finish yesterday. I know you can't stand being with me at the moment. Here's the safe written version to make it less nauseous. And I guess this is my last chance, so I'd better be explicit. So much for my pride.

You know I'm sorry. There's no way I can write anything to prove it. But if you have a fraction of the sensitivity that I believe you have, you know exactly how I'm feeling. Guilt is a fucking disaster in someone like me. Too self-assured to take it. No one else believes I'm capable of it (including you?), and as for me – I haven't the first idea how to deal with it. It just sits in my gut making me physically sick and desperate to see you all at the same time. Don't worry. I won't come running round and camping on your doorstep. You don't want to talk to me. I'm too scared to talk to you. So that settles that.

This is going nowhere. I've left James. You already know

that. Does it make any difference? Am I still a bitch? Logic-
ally, yes – I can't undo what I've done. But do you under-
stand why I left James? Does that make any difference? Is
forgiveness possible? I'll say it again. I am sorry. I am sorry
for every single tiny or enormous piece of his jigsaw that I
helped to put in place, and I mean sorry in the sense of real
regret. I would undo it all if I could, and that is why I left
him. And because of you.

   Look, you know what I am. I've set you up, hidden stuff
from you, deceived you, but despite all that you know me.
You've woken up beside me sixteen times. Did you know
that? You've seen me happy, you've seen me freak out,
you've seen me destroyed with regret. What's the use of these
fucking emotions if they don't tell the guy you love what you
are and how much you love him and that he should love you
still? Whatever part I've had to play, you know what I
really am, and there was a time when you liked that person.
Trust me enough to look for that person again.

There was no signature. I dropped the letter on the
table.

'Does it make any difference?' he asked.

'No.'

He nodded, pushing the letter aside in case he should
happen to catch sight of a couple of words. 'So, what's
the lead?'

'The people who built the sensor. I saw a logo and a
name when Fieldhead was showing me the program. It
began with S. Something like Semantic. It's probably
American. We can find them from International Direc-
tory Enquiries.'

Sammy shook his head. 'There's no way they're called Semantic.'

'Well, it was something like that. It definitely began with S and ended in -tic. Or maybe – tec, for technology. I can see it distinctly. Big yellow letters above a cartoon monkey.'

'A monkey? How about Simiantec?'

'Not bad. And you're not even a biologist. Let's try it.' I reached for the phone.

'Simiantec?' said the voice. 'No, there's nothing listed in the United States under that name.'

'How about something close? Are there any names that look like that?'

'I'm sorry,' said the voice, 'but we have to have an actual name.'

'Then how about Simintec?' I tried.

Again the response was negative. I suggested a couple more variations. The voice was getting bored.

'Semantic?' I avoided Sammy's eye.

'Look,' said the voice. 'Give me a moment.' The line went dead. Was there a means after all? Something kept in reserve for family friends and annoyingly persistent strangers? An experimental phonetic search device?

'Would it be Simatec in Northern California?' asked the voice.

'Yes!' I said. 'Yes, I'm sure that's right. Thank you.'

'Here's the number, then,' said the voice, enunciating it carefully.

Sammy didn't say anything. He got up and walked to the kitchen, reappearing a minute later with a bottle of wine and two glasses. He sliced away the foil and pulled out the cork in the precise, elegant way that our father had insisted upon. Each glass exactly half full.

'We've got them,' I said as I raised the glass to my lips. 'It's in the bag.'

Sammy tasted the wine and shook his head. 'Not really,' he said softly. 'All you have is a name.'

'The name is everything. With that, we can start searching. Find out what the company does. What it's working on. Where it's spending its money.'

'I doubt it. If Fieldhead is that secretive, what makes you think Simatec publish their plans?'

I waved away the concern impatiently. 'Christ, if necessary I'll go out there and ask them myself.'

'And you think they'll tell you?' Sammy smiled and gestured to Philip's room – Philip's PC. 'Shall we do the groundwork first?'

His Internet search proved one thing conclusively. If a privately owned American company wishes to be discreet, it has every right to be. Freedom of non-information. There were no neat company listings to be perused, no State Department records, no Chamber of Commerce indices. By the end, I was beginning to doubt the company even existed.

It took Sammy's patience to find it.

'Have a look at this,' he said a good hour later, as I walked back from the kitchen. Sammy had given up the direct search and was scanning the business press archives for references. The only gold – of a sort – to be struck was a brief mention in the *Financial Times*.

It was a long article about venture capital firms –

the high-risk investors who provide start-up capital to embryonic companies in return for a large chunk of their stock. The writer bemoaned the fact that London VC firms were throwing all their capital at foreign entre-preneurs, particularly those in Silicon Valley. A few examples were cited; a few Internet hopefuls. And then: *Other investments include the 30 per cent stake of hi-tech newcomer Simatec, recently purchased by Everest Ventures.*

'This is two years old.'

'It's all there is. Everest Ventures. Have you heard of them?'

I shook my head. 'See if they're on the Net.'

Sammy typed in a new search command and selected the Everest Ventures home page. It was sparse, straight-forward: down to earth. A young player. Modest resources. Senior partners: Artonby, Samuels and Taylor-Mason. No mention of Simatec.

'This is interesting,' he said. 'They've sold off quite a few investments recently, without taking positions in any new companies. As if they were contracting.'

I looked down the list of divestments. Everest had an excellent record for picking winners: small start-ups that had yielded high returns. So why weren't they investing in more? And where was Simatec?

'They're hiding it,' I guessed. 'It's that important to them. Can't even be named. Perhaps they're getting out of other businesses to concentrate their resources on Simatec.'

'Putting all their eggs in one basket?'

'Exactly. Whatever Simatec is doing, Everest are expecting to make a fortune from their stake. Perhaps they're channelling more money into the company to get hold of an even bigger slice of the pie.'

'It's not just the money.' Sammy had opened up a list of employees. 'Look at these starting dates. They've hired five new professionals – all aged above thirty-five – in the last eighteen months. If they're not making new investments, those people must all be working on Simatec.'

'Managing Simatec?'

'Could be. If the company itself is mainly technical people, Everest may have taken over all of the administrative work.'

'That would make sense if they want to keep it secret. It's probably easier to run a company discreetly from a distance. Any enquiries can just be referred to some faceless voice in London.'

'Then do you think it was Everest that arranged the project with Fieldhead?'

'Probably. It would explain why they went for a British researcher.' I stopped and stared at the screen. 'That would mean . . .' I picked up a notepad and scribbled down the phone number of Everest Ventures together with the names of its senior partners. 'Just a moment.'

The number clicked straight through to a voice message: *The offices of Everest Ventures are closed until the fourth of January. If your call is urgent, please contact . . .*

'They've all gone home for Christmas.' I turned to Sammy. 'If Simatec are still working, there may be a small window of opportunity. It's just possible, if they're really into the technology and nothing else . . .'

He nodded, immediately understanding. 'What do you need?'

'A plane ticket. I've got that five thousand from Field-head in the bank, so it shouldn't be too difficult to find one. And I need you to make a phone call.'

San Francisco International Airport, ten and a half hours before the New Year, Pacific Standard Time, was pleas-antly warm and unpleasantly crowded. The morning fog had closed the runways, delaying all incoming flights, with the result that the Arrivals hall was full of angry, tired travellers. The baggage carousels had chosen this moment to grind to a standstill, and as I wandered past with my small overnight bag, tempers were erupting in all directions. By contrast, the Simatec receptionist was sweetness itself, recognizing my name over the phone, providing directions, introducing herself as Malya, and promising to have the red carpet laid out by the time I got there. Not a glimmer of suspicion.

The taxi dropped me in the landscaped car park of a steel-and-glass building in Redwood City, at the northern end of Silicon Valley. It seemed a little more permanent than the hastily thrown up offices that lay all around: a sign that Simatec was not just any fly-by-night Internet start-up. The roof was low, curved and shining in the sun. Evergreens filled double-lined flowerbeds on either side of the entrance. Four young men in white coats over T-shirts and jeans were slouched on a bench, enjoying the last rays of the year. The glass double doors of the reception had been fixed open.

'Welcome to Simatec,' said the gushing, delicious

Malya. Her white-blonde tresses cascaded from dark roots all the way down to her shrink-wrapped breasts. Behind her, the wall simply held the Simatec monkey logo: no pictures of products, no mission statements, no clues. 'Nico's just stepped out for a burrito, but he'll be back in a second. He's our operations manager. He's very excited to finally meet you.'

I nodded, accepting the visitor's pass, and sat down to wait. Already things weren't quite working out the way I'd expected. After weeks of manipulation and suspicion, I had imagined a detachment of coldly hostile troops defending a fortress of a research centre, not this open-door, open-arms workplace where staff sunbathed or wandered down to the local fast-food joint.

When Nico arrived, he accentuated the impression of casual openness. Gripping a half-eaten tortilla-wrapped tube of rice, black beans and chicken, he held out his free left hand and grasped mine.

'Ben!' he said. 'This is a real pleasure!'

Nico's Mexican origins were visible only in his thick black hair and small stature. In manner, he was entirely Californian. Still wielding his stub of burrito, he seemed to want to press his right hand against my shoulder, but luckily thought better of it. I took in the Hawaiian shirt, the smart but casual suede leather jacket and the wrinkled slacks, wondering at the same time how best to respond to this energetic geniality.

'Thank you,' I said, half-watching the progress of the burrito as I smiled back.

'No way. Thank *you*. It's so great to have the chance to say that to you myself. Me, I'm so impressed by that stuff you did, I'm really happy Everest unbuttoned a little and let you visit us.'

'Yes, well, I asked them nicely.'

'Of course you did, Ben. Of course you did.' He was nodding vigorously, ecstatic smile locked in place. Behind him, Malya had one finger wrapped inside a few strands of hair, one eye on her computer, and a big grin aimed at me. 'So what are you doing in California?'

'Seeing relatives. There's a big New Year's Day reunion in Santa Barbara. I thought I'd come a day early and visit you guys.'

'Ben, it's so cool you did. We don't get many visitors, for obvious reasons, so it's fun for us to be able to show someone what we're doing.'

'How's the next phase going?' I asked as casually as I could.

'Oh, great, excellent. About two months behind, but no technical problems we didn't anticipate.'

'I'd love to hear what it's going to look like in the end.'

'Yeah, sure Ben, but come and meet some of the team first. They're all dying to see you in the flesh.'

Nico led me up to the first floor – or second floor, as he called it – where the Software Department was housed in a hangar-like room. Six five-foot high mud-brown cubicles lined the wall. In the centre of the room, transparent inflatable armchairs and beanbags surrounded a low table carrying a vast bowl of cookies and giant day-glo Gummi Worms. Nico pointed me to the nearest chair and called in the direction of the cubicles.

'Boys and girls, we have a guest.'

There was no response. I decided not to risk the flimsy-looking seat. Nico repeated his call, this time giving my name and injecting a little stridency into his voice. Immediately, a head appeared above one of the cubicle walls. The face was young, the hair dark, lank and swept over to one side.

'No way!' said the man.

On either side of him, two more heads appeared: one male, one female; both under twenty-five.

'What's up?' said the second man as he stepped out of his cubicle and walked over to the table. His head was shaved clean, except for a small goatee and a few missed wisps in front of his left ear. He wore a white T-shirt with the logo *not.com* printed in big pink letters.

'This is Andy,' said Nico as the programmer reached us. 'He's been here since the beginning.' He waited a moment as I shook hands with Andy. 'This is Danielle . . .'

'Wow. Hi!' said the girl, drawing each word out long and breathy.

'. . . And this is Christof.' A slight laugh as he said it.

Christof didn't notice. As if to beat his colleagues in enthusiasm, the third programmer gripped my hand between both of his. 'You're very welcome, Ben,' he said.

'We heard that experiment was awesome,' said Andy, his eyes alight.

'Really exceptional,' added Christof.

'Christof is your biggest fan,' said Andy. 'He was so impressed by the way you handled that prison he wrote you a . . .' he lifted both hands and curled his fingers down twice to seal the following word in virtual inverted commas: '. . . "love" letter.'

'Not true, dude,' said Christof. His face had turned red and licks of hair were tumbling over his forehead.

'Yes true. We "found" it in your personal file when you went for pizza.'

I began to realize that Andy's inverted-comma motions were not meant to signify doubt or double meaning. They were just habit: a nervous tic. His fingers would leap up in every other sentence to accompany some random, innocent word. I don't think he even knew he was doing it.

'Dude, you sneak around way too much. You should learn to let it go. You should, like, do Zen or something. It's bad for your heart.'

'Guys, shut up,' said Danielle. She had a long hourglass figure carefully displayed in tight blue jeans, and when she raised her voice the others always listened. 'He really doesn't want to hear it. Christof, why don't you offer him some refreshments?'

'Oh, yeah,' said Christof, blushing again. 'What would you like, Ben? Odwalla? Frappuccino? Or we can send Malya over to Jamba Juice for smoothies and wheatgrass juice.'

I was almost silenced by his canine enthusiasm. 'I have no idea what you're talking about,' I finally admitted.

'Oh! You don't have wheatgrass juice in England? Hey, you should try it, Ben. A shot of that shit is like six pounds of vegetables. It really gets you going. They grow the grass in the shop and they mash it right there in front of you.' His voice was rising to a dangerously excited pitch.

'A coffee would be great,' I said weakly.

His enthusiasm never faltered. 'You got it. Double or triple strength?'

I wanted to get back to the reason for the research, and when Christof had bounded off to the espresso machine I turned to Nico and asked about the company's origins. He pointed me towards one of the blow-up chairs and then sat on a beanbag. I tested the seat apprehensively, convinced it would burst the moment I lowered my full weight on to it. Beside me, Andy dropped like a rock into an identical see-through bag of air. Scary.

'It all started two years ago when Donald – he's one of the hardware boys – was looking for investors for his emotion-sensing idea,' said Nico. 'He used to work at a medical diagnosis company that made neural sensors for brain surgery. No one in the scientific community believed his model would work, so he set up his own company and started calling round the VC firms.

'Everest responded immediately, and put up the first two million. Then, when we suddenly realized what the potential applications of the technology were, Everest basically closed up shop, re-financed us, and took over the running of the company.'

'So they reckon it's going to be very profitable?'

'Like, "big" money,' said Andy, his fingers dancing in front of his face.

I was in a quandary: knowing none of the things they assumed I knew – the answers to all of my questions.

But if they discovered my ignorance, what then? Would they all rush to explain, or would they suddenly become suspicious of Sammy's 9.00 am PST – 5.00 pm GMT – phone call? Would they suddenly wonder why Mr Taylor-Mason had not bothered to phone himself? Would they recall their surprise that he had delegated his request for hospitality to a 'new assistant'? *I do not know what you are talking about – please explain*, I longed – but didn't dare – to shout.

'So, what are you calling the next-phase hardware?' I asked, the language sounding ridiculous on my Oxford tongue.

'Oh, we just call it by the development code, RX582. The name's up to the marketing guys that Everest brought in, I guess,' said Danielle.

Marketing guys? *Marketing*? What the hell was this? Consumer goods?

'Your espresso, Ben,' said Christof, walking back into the room. 'I forgot to ask if you like sugar. Here.' He handed me a fistful of individually wrapped sugar cubes and a thin plastic stick. 'I take three in mine. Two tastes too sweet, but three goes beyond sweetness. It gives the coffee a whole new dimension. Like a kind of flavour backdrop to highlight the beans.'

'Um . . . yes. Thanks,' I mumbled, already losing track of that precious flow. I turned back to Danielle, searching for some open-ended question that might unearth an explanation. 'How would they market it?'

The programmer stuck her tongue out. 'What would I know?' she said. 'I write code. I'm not some catch-phrase jockey.'

'She can barely write her own name,' joked Andy. 'Prose is not Danielle's big button.'

'I seem to remember helping you with your résumé at Cal,' said Danielle calmly. 'Just before you dropped out of the course.'

'Hey, and I'm grateful. Why else would I get them to hire you as well? But you know how many complete sentences my résumé had by the time you'd finished with it?'

'Résumés aren't supposed to have complete sentences.'

Andy laughed full at her, trying to get a rise. 'What century are you coming from, hon? A résumé's a work of art: you "express" yourself through your résumé. You show your inner self through your résumé. What kind of inner self produces a list of bullet points?'

'To see your inner self expressed on paper would be a punishment beyond death,' replied Danielle sweetly.

The word contest was sharp and fast, but no amount of abuse could disguise the underlying comradeship between the three programmers. These were people who knew each other intimately and never tired of each other's company. Nico sat comfortably erect on his beanbag, watching his troops with a mixture of amusement and paternal pride. A curious sight, given that he could only have been about twenty-seven himself.

When there was a brief pause in the conversation, I tried again. 'Will Simatec . . .'

'Oh wait, Ben,' interrupted Christof, slapping the table suddenly. 'I have to show you something.' He leaped up and scampered over to his cubicle.

'I knew he'd have to show you this,' smiled Danielle.

'What?'

'His pride and joy.'

When Christof got back to the table, he held out a photograph to me; reverently, as if it was a sacred relic.

'You like it?'

'Yes.'

'I've been there,' he added.

'I can see that.'

'Oh! Yeah. Duh! Cool though, huh?'

'Definitely.' It was a picture of Christof standing next to a guard at Buckingham Palace, looking ridiculous in a I-love-London T-shirt and bright yellow Bermuda shorts: but what else could I say?

'Dude, London is so cool.'

'Yes . . .'

'Do you want to see it?' said Nico suddenly.

'Excuse me?' See London? This was getting weird, not to mention way off track.

'The RX582. Do you want to see it, as you're here?'

I stared at him for a moment, stunned by this new focus. 'Yes. I'd love to,' I said quickly. Perhaps too quickly.

'Let's go then. You sure you've finished that coffee?'

'Sure.'

'Sure? We can get you another if you'd like it?'

'No, I'm fine. Thanks,' I said.

'If you're sure. I know you've had a long trip. Me, I have to drown myself in caffeine after a Europe flight.'

'I'm fine,' I said again, a little too strongly.

Nico rocked his head to one side and gave a shrug. 'OK. Anytime you want something, just say.' Then he motioned me towards the far door.

19

The Simatec building was centred on a large atrium, with a fountain in the centre and a straight run upwards to the heavens. Nico led me down a corridor, where light poured through glass walls, round to the other side of the building. Stopping at a heavy steel door, Nico pointed through a Perspex panel.

'We can't go in without special clothing, but you can look from here,' he said. 'There it is. It's still just a baby. First trials are years away.'

Whatever the baby was, I couldn't see it. Three white-suited men were stationed around a broad, gleaming surface on which robotic arms slid noiselessly back and forth. The laboratory was impressive. The baby was not.

But Nico was beaming with happiness. 'I really envy those guys. To be building the future like that. It's exciting just to watch, isn't it? I mean, this is going to be even bigger than Walkmans.'

I was about to phrase another subtle question. Something to tease the answer out by guile. Then my brain caught up with his words and I suddenly realized it wasn't necessary. With that one oblique comparison, Nico had just given the whole game away. I stared at his sunny face and knew I had come to the end of the trail. How simple. How obvious. How commercially perfect.

And how stupid of me not to have put the pieces together before.

Because really I had had them ever since Professor Carrington sent me hurtling down the wrong track. Dictating emotions, he had said. Right idea, wrong sense. He had used a word that brought every paranoia to the surface, and cemented that impression with a reference to Mao. But this wasn't about authoritarian regimes or manipulative companies. This was about consumerism. People were actually going to buy this thing: bring it upon themselves. Marketing! Give the consumers what they want. *This is going to be bigger than Walkmans*. Who wouldn't buy a neat new consumer durable that allowed instant gratification at the touch of a switch? How many people could resist the temptation to escape reality?

Packaged happiness, boxed amusement. Personal emotion-controllers to wear on your belt and adjust to achieve the perfect emotional condition. Buy them in the hi-fi store – you'll find them between the digital cameras and the PalmPilots. Tune into bliss. The logical development in high-street offerings. After all, every other non-essential consumer offering was effectively an emotion controller. The sports car that delivered excitement, the tropical holiday that delivered pleasure and happiness, the cinema that delivered everything. Emotion controllers, all of them – just imprecise, expensive emotion-controllers. Enter Simatec, offering instead the chance to make a one-off investment that allowed perfect control in the comfort of your own living room. Forget the alcoholic binge, the crowded, ear-damaging nightclub. Get the same trip by sitting down and plugging in.

I shuddered at the thought of people the world over renouncing normal life and living an existence filled by artificial emotion: millions and millions of couch potatoes. Voluntary vegetables. Would I ever use such a device? Irrelevant question: there was no doubt that many would.

'What's up?' asked Nico. 'You look kinda strained.'

'I'm just trying to imagine what life will be like when everyone stops doing anything and just sits around with artificial emotions pouring into their heads.'

'Yeah, we thought about that, too. We've decided to put a two-hour per day limit on use. It'll be like a meter – once you've used a unit for two hours, it switches off automatically until the following day. Of course, a few people will just buy twelve of them, but we're going to keep the price high, so that won't happen much.'

I hadn't even been looking for confirmation, but now I had as much as I could possibly need.

'Also, we're designing the headpiece to be quite bulky, so that it's inconvenient and uncomfortable to wear for long periods. We may even issue a warning about a possible danger of cancer from excessive usage, although that's obviously a difficult message to get right.'

'It just seems so unnatural,' I said. 'It's going to stop people from doing all the normal things they've been doing for thousands of years.'

'Sure it's unnatural, but why assume nature is so great?' Nico held up his hands. 'We live for our emotions, but they trick us into doing all kinds of useless things

394

that stopped being relevant the moment we left the savannah. We get our pleasure from eating fat, from having power over others, from beating up on people who don't belong to our group, from killing animals, from gossiping, from belittling our rivals, from accumulating possessions. Why?' He breathed in quickly. 'Why? None of these things is useful in modern society. Most of them are harmful. If not to us then to others. Nature is not perfect. It's extremely *un*-perfect now. Why shouldn't we try and improve on it?'

'But doesn't it scare you? The idea of people getting their strongest emotional experiences from a black box?' I tried to phrase my instinctive repulsion in polite, reasonable terms.

'Ben, a lot of people don't get any strong emotional experiences at the moment: at least not positive ones,' said Nico. 'Anyway, it's the only answer to the excessive consumption that the Western world loves. It might just safeguard some of the last remaining resources on the planet. Every charter plane burns gallons of non-replaceable fuel. Every bar throws away tonnes of glass and aluminum that required enormous amounts of energy to create. If artificial emotion stimulation can replace some of that consumption at the cost of a few batteries, then we should celebrate.'

I began to feel very tired. The search for the truth was over. There was no illegal planning, no immoral conspiracy. Just a new product, coming to the planet in less than a decade, perhaps enjoying world-wide popularity by the time my children were old enough to know what they wanted for Christmas. A revolutionary, possibly irresistible device that would destroy the natural way of life completely. Why leave your home at all when you could simply line up your twelve RX582s beside your tin of complete-nutrient meal-substitute and spend your whole life ecstatic on the couch? Vile, vile thought.

Now that I had the answer, being in the company of the people who were building it was uncomfortable. 'Well, thank you for showing me around,' I said to Nico. 'It's interesting to see the next stage. But I mustn't use up any more of your time.'

'No worries. It's been excellent to meet you. Where are you partying tonight?'

'Oh I'm just . . .' I shrugged. 'I'll just get an early night at the hotel.'

'Are you kidding? You can't come to California and spend New Year's in a hotel. Don't you realize this is the party capital of the world?'

'Yeah, well, I'll wander about a bit.'

'Uh-uh, you gotta come with us. Get a shower downstairs; sleep if you want. Then at seven we'll head for the Triple Bar in North Beach. A really cool place – you'll love it. Come on,' he added when I was about to refuse. 'The others loved meeting you. They'll be really glad for you to come.'

I very nearly said no, and that would have been it. I would have gone back to England, wrought some havoc with the newspapers and left it at that. I wanted to say no. Instead, I looked at his young, sincere, it'd-make-me-so-happy face and nodded.

*

New Year had brought Highway 101 to a near standstill. By the time our convoy of cars and jeeps left the Simatec grounds it was already dark and the fog had rolled back in. But all along the road, floodlights illuminated Internet company billboards advertising every kind of online service. Not one sign was free of the mandatory dot-com label. Conversation in Andy's Ford was easy flowing and low-brain. Danielle had her own car, but Christof sat behind me with one of the white-suited engineers called Matt.

'Light 'em up and fire 'em away!' shouted Matt. There wasn't really any context.

At first San Francisco seemed dead. Our route off the freeway led us through the Financial District, its skyscrapers beheaded by the fog, with only an occasional group of yuppies around a bar to liven up the empty streets. Then we turned into Columbus and the whole world seemed to appear. Suddenly, the city was alive with music and celebration.

'Welcome to the land of the free!' said Andy, lifting his hands off the wheel to embrace the crowds. From that moment, his fingers were permanently twitching up: 'Up there's Chinatown and Nob Hill – "smart". That's Russian Hill. Oh! Check out those "clown" people.' His hands darted between direction pointing, inverted comma forming, and vehicle steering. 'And behind those buildings is Telegraph Hill. Lots of hills,' he laughed. 'And here,' he said, pulling up on the crest of Columbus beside a high white stone building leaking coloured light, 'is the Triple Bar. Guys, take Ben inside. I have to go "park".'

'I got to tell you,' said Matt, 'you are real lucky to be with us. This place always has great New Year's parties, and it's difficult to get in. But RJ is best buddies with the manager, so we should be fine.'

A long queue of under-thirties snaked out from the building, but my hosts ignored it and walked straight up to the bouncers. A magic word, breathed quietly in one of their ears, was all that was needed. A door opened and Christof's hand between my shoulder blades propelled me in. It lingered there a couple of seconds longer than necessary: maybe Andy was right about that letter. I took a firm step forwards and forced my way into the crush.

The Triple Bar was a cavernous venue, so named for its three floors, each featuring a different atmosphere and music genre. The ground floor was dedicated to house music and held most of the crowd, too short-sighted or lazy to find the stairs. They were pressed shoulder-to-shoulder, hands gripping Budweiser bottles at neck height, mouths shouting good-humoured but inaudible conversation at everyone around them. Streamers hung from the ceiling and tangled into the crowd of hair below. I started to press my way towards the bar, but Christof gripped my arm, pointing to the stairway.

'Come upstairs,' he mouthed. Then, bringing his lips to my ear: 'There's more room. Salsa.'

I checked to make sure the rest of the group were also headed that way, then followed him up. The middle floor was still noisy, but the bodies were spaced a little further apart and conversation was suddenly possible again. The atmosphere was amazingly friendly. Half the people had their arms round each other: everyone smiling or laughing, everyone happy. The area nearest the street was given over to salsa dancing, although the Latin beat reached into every corner of the room, making bodies shimmer, rock and sway.

'Can I get you a drink?' I asked Christof, politeness overcoming wisdom.

'Well, thank you, Ben,' he said in a delighted voice, intonation rising in surprise. 'I'll have what you're having.'

No, his smile was definitely too friendly.

I moved to the bar and ordered two beers. Thankfully there were other options besides Bud. The bartender's T-shirt also bore the legend *not.com*: apparently a favourite among the cyber-unchosen ones. Beside me, a man in a maroon polo shirt was jabbering wildly to a man in a blue polo shirt.

'It's a great idea,' said Maroon.

'It's a *really* great idea,' said Blue.

'There is *nothing* out there yet. Just *nothing*.'

'God. Forget IPOs,' said Blue, in one of those deep, national-security-serious voices. 'You know who would want to swallow this up . . . ?'

'You got it. They would have to acquire. Seller's price.' A shifty look over his shoulder at me. 'If we can just get the website up and running with basic functionality, and the brand out there in the next six months . . .'

'Yeah, we've just gotta get the brand out there before *they* wake up.' Another suspicious glance from Blue.

'I have to bring Marty in on this,' said Maroon, pulling

out a cellphone. 'Shit. No signal. What are these walls made of ?'

My beers arrived. I took my time paying.

'You sure you want to do that?' asked Blue.

'You got a bad feeling about Marty?'

'No . . .'

'You're right,' said Maroon, putting the phone back in his pocket. 'I've got a bad feeling about Marty. This is way too great to blow it. We should keep it tight right now.' This time he stared directly at me. I smiled and picked up the beers.

Christof appeared by my side. He thanked me again for the beer and then put one arm round my shoulder to guide me over to the Simatec camp. Danielle immediately stepped forward and grabbed the beer from his hand.

'Thanks. Just what I wanted,' she smiled. 'Now let go of him and go get yourself another.'

Christof made a face, but turned and obeyed her. When he was out of earshot, Danielle threaded her arm through mine and led me a couple of steps away from the others.

'Ignore him,' she said. 'He's on heat.'

'Right.'

'He's so funny. This is the perfect city for us to be gay but he has to go after more exotic targets.'

'Us?'

'Us,' she said firmly.

'Oh.' I tried not to think any more about Danielle's narrow waist or the curve around her hips. Still, the interest had to be a good sign: some things were getting back to normal. 'Who are these other people?' I asked, nodding at the guys who had joined the Simatec party.

'A bunch of Internet geeks. They have an office near ours: we play volleyball with them occasionally.'

As she spoke, Andy arrived and grabbed one of the geeks from behind in a bear hug, lifting him clear of the floor. 'Jay! How's life?' he cried.

Jay was a short man in a chocolate duffel, with hair that looked as if it had been purposefully greased forward into his eyes. Hard to imagine anyone actually doing that to themselves.

'Andy. Give me some space,' said Jay, when he'd been released. 'Please? It's New Year's Eve.'

'Sure, Jay. All the space you need.' Andy lifted up his hands as if about to form a couple of inverted commas, then used them to brush down Jay's arms.

'Andy likes giving the Internet guys a hard time,' muttered Danielle. 'Makes him feel better about spending the most exciting period in Silicon Valley history labelled as a medical diagnostics equipment loser.'

'Medical diagnostics?'

'Well, it's almost true, isn't it?' she grinned. 'Great camouflage. People's eyes glaze over the moment you say those two words, and that's the end of any interrogation about your work. It's really important, because that's all anyone talks about here now: programming skills; IPO date; option packages.'

Jay's colleagues were drawn from the same mould. Their taste in clothes and style of hair varied from reasonably normal to even-worse-than-Jay. Lots of company logos, lots of synthetic coats, lots of nasty-framed glasses.

'Lots of money,' murmured Danielle.

'What?'

'These guys. They just went public. Serious bucks all round. Jay's already worth twelve million.'

I stared at the cyber-geek in the chocolate duffel. 'You're joking.' He looked even younger than me. 'What does the company do?'

'Runs a website, provides a free but pointless service, operates at a net loss: the usual criteria for a high-valuation Internet IPO. They'll probably go under within eight months.'

Her casual tone made the prediction sound perfectly normal. 'Why?' I asked.

'Because they don't do anything anyone's willing to pay for. Everyone but the VC firms and Wall Street can see that. It's the same with half the stupid ideas in the Valley, but it doesn't seem to put off the investors. I get really pissed seeing these guys buying mansions and Ferraris because they thought of a new way to offer virtual card games for free, when we're working our butts off on zero pay to bring happiness to the world.' She lowered her voice automatically for that oblique reference to Simatec, even though there was no one close enough to hear a word we said over the noise of the salsa. Ingrained secrecy.

'Zero pay? I thought Everest were throwing money at you.'

Danielle shook her head, letting her dark hair fly loose around her. 'Everest are throwing money at the equipment and the materials. There's nothing left over for the people except stock options and bread-line wages. Our take-home has to be the lowest in the Valley. Even the founders still share the apartment they had when they were at Berkeley. Nico is employee number three and he can't even afford to get his car door fixed. He's been climbing in over the passenger seat since the fall.'

'Then why haven't you run off to join an Internet company?' I asked.

She tilted her head to one side and looked at me in surprise. 'I just told you; most of them are a sack of hot air. Simatec is doing something so important, way more important than any of those dot-coms. What does it matter if you can book concert tickets online when an RX582 will make going to the concert redundant? Huh? That's why we've been working fourteen-hour days, seven days a week, for the last two years.' I nodded, unsure how to answer. But Danielle was smiling again. 'And anyway, if it all works we'll have our pay-day when Simatec gets its listing on NASDAQ.'

'When is that?'

'Absolute inside: five years,' she said.

'A long time to survive on your parents' generosity in hope of an uncertain reward.'

She looked a little cross at that. 'We do a lot of praying,' she said.

That was an uncomfortable thought. I was starting to sense the extent of my power. Not all the consequences of my plans were going to be pleasant.

'Exactly,' shouted Andy to Christof, a heavy emphasis on the first syllable.

'Even Evil People,' replied Christof. Again, that heavy first syllable.

'Whatever,' said Jay. 'But you can't deny people the right to buy cheaper doughnuts, just because they're in a different state. Don't you believe everyone should be able to get a good deal off the web?'

'Eeeventually,' said Christof, causing Matt to roar with laughter.

Jay was looking as confused as I felt.

'What's going on?' I whispered to Danielle.

'It's just a dumb game they like to play. Putting as many e-words as possible into the conversation to wind up the dot-com boys. You know, like email or ecommerce. Always works.'

'Eee-xcept "Eee-lephants",' said Andy, his fingers bobbing up to accentuate the nonsensical statement.

'You guys really suck,' said Jay angrily, catching on and making off in rapid succession.

'Goodbye, Jay!' chorused Christof and Andy. 'Happy New Year!'

Grinning, Christof turned back to me. 'OK, now that dude hates us, too. We're slowly alienating the whole dot-com community so we don't have to go swim in their giant pools or share their Jacuzzis when their IPOs fly.'

'Like we'd have time to,' muttered Matt.

'Right. Why spend our free time in a pool?'

At that, all the Simatec crew – even Danielle – burst out laughing. When she caught sight of my puzzled expression she shouted 'Free time!', prompting a new burst of hysteria. Fourteen-hour days, seven days a week, was a hell of a commitment.

While they were laughing and hugging each other, a girl appeared beside me and watched the scene with a cheery grin on her face. 'How are you surviving the time difference?' she asked. 'You just flew in, right?'

I nodded. 'How did you know?'

'Oh, Matt told me,' she replied, holding up a beer. 'This was for him but he doesn't look like he needs it as much as you. My name's Amy.'

'Thanks. I think.' I glanced at Matt, but he was ensconced with the rest of the programmers and engineers in a series of one-line in-jokes about slave-labour working hours in the Valley. 'I'm Ben.'

'Yeah, he told me that, too. Short but sweet. Great name. Ben the Benelov . . . God, what is that word?'

'Benevolent?'

'Right!' she grinned. Under a fringe of strawberry blonde hair, her eyes beamed trusting fun straight into me. 'Are you?'

I laughed. 'Occasionally, maybe.'

'Whatever. Don't even really know what it means. How d'you like this place? Isn't it wild?'

Amy was overflowing with life, unstoppable in her enthusiasm for the wonders of California and, most especially, the Bay Area. 'It's the best place in the world. You can surf in the morning, drive to Lake Tahoe and ski in the afternoon. We used to spend half the summer sleeping out on Mount Tam. It's real heaven, I tell you.'

I shuddered briefly as I wondered whether it too had a hell to complement the heaven. But I found I could quickly push the subject out of my mind. Amy's shining eyes and teeth were very distracting.

'So, what do you do when you're not running around the wilds?'

'Oh, I'm the polymer matrix composite specialist at Simatec. When I'm not running around the wilds I build emotion sensors for charming English boys.' She waited a moment to enjoy the surprise in my eyes. 'Pretty good reaction. Some guys get really freaked out when I admit I'm an engineer,' she laughed. 'I just love playing that bimbo routine. Will you still flirt with me?'

'Um,' I mumbled. 'Am I . . . ? I mean . . . aren't you with Matt?'

'No way! I grew up with him. He's like my brother. *And* we were at Cal together – University of California,' she added when she saw the question in my eyes. 'Berkeley, across the bay. All these guys were there. That's why we're all such good buddies. So?'

So?

'You ever tried salsa?' she asked, glancing towards the end of the room where a growing number of couples were linking arms and moving around the floor. I shook my head. 'You want to give it a go?' she suggested, an inviting smile playing on her lips.

I nodded without thinking. As the old desire came tearing back, I was shocked to realize how removed from normal feeling I had been over the last ten days. The horror of Fieldhead's deceptions, and the memories of that nightmare, had swamped every regular impulse. My thoughts had been dominated by paranoia and cold-blooded plans for revenge. Now in the warm, relaxed atmosphere of the Triple Bar, surrounded by hundreds of friendly people, I melted.

Suddenly I was looking at Amy with new eyes and responding to her flirtation as we walked towards the dancers. I found myself moving from idle speculation to absolute certainty that I wanted her, not for herself but for the antidote that she represented: the final cure to dispel the pain of Cara.

Amy was nothing unusual: a pretty girl with a bubbly personality and a fun attitude. In my newly recovered state, I found her irresistible. While she showed me the basic steps, I felt my desire explode, built up out of all proportion after such a long period of inaction. I had to resist the urge to run my hands inside her clothing.

'You know, it's real hard to find a straight guy who isn't a computer geek around here,' she murmured. That was too much.

I stopped dancing and whispered in her ear, 'What's upstairs?'

She giggled and took my hand. 'Come and find out.'

The Simatec crowd were waving enthusiastic signs, urging me on. Embarrassing, but also quite warming. Only Christof looked a little subdued, his hair tumbling over a creased forehead; but there was no way I was going to feel bad about that. Amy climbed the stairs ahead of me, brown legs below the tiniest of leather skirts, knowing that she was giving me ample opportunity for study.

On the top floor, a heavy door sheltered the room from the lively sounds of the salsa. Inside, sultry jazz floated from ceiling speakers, under which couples swayed drunkenly around the room. Amy turned, and I pulled her into my arms, my lips closing on hers before we had even begun to dance. She felt warm and sensual as we circled the room in small, unhurried steps. I watched her eyes close and sensed her hands run over my trousers. She wore a loose cotton shirt, tied above the waist. I brought one hand round to open the top buttons and explore inside. Then I closed my eyes and concentrated on her mouth.

I had a lover in Africa.

I once knew a pretty girl named Cara.

There was definitely something there, but things change. You know how it is.

A little beer, a little dancing, a lot of kissing, and Cara was a distant memory. It almost seemed laughable to remember the pain she had caused me. How powerful was the affection of another human being, an identity-free piece of the New World. How quickly it erased the other.

And instead of pain there was even guilt. Astonishing! Guilt for Cara? Guilt for the most guilty of them all? *Trust me enough to look for that person again.* With another girl in my arms, I knew I would never do it.

Suddenly unsettled, I pulled away from Amy. She opened her eyes and looked at me, a slight frown adding to – not replacing – the warm glow of happiness on her face.

'What's up? You don't look too good. Wasn't anything you swallowed, I hope?' And she laughed an all-refreshing all-American laugh that cleared away most of the Cara-confusion in my head.

'No.' I laughed with her. 'Just coming up for air. Shall we go downstairs and be sociable for a bit? It's almost midnight.'

She made a face. 'God, I was really enjoying that, though.' She smiled sweetly to deny the tone, not the meaning, of the words.

'Well, there's plenty of time afterwards,' I offered.

She grinned. 'That's better. I was beginning to think you were going to be all British on me.'

She turned and led the way down the stairs, only bothering to do up one of the buttons on her shirt. Half of the Simatec crowd had taken over a circle of seats under the stairs and they raised a cheer when we showed up. The salsa had given up and the ground-floor music had invaded their den. Television screens lit up to show streamer-ridden studios in Los Angeles filled with semi-drunken semi-celebrities gazing at the clock.

Amy's face spun round to mine. Her nose rubbed my cheek. 'You want another beer?'

'Thanks.' I smiled and took the chair beside Danielle.

Christof and Matt waited about two seconds after Amy had left.

'Shit, Ben, you were fast!' said Matt.

'Unbelievable!' added Christof.

I shrugged. 'She's a really nice girl.'

'Oh yeah,' agreed Matt. 'But what is it about you English? Are you all on Viagra or what? The project manager from Everest was over here a few days ago and it was just the same. Work over, into a bar, and giving a stranger the line before we'd sat down.'

'Successfully?' I said, more out of conversational politeness than interest.

Matt nodded. 'Sure. No time at all. Amazing babe. Quite intimidating 'cause she knows exactly what she wants, but real nice with it. She just has to smile at you to make you want to work twenty-four hours a day for her.'

In my beer-sodden, sex-filled brain, a seed of a thought took root. It grew rapidly, racing through possibilities, becoming stronger with every matching clue, developing into near-certainty in the space of an instant.

'What's her name?'

My voice was obliterated by a warning bell from the bar: 11.59.

'What's her name?' I shouted at Matt.

'Her name. God, something cool, foreign, what was it? I never got to speak to her. Nico will know.'

I leaped up and searched the room. Nico was standing at the bar with three other Simatec men. The celebrities on the screens were panting with excitement. Their enthusiasm spread across the room. I pushed through the crowd as the figures started to fall.

'Ten! Nine! Eight! . . .' shouted the Triple Bar of San Francisco, California.

'Nico!' I called out as I reached him. 'The project manager. English girl from Everest. What's her name?'

'Six! Five! Four! . . .'

'Count, Ben!'

'Three! Two! . . .' shouted the crowd.

'Her name, Nico!'

'Who? Cara? You never met her?'

'HAPPY NEW YEAR!!' yelled the crowd. And I yelled with them. I yelled in astonishment, in excitement, in shock, in delight, in outrage. I yelled in all the colours of the emotional rainbow that had hung over me for so long. I yelled in congratulation of the greatest player of them all. The ultimate artist. But I yelled loudest in elation. For I knew without question that she had deceived Fieldhead, too.

And the next moment a pair of arms came round my neck and shining lips rose up to meet me. 'I want you to be the first person I kiss this year,' said Amy, a wide smile balanced across her mouth. I kissed her back, joyfully, sensing the total freedom of the moment, drunk on the wonder of the thing.

I kissed her back and adored her, even though every moment we spent together I was overwhelmed with respect for the other. What a player! Every expression, every emotion, perfectly performed. Layers of deceit, draped like a magical cave around me. And, crucially, around Fieldhead as well.

'Come on,' said Amy through the noise. 'Let's get out of here.'

Grinning crazily I followed her to the stairs. My Simatec friends watched me go, smiling their blessings, unaware of the revelation they had just provided for me. Out in the road, I kissed her again, listening to the noise from the bar gradually fading away. San Francisco suddenly seemed very peaceful.

'Look at that,' said Amy, pointing to the great Transamerica Pyramid that rose high above the rest of the skyscrapers, marking the southern end of Columbus. The fog had disappeared, leaving the magnificent illuminated apex of the structure gleaming against the dark sky. 'It's so beautiful at night. You know it's built on rollers to protect it from earthquakes?'

A couple of other revellers tumbled out of the Triple Bar and howled at the sky like wolves.

'It's a bit like my life,' said Amy. 'Shaky, but immune to collapse. Often in the fog, but occasionally bright, wonderful and beautiful to behold.' She grinned and turned to me. 'So, where are we going to spend the night?'

20

'Tell me again,' said Sammy, quietly fascinated, generously pandering to a recently recovered ego as only a brother could. 'Not only did you find the answer but you got laid as well?'

'Wonderful,' I smiled. 'It was all wonderful. And the best is still to come.'

'Fieldhead?'

'Fieldhead.'

'When?'

'This afternoon. Why not? I can't wait to break the bad news about his innocent little girlfriend to him.'

Sammy smiled. 'Can you delay your revenge by a few minutes? Piers is going to drop by at lunchtime.' He sensed me stiffen beside him and looked round, taking his eyes off the road for just a second. 'Relax, Ben. He's coming to apologize.'

'Apologize?'

'That's what he said.'

'When did you speak to him?'

'He came round yesterday morning, just as I was taking Jenni back.'

'What!?'

'Didn't I say? I asked her over to your place for New Year's Eve. We had a little party. She finally got to sleep in your bed,' he added, laughing to himself as he turned off the motorway. 'You don't mind, do you?'

'You didn't . . .'

'No I didn't. God, Ben, why do you always assume that?' But he was still smiling, and I knew he'd meant me to fall into that trap. 'No, I just thought she might be a bit lonely, stuck in that dreary old college over New Year. I didn't have anything planned, so I popped round, scooped her up, and carried her over your threshold. A couple of bottles of that disgusting Spanish wine you like and we made quite a night of it.'

I had, once again, forgotten Jenni. Twice I had done her harm, each time choosing to live with the guilt by erasing it from my mind. How light-hearted would I have felt in Amy's bed if I had remembered the sound of my hand crashing into her face?

'How . . . What did she say about me? About what happened?'

'You know, I think we completely forgot to mention you all night. Isn't that extraordinary?'

'Oh.' That left me feeling leaden inside.

'Smile, Ben, I'm pulling your leg. She couldn't stop going on about you.'

'Jesus!'

Sammy looked round again and winked. 'You know, I think it's the first time she's ever actually talked about it. Strange, huh? All those doctors and psychiatrists, and she wouldn't let them in. But the moment she was in your flat, it all came flooding out.'

'Do I want to hear this?'

'Yes, I think you do. Well, you should, anyway. If

someone has feelings that strong about you, you should know about them.'

So I let him tell me. Sammy described the board games they'd played, the microwaved spring rolls they'd eaten, the party hats he'd found. They insulted the CD collection and then chose the Lightning Seeds for an irreverent, spirited atmosphere. Jenni sat back with her leg supported on the sofa and began to talk. She repeated the kind words that I'd once offered her, long since forgotten by me but stored away as the first entry in her mental logbook. She described the frustrations of that first term, wanting every time we met to talk about her feelings, failing each time to find the courage. Then, finally, an alcoholic overdose and the curtains of inhibition lifted.

'She was so convinced you were going to get off with her that night,' said Sammy. 'Everything you did seemed to suggest it. So when you . . . when you demonstrated how wrong she was, she said her mind just kind of shut down. And then she found herself lying in a hospital bed with a shattered leg.'

'And me floating around with a gorgeous new girl.' I sank a little lower in the passenger seat, my San Francisco elation wiped out by the memory.

'Yeah. Didn't help. But in a way it did, because it took her to the very bottom. The only way out was upwards, and that's the way she's been heading ever since.'

'Is that your professional opinion?' I asked, my voice heavy with sarcasm.

'I talked to her for a long time. Most of the night, in fact. She's doing OK.'

'What about the slap?'

'Weird, that. It almost seemed to help. When you did that, she suddenly saw another human being who was as messed up as she was. In fact, not just any human being – the one that she'd been idolizing all this time. Seeing you fall apart over that slap was, well, therapeutic I suppose.' He paused to remember her words: ' "I needed that more than anything." That's what she said. So maybe it wasn't such a terrible thing to do.'

It was kind of her, of him, to see it that way. But yes, it *was* such a terrible thing to do.

'What now?' I asked.

'What do you mean?'

'What will she do now? What does she think of me?'

'Oh, nothing very dramatic, on either count. Carry on with university life, get that First, find that perfect job. And she's over you, if that's what you're worrying about. In fact, she's more anxious about your mental health than her own. Which,' he said, flicking his eyes round once more, 'can only be good. I've no idea what the shrinks would say, but having something to take her mind off herself must help. If I were you, I'd go round there in a week or so and have a chat. She's a nice girl – she'd make a good friend.'

I nodded. Sammy's judgement I trusted more than anyone else's in matters of emotional stability and therapy. If he prescribed contact between the wounded then that suited me fine. I would suggest that dinner again. This time, she wouldn't throw it back in my face. Or perhaps something gentler. Perhaps I would follow in the steps of my younger brother and invite her round for microwaved spring rolls and Spanish wine. Start at the beginning, and tell it slowly this time, the wisdom of hindsight clearing away the confusion of conspiracy and leaving me free to examine all my stupidities and rushed conclusions within the context of that great game. Together we would drink a toast to the girl who was Cara: the ultimate artist, who knew better than anyone how to boil a frog.

Piers was already standing on the pavement outside my flat, hands stuffed into his jacket pockets as he waited for us. He came forward and offered his hand, rather roughly I thought. I took it.

'Come in,' I said, gesturing him to the front door.

'No. No, thank you. I just wanted to straighten things up a little.'

'What things?' I asked innocently.

He looked down as Sammy walked past and opened the door. 'Stupid things,' he said at last. 'I just got a bit jealous, I'm afraid.'

It seemed slightly surreal to be standing in a street of modern, suburban semi-detached houses and listening to the king of the elite confessing jealousy. Certainly, Piers was not used to it. His jaw was moving from side to side like some kind of ungulate, and spots of pink had appeared on his cheeks. The grandiose certainty of his arrogance had vanished.

'You see, I'd told everyone I was going to pull that girl. I was sure of it. Jesus, she was the one who came on to me in the Union bar, Christ's sakes. Then you go and get off with her in front of everybody. It was too humiliating.'

'Wait a minute,' I said, confused. 'You're telling me you weren't in on the plan?'

'What plan?'

'The plan to set me up with Cara for the emotions experiment.'

'She was part of it?' he said in genuine astonishment. 'Jesus, Ben, no. Is that what you thought? Didn't you know I'd invited you to that party long before I met her? She just – well, I thought it was by chance – happened to be in the frame at the time.'

'Then what are you apologizing for?'

'For deciding to screw you as a payback for taking Cara. It was nothing big. Just that password thing. That evening, after you'd been round for brunch, I went into college furious with you still – even more so as you'd decided to ignore my advice. It would have all faded away to nothing, I'm sure, except I happened to bump into your tutor.'

'And you told him?'

'I couldn't help it. The opportunity was there. A spontaneous chance to get my own back. Just asked him if he'd seen Ben Ashurst today.'

'And he said yes.'

'So I asked if you'd seemed interested in his keyboard. "What are you talking about?" he asked. "Oh, nothing," I said. "Only he's been round at my place all morning learning how to read your password as you type it: something to do with emotion manipulation."'

'And that got his attention, I imagine.'

'He wouldn't let me go until I'd told him everything you said.'

'Did it make you feel good?'

'No. It made me feel pathetic. Which wouldn't have been too bad, except that I then found out from the others what a bad shape you'd got into and I suddenly realized I'd been interfering in something way more serious than I'd imagined. I know you well enough to see if you were shouting at people and breaking down doors then I should be helping you, not screwing you.'

'What was going on in your house?'

'New Year celebrations. I've had a bunch of people staying for the last few days. Everyone had just arrived when you got there. Ripper'd been gossiping about your story. I'm sorry; I heard they got out of control. Pack mentality. We'd drunk so much I was already collapsed on my bed upstairs. But Sal told me what happened and I tried to find you, see if you were OK.'

I thought about the terror that had been going through my mind as Piers stood outside my door that afternoon. I thought about the sense of persecution I'd felt in his dining room, faced with that onslaught of abuse and air of menace. The power of the mind to unhinge itself is frightening. Then I thought about the man who'd started it all. It was time to pay him one last visit.

'Well, thanks for coming round,' I said, as generously as the circumstances allowed. 'Don't worry about it. It's all working out fine.'

So. What does an all-time dupe do when he finally holds the strongest cards? Gracefully put them in his back pocket and offer a draw? Too charitable. Throw them all on the table at once, in a massive, destructive show of strength? Better. Or produce them one by one, keeping the Ace to the end, prolonging the opponent's agony to maximum effect? Sweet vengeance. The very best.

On the second day of the year, one man is working in the Zoology Department. One man, who has not suffered the seasonal hangovers and stomach ulcers of his colleagues, who has remained at his desk throughout the holiday period, driven to work by the excitement of his data and the absence of his lover. The analysis is complete. A student's head has been plundered, the contents mapped out, and the distilled essence made ready for distribution to the masses. Reams and reams of data fill appendices, but the report itself is daringly short for the fees paid. Just a few, simple sheets, with a long list of frequencies and some rather brilliant insights. Of course, the academic papers will be much wordier, when they are finally released in five years' time. But the writer knows his current audience, understands their needs. All they want are the frequencies.

A perfect anatomy of human feeling. Numbers, figures, data and more data. Data to be processed, to be picked over, to be modulated, sorted, manipulated. Lots and lots of data.

And just occasionally, in some polished office in London, or in some glass-walled laboratory in California, just occasionally someone might remember what those data once were. And just occasionally they might spare a thought for the sick, lonesome, terrified, persecuted, betrayed young man who cowered on the floor of a darkened cell, waiting for the guards to come for him with the machete, so that the world might own a daily two-hour ration of happiness.

The betrayed young man knocks on the only unlocked office door in the building and prepares for battle.

'Good heavens!' he started. 'What on earth are you doing here? Aren't you supposed to be recovering from a party?' He smiled a conciliatory smile.

'I recover quickly,' I said, returning the smile.

'I'm glad to hear it,' he said, reading the double meaning. 'I didn't expect to see you again after that rapid disappearance.'

'I looked over your letter again.'

'I hope it helped. It was meant in kindness,' he said.

'I particularly liked the bit about you all being extremely grateful to me.'

'It's true. We are.'

'Good. Because I'm here to negotiate.'

'Negotiate? But what is there to negotiate? As I said, I'd be delighted if you would like to continue with our tutorials.'

'I'd like to put a value on your gratitude.'

Fieldhead stopped still. His hands were resting on the desk. A sheaf of papers had been hurriedly turned over when I knocked. The computer screen was blank.

'A value?' He raised an eyebrow.

'Yes. A value. I'd like to discuss how much my participation in this project was worth to your sponsors.'

His face had lost the earlier traces of friendliness. 'Ben, I don't think you understand. I cannot discuss anything to do with the project. I thought I had made that clear. In five years' time, we'll meet up and I'll tell you all about it. But at the moment . . .'

'So just give me an opening figure. No need to discuss the project. We'll take it from there.'

He was definitely uncomfortable. After a while the deceived can read the deceiver like a book. The normal fluency of argument had deserted him in the face of these unsettling demands.

'Well, the sum agreed was £5,000. We paid it into your bank account before Christmas.'

'Is that a reasonable value?'

'I suppose so. I mean, I suppose I could ask for a bit more if –' I cut him off. Time for the first card. 'Tell me, how much will the units sell for?'

His mouth opened to answer, but no sound came out. His pupils seemed to contract to tiny points. He leaned forward, a look of incredulity on his face.

'What are you talking about?' he said quietly.

'The units. Whatever they're called. RX582s. I mean, I imagine they'll be priced quite high for the first few years. With a complete monopoly and a whole new concept in consumer durables, you could probably sell them for a thousand apiece, don't you think?'

Fieldhead didn't answer. His face was looking unnaturally white.

'And if that's the case, then I'm worth a total of only five units. With worldwide sales probably reaching into the millions, that makes me feel pretty damn unimportant to your sponsors. I'm not saying I can't live with that. But it does contradict all the effort you've been putting in on my behalf, doesn't it? After all, why go to so much trouble for a five-unit guy?'

'Who have you been talking to?' His voice was strained, the first bruises appearing.

'What if I said Cara?'

'Cara knows nothing about this. Who have you been talking to?' he demanded, suddenly very loud.

Yes! His response had been immediate and absolute. He really didn't know about her role at Everest. The Ace was solid. Just the thought of revealing it in a few moments made me smile. That infuriated him.

'Tell me!'

I ignored the shout and put on a bored expression. Time for the second card.

'Look, I'm sorry to hear things aren't working out between you and her. You must have been a great couple.'

Up to that point, Fieldhead had been concerned, even angry, but all within a professional context. Now, I had touched a personal nerve.

'Be careful, Ben,' he growled. 'You're about to get out of your depth.'

'Oh, unlikely,' I laughed. 'I've never seen a shallower relationship. She used you and now she's bored with you: it's the oldest story in the book.'

I fingered the final card. The Ace. It was almost time.

'Face it, James. You've lost her. She's gone. Got better things to do than hang around you now that all the fun's over.'

He looked as though he was about to hit me. When he spoke his voice was cold fury.

'What the hell could you possibly know about it?'

When you grow up, and if you're lucky enough to find some half-blind moron, you'll discover that women in love don't disappear the moment "the fun's over", whatever that adolescent phrase means to you.'

My fingers closed around that last card. 'You really believe she ever loved you?' I laughed. 'I thought you were supposed to be smarter than that.'

'If you think you know anything about our relationship . . .' he growled.

The card was hot, about to burst out, set the table alight. I started to lift it. 'Let me tell you about your relationship,' I began.

As the card stood balanced on its edge, ready for my fingers to flick it face-up across the baize, the door opened. No knock. Total intimacy. And in she walked.

The ultimate artist was wearing a tailored jacket, medium heels and black silk trousers. Her hair was loose, her face still perfectly tanned. A prize straight off a catwalk.

For a moment, neither opponent spoke. Each was equally surprised. But knowledge is power and the one with most recovered first. While the genius struggled to adjust his emotions to this reappearance of a lost lover, the student smiled up at the ultimate artist and wondered absently how long she had been standing outside the door. Wondered when exactly a call had come through from California; a comment on the young English guy that Everest had sent over; a moment of confusion; a reference to a non-existent temporary assistant placing calls on behalf of Mr Taylor-Mason; a sudden understanding. Wondered how the game was going to end.

'Ben, would you excuse us?' Fieldhead had recovered his poise, even managing a pleasant tone.

But Cara placed a hand on my shoulder, restraining me. I looked across at Fieldhead. He seemed angry, but he knew better than to show it at this critical moment.

'So, how have you been?' he tried. She smiled her beatific smile at us both but didn't answer. Instead, she walked past me and stood beside him, almost behind him.

When she dangled one arm over his shoulder, I recognized the re-enactment from that first night with Piers. And in his face I saw the same unsuspecting look of triumph.

'Thanks for everything,' she murmured, just as I knew she would.

Fieldhead understood the tone immediately, and his expression froze. 'You're leaving?'

'I don't know,' she said, as I knew she would. When she walked back towards me, I gave a tiny – imperceptible to him – nod of understanding, of cooperation.

'You'll probably want me to,' she added as she reached me. This time, I didn't wait for the hand. I dropped my head backwards and watched her mouth descend towards mine. One final, graphic kiss: easily as powerful as that third card, which I now understood was to be stored away for ever. When our lips met, I heard his fist crash down on his keyboard, heard the fury, heard the destruction, savoured every part of the vengeance through my ears.

Then her lips pulled away, and she whispered, 'Let's go.'

I stood up and followed her to the door. I didn't look back. The sound had been enough.

Cara chose FREVD, the site of my original, humbling introduction to practical game theory. I don't know if it was meant to be ironic, or if the choice was made purely on the grounds of privacy. Either way, it seemed a fitting place to finish the game. She drove the MG smoothly and cleanly, her mood quite different from the girlish excitement of December.

'I should be furious at you,' I said. 'Why aren't I angry?'

'Good question.' She smiled at the road.

'I've spent the last two weeks wanting to rip James apart for what he did. Now I find you were running the whole show, yet there's no anger.'

'Emotions are weird like that. They often don't keep up with the shifting course of events.' She pulled up outside FREVD, in the same illegal position I had taken a month earlier. 'You've spent too long focusing your hatred on one person to be able to transfer it just because of some new piece of information.'

'So now you're an expert in emotions?'

'I have a PhD in behavioural psychology.'

'Of course.' Strained laughter, but now even more impressed. 'I thought you said I knew what you were.'

'I said a lot of things.' She smiled lightly and led the way up the steps. 'Tea?'

'What was that letter about, anyway?'

'A last-ditch attempt to contain a liability. Just like the new affection on the meadow and the pleading on my

426

doorstep. James's doorstep, I should say. He bought the house for me, thinking I was a penniless student.' She laughed. 'He would be mortified if he knew it was me that authorized his contract with Everest.'

'What would you have done if I'd responded?'

'Had a full relationship with you until you were over the experience and no longer emotionally driven to uncover all our dirty secrets. After a couple of months, you would have got bored with me.'

'I doubt it.'

'Trust me. I would have made certain of it.'

Her eyes held the same mocking humour of that first night, before it all began. That at least was real. I watched her order a tray of tea then remove her jacket, every movement efficient. Her face was calm and controlled, the amusement of the moment balanced by a professionalism that I was astonished I'd missed before.

'Have you ever been an actress?'

'No.'

'How old are you?'

'Twenty-eight.' Five years more than before.

'How long have you been working on this project?'

'Four years.'

'Should I believe anything you say?'

She shrugged, the smile still in place. 'You might as well. It's all harmless so far, and you won't hear anything to contradict it.'

I watched her eyes. I knew I had no better idea of what was going on in her mind than during that original truth game. Enigmatic pools of street wisdom. The waitress set a tray of tea in front of us.

'So what was that scene all about back there?'

'It was mainly for your benefit.'

'Oh, really? You know, I can get snogs elsewhere.'

'So I heard.' She raised her eyebrows. 'You wanted revenge on James. More than we'd expected, and it was threatening the whole project. So I gave you revenge.' She took a sip of tea. 'Besides, I needed to get him off my back. The plan was that I should go out with him for the duration of the project, to monitor progress from the inside and check he wasn't screwing us around. But now that it's over, I have to get back to my own life. He's been calling me constantly since I dropped him. You were a good story for him to swallow – the experiment backfires and the experimenter loses his bait to the fish – this way, he won't find out I work with Simatec, so the good relationship is still there if the company needs him again.'

'Why him in the first place? Why not a psychologist?'

'There aren't many good scientists with the capability or willingness to indulge in deception and manipulation of fellow humans. Psychologists tend to be too concerned with the individual's well-being. Experimental biologists are trained to think about their subjects in a much more utilitarian way. And besides, he's probably the best empirical researcher alive today. I sketched out some ideas for the project and had them sent to James, but he was the one who perfected the details, ensured that every emotion was displayed in contexts that allowed clear, uncorrupted recording. The gaol was a stroke of genius.'

I shuddered to hear such a casual reference to that

horrific experience. 'If this is all about making people happy, why did you need to put me through that hell? Why did you need the negative emotions?'

'Creating artificial emotional states isn't just about injecting what you want. It's also about removing what you don't want. The RX582 is designed to suppress negative emotions as well as enhance positive ones. It will emit opposing frequencies that cancel out those negative emotions we measured in you.'

'You make it sound even more clinical than James does.'

She shrugged. 'It's just a job. A very interesting and challenging job, but if I allowed myself to get emotionally involved, I'd be finished.'

'Did you really never feel anything?' It was supposed to be a disinterested question, but we both detected a fragment of a plea in my voice.

She eyed me curiously for a moment. 'Do you really need to ask?'

'Then what about your relationship with James?'

'The same,' she said coolly.

'Did he meet you at a friend's house party? During a truth game?'

'He gave a visiting lecture and saw a very keen student in the front row.' For a moment, the grin turned almost impish.

'At Edinburgh?'

'Or Cambridge . . . or Newcastle . . . wherever it was that we eventually ensnared him.'

'How long ago?' Crazy to be worried by the length of someone else's fake relationship.

'April.'

'Quite a commitment to the project.'

She nodded. 'I have a few Simatec stock options. Believe me, that encourages commitment.'

'And he never found out about you? He never discovered you were working for Everest?'

'There was no reason why he should. His contacts at Everest are both serious, middle-aged men – the sort of stereotype executive he expects to deal with. To him I'm just a pretty student. He arranged for me to get a post-grad place here, and as far as he knew I was spending all my hours dreaming of fruit-fly genes – when I wasn't being deceitfully over-impressed by his sexual ability.'

I winced at that, remembering her enthusiasm for my own lovemaking.

'And it was his idea that you should have a relationship with me?'

'He thought it was his idea. He did so like talking about his work in bed. That was another reason why I had to become his partner. Even though he signed a secrecy agreement, we knew he would need to chatter about the project to someone.'

'So what skills does the project manager have to have, other than superhuman seduction talents?'

'I'm not really *the* project manager. That's my boss – you remember David? On the plane back? Not actually from St Albans. But wanted his Hitchcock moment. No, I'm just the only one that the guys at Simatec usually see. The project is much bigger than the technological development. Planning for the launch of a breakthrough personal appliance is a huge task. Regulatory approval, marketing plans, distribution channels, and everything has to be kept secret.'

'Why? Why the secrecy?'

'Surely you can see that. After your paranoid ideas? If the suggestion of thought control leaks out to the media before we've had a chance to educate the public, it could kill the company at birth. We have to control the information flow, and it's still far too early to release anything. The Public Information Plan is incredibly complex: hundreds of pieces in all areas of the media to get people comfortable with the idea of emotion management long before we start trying to make them want to buy our product.'

'It isn't going to stay secret, Cara.'

For some reason, it was extraordinarily hard to say it.

'You're not planning to blow the whistle on us, are you?' she asked, a demure smile on her lips, not a trace of anxiety in her eyes.

'What you're doing is unnatural. It's messing with the mind. It's preparing the way for every kind of thought control, however much you want to wrap it up in some consumer electronics right-to-choose veneer. To tell the truth, I find the whole idea disgusting.'

'You can't judge its worth by your own standards. You're lucky enough to have a reasonably balanced emotional profile. Many don't. Without understanding them, how can you decide the merits of this technology?'

'You're right. I can't,' I admitted. 'No single person can. Which is why it shouldn't remain secret. This has to be debated openly. Before your marketing experts start playing their games with public opinion and brainwashing people into accepting it, there should be a serious investigation into the long-term consequences. That is why I am going to blow the whistle.'

Cara's expression remained unchanged. The confidence in her jawline didn't falter. It was as if she'd anticipated my reaction exactly.

'You talk about consequences,' she said evenly. 'Let me tell you what the consequences will be if you take this story to the press. Assuming they believe you – which is reasonably likely, given your intelligence – two things will happen. First, the papers will publish a doomsday splash about Simatec, distorting their aims and values until they come to be seen as public enemy number one. This will finish Simatec, and with it Everest Ventures – our commitment to Simatec is too large to survive its total annihilation. That brings us to the second consequence: the receivers will sell off all assets of any value belonging to the two companies, the most significant being the patents and designs for the emotion technology. Who will buy them? Some vast corporation that can see the long-term commercial potential in emotion management and that can afford to invest sufficient PR money over the next few years to turn public opinion around.'

'It won't happen. No one will buy it.'

'Of course it will happen. No technology, once invented, has ever been de-invented. You can't kill emotion control, Ben. No one can, now that it exists. All you can do is determine who ultimately owns it and benefits from it. Keep quiet, and Simatec will launch it, together with all the safeguards and public health warnings that, as responsible citizens, they believe to be necessary. Announce the technology now – prematurely and coarsely – and some unknown corporate giant will pick it up for a song and do with it whatever they see fit.'

She paused, and the smile disappeared from her face. Her voice dropped lower. 'And in the process, you will have destroyed the lives and dreams of all those hard-working, well-intentioned people that you met in California. You'll get your revenge and enjoy the pleasure of the moral high ground for a few days. But the people whose genius and dedication have achieved an extraordinary scientific advance will be left penniless and reviled by the media, forced to grow old watching their innovation lining the pockets of someone else.'

The memory of those laughing, almost innocent faces welcoming me to their country and their company was so fresh I could see each one of them clearly. Christof with his sweet affection. Andy's dancing fingers. Danielle, Matt, Nico, Amy.

Amy.

Their charming enthusiasm, their immense pride in their groundbreaking work: these were real qualities, which even I could value. Cara knew that. More than anyone else, she knew what I valued. And, as always, she knew how to use that knowledge.

It was ironic, really. By going to San Francisco and penetrating Simatec's secret, I had given her one final hold over me. Before, the manufacturers had been face-less manipulators, assigned in my imagination all of Fieldhead's worst streaks but lacking his charm and scientific status. Now, I had seen the real people behind that image, and critically, wretchedly, had found myself liking them. Cara couldn't have planned it better if she'd tried.

And that made me wonder. Suspicion came easily to me now. Wondering was almost an academic exercise: a game of 'what if?' played with the evidence of the past. An analysis of any slight discrepancy that might have been left unexplained, forgotten temporarily in the rush of events. A curious lack of interest in security. A surprisingly warm welcome. A rather neat variety of arguments in favour of the technology. An abnormal degree of niceness. Perhaps even – or was this too paranoid? – yet another unusually eager girl. What if?

What if a game player were faced with two options? She and her colleagues could be dismissive, secretive, hostile; or they could be warm, welcoming, open. What would be the effect on her opponent's later decision? *Use backwards induction to work out what action will induce him to behave in the way that best favours you.* The counter-intuitive choice often makes the superior strategy.

He has signalled his intention to keep searching. He has proved himself persistent and capable of uncovering what was never meant to be uncovered. He is on his way to San Francisco and he knows the name. He knows the name, for Christ's sake! What use is hostility and secrecy now? It will merely justify the use of that whistle in his mind. Better to be friendly, kind, disarming. Pretend that a bunch of cynical, argumentative engineers are the sweetest, loveliest flowers on God's Earth. Perhaps even substitute them with actors from the local charm school? Then let slip her name at the end of the evening. Offer him a different kind of revenge. Win him over without him even realizing it.

Cara was glancing at her watch.

It's always easier to influence someone's decision if they don't know they're being influenced.

'I have to go now. I'm flying to San Francisco tonight.' She stood up and smiled again, resting her hand on my arm. The touch was soothing. It reminded me of that last, dark night in the beach house. It was tempting to enjoy it.

'Have a good trip,' I said curtly.

'Thank you, Ben,' she said. 'It's been fun. You're a great guy. Really great. But please think about the consequences. Think about those people in California who have worked the best years of their lives for this. Think about their dreams. I hope you'll make the right decision.'

She bent down to give me one final kiss, then picked up her bag. As her eyes met mine for the last time, I smiled back and gave her a look I hoped she would remember: a mixture of humour and defiant challenge, to plant a first seed of doubt in her mind. A question mark.

'Maybe I will,' I said.

Recording No: 45

Date: 19/20 December   **Time:** After Midnight

Situation: In bed – Cara is asleep

Sensory Context: Auditory: waves on shore, distant disco, C's breathing; Olfactory: C's perfume; Tactile: C's warmth against me

Cognitive Context: I love her
Emotional Context: I love her
Somatic Response: I love her
Facial Response: I love her
Global Viewpoint: I love her
Action Impulse: I love her

ACKNOWLEDGEMENTS

The Mind Game delves into the fascinating but complex fields of neurology, evolutionary psychology and game theory. To keep the book entertaining to non-scientific readers, I have simplified, omitted, and selectively amplified. The scientific study of emotions is a murky and disputed territory, and for the sake of the narrative I have chosen to take certain positions that are by no means accepted by all specialists in the field. For those positions, and for any mistakes or misrepresentations I have made, I take all responsibility and beg forgiveness from those who know better. That said, I would like to thank: Richard Dawkins, for critiquing my portrayal of the scientific method and Oxford Zoology, and for providing the excellent tennis 'game'; George Mandler, for bringing professional rigour to my interpretation of emotion science; and Andrew John, for his advice on game theory. I have drawn on the efforts of too many scientific thinkers and experimenters to list the complete literature here, but readers interested in reviewing the science in detail should read Joseph Ledoux's *The Emotional Brain* (Phoenix Press, 1998), Steven Pinker's *How the Mind Works* (Penguin, 1999), and Daniel Goleman's *Emotional Intelligence* (Bloomsbury, 1996). Matt Ridley's *The Origins of Virtue* (Penguin, 1996) gives an excellent summary of both the Prisoner's Dilemma and the intriguing theories on the evolutionary roles of emotion put forward by Robert Trivers and Robert Frank.

The description of the Kenyan political environment is loosely based on the events that took place in the run-up to the 1997 General Election. However, the Kenya Freedom Party does not exist and the general security situation in the country remains among the most stable in the region. The welcome extended to visitors is as warm as always.

My thanks to Richard Marriott for reading the first draft and for giving me the crucial encouragement and advice that – as a complete beginner in the world of creative writing – I badly needed. Since then, several friends have been kind enough to read later drafts and offer important feedback, most notably Bruno Shovelton and Matt Nelson. Many others have helped me track down numerous details, especially Katja Stout, Gretchen Maddox, Richard Harding and Brett Lee. I am also grateful to the Swann and Scott-Bolton families for providing a quiet place to work when the distractions at home became just too great.

I would like to thank Tom Weldon at Michael Joseph for believing in the book and patiently guiding me through the editing process. Finally, I am indebted to my agent, Patrick Walsh, for excellent structural advice and for working miracles on my behalf. Thank you.